BLUE CRUCIBLE
BOOK SEVEN OF THE THE FALLEN WORLD

Benjamin Tyler Smith

Blood Moon Press
Virginia Beach, VA

Copyright © 2020 by Benjamin Tyler Smith.

All rights reserved. No part of this publication may be reproduced, distributed or transmitted in any form or by any means, including photocopying, recording, or other electronic or mechanical methods, without the prior written permission of the publisher, except in the case of brief quotations embodied in critical reviews and certain other noncommercial uses permitted by copyright law. For permission requests, write to the publisher, addressed "Attention: Permissions Coordinator," at the address below.

Chris Kennedy/Blood Moon Press
2052 Bierce Dr.
Virginia Beach, VA 23454
http://chriskennedypublishing.com/

Publisher's Note: This is a work of fiction. Names, characters, places, and incidents are a product of the author's imagination. Locales and public names are sometimes used for atmospheric purposes. Any resemblance to actual people, living or dead, or to businesses, companies, events, institutions, or locales is completely coincidental.

Cover Design by Elartwyne Estole.

Ordering Information:
Quantity sales. Special discounts are available on quantity purchases by corporations, associations, and others. For details, contact the "Special Sales Department" at the address above.

The Fallen World/Benjamin Tyler Smith -- 1st ed.
ISBN: 978-1648550010

To my Lord and Savior, from whom all blessings flow. Hosanna in the highest.

Chapter One

I raised my riot shield just in time to catch my armored opponent's sword on its clear, rounded surface. As I swung my nightstick in response, my only thought was, *How the hell did I end up in this mess?*

My nightstick struck the side of my opponent's mail shirt. He shrugged the blow off and lashed out again. We traded blows back and forth for several seconds, neither of us giving ground.

I thrust my nightstick at the man's chest like it was a sword, hoping for a quick "kill." He stepped to the side, and I overextended. Before I could recover, he struck my padded arm with his dull blade. The force of the impact sent a wave of shock up my arm, and my hand reflexively released the nightstick. It fell, but the loop around my numb wrist kept it from hitting the trampled grass at our booted feet.

I whipped my arm in a tight circle and snatched the nightstick as it sailed upward. I then cracked it across the brim of the man's kettle helm, a solid, clean blow.

The man cursed, then curled up on the ground with his shield raised over him. He would feign death until the marshals called him off the field.

I stepped forward to engage the next man-at-arms, but a hand clamped on my padded shoulder and pulled me back. My brother, Sergeant Danny Ward of the Mobile Police Department, grinned at me from behind his faceguard. "Getting caught up in the excitement, Nate?"

"How'd I let you talk me into this?" I adjusted my footing until I was lined up with the rest of the men and women in the police shield wall. "This is ridiculous!"

"Ridiculously fun, you mean!" Danny laughed. "Come on, man, live a little! We were here, they were here. Some words got thrown around—"

"By you, I seem to recall."

"*And* others. One thing led to another, and now we're in a mass melee." He lifted his armored shoulders in an exaggerated shrug. "These things happen."

Chaos reigned throughout the grassy field. Police officers in full riot gear clashed with fighters draped in chainmail or clad in plate armor. Padded nightsticks and swords made of rattan rose and fell with wild abandon.

A throng of spectators clad in everything from tunic and hose to T-shirts and shorts cheered at the display. More than a few held up tablets and phones to take pictures and record video. Over the PA system, a bubbly female announcer delivered a rolling commentary. *"Folks, who knew the May Day Melee would begin with such a bang? Before the main event even starts, we have officers of nine police departments from across the fruited plain pitted against brave volunteers from the ranks of the Society of Creative Anachronisms!"*

"You forgot the London police, lass!" Lieutenant Gregory Blackwood shouted from his position in the shield wall. "It's not just Yanks here, you know!"

"Yeah, don't forget about the international presence!" Sergeant Mosher of the Tel Aviv Police called.

To be fair to the announcer, all of this had been a last-minute addition to the Three Rivers Renaissance Fair's lineup, including which departments decided to join. I'd have preferred to stay out of it entirely and carry out our mounted patrol and demonstration like we were here to do, but Danny was right: a challenge had been issued by the SCA, and it was hard to say no to a chance to fight against opponents as well-equipped as a unit of riot police. It made for good experience.

It was also hard to say no when my kids were so excited by the idea.

A whistle blew, and the fighting stopped. Marshals worked their way through the line, yelling, "Clear the dead!"

The man I'd defeated got up and headed for the sideline along with several others.

The SCA fighters retreated about twenty yards and formed up for another charge. "Steady, everyone," I said to the eight Mobile PD officers who had volunteered to join me on the field. "We just need to hold this patch of ground, and we've won!"

A chorus of "Roger, LT," and "Ten-Four!" answered me.

"The opening clash has occurred, and first blood is to the officers!" the announcer continued. *"But it's not over yet! Each side still has around sixty members, and the contest will continue until either the defender's castle is captured, or the attacker's general is captured. Who will win: Richard's Raiders of the SCA on offense, or the dismounted officers of Phillips' Phalanx on defense?"*

Our "castle" was the United States Border Patrol's command van, brought to Columbia with Captain Phillips and his men. The agreed-upon rules were that we would defend against all attacks by the SCA fighters as if we were engaged in riot control. We won if we could outlast the enemy, but we would also win if we could take out the riot's ringleader. I don't think "Capture the General" was part of a normal tournament's lineup, but the SCA's leadership had agreed, so here we were.

Danny whooped. "Let's give 'em hell, boys!"

The officers from Mobile cheered, as did a few from Blackwood's group. The other cops in the line either hadn't heard Danny, or they were out of breath from the previous skirmish. That worried me. If a few minutes of combat were enough to get them winded, how would the next bout go?

With a roar, Richard's Raiders charged across the clearing.

"Brace yourselves!" I shifted my right leg back and leaned my weight forward to absorb the shock of the anticipated impact.

"There's General Richard!" an officer from the Houston PD shouted. "Capture him, and we win!"

"Yeah, best defense is a good offense!" another answered.

"No!" Captain Phillips barked, his voice carrying over the shouts of the approaching enemy. "Stay on the defensive!"

The command from our "general" came too late. Three of the nine departments charged. After a moment's hesitation, two more followed, totaling half our number. A staggered line rushed to meet the solid mass of Richard's Raiders.

When both sides met, Phillips' Phalanx shattered. Fighters swarmed the five officers of the Lancaster PD and quickly beat them down with blunted weapons. The four officers from Charlotte brought down twice their number before being overwhelmed. All fifteen officers from the Philadelphia PD disappeared from view as SCA fighters surrounded them.

While the center of the Raiders' formation was bogged down, both its flanks pressed the attack. My squad of Mobile officers was positioned on the rightmost flank of the Phalanx, alongside the London officers. "Let's show these Yanks what we can do!" Blackwood shouted.

Fighters rushed our position. A chunky man who had to weigh nearly three hundred pounds lunged at me with frightening speed. I brought my shield up in time to block his greatsword, but the blow staggered me.

He swung again and again, aiming for my head, my side, wherever I was exposed. Each blow I managed to block, just barely. I was breathing hard after just a minute of this intense assault. Sweat dripped down my face and stung my eyes.

My opponent's attacks slowed as his breathing grew labored. He raised his sword for another overhand blow. As soon as he brought it down, I sidestepped. He chopped empty air and overextended himself.

I gently rapped him on the helmet.

"Damnation!" The rotund man dropped to his knees, then curled up in a ball. "Nice one, but we'll win this!"

I couldn't argue with the man. The field we were on was completely flat, making it difficult to see beyond the line of combat immediately in front of us. I could make out the colors of the different kingdoms or provinces or whatever they were called, but I had no idea who was who, other than that they were SCA. And they were everywhere.

Danny fought against two opponents whose mail shirts were draped in the white and red tabards of the Knights Templar. I charged at the one closest to me. He saw the blow coming and blocked it with his shield. He turned to attack me, then Danny stepped in and jabbed the man in his exposed armpit.

The other Templar didn't give in so easily. He rushed at Danny, and they exchanged a flurry of blows: sword struck shield, nightstick smacked side. Nightstick jabbed stomach, sword bounced off shield. Back and forth they went, officers and Raiders on either side giving them a wide berth.

As the battle raged, the excited announcer continued her blow-by-blow account of the action. *"More officers have quit the field! Their poorly executed charge at the center of the Raiders' formation has cost the Phalanx dearly! Three departments are down, but the Philadelphia police are holding their own in the center! One officer in particular is making the Raiders pay for every inch of ground they take!"*

I grinned. That had to be Sergeant Jake Morris, a childhood friend from when Danny and I lived in Philadelphia. He'd always been good in a fight, even before he and Danny had trained together for Obsidian's Armed Forces.

"But I don't think that's going to be enough to stop Richard Cates and his raiders from winning! SCA fighters have broken through the police line and have Captain Phillips surrounded!"

"To me!" Captain Phillips bellowed, his voice almost lost in the cacophony of banging metal and screaming combatants. "All officers, to me!"

"We have to get to Captain Phillips!" I shouted. "He's surrounded!"

"Hate to break it to you, Nate, but so are we!" Blackburn called back. "Ow, bloody hell. That hurt!" There was a loud crack, followed by a string of curses. "Anyone have an extra billy club?"

I gritted my teeth and swung my nightstick at the next man to attack me. We were going to lose if we couldn't get to Phillips. If we'd had our horses, this wouldn't have been a problem.

"*Uh oh, folks, it looks like things are finally coming to a conclusion!*" the announcer chimed in. "*Maybe, if our boys and girls in blue had their horses, it'd be another story!*"

"Is she a mind reader?" Danny demanded. "I was thinking the same thing!"

"*General Richard Cates is on the move! He and his knights are coming in for the kill!*"

I strained to see above the enemy's shield wall in front of us, but I couldn't see anything. "Jones, you're the tallest man here!" I shouted. "Can you see the general?"

Patrolman Jeremiah Jones was six-foot-eight, a former linebacker for Alabama and a current assistant basketball coach at his niece's school. And he must've spent some time on a baseball diamond, if the way he swung his nightstick was any indicator. He knocked over two fighters at once with his powerful swing, then stood on his toes to peer over the melee. "I see him, LT! Surrounded by some guards! And all that's between us and them is green grass!"

"How many?"

"Eight dudes dressed up like they're ready for a feast at the Round Table!"

"We're going up against knights?" Danny asked.

"Or people dressed like them," I said. Just because they had the armor didn't mean they had the skill. Just rich parents or high-paying jobs.

Danny laughed. "Well, hell, let's get 'em! When's a chance like this going to come again?"

I couldn't fight back a grin. Why not give it a shot?

"Mobilians, Londoners, listen up!" I shouted. "We're going after the enemy general! It's our only chance to win!"

"You won't get past us!" one of the SCA fighters called.

Blackburn bashed the fighter's helm with a nightstick he took off one of his "dead" officers. "Nate, take your squad and go! We'll hold them here."

We were up against an equal number of fighters. If we left things like this, the Londoners would quickly fall, and our backs would be exposed. "Jones! Give these guys a run for their money!"

Jones didn't need to be told twice. He slammed his nightstick against his opponent's shield with enough force to knock him off balance, then did the same to the man next to him. He pushed into the enemy's shield wall, his nightstick rising and falling.

One SCA fighter rapped Jones on the helm, but Jones kept swinging. "That was a clean hit!" the man objected.

"What hit? I didn't feel a thing!"

Another "stabbed" Jones in the chest with a sword, then a third struck him in the side with a two-handed axe. He wouldn't lie down.

"Son of a bitch is Rhino Hiding!" one of the fighters yelled.

More took up the call of "Rhino Hider!" and "Clean hit!" The SCA's shield wall swarmed around Jones trying to bring him down.

Jones shrugged off the insults and the blows with a laugh. "Momma always said I was pretty thick!"

"You lousy cheater!"

"All's fair in love and police work!"

Blackburn and his Londoners formed up around Jones as the big, black man continued to knock around the SCA fighters with his immense strength.

"Let's go!" I shouted.

We ran around the swirling melee and out into the open.

Richard and his knights jogged toward the center of our line, where Captain Phillips and his beleaguered men tried to protect the command van. Their attention was split between the fight ahead of them and a knot of Philadelphia officers off to the right, who were still battling their SCA opponents. Not one of them ever looked left, the direction we approached from.

We crashed into their formation at full-speed, nightsticks swinging. I struck the first knight's helm, then blocked the second knight's slash. Danny swung at him, and the two squared off as the rest of the squad joined the engagement.

Richard charged at me. He wore high quality plate armor, and he wielded a two-handed sword. I raised my shield in time to block his first strike, but the force of the blow sent a shock up my shoulder. I gasped in pain.

"Better men than you have fallen at my blade, boy!" The voice that boomed from the depths of the great helm sounded amused.

"We'll see about that!"

I swung my nightstick. He parried, then slashed at my side. I brought my shield across my body and blocked what would have been a "fatal" blow, just barely. I pushed his blade away with my shield, then backed away.

Richard stalked forward, his sword swinging. Before he could connect, Danny crashed into him as his fight spilled over into our section of grass. Danny reflexively jumped forward to get away from Richard and slammed into the knight he was fighting. Both of them went down in a tangle of armored limbs.

I wasted no time. I ran straight at Richard as he turned back to face me. I held my shield up to block his incoming strike and then lunged with my nightstick aimed at his chest. Excitement burned within me. We had this!

A whistle blew.

I staggered to a halt, my nightstick a couple inches from Richard's breastplate.

"*Folks, I wish I could say this was a great turnaround for the police,*" the announcer said, "*but it looks like Captain Phillips was defeated just seconds before Richard could fall! It was an amazing gambit by the Mobile Police Department, but the winner of this impromptu match is Richard's Raiders!*"

The SCA fighters and the audience cheered.

The elation I had felt withered and died.

"I know that look." Richard's laughter echoed from inside his helm. "Worn it many times myself. Defeat from the jaws of victory and all that." He clapped me on the shoulder. "Hell of a fight, kid. Maybe next time will be different, eh?"

* * * * *

Chapter Two

"Well, that could've gone a lot better," I grumbled as we trudged back toward the police transport vans and the accompanying horse trailers parked on the north end of Cedar Lake Park, a newly opened park south of Columbia.

"Could've gone a lot worse, too," Danny said. "Could've been a total rout after that mess of a charge." He glanced sidelong at the man next to him. "Have anything to say, Mr. Philadelphia?"

"Hey." Jake Morris raised his hands. "I just followed Lieutenant Stallings' lead. She wanted to charge, so we charged."

"Yes, but Captain Phillips said to stay put." Danny rested his nightstick against his shoulder. "We should've obeyed his orders."

"I agree, but I wasn't about to leave the boys high and dry by staying put, you know?"

"Mark it down as a lesson learned," I said. "Internal unit cohesion is important, but so is inter-unit cohesion. You can't ignore one in favor of the other, especially during a large exercise like this."

After a long pause, Danny muttered, "Says the man who charged against orders, too."

Jake snorted, then busted out laughing. I cracked a smile, then thumped Danny on the shoulder. "Smartass."

Captain Phillips had told me just as much during our debriefing a few moments ago. While the older Border Patrol agent had clearly enjoyed himself, he was more than a little disappointed at the poor overall display. "This might have worked had we been up against your typical mob of looters, thugs, and civil agitators, but we were pitted against an equal number of men and women just as well-equipped as we were. And instead of discipline, we relied on ballsy maneuvers like those the Ward brothers executed."

That had brought a cheer from all the Mobile officers and a smattering of officers from other departments.

"And sometimes those maneuvers are necessary," Phillips had continued. "But, better if that was Plan B or C rather than the only plan available. So, Lieutenant Ward, I hope you will take this to heart as you plan our joint maneuvers over the coming days of training."

The training he was referring to was one of our main reasons for being out here in Missouri. This was the third annual International Mounted Police Officers' Summit, a two-week convention where officers from around the globe gathered to train, compare tactics, and purchase new equipment and even horses. At last count, we had four hundred and twenty officers participating, from as close as St. Louis and Kansas City to as far away as Tokyo and Tel Aviv.

And with them came close to five hundred horses and other mounts. It was a good thing the University of Missouri had a huge granary just for equines and enough stables for more than three-quarters of them. The remaining mounts were housed at two large horse farms, one to the south of the university in the Newfarm area, and the other on the eastern outskirts of the city along I-70.

"Well, at least you put on a good show at the end, Nate," Jake said, bringing me back to the present. He clapped me on the shoulder. "We'll be talking about it for the rest of the convention."

I rubbed my shoulder, thankful for the padded riot armor. His friendly pats could knock a German shepherd out cold.

Patrolman Jones caught up to us a few minutes later. The giant carried a couple of stuffed animals in his hands. "Are those rhinos?" I asked.

"Yes, sir. Couple of the SCA fighters said I earned 'em for my actions back on the field." He looked off into the distance. "They're callin' me Jeremiah Jones, the man with the Rhino Hide."

Danny and I shared a look. "I don't think that was meant as a compliment," I said.

"Well, hell, why not?" Danny raised his voice. "Let's hear it for Rhino Hide Jones!"

The Mobile officers cheered. A bit further back, the Philadelphia and London officers laughed.

"Daddy!" a high-pitched voice called as we neared the MPD transport van.

I let my riot shield and helmet drop to the grass and knelt just as my five-year-old son, Jason, threw himself into my arms. He looked up at me, his mouth wide in a gap-toothed grin. "You were great! You, too, Uncle Danny!"

"Glad you approve, little guy," I said, ruffling his short, black hair with my gloved fingers. "Not every day you get to see your relatives beat on some knights, right?"

"Yeah!" He paused. "But aren't knights the good guys?"

"They can be," Danny said. "Depends on what they're fighting for."

Jason let go of me and stood back, his face scrunched up as he thought about this deep issue. "So some knights are bad."

"If they're bad," I said, "they're not real knights. They just look like them."

Danny knelt next to Jason. "This was a play fight. Those knights are good guys just like us."

Jason's grin returned. "Yeah, good guys just like us!" Then he turned his head and pointed. "Who's he?"

"That's Sergeant Jake Morris of the Philadelphia Police," Danny said. "He's also a friend of ours from back when we were your age."

Jake held out a hand. "Pleasure to meet you, Jason Ward."

I smiled as they shook hands. Jason had actually met Jake a few years ago, but he didn't remember much of his toddler years.

"Dad! Uncle Danny! And—Gosh, Uncle *Jake?*"

Nine year-old Helen Ward appeared from behind the van and ran toward us, her long, auburn hair flying behind her like a banner. A familiar tightness formed in my chest. She looked more and more like Regina with each passing day.

She stopped a few feet short of us and pressed her hands against her long skirt. The tightness in my chest eased, and I smiled. Helen could be just as in-your-face as Jason, but then she would suddenly have her shy moments. "It's good to see you, Uncle Jake."

"And it's good to see you, too." Jake made as if to shake her hand, then snatched her up into a sudden bear hug.

She screamed as her feet left the ground, then that scream turned to laughter as he spun them both in a circle. "Uncle Jake, stop! I'm going to get dizzy!"

"That makes two of us, kid." Jake laughed but set her down. "I had to chase the shies away. Did it work?"

Helen's pale face flushed, but her answering grin said it all. I asked her, "Where's Brother Stephen?"

"Over here!"

A tan man in an MPD polo shirt and slacks walked over from the horse trailers. He held the reins to a charcoal mustang with one hand and a brush in the other. "We were just giving Gared a good brushing before the morning patrol began," Stephen Pham said.

"Were you now? And did you do a good job?"

Helen planted her hands on her hips and looked up at me. "I learned from you, didn't I?"

Jake whistled softly. "Looks like she put it back on you, old man."

"She has that way about her." I ran a hand through her hair. "All right, then. Go and finish brushing down his horse while we strip out of this gear. Then we ride!"

"Stop that!" Helen ducked away from my grasp and straightened her hair. "Are you coming along, too, Uncle Jake?"

Jake looked back to where his fellow Philadelphia officers had gathered. "I'll have to see."

"I'll go talk to Lieutenant Stallings, if you want," I said. "See if we can't patrol together, or at least mix the units. Anything to help build inter-unit cohesion, right?"

Fifteen minutes later, our mixed squad of officers rode out of the parking green toward the entrance to the Three Rivers Renaissance Fair, an imposing gatehouse constructed of sturdy timbers with a stone veneer. A pair of men with crossbows waved at us from the parapet as we approached.

I rode a tri-colored American I'd named Calico Countess for the blend of black, white, and brown hair that covered her body. She wasn't the tallest horse at fifteen hands, but she was one of the fastest I'd ever ridden, in or out of her riot barding. Gunfire never scared her, and she had no problem charging into a mass of angry people, both of which had come in handy during our tenure with the mounted unit.

Danny rode next to me on a young, black filly named Noir. Noir had come from the same horse farm as Countess, but that was where the similarities ended. Where Countess was almost always calm under fire, Noir was quick to go on the attack. Sort of like her human partner. At only three years of age, I expected her to grow out of some of that. Then again, I'd expected my little brother to grow out of a lot of things, too.

"Something on your mind?" Danny asked.

"Oh, nothing."

"Uh-huh." He eyed me suspiciously but said no more.

Pastor Stephen and Jake rode behind us, the pastor on Gared and Jake on a red roan he called Sanguine. Jason rode in front of Jake, while Helen clung to Stephen's back.

We greeted the Columbia officers standing guard at the fair's entrance, alongside two armored men wielding shiny, blunted halberds. They ordered the visitors waiting in line to the side, then waved us through. Some of the onlookers cheered as we rode past, while others quietly took pictures or video with their tablets.

Once inside, Lieutenant Stallings split off from us with half the Mobile and Philadelphia contingents while I took the other half. "We'll meet back at the transports in an hour," she said.

"Sounds good." I waved at her, then turned Countess down the main avenue cutting through the fairgrounds. Brightly colored tents lined either side of the avenue, each staffed by exhibitors demonstrating old trades or vendors hawking a variety of wares. We shifted our formation to a single-file column and kept to the center as we worked our way through the throngs of visitors.

Most of the wares tended toward historical reproductions or fantasy costume gear and jewelry, but we also came across a group of vendors who were set up at our convention. A lot of what they sold was for law enforcement equestrians, but there was definitely a crossover market for private citizens: dietary supplements, horse trailers of varying sizes, tack and bridles, composite shoes, and whole-hoof boots that protected against glass and other sharp hazards were all on display, both here and back at the university.

Pretty women in white coats from VetTech were handing out pamphlets and showing videos of experimental nanite treatments for horses and other farm livestock, capable of healing grievous injuries and extending prime-of-life well beyond the normal life expectancy. "Frisky at Fifty!" read one of the banners set up in front of the booth.

I was more than a little proud that our convention was one of the few in the country that drew support and sponsorship from both Teledyne and Obsidian. It was also one of the few places where the two Corporations and their subsidiaries could sit elbow-to-elbow and not have events devolve into a shouting match or a gunfight.

Even D&H Equipment had set up a booth at the Renaissance fair this weekend, wedged between a leatherworks stall and a costume armorer. With the exception of Combined Arms Conglomerate, D&H was the only other company attending our convention that wasn't owned by either Corporation, and both had tried to acquire it. Neither had risked a hostile takeover, though. It wasn't wise to get violent with a company that supplied hundreds of police departments and private militaries.

"Yo, Nate!" the D&H company rep shouted, a grin splitting his bushy beard. "How's the retention attachment holding up?"

I patted my holster. It was secured to my duty belt by one of the company's adapters. "Still alive and kicking after how many years? Five?"

"Six! Since we saw each other in Richmond. Hey, what is Mobile's SWAT team saying about switching over to our plate carriers?"

"They've been working fine for my squad. I'll have to check with Captain Cochran when I get back."

"You sure do know how to smooth talk everyone," Jake said after we rode past.

Danny chuckled. "More like the sales reps know how to smooth talk him. Department's made a lot of equipment investments based on his recommendations. Wouldn't surprise me if some of these companies have him on the wall as their salesman of the month!"

"Hey, I call it like I see it," I said. "If it's the best, then everyone should have it."

Before Danny could reply, the squeaky tones of some nameless pop singer emitted from his pocket in a loud screech. He cursed under his breath and pulled out his phone.

"Is that Riley Virus?" Jake asked.

"I'm not sure what's worse," Danny said, "my having this ringtone or you knowing the singer's name. She's my wife's favorite at the moment." He pushed a button, then put the phone to his ear. "Hey, darlin'. How's the Mighty A today? Change of plans? Well, listen, I'm kind of in the middle of a patrol right now. Can we talk a little later? Great. Love ya. Bye!"

Danny let out a deep sigh as he pocketed the phone. "Sorry about that. Told her to send me a picture when she got to Battleship Park, but she wanted to talk."

"You could've spoken with her for a bit," I said. "No harm in it."

"With the public around?" He waved his arm to encompass the people walking down the avenue with them. "Sets a bad example."

"Why?" Brother Stephen asked. "Most of the people are on their phones anyway, walking around like there's nothing else going on."

"He's got a point," Jake said.

The fairgrounds opened up into a series of fenced-off clearings where equine demonstrations were taking place. A dozen buffalo riders from the Marajo military police had the smallest field to themselves. The Brazilian soldiers were surrounded by curious and excited onlookers who were likely seeing a water buffalo for the first time, outside of videos posted online. The giant, yet placid, buffalo looked slow and lumbering, but I'd seen them at full gallop. They could keep pace with any of the horses we had. Their commander, Sergeant Berengár Silva, held a child in either arm as he sat in the saddle. He grinned for the cameras.

Knights in full plate mail jousted at the lists. The bleachers on the other side of the field were packed with spectators, and the wooden fence on our side was lined with even more. Every time the charging knights met, the double crack of lances shattering against shields resounded, followed by a hearty cheer from the crowd.

A number of mounted officers from different departments sat atop their horses behind the pedestrians near the fence. I recognized one red-uniformed gentleman as Captain Andrew Graham, commander of the Royal Canadian Mounted Police detachment that had come to Columbia. His was the largest force at forty-eight men and women, seconded by Captain Phillips' Border Patrol at thirty-three. I waved to him. "Captain Graham, when's the Music Ride?"

He smiled and returned the wave. "Later this afternoon. It'll be our first time performing in the United States, so we're pulling out all the stops. Expect quite a show!"

"I'm looking forward to it!" And I was. I'd been blessed to see them perform a couple years back when I was up in Edmonton, training their municipal mounted unit. The Music Ride had come to town just before I left. It was a full half-hour of thirty-two Mounties maneuvering their horses to a wide variety of musical pieces. The choreography of some of their more complex formations had been astounding. Jason and Helen were going to love it.

We spent the rest of the hour wending our way through as many lanes and avenues of the fair as we could comfortably fit down. I arranged it so that Mobilians and Philadelphians rode one behind the other. The Philadelphian horses weren't as used to crowds of this size as our horses were. While Philadelphia was much larger than Mobile, they didn't have Mardi Gras to contend with each year. Weeks of parades and near-riotous crowds would turn any timid horse into a veteran within a season. The Philadelphian horses drew strength from the Mobilian mounts' quiet confidence.

"I'm hungry!" Jason announced as we neared the fair entrance.

"I could go for some breakfast as well." Jake ruffled Jason's short, black hair. "Want to split a breakfast burrito?"

"Yeah! Do they have breakfast burritos here?"

"Good question. Well, we'll get something good to eat. Maybe some kind of Polish sausage."

My stomach growled at that. I stood in my stirrups and looked around. "All right, I think if we turn left at the next intersection, we can head to one of the food courts." We'd passed about six of them, and each time it had been a struggle not to drool.

"Hey, look! Camels!" Helen pointed.

Four tan-skinned officers in green uniforms, wearing red and white *shemagh* on their heads, trotted toward the entrance, their bodies swaying from side to side in time with their large animals' rolling gaits. People hurried to get out of the way, their annoyed shouts turning into surprised laughs and cries of "Woah, look at that!" when they realized the men were riding camels. I recognized the man in the lead as Lieutenant Yousef Saleh of the Jordanian Royal Desert Forces. I raised my hand and opened my mouth to shout a greeting.

"Something's not right," Jake said. He tilted his head to the side, listening. "There's a commotion at the gate."

"Want to go check it out?" Danny asked.

"Oh, of course." I smiled. "Gotta back up our fellow officers, after all." To the others I said, "Form up just inside the gate and get the civilians out of the way. Sergeant Ward and I will go out. Be ready to charge in on my command, except for you two." I pointed at Jake and Stephen. "Keep my kids out of trouble."

Danny and I led the way, cutting through the crowd. As we drew closer to the gatehouse, the unmistakable sounds of a heated argument rose above the din. "Police, make way!" I shouted, and the command was echoed by the others behind us.

Through the gatehouse, I could see that Saleh and his fellow camel cops had formed up with the Columbia officers on foot. They half-surrounded a group of men and women dressed in tailored suits, most of whom wore sunglasses.

"Get these unsightly beasts away from me!" a reedy voice shouted. "Do you know who I am?"

"I have an idea," the Columbia sergeant said, "and it doesn't matter, sir. The ticket master told you the rules. Everyone pays to enter, or they're not allowed in."

"Why should I have to pay to enter this festival for the rabble?" A slight man in an expensive suit glared at the cop, then waved a hand. "Now, get these disgusting animals away from me!"

One of the camels snorted. "Don't insult our mounts, sir," Saleh said. "They understand your tone very well."

"What are you, its lover?" The man sneered. "I'll say what I damn well please about your smelly, nasty beasts. And I'll have them out of my city—"

One of the other riders' camels grunted, then reared its head back. There was a loud hawking sound and then it spit a wad of *something* at the angry, little man.

A white-haired, young woman in a fitted, black, three-piece suit threw herself between the man and the camel. The wad of slimy spit struck her squarely in the chest, but before it even had time to settle onto her dark gray shirt and vest, she was on the move. In the blink of an eye, she stood in front of the offending camel, her gloved hand balled into a fist and cocked back.

The petite woman struck the camel with enough force to snap its head completely to the side. It staggered, groaned, and collapsed. Its rider tumbled from the saddle and rolled along the ground.

I sat there, my mouth agape. Now *that* wasn't something you saw every day.

* * * * *

Chapter Three

Shouting erupted among the other camel cops, the Columbia cops, and even the halberdiers and crossbowmen on the parapet above. The downed Jordan officer jumped to his feet and ran to the stricken camel's side. Saleh screamed in a mix of Arabic and English, first at his officer, then at the alabaster-skinned woman.

She turned her gaze on me as I approached, and it was then I realized her irises were a brilliant purple. Her gaze dropped to Countess, then back up to me, before she turned back to the irate Jordanians. Even from high up, I could tell she was short, probably no taller than five feet. Her black, hand-tailored, three-piece suit clung to her curvy, yet petite, frame. Her coat hung open, and I saw a hint of black leather hugging the sides of her breasts: a shoulder holster, with what I assumed was a spare magazine pouch on one side. Definitely a bodyguard.

"Holy shit," Danny muttered. "That's Teledyne's Battle Flower. Specialist Aster, the Lady in Black, herself."

"Is it normal for Specialists to be able to cold-cock a half-ton dromedary with one punch from a tiny fist?"

"That isn't the half of it, Nate. She was going easy on the animal."

"Well, then we better get out there and explain that to Saleh. Poor man looks like he's about ready to shoot her where she stands."

"He would not survive the attempt."

I shivered. If my brother was spooked, there was reason to tread lightly. "Let's deal with this, then." I nudged Countess forward, then raised my voice. "What seems to be the problem here?"

The Columbia sergeant in charge turned to face me. The nameplate above his badge read "Felix." He waved us back. "Lieutenant, we have this under control. It's just a minor disturbance."

"Minor disturbance?" the well-dressed man snapped. "I'll have you know that I'm Roland Strohl, senior manager of Tower Floor Seventeen."

"Is that supposed to mean something?" I asked Danny, loud enough for everyone to hear. "Isn't Teledyne Tower thirty-nine stories tall?"

Sergeant Felix cast a baleful glance my way. "You're not helping, Lieutenant."

"Yes, this situation doesn't need any more low-rent security in the mix." Strohl threw up his hands. "I've got an important client to meet with in there, and you lot are—" He paused, then studied me. "Where are you from?"

"Mobile, Alabama," Danny said.

"*And* Philadelphia."

Jake pulled Sanguine up next to Danny and me. I looked back and saw Jason standing with Stephen and Helen. The pastor had dismounted and moved to the side, well out of any potential line of fire.

Strohl's eyes narrowed. "You're all from Obsidian territory."

Aster stiffened, as did the other bodyguards.

"We're servants of the people," I said. "The taxpayers fund our departments."

"And who do you think funds the taxpayers, my blue-uniformed friend?" Strohl touched his chest. "We do. The Corporations employ most of this nation's workforce, who in turn fund what little government we allow to exist, like the good, little cash cows they are. Am I wrong?"

I gripped Countess's reins tightly. Damn him.

He smiled. "Yes, exactly. And you understand who your master is, right, Corporal Felix?"

Felix blinked. He pointed to his stripes. "Excuse me, sir, but I'm a sergeant—"

"Not anymore." He raised a hand, and one of his entourage removed a phone from her pocket and stepped away with it to her ear.

Strohl pointed at us. "Obsidian owns them." Then his finger drifted toward Felix. "And we own you. Be grateful you're not being terminated and blacklisted for daring to question a member of Teledyne's upper management."

Felix's face turned beet red, and his hands balled into fists. He lowered his head and muttered, "Yes, sir. Thank you, sir."

Strohl beamed. "That's the spirit. And now that we're all on the same page, we'll—"

"We're not on the same page." Saleh pointed at the downed camel. "Your little girl assaulted one of my animals. If he's been injured, my government will demand recompense." He leaned forward in his saddle. "And my people aren't owned by either of your godless Corporations."

"No, they're owned by a royal family instead," Strohl retorted. "How is that any better?"

Aster suddenly cocked her head to the side, as if listening to something. Behind her, Strohl's remaining bodyguards put hands to their earpieces.

My radio suddenly squawked a high-pitched emergency signal. The noise was a lot louder than I remembered it being, but when I muted it, I realized it wasn't just my radio going off. The radio of every officer within earshot was going nuts. I pulled my radio free and switched to the emergency band.

"*—grounds immediately. I repeat, a state of emergency has been declared. All active duty police and first responders, report to your respective departments and supervisors for further instruction. All visiting mounted officers and their handlers, return to the university grounds immediately. Over.*"

"Well, that doesn't sound good," Danny said.

No, it didn't. What in the world was going on?

* * * * *

Chapter Four

I tuned my radio to the squad's frequency. "You all heard the call. Let's get our mounts to the trucks."

One of Manager Strohl's bodyguards whispered in his ear. He sighed, then nodded. "Oh, very well. We'll do as he asks and meet with the mayor. We're leaving, everyone." He looked at Aster. "Except for you. There's no way you're riding with me, smelling and looking like that."

He turned away, and his other bodyguards followed closely behind. "You can run along behind the vehicle, Aster. Or you can ride on the roof."

If Aster felt anger or shame at the mistreatment, she gave no outward sign. She turned to follow.

"Wait just a minute," I said. "You'd treat one of your own that way, after she protected you? Without even a word of thanks?"

Strohl stopped mid-step. "She only did as she was trained. There was no thought involved, only ingrained reflex." He looked over his shoulder at me. "Should a father thank his six year-old for using the toilet the way he was taught to when he was two? Where's the sense in that?"

I didn't know what to say to that. These Corporate types were real assholes.

He considered me a moment longer, then started walking again. "Very well. If an Obsidian mutt is so worried about the safety of a Teledyne purebred, who am I to judge? Clean her up and return her to me at City Hall. I will be there for the duration of this 'state of emergency.'"

We watched as the Teledyne manager and his entourage walked down the path toward a waiting executive sedan, its long, sleek body painted a dark blue. The vehicle's hood ornament bore Teledyne's logo, as did the antenna rising from the rear fender. There was no mistaking who owned that vehicle.

Sergeant—*Corporal* Felix heaved a sigh. "God, I hate that stuffed-shirted son of a…" His voice trailed off, and he looked at Aster.

Aster ignored him. Her purple eyes flicked from me to Danny to Jake. She said nothing, and there was a long pause.

"I should arrest her for assault!" Saleh said into the awkward silence. "Your government has given my men full powers of arrest, and striking a police animal in this country is the same as attacking a sworn officer, yes?"

"It is, but that isn't the problem." I nodded to Danny.

"You saw what she did to your man's camel. What does it weigh, nearly fifteen hundred pounds?"

"A lucky strike," Saleh snapped.

"She was holding back, I assure you."

Saleh started to scoff, then hesitated. He looked down at Aster, an appraising look in his eye. "Is this true?"

Aster turned her gaze toward Saleh. She stared at him for a few seconds, then looked forward, her body sliding into a parade-rest stance. "I didn't want to kill him."

Her voice was soft, graceful, and very feminine. It matched her outward appearance, but not the raw physical power she had displayed. And she had been holding back, to hear her tell it. I shivered again.

"Get the kids and the others back to the university," I said to Danny. "I'll take the command vehicle and get her over to city hall."

"You sure you don't want any backup?" He eyed Aster suspiciously.

"If it came down to it, would it really matter?"

"I suppose not."

"Then stay with the kids." I looked at Jake. "You, too, if you would. Jason's really taken a liking to you."

"I'll check with the LT," he said, "but I don't think it'll be a problem. Both units have their horses stabled on the university grounds. I'll see if Jake wants to help brush Sanguine."

I smiled. "He'd like that." To Felix I said, "Sorry about all that."

"Wasn't your fault, sir." Felix still looked like he was ready to spit nails at the next Corporate toad he came across. "It's just how it is. I'm sure Captain Bradley will get it straightened out. He's good people."

We formed up and rode back to the horse trailers. I let Danny ride in the lead and hung back a bit, more to keep an eye on Aster than anything. She walked to the side of our column, well out of the way of the horses.

Jason sat in front of Jake again, and he couldn't keep his eyes off Aster. He first tried waving at her, then began shadow-boxing at imaginary camels, adding more punches than Aster had used. "Bang, zap! Right in the camel's trap!"

Jake shushed him as some of the other officers chuckled. The merriment was tinged with more than a little trepidation. Most of them had seen what Aster did, and the same thought that was running through my mind had to be running through theirs.

If she could do that to a camel, what could she do to us?

I dismounted and led Countess up into one of the trailers we brought, then returned to the command van. Aster stood at the rear door, her folded coat resting on the van's chrome bumper, her tie rolled up and placed to the side. She removed her shoulder holster next, then her slime-covered vest.

Brother Stephen rummaged around the inside of the van. "Where do I remember seeing... Ah, here it is."

He came out with a button-down MPD uniform shirt, devoid of any medals or insignia. "One of Patrolman Pierce's. She's about the same size as Miss Aster, wouldn't you say?"

Close enough that it made no difference. Kelly Pierce was out on maternity leave, and she wouldn't miss the shirt for some time. "That should work in a pinch. What do you think?"

Aster took the offered shirt and ran her fingers along the fabric. She nodded, then set it down on the bumper. "This will do."

In a blink, she had her spit-soaked shirt unbuttoned and stripped off. She wore no undershirt, just a sports bra that kept her breasts snug and out of the way if she needed to fight. The sunlight gleamed off her smooth, white skin as she reached up and started to peel off her bra.

"Woah, woah, woah!" both Stephen and I shouted in unison. "Get in the van first!"

She froze, her thumbs hooked under the front of her bra. She looked at us for a long moment, one twitch away from being publicly indecent. Finally, she picked up the police shirt and shoulder holster and stepped into the van. As she did so, I saw that she had another pistol tucked into the small of her back, along with a knife or dagger of some sort. How much heat was she packing?

Stephen stepped out. "There's a towel for you to wipe down with over there," he said.

Her sports bra dropped to the metal floor of the van, and she turned to face us, her mouth open to say—

Stephen and I slammed the doors shut. We looked at each other for a long time, then sighed. This was *not* an experience an officer and his chaplain wanted to share.

At least it answered my earlier question, in a way: Aster was packing *a lot* of heat.

"Daddy's face is red!" Jason called from the horse trailers.

"Brother Stephen's, too!" Helen added.

Danny looked at us. "Yeah, both of you do look a little flushed. See anything good?"

"That's enough out of you," we snapped in unison.

"Oh, ho, I was right!"

The van doors opened, and Aster stepped out. She had donned both shirt and shoulder holster. "Thank you," she said quietly as she pulled on her coat.

"Don't mention it," Brother Stephen said, a bit of red still showing on his otherwise tan cheeks. He looked everywhere but at her.

That made two of us. "If you're both ready to go, let's make tracks."

* * *

City hall stood in the center of Columbia's Old Town district. Surrounded by banks, restaurants, and theaters, it stood eight stories high. A few of those floors had only been added in recent years, from what I'd been told.

The building took up an entire city block, with the entrance at the intersection of East Broadway and North 8th Street. The corner of the building was set back from the street in a concave design. A decorative arch in the shape of a keyhole stood between the building and the street. This "gate" served as an artistic symbol of who held the key to the city.

At least, it had. The mayor's office hadn't controlled the city in at least twenty years, not since JalCom had first taken over and then Teledyne. The real seat of power in Columbia lay more than two miles away in the penthouse of Teledyne Tower, a glass and steel building that dwarfed everything in the region.

Still, the Corporations sometimes liked to maintain appearances for the sake of tradition and to keep the masses in line. If the people wanted a mayor, they got a mayor. Even if he was just a figurehead.

Several police vehicles had been parked alongside city hall, and a squad of Columbia officers stood guard outside the main entrance. Police tape blocked access through anywhere except the keyhole gate. A line of men and women in business attire and casual dress waited for their chance to enter.

Stephen and I followed Aster as she cut to the head of the line, heedless of the objections thrown her way. A Columbia officer held up a hand to forestall her, then did a double-take. "Specialist, how can I help you?"

"Manager Strohl ordered me to attend him. He's in the command post."

He let her pass, then blocked Stephen and me as we attempted to follow. "Sorry, sirs, you'll have to go to the back of the line."

Aster stopped and turned. "These men are my escorts."

"Ma'am, we're happy to let you in, but we weren't given orders to let anyone else through without proper vetting. Visiting officers need special permission to get in."

"He was very specific with his orders." She cocked her head to the side. "Something to do with Director Ingersoll, if I remember right."

That brought the officer up short. "Yes, ma'am. Please, come through. You, too, Lieutenant, and—"

"Chaplain," Stephen said. He touched the collar of his uniform shirt. "Baptist, so no white collar for me."

"Yes, of course. Please, come through."

As we entered the lobby, she turned and led us away from the main set of elevators. We rounded a corner and were met by a pair of Columbia SWAT officers, guarding what looked like a utility closet. They opened the door and stood out of the way, revealing a set of stairs leading down to a basement level.

The stairwell descended for several flights, until we were at least fifty feet underground. We walked in silence, the only sound that of our riding boots and Aster's wingtips clicking on concrete. My curiosity grew with each passing moment, along with my sense of worry.

"Why did you tell the gate officer that?" I asked.

"Manager Strohl did tell you to escort me to him, did he not?" She glanced back at us. "Besides, I thought you would want to see what was going on."

"Of course, I do. In a crisis, the more information, the better."

"You may have a different opinion in a short while."

A chill ran down my spine. "Do you know what's going on?" Strohl's other bodyguards had earpieces. Did she have one hidden behind her long, white hair?

"Very little. What I do know isn't good."

Another pair of SWAT officers met us at the bottom. They guarded what looked like a vault door stolen from a bank. Beyond it was a corridor lined with steel doors on either side. Aster led us past all of them to a door on the far end.

We stepped into a dimly lit room filled with seats facing a glass window, overlooking a command center like you'd find at Obsidian's Space Center in Huntsville: row upon row of technicians at computers, each studying a specific part of a greater situation. And that greater situation was nationwide, if the projection on the screen on the far wall was any indicator. A map of the continental United States took up the entire wall, divided between Obsidian on the East Coast, Teledyne on the West Coast, and a smattering of smaller Corporations in the contested lands of the Midwest. Several city names were highlighted on the map all over the country, the letters written in either red or black. There were also lines criss-crossing the nation, with indicators showing projected points of impact. Satellite imagery and traffic camera footage appeared on big screens below the projections, the feeds rotating after a few replays.

"Lieutenant Ward?"

Captain Graham's bright red Mounty uniform stood out, even in the gloom. He waved us over to a corner filled with other mounted police officers, including Captain Mike DiAngelo of the NYPD, Lieutenant Kevin Hanson of the St. Louis PD, Captain Ko Hsu of the Philadelphia PD, Lieutenant Cassandra Martinez of the LAPD, and Captain Eugene Phillips of the Border Patrol and the short-lived Phillips' Phalanx.

Phillips still wore most of his riot gear from the melee, minus the helmet. He shook my hand. "Nate, didn't expect to see you here."

"And in such esteemed company," Cassandra Martinez said. "The Lady in Black is a legend in the LAPD. She and her 'Party of Nine' helped us with the sandbagging of Spring Street during the market turbulence a couple years back. Saved a lot of officers' lives." The tall woman snapped to attention and saluted. "Ma'am, it's an honor."

Aster returned the salute, the slight hint of a smile on her pink lips. "Section Nine goes where our handlers send us. We were happy to be of assistance."

"Aster!" a voice hissed from the front of the room. It was Strohl. He motioned for her to join him.

Aster took one last look at me and then took up position close to Strohl. She turned her back to the glass and faced toward the door we had come through, gloved hands crossed in front of her belt buckle. She stared straight ahead, her purple eyes seeming to glow in the dim light.

Strohl turned his attention forward again. Two older men in suits sat to his right: one was Mayor Reynolds, and the other was Chief Ballantine.

"Another one just popped!" a tech on the other side of the glass shouted. "And another! My God, there are so many!"

"Track them!" a deep voice boomed.

I turned back to the projection as a new set of lines appeared on the country map. Arrows extended out from the heads of those lines, showing the path of something moving from east to west. Missile-shaped icons appeared on those lines, and it was only then that I noticed them on the already existing lines.

My blood ran cold. "My God, they've finally done it, haven't they?"

"So it would seem," Captain Hsu said. "Who fired first?"

Captain Graham shook his head. "Does it matter? Won't the result be the same?"

"God, I thought it was just a few." Martinez put a hand to her mouth and whispered, "The world's about to fall, isn't it?"

* * * * *

Chapter Five

If the map was correct, more than forty cities had vanished in the span of just a few minutes, including Chicago, Atlanta, Charlotte, and Miami.

And still more missiles flew, from Teledyne, from Obsidian, and from any other Corporation big enough to have even a single nuke. It seemed like the whole damned arsenal was being used in an absolutely insane display of destructive power. Cities in the crosshairs only had minutes left, too short a time to mobilize evacuations.

Every few seconds, my gaze drifted down to southern Alabama. The state's geographic outline was cloaked in the black of Obsidian's sphere of influence, but no city names had appeared yet. No missiles tracked toward it. I prayed that Mobile and the cities surrounding her would somehow survive this.

"Lord, let these missiles not find their targets," Brother Stephen quietly prayed. "Protect the faithful. Protect your children. Lord, just protect *everyone*."

"Amen," Martinez, Graham, and Hsu said in unison.

A deep alarm blared through the command center. A new projection appeared on the wall to the left of the nationwide map. This map was of the state of Missouri, with the city of Columbia highlighted in orange. Two more cities—Kansas City to the west and St. Louis to the east—were also highlighted. Several missiles approached each city, Teledyne missiles bound for St. Louis from the west and

Obsidian missiles sailing toward Columbia and Kansas City from the east and north.

"Targets designated as Missiles 07 to 10 have targeted Columbia!" one of the techs shouted. "Closest is three minutes away!"

My stomach tied itself into a knot. Phillips cursed under his breath. Martinez and Hsu closed their eyes and joined Brother Stephen in his near-constant, whispered prayer. Mayor Reynolds and Chief Ballantine jumped to their feet and started talking over one another.

Strohl put a phone to his ear, said a few words into it, then raised his voice. "Silence!"

That startled Reynolds and Ballantine enough to shut them up. The only sounds in the observation room were the whispered prayers of Brother Stephen.

Strohl gave Stephen a disgusted look, then flipped a switch next to the glass. "Permission to use CBMs granted. Destroy these Obsidian lances before they have a chance to poke us."

His voice echoed in the command room. The man in charge down below looked up, saw who had spoken, and snapped to attention. "Sir!"

Strohl waved him away, then turned off the mic. "Well, now, all we can do is wait," he said, his voice as cool as ice.

Still, I couldn't help but notice his left leg bouncing up and down. The unconscious display of fear blunted the surge of hope I felt at the idea of countermeasures.

* * *

A servant popped the cork on the champagne bottle and poured a glass for Director Lloyd, head of Obsidian's St. Louis branch. The servant then placed the bottle back into a chilled bucket and left the executive's vast office.

Lloyd spun his chair around to look out the floor-to-ceiling windows. The fifty-three story building was small by his standards, but at least it towered over the rest of the city, including the St. Louis Arch. He looked down at it as he sipped the champagne. *Ah, chilled to the perfect temperature.*

"Jacobs, would you like a glass?" Lloyd asked.

Agent Jacobs stood in the corner of the room, silent as a shadow. His face lit up at the prospect. "Sir, I won't say no if you're offering."

Lloyd waved a hand at the bucket. "By all means. We're on the cusp of greatness, and a lot of it's thanks to your efforts."

"Thank you, sir."

As Jacobs poured himself a glass, Lloyd turned his head to the west. A wall lined with bookcases blocked his view, but he wasn't looking at anything within eyesight. He had his sights set on something more than a hundred miles away, something he had only just learned about that morning, from a former JalCom employee who knew a little too much about the defunct Corporation's secret projects.

Once they let the doctors finish healing him, he and Jacobs would return to the sublevels for further questioning.

2067 was going to be a great year, indeed.

The champagne bottle dropped into the bucket with a loud crash. Lloyd jumped and glared at the Agent. "Easy, man," he started to say, then trailed off.

Jacobs held a hand to his ear, his eyes distant as he listened to someone. "Understood," he said.

The Agent then ran to the bookcases on the western wall and flung one of them aside. Finance and productivity books flew everywhere, and the bookcase crashed into the corner of the room.

A hatch occupied the bare space on the wall. Jacobs pushed the button to open it, revealing a padded tube large enough for a man.

Fear seized Lloyd. "What's going on?" he demanded.

"Teledyne strike," Jacobs said, his voice deadpan. "Early warning systems failed to detect it. We only have seconds."

Lloyd jumped to his feet and looked out the window. In the streets below, the air raid alarms started wailing. He opened his mouth to say something.

Jacobs grabbed him by the collar and shoved him into the tube. "This'll get you to the subfloors, sir." Though the Agent's voice was calm, his eyes were wide. He pushed the button. "Good luck."

The hatch sealed, and the last thing Lloyd heard was the muffled moan of the siren.

Then he fell.

* * *

"Do you think Daddy's gonna be okay with the Camel Lady?" Jason asked. He sat in the center seat of the police truck, sandwiched between Danny and Helen.

Danny pulled in line with the other vehicles parked near the university's stable complex and checked the mirror to make sure the horse trailer he was hauling was also lined up. He reached over and patted Jason on the knee. "Your father's a tough man. He'll be fine."

"Yeah, but she punched a *camel!* They're big! What if she hits Dad?"

Then he'd go down like a sack of potatoes. "Aster hit that camel because it tried to spit on the man she was guarding. As long as your father keeps the peace and doesn't trouble Mr. Strohl, she won't have any reason to hit him."

"He didn't seem very nice," Helen said. "He seemed rather mean."

"Can't argue with you there," Danny said.

He hopped out of the truck, then ran around to the other side to help Helen and then Jason get out. "Come on, y'all. Let's get Countess and the others out."

It had taken a few minutes to load up all the animals and start the short drive back to the university from Cedar Lake Park. Much of what had been the southern portion of the city limits had been given over to farmland after the urban reclamation fads of the '30s and '40s. They had driven past fields with the beginning growth of corn and wheat, and by pastureland where cattle and horses grazed. Farmers stopped what they were doing to stare and wave at the police convoy.

Pedestrian traffic had grown heavy once they reached the university grounds. Even for a Sunday, many of the school's twenty-five thousand students were on campus, either because they lived there or because they were busy studying for finals. It seemed like all of them were outside, huddled together in groups or shouting questions to Danny and the other cops as they passed. Everyone wanted to know about the state of emergency.

A few stable hands joined Danny as he lowered the trailer's ramp. "Sergeant, any idea what's going on?" one asked.

Just then Danny's phone started ringing with that stupid Riley Virus ringtone his wife had set. The students looked at each other, then back at him. It was obvious they were trying to contain smiles and grins.

"Wish I knew," he said with a flash of annoyance. He fumbled in his pocket and muted the phone. *Sorry, darlin'. Little busy.*

"It's Uncle Jake!" Jason cried suddenly, and off he ran.

Danny turned to chase after his nephew, but then he saw Jake scoop him up in one arm. His other hand held the reins of Sanguine. "There you are, little guy! Ready to give Sang a brushing?"

"Yeah!"

"Good, because he could use it!" Jake looked at Danny. "Haven't heard anything since the initial call on our end. You?"

"Nope. Must be one of those 'need to know' kind of things."

"Well, we learned all about that when we were in Obsidian, right?" Jake shook his head and chuckled. "Not much changes."

"You worked with Obsidian, too?" Helen asked.

"Sure did! We even went to boot camp together. Didn't see each other much after that, though. Different departments, and Obsidian's a big Corporation."

In the distance, a low hum resolved itself into the high-pitched scream of a siren. Danny and Helen froze, and looked at one another. "Sounds like the Friday Noon alarm," she said.

"*Vrrrrrrrooooooooooo OOOOOO!*" Jason howled, imitating the sound of Mobile's civil defense air raid alarm as it powered up to full output. A relic of the First Cold War, it had been a part of city life for many decades, its deafening tone piercing the sky for a full minute every Friday at 12:00 PM on the dot. It was deactivated sometime after the year 2000, only to be brought back once the Second Cold War, the Corporate Cold War, began.

Danny checked his watch. 10:23 AM. Not exactly the time one would expect for a regularly scheduled siren test.

The alarm's high-pitched screech was joined by a deep rumble, both sounds coming from Teledyne Tower to the northwest. The building was clearly visible even a few miles away, the top third of the structure gleaming in the sunlight as it rose above the tree line. *What the hell?*

A missile shot into the sky, a trail of white smoke chasing after it. Three more missiles rose to join it.

Danny's heart skipped a beat. Was Teledyne launching nukes? Or were they CBMs?

"Woah, fireworks!" Jason squealed.

"Don't be stupid!" Helen snapped. "Those are rockets! Like what we saw in Huntsville!" She frowned and looked up at me. "What are they launching rockets for?"

"I wish I knew, darlin'." Danny patted her on the head, then pulled her close. The sense of dread he felt when he first heard the siren continued to grow. "I wish I knew."

* * *

"CBMs away!" one of the techs called.

A third projection appeared to the right of the nationwide missile tracking map. This showed a radar screen for the immediate area. The four missiles speeding toward Columbia appeared as blips on the screen. Rising from the center of the radar projection were four new blips, each sailing toward a different target.

"Contact for Missile 07, fifteen seconds! Contact for Missile 08, twenty-six seconds! Contact for—"

Four countdowns appeared on the screen near each of the approaching missiles. I leaned forward, arms across my chest, fingers digging into my biceps as I watched Missile 07's countdown go from fifteen to ten, then to five.

When five turned to zero, the two blips that represented the missile and the CBM merged. There was a bright flash on the radar screen and then both blips vanished. "Missile 07, destroyed!"

Missiles 08 and 09 vanished seconds later, and it was only then I realized I'd been holding my breath. I quickly exhaled, then sucked in a lungful of air to ease my aching chest. "One more missile," I whispered.

Missile 10 was the farthest away, with an estimated fifty seconds to impact. The final CBM soared toward it at a speed much greater than the Obsidian missile's. "CBM is ten seconds from target!"

"Prepare another volley," Strohl said into the intercom. "I don't want to take any chances."

"Five, four, three—Wait, what?"

Missile 10 suddenly vanished from the radar. The CBM disappeared an instant later as well.

Then the power cut out, casting us into near-total darkness. Two purple lights glowed in the darkness, and after a moment, I realized they were Aster's eyes. The luminescence in them was quickly fading, but it was there.

"Switching to emergency power!" a tech called.

After a moment, emergency lights came on, bathing the observation room and the command center in red. The two maps and the radar projection reappeared on the far wall, but something was wrong. The radar screen's details were fuzzed out, with the words "No Signal" stamped over the image.

The Missouri map was frozen, the missile trajectories revealing data seconds or minutes old, before the satellite connection was severed. St. Louis was splashed in red, and Kansas City had three missiles seconds from impact. Both cities were likely lost.

"My God," Hanson whispered. "That can't be true, can it?"

"Shit, Manhattan got hit," DiAngelo said. "My wife and kids are in the Poconos, but my parents are on Staten Island. You think they're all right?"

Martinez pressed a hand to her forehead. "LA's a big city. It's possible Rick's all right."

I looked at the nationwide map in the center of the screen. I started on the west coast and moved quickly east, my eyes falling on each city marked in red, my heart growing heavier with each name: Los Angeles, Prescott, Santa Fe, Lubbock, Fort Worth, Jasper, Shreveport.

Mobile.

My legs grew wobbly, and I had to lean against the wall to keep from falling over. I felt a hand grip my shoulder and saw it was Captain Graham. The RCMP officer had one hand on me and the other on Brother Stephen. Stephen continued to pray, eyes wide, tears running down his cheeks.

How could Mobile be gone? Lord, how could half the country be gone?

Aster stared at me, her expression unreadable. I remembered her words from the stairwell. She was right. I'd rather have not known any of this.

"Estimated impact of Missile 10 has elapsed, with an extra thirty seconds on the clock," one of the techs called. "It must have self-detonated high in the atmosphere."

"EMP?" another tech asked.

"It would explain the grid failure up above."

"Any reading from the radiation sniffers?" the command center leader demanded.

"Negative, sir. Air is clean."

A cheer rose up from the command center. I'll admit, I felt a momentary elation at having survived the nuclear attack meant for us, but it quickly died. So many cities and so, *so* many people we knew and loved were gone, their bodies atomized or burned to ash in a nuclear hellfire they never saw coming.

One minute they were enjoying life or struggling at work or suffering from an illness. The next minute, they were in the next world.

Lieutenant Martinez was right. We may have survived, but the world had fallen.

* * * * *

Chapter Six

"Nothing will leave this room," Mayor Reynolds said. "We'll pretend it's a local event and go from there."

That hit me like a punch to the gut. "Sir, we're not even allowed to tell our own people?"

"That's preposterous!" Captain Hsu snapped. "We should at least be able to inform the ones under our command!"

Chief Ballantine held up a hand to forestall any further grumbling. "I understand your feelings, but it'll be pandemonium if the people learn about the extent of the devastation."

"My men have a right to know their homes and families are gone!" DiAngelo jabbed a finger at Manager Strohl. "Killed by Teledyne bastards like him!"

"Obsidian's no better!" Lieutenant Martinez glared at DiAngelo. "The Corporate assholes who sign the NYPD's checks just cratered half of California!"

"Is that really a problem?"

"Why, you—"

Captains Phillips and Hsu stepped between the two officers. All four shouted at one another. Lieutenant Hanson stomped toward Manager Strohl, but Ballantine intercepted him. Hanson stuck a finger in the chief's face, his own face beet-red with anger. Captain Graham tried to restore order, but his voice was lost in the chaos of the room.

Numbness spread through my chest and into my head. The shock and grief I felt at what we'd just witnessed didn't disappear, but it took a backseat to the present situation. Someone needed to restore order, or it was going to come to blows.

Or worse.

Aster placed herself between Manager Strohl and the rest of the room, her hands at her side. Strohl's other bodyguards flanked her.

I tucked my thumb and forefinger into my mouth and whistled. The shrill sound brought everyone up short, and more than one set of eyes turned to study me. "The mayor and chief are right, much as I hate to admit it. Look at how much we're fighting. How do you think those under us would react? Or the citizens?"

No one said anything for a long moment. Then Captain Hsu lowered his head. "He's right."

"Thank you, Lieutenant Ward," Chief Ballantine said. "We're going to have to ease this into the public's consciousness. Hell, *I* need time to process it." He laughed nervously. "Hey, there's one upside to this for me. No more Thanksgiving dinners up in cold-ass Minneapolis with the in-laws, right?"

No one laughed. Mayor Reynolds cringed, but I understood the attempt at humor. One didn't walk the beat without learning to appreciate gallows humor. It still didn't make it funny, though; not this time.

"Give my office some time to come up with a proper statement," Reynolds said. "Until then, everyone return to your posts."

He turned back toward Manager Strohl, and the two men put their heads together. Chief Ballantine motioned us toward the door. "All right, then, you heard the mayor. All of you, return to your men and your billets. We'll figure out how best to utilize you shortly."

"Sir, if I may," Phillips said, "I'd like to offer some suggestions on how we can survive the present situation. Would you mind if I followed you back to headquarters?"

"I won't be leaving here for some time," Ballantine said, "but Captain Bradley can help you back at HQ."

The noon sun beat down on us as we left city hall. The frantic, but purposeful, energy of the command center gave way to frustrated chaos on the streets. The traffic along East Broadway had ground to a halt the instant Missile 10's electromagnetic pulse hit the city. The blast hadn't irradiated or vaporized us, but it had fried most electronics in the region. At least, that was the assumption we were working under, and the pile-up of disabled vehicles and confused, irate drivers only added to the pile of evidence.

"I trust you can see to my men?" Phillips asked as he turned to the right to follow East Broadway to Columbia's police headquarters, which was located a few buildings down.

"I'll let them know you're dealing with the situation," I promised.

"Lord, how are we supposed to keep this from everyone?" Brother Stephen whispered to me as we crossed the street to the parked van.

I bit back the reply I wanted to give and said, "It's gonna be tough; that's for sure."

The van wouldn't start, much as I'd feared. We opened up the back, and I was thankful we didn't have much equipment to lug back: just two sets of riot armor and a pair of shields. Most of the squad had carried their riot gear in the trucks hauling the horse trailers. The idea had been to keep this rear compartment clear so Corporal Stacey Ferris and Patrolman Christine Williams had a place to change, away from the prying eyes of the men.

That thought summoned an image of Aster in the van, turning toward us, her eyes questioning, her bare chest—

I shook my head to clear it. *Keep it together, Nate. You're not a horny, little teenager anymore.*

Brother Stephen slung a duffel bag full of riot gear over his shoulder. He held up the clear riot shield. "I'm surprised you can run around in all that gear."

I slung a matching bag over my shoulder. "The shield can get cumbersome after a while, but the armor isn't so bad. It's evenly distributed over the body, sort of like a knight's plate mail."

"I always thought *that* was heavy, too."

"We'll get you suited up one day, and you can tell me what you think." I lifted the shield and grimaced. "Yeah, like I said, cumbersome. But, it's a lot better than what our predecessors carried years back. It can also absorb most small arms fire, even at point blank range. Similar to the barding our horses wear."

We joined the other commanders and their escorts a few minutes later. Each was loaded down with various amounts of gear, suitcases, and paperwork taken from their disabled vehicles. None of us needed to wait for the others before returning to the university, but there was an unspoken desire to stick together.

It was a good thing we did, too. More than once during our walk back, we were stopped by scared or irate citizens demanding to know what happened, and when it was going to be fixed. Everyone had a different, urgent reason: "We have a church service to get to! Do something about this!" or "My kid's home alone! Can you go check on him?" or "My grandpa's in the hospital! Do they still have power?"

"The mayor and chief of police are working on it," I'd said each time, with much more confidence than I actually felt. "Proceed to your homes or to the nearest shelter and wait for further instructions."

"I can't believe it's gone," Lieutenant Hanson muttered. The St. Louis officer shambled along beside me, his eyes unseeing, as he placed one unsteady foot in front of the other. "I can't believe it's gone," he repeated, a little louder.

"Quiet!" Captain DiAngelo hissed. The NYPD officer glared at Hanson. "You heard the chief! Keep this to yourself."

Hanson's eyes focused on DiAngelo for a moment, then grew distant. He opened his mouth to speak, then snapped it shut and shook his head.

DiAngelo glared at Hanson a moment longer, then he turned his gaze to me. "You holding up all right, Teach?"

In spite of the situation, I smiled. DiAngelo had been calling me "Teach" since he and a bunch of other NYPD officers visited for Mardi Gras training a few years back. It had started as an insult, but he'd grown to respect me in the time we'd known each other.

There won't be any more Mardi Gras parades, a voice whispered inside my head.

The smile disappeared from my face. I focused on DiAngelo. "Yeah, I'm okay."

It was a long, long walk back.

* * *

"No good, LT." Corporal Collins stuck his head out of the door of the police truck and shook it. "It's dead, just like the others."

"Damn," I muttered. All our trucks and the command vehicle were down, their electronics fried like so many other vehicles in the city and surrounding area. I wondered how the other departments had fared. Even one working vehicle could make a huge difference.

"At least we made it back before the lights went out." Patrolman Williams put her hands on her hips and glared at the truck. "Think we can get it running again?"

"I doubt it," Danny said. "Not without parts that weren't also affected."

"Damn."

"Hey, LT, do you think we'll be stationed here awhile?" Collins asked.

"Oh, I imagine so." As far as I could tell, the university grounds was one of the only places in the city with electricity. As the afternoon slowly turned to evening, it was evident that lights were on in some—but not all—of the university's buildings. The only other building I could see from here that had any lights on was Teledyne Tower back over near city hall. It made sense they would have backup generators just like the university's hospital and command center.

"We'll stay here until we're told what else to do," I said.

"The university will need protecting," Danny added, "especially once the rest of the city realizes where the lights are on."

"It's as good a place as any to billet." Williams sighed. "At least we'll be able to take hot showers, unlike when Henrietta blew through. Remember that? Three weeks without power, except for those Obsidian jackasses in the RSA Tower. And they weren't sharing. Not electricity, and definitely not the food and ice being flown in by helicopter every day."

"And who was on duty keeping them safe from the hungry, smelly masses?" Patrolman Jones placed a hand on his chest. "Us."

"All right, enough of that," I snapped. "Stay focused on the present, not the past."

"LT's right," Danny said. "We need to keep our heads in the moment. Columbia doesn't have a large police force, and the university has even less. With most vehicles down, the mounted units have a great advantage. We could really make a difference in the days ahead, while we wait for relief to come."

I grimaced at that last part. Relief wasn't coming.

Corporal Ferris stretched and popped her shoulders. "It would certainly pass the time while we wait for orders to arrive from Mobile."

I turned away to hide my scowl. Orders weren't coming, either.

Still, she and Danny had a good point. We could do more than just sit around, waiting for someone to give us orders. And it would distract me from, well, everything. "Since we're all so eager to get off our butts and do something, I'll go see what the university needs." I walked west, toward the center of campus. "Y'all hold down the fort until I get back."

"Sure thing, LT!" Ferris called.

"Well, I guess we'll be here a few days longer than we thought, right?" Collins asked, his voice carrying to where I was. "Sarge, you able to catch your woman on your phone?"

"Nah, haven't had any luck since this morning. No service at all, so I imagine the cell towers are down."

"At least your phone still works! Mine's toast. Can't access my pictures or even play City Slacker 4!"

Ferris's laugh cut through the air. "Oh, poor baby!"

My stomach churned. None of them knew, and I couldn't tell them. Not yet. Maybe not ever. Chief Ballantine was right: if word got out to our subordinates, it would shatter morale. And if word got out to the public, it would send the citizens into a panic. And if police morale was shattered when the general populous spiraled into panic-fueled chaos...

I shook my head to clear it. No. That had to be avoided at all cost. Even if it meant hiding the fate of Ferris's parents and boyfriend, of Collins' nephews and dogs, of—

Of Danny's wife, Amy. Of Mom and Dad. Dear God, of *everyone* we knew. How could Mobile be gone? And in the blink of an eye. I could just imagine the smoking crater that was downtown. The RSA Tower and Admiral Semmes hotel, reduced to rubble. Battleship Park blasted clean, its namesake rolled over into Mobile Bay and capsized before its renovations could be completed. Amy had been working hard on that, with just a week or so to go before its shakedown cruise.

How was I going to tell Helen and Jason that their aunt, their cousins, and all their friends were dead?

Bile suddenly rose up in my throat. I stopped and clamped a hand over my mouth. Tears stung my eyes. How in the name of all that was holy were we going to recover from this? And why were we spared?

Focus. I took a shuddering breath, held it, then released it slowly. The next breath was steadier, as was the one after that. After the fourth breath I started walking again. My head cleared, though the thickness in my throat remained.

I looked over my shoulder and saw Danny, Williams, Ferris, and Collins chatting with the other Mobile officers who had gathered around the stricken trailers in their permanent resting spots on the grass outside the stables. None of them had looked my way and seen me nearly lose it. Good. I had to be strong for them. They deserved no less than that.

What I needed was something to distract me from the thoughts seeking to tear me down.

I walked past several student housing buildings and over a footbridge before arriving at the main dining hall on campus. A group of students and administrators had gathered near the entrance off Virginia Avenue. An older man stood on top of a milk crate in front of the gathered body of people. His tie hung loose and his shirt sleeves were rolled up to the elbow. He held a megaphone at his side in one hand, a clipboard in the other. I could only assume the device was another casualty of the EMP, as he wasn't using it to address the crowd.

"—the backup generators are supplying both hospitals just fine," the man said, "so don't worry about the patients who are there. What we need to be focused on is assessing which rooms and buildings throughout the rest of the campus still have power, and which ones have working equipment. Computers, copiers, kitchen appliances. All of it's going to be important in the days to come."

It was Dr. Schneider, I realized belatedly. He was head of the electrical engineering department, a member of the university's board of directors, and one of the mounted police convention's sponsors. I'd only met him once, on the day we arrived, and he had been wearing a full suit, hat, and glasses. He looked a bit disheveled now, but it was definitely him.

Dr. Schneider checked his clipboard. "Of top priority is checking all the refrigerators and freezers in the kitchen, the food warehouse, and the science and medical labs. The kitchen staff is working on it right now, but they need volunteers. We also want to check the refrigerators in all staff and student areas and consolidate any food in the kitchen. Anything perishable that can't fit in cold storage will be eaten first."

I couldn't help but smile a little at that. How many after-hurricane barbecues had I been to, where neighbors would grill up all the meat left in their unpowered fridges and freezers?

Around me, the students joked and laughed like this was going to be a fun party. "Hey, you think we'll be able to avoid finals?" one asked.

"I hope so!" another said. "If it means skipping that biology exam, I could live without power in the dorms for a couple weeks."

My smile faded. It was going to take longer than a couple weeks to restore power, if it was even possible. How long could the backup generators last?

"What do you think is really going on?" someone asked in a hushed tone. "Missiles launching and then that bright flash up in the sky?"

"I don't know, but my phone hasn't worked since."

"I couldn't get my car started," a third person said. "Neither could anyone else in the lot. Is it a terrorist attack?"

So, some of the students were as worried as I was. And they didn't know the whole truth. They needed a distraction, a task with a purpose. That was probably why Dr. Schneider was here, requesting the help of any students willing to volunteer.

Maybe that's what I needed, as well.

I raised my hand. "Dr. Schneider."

"Ah, Officer Warren, was it?"

"Ward. Lieutenant Ward." I couldn't blame the guy for not remembering.

"Oh, right. Sorry, Lieutenant Ward. What can I do for you?"

"How much space do you think you'll have for extra perishables?"

"I would have to see." He looked at me over his clipboard. "Why do you ask?"

I smiled. "I was considering going on a food run."

* * *

"You can't do this!" The store manager crossed his arms and glared up at me. The nameplate on his chest read T. Fredrickson.

"Tel-Mart will be compensated, Mr. Fredrickson," I assured him.

Fredrickson tried to block the door with his body, but Danny used Noir to push him out of the way. "Send the bill to the university. What we're doing is aboveboard."

I turned my head to the working station wagon we had found in the campus's underground parking garage. The white, wood-grained Buick Roadmaster was owned by a professor of creative writing, and he had been more than willing to loan the antique vehicle to us, as long as he got to drive it. He sat on the open tailgate, enjoying a glass of sweet iced tea while he waited. He saw me looking at him and waved.

Twelve mounted officers had escorted about thirty students who had walked here. Fortunately the nearest Tel-Mart was right off campus, so it wasn't a long walk. I whistled sharply to get their attention. Countess's ears perked up. The whistle was usually my treat call. I stroked her neck and promised her one later, then said, "Come on, boys and girls, get in there. And hustle! I don't want us out here any longer than we have to be."

Fredrickson again tried to block the door, but Noir snorted in his face and started forward. The manager backed away, and the students filed in. Flashlight beams shined through the windows, proof that the store had no electricity and no means of keeping perishables from spoiling.

"Look, I don't like this any more than you," I said, "but what I like even less is good food spoiling. Good food that could feed a lot of people, your family included."

Frederickson flinched. "My family has already evacuated to Teledyne Tower. They're safe there."

"And thank God for that. I'm sure they're ready to weather this storm. Not everyone in Columbia is as fortunate, but that's what we're here for. The city will set up distribution points in the next few days." I wasn't too sure about that last part, but I expected Columbia had some kind of disaster contingency plan in place. After FEMA was defunded and eliminated, most municipalities of any decent size had worked with Corporate planners to determine the best means of providing for the people in a disaster.

Frederickson opened his mouth to protest, then fell silent. He leaned against the window and lowered his head.

I walked Countess over to where Morris sat astride Sanguine, the leather saddle creaking with each step. Morris smirked at me and nodded toward the manager. "He looks like you just kicked his puppy."

Countess snorted, and I returned the smile. "Yeah, well, I wouldn't want to be him when he has to explain to his betters what's going on."

"You think Teledyne really cares at the moment?" Morris looked to the northwest. Teledyne Tower shined like a lighthouse in the evening gloom. "I imagine they've got bigger things to worry about."

"Other than being the heroes who saved Columbia?" Patrolman Jones said. "You should've seen those CBMs, LT! *Fwoosh, fwoosh, fwoosh, fwoosh!*" He imitated rockets launching up from the ground and into the air. "Damn, it was quite a show. Wish it had been at night."

"I wish they had managed to get all the missiles," I said, surprised by the bitterness in my tone. Was I talking about the Columbia area, or elsewhere? "If they'd been able to take out that last one, we wouldn't be in this mess."

"Well, better in this mess than how it would've been had that last nuke hit," the Philadelphia officer said. "Teledyne's got my vote, even if they're on the West Coast."

My back went rigid, and Countess tensed beneath me. I forced myself to relax and gave her a reassuring pat on the neck. I kept my face placid as anger boiled within me. How was I supposed to forgive Teledyne after what they did to Mobile?

"Hey, you! Get back! I said, get back!" a voice shouted on the other side of the parking lot.

A few officers from the Philadelphia PD had ridden around the perimeter of the vast Tel-Mart parking lot, and now they had their horses turned toward a mob of people approaching the store. It was a bunch of teens armed with bats and clubs, each wearing backpacks already stuffed with goods. There had to be at least sixty of them.

"Come on, get 'em!" one of the teens shouted. "It's just a couple pigs on horseback."

"Yeah, they can't stop all of us!" another called.

"Get back!" the Philadelphia officer yelled again.

"Shit," Morris muttered.

"Form up!" I shouted.

Morris, Danny, Collins, Ferris, and four others pulled their mounts alongside mine. We drew our nightsticks and kicked our horses into a canter. With barely a foot between us, we approached as a solid line.

"Oh, shit, there's more of them!" one of the teens squealed.

"Who cares?" the leader called. "There's nearly a hundred of us! We can take 'em!"

There weren't that many of them. And even if there were, they didn't realize one mounted cop was worth ten on foot in a crowd control situation. And there were twelve of us. I grinned. That meant we were worth a hundred and twenty to their sixty or seventy. I liked those odds.

I squeezed Countess with my heels, and she increased her speed to a gallop. The others quickly followed suit. We covered the ground between us and the mob in seconds.

People in a mob act brave, but it doesn't take much to break them. Twelve horsemen charging at a gallop would unnerve most people, and it was no different here. The mob scattered in three directions.

"Get back here!" their leader shouted. He looked like a classic punk rocker, with a leather jacket and sunglasses that went out of style decades ago. "They ain't so tough! They'll be just like those other pigs we jumped!"

Morris's nightstick caught the punk in the side of the head. He went down like a sack of potatoes and lay still.

We broke into three groups and chased the fleeing looters away from the Tel-Mart. Satisfied they wouldn't return, I shouted for everyone to turn back.

One of the Philly officers had dismounted and had the ringleader handcuffed when we rode back into the parking lot. "We'll question him when he comes to," he told me as I approached.

The sound of an engine caught my attention. A moment later, a patrol SUV from the Columbia Police Department rolled up, its blue lights flashing. The side-mounted lamp turned on and beamed bright light into the parking lot. I held up a hand to shield my eyes from the glare. Countess snorted and turned her head.

Just as suddenly as the light was on us, it was turned off, and the vehicle pulled into the parking lot. It parked in a space near us, and the door opened. A couple of officers in Columbia PD uniforms got out and walked over. "What's going on here?" the driver, a dark-skinned young lady, demanded. She had corporal's stripes on the sleeve of her uniform shirt.

"Moving perishables from here back to the university, where there's electricity," I explained. "University admins thought it made more sense to do that than to leave the food to rot, Corporal—?" I squinted, but couldn't make out her nameplate in the gloom.

"Chloe Reed."

"Lieutenant Nathan Ward, Mobile PD. Nice to see you've got a vehicle in operation." I nodded to the SUV, then patted Countess. "We're having to rely on the horses we brought with us."

"I fear we'll all be relying on them in the days to come, Lieutenant." Reed took off her hat and ran a hand through her dark cornrows. "We've got three cars in service. Five, if you count a couple of personal vehicles the detectives have. That's out of a hundred."

"Yeah, it's the same at the university. Most of the vehicles are fried. It's gonna make getting around the city difficult."

"You're not kidding. That bomb went off just as church traffic was at its height. Our streets aren't nearly as heavily trafficked as some of the bigger cities out there, but our roads aren't built to handle high volume, at least in the old downtown district. It was gridlock along the main roads. Permanent gridlock, now," she added with a harsh laugh.

I smiled, but didn't feel much mirth. "Well, we're happy to assist however we can."

"I see that you already are." She pointed at the handcuffed thug. "Is he part of that mob that came this way?"

"The ringleader, from what we could gather," Morris said. He walked over and touched the side of his helmet. "Sergeant Jake Morris, Philadelphia PD."

"A pleasure, Sergeant." She glowered at the unconscious punk. "That mob had already knocked over a couple stores, and they attacked two of our officers while they were at it." She rested her hands on her gun and nightstick. "Days like this really test my patience, you know?"

"I've been an officer through four hurricanes," I said. "Believe me, I know how trying it can be to deal with looters."

"Four hurricanes? Even Patricia?"

"Patricia went a little to the east of us. Gave Pensacola and Destin a real walloping. We got hit, but not nearly as bad as they did. And the looting was a lot less of a problem." I grinned. "Our governor ordered them shot on sight."

"No shit? Did you have to follow through on that?"

"Nah. Oftentimes, the threat alone is enough. That, and the order extended to civilians. Usually, we just took care of the cleanup after a private citizen defended their own property or their neighbors' property."

"Be a lot less crime if we let folks do that more often."

"Amen to that," Morris and I muttered.

"Well, we'll take this piece of crap off your hands if you're done with him," Reed said.

I looked at Morris, who nodded. "He's all yours."

"We'll make sure your departments get the credit." Reed and her partner picked up the unconscious teen and dragged him to their SUV. They unceremoniously threw him into the backseat and slammed the door before climbing into the front seats. Reed picked up her radio, then dropped it with a grimace. "Force of habit."

I turned back to the Tel-Mart as the students came out with the first load of cold goods. I noticed that Manager Fredrickson was helping them load. He nodded to me. "Thank you for protecting the store."

"It was the least we could do," I told him. "Would you like us to keep someone posted here through the night?"

"No, we've got a security detail from Teledyne Tower scheduled to stop by later."

"Glad to hear it. And I'll see to it that the university reimburses you for all this. We're not thieves."

"I know. Thank you."

I walked Countess up to the Roadmaster and peered in. "Ice cream?" I asked with an arched eyebrow.

The student loading it had the good grace to look sheepish. "We figured the most perishable stuff first, right? Don't want it to melt."

I shined my flashlight in and said, "Hand me a couple of those tubs. And that box of popsicles, if you don't mind."

The student quickly complied, and I rode back to the other officers. I pulled Countess up to the SUV and waited for Reed to roll down the window. "Headed back to the station?"

"Yeah, what's up, Lieutenant?"

"Tribute." I passed her the two tubs of ice cream. "Compliments of Teledyne and the Mobile and Philadelphia police departments."

"We won't say no, that's for sure! Thanks, Lieutenant!"

With a wave, Reed drove off, headed back the way they had come. The side-mounted lamps flicked on, and both officers scanned the sides of the roadway with high-powered LED beams.

I walked Countess over to the other officers and opened up the box of popsicles. "Something to cool our throats," I said, passing the box around.

There was a chorus of, "Thanks, LT!" from the assembled officers.

Countess snorted. I smiled and leaned over so she could take a bite of my watermelon popsicle. She nodded approvingly.

I let her eat the whole thing. She'd certainly earned the treat on her first night in this Fallen World.

* * * * *

Chapter Seven

"All right, Countess, let's get you brushed down." I led Countess into her stall and closed the gate behind her. She walked over to the hay left out for her and grazed, one mouthful at a time. All around us, horses snorted and whinnied while officers and stable hands laughed and conversed. More than one Mobile or Philadelphia officer yawned. I stifled one of my own and picked up the brush.

"Sorry for the late night, girl. It's been a day." I tried to keep the quaver from my voice. "One hell of a day. I fear you and I will be needed for harder duty in the days to come."

She flicked her ears at me, then flicked the brush with her nose before she turned back to her food.

I ran my hand along her sleek back, then applied the brush. It always amazed me how soft her hair was, like one of Helen's teddy bears, or one of the anime plush dolls my wife had liked to collect.

My time brushing Countess each day was a time of quiet reflection and prayer. No matter how much paperwork needed to be done or how late we were out dealing with last-minute calls, Countess needed her brush-down time. And so did I, especially on a day like today.

It had taken a couple hours to pack the professor's station wagon, get it back to the university, and secure all the perishables in the kitchen freezers. We had hundreds of pounds of frozen vegetables and microwave dinners and enough gallons of ice cream to make a herd of elephants lactose intolerant and diabetic all at once. I was amazed at how much that old vehicle could hold. It had been stuffed to the gills, only leaving room for the professor and his sweet tea. Ice chests had been strapped to the roof in some sort of weird plastic pyramid. By the time we rolled into the university, it looked like we were escorting a lone Mardi Gras parade float, except instead of Moon Pies and beads we had Klondike bars and Stouffer's French bread pizzas.

I opened my heart and mind to prayer as I always did when troubled: *Lord, Lord, hear my prayer.* Normally the words would pour forth, allowing me to unburden myself of all doubt, of all fear, of all the little nagging worries that plagued me day-to-day.

Nothing came. As I brushed Countess's black-and-white mane, I kept repeating that phrase in my head: *Lord, Lord, hear my prayer.* But no prayer would come forth. It was as if someone had jammed my connection to the Almighty. The only word I could form in my mind was *Why?*

The map of the United States appeared in my mind, covered in missile lines. When backup power was restored, it had revealed hundreds of strikes, and hundreds more missiles inbound to targets all over the country. Lines had even extended across the oceans to targets unknown.

Why?

Satellite imagery appeared on the screens next, showing smoke plumes over cities that no longer existed.

Why, Lord?

Traffic camera footage from around the country showed panic-stricken citizens running as destruction rained down on them. One image in particular had burned itself in my mind: a little, redheaded girl in Los Angeles, reaching out for her mother after she fell in the street. The two were about to touch hands when the feed went orange and yellow and then cut out.

Why?!

Countess snorted and sidestepped away from me. I realized with a start that I'd been digging into her with the brush. I murmured an apology went back to gentle strokes, tears stinging my eyes. I let them well up and fall. No one was here to see them, and if I had to, I could blame them on the nagging horsehair allergy of mine. It was bad enough to give me the sniffles, but not bad enough to override my love of horses.

I finished up the brushing and gave Countess a playful slap on the rump. "Have a good night, girl," I said, my voice still a bit unsteady. "We can do it all again in the morning."

Before I could make for the gate, Countess turned around and hooked her neck around my shoulder. She pulled me in close, her chin against the small of my back.

I put my arms around her neck and pulled her in for a hug. I pressed my face against her hair and let it soak up my tears. I breathed in her scent, like that of freshly cut grass. God, what were we going to do? How were we going to recover?

Those questions plagued me, but for the moment, I felt at peace. Countess had been there for me when Regina died, at the lowest point of my life. I'd thought nothing would ever top that, then today happened.

"Thank you, girl," I whispered. "We'll get through this together. You, Helen, Jason, Danny, and me."

Countess snorted.

* * *

A few minutes later, I stepped out of the stable and into the cool night air. Half the officers had finished before me and returned to the dorm we were using as a billet. Danny was still inside, so I thought I would wait for him.

Our horse trailers lined one end of the grassy commons that was shared by three large stables. All of these buildings were relatively new, a necessary addition for the university's growing equine research and breeding program. The ability to house almost all of the visiting horses was a big reason why Columbia had won out over other cities vying to host the mounted police convention.

And given what had happened to most of those other cities, I could only thank God we had chosen Columbia.

The doors to the stable across the commons opened, and seven figures filed out, each leading one or two horses by lead ropes.

I frowned. Something wasn't right.

As I walked across the grass, I pulled out my flashlight and shined it. The people at the stable door looked away from the light. They were wearing the uniforms of the St. Louis PD. I turned the light off. "Kevin?" I called.

"Nate?" Lieutenant Kevin Hanson pulled himself up into the saddle and walked his horse over to me. He looked down. "Busy night?"

"Just finished. What about you?" I pointed at the officers behind Hanson. Four men, two women, each on a horse loaded down with saddlebags. Two of the officers led pairs of remounts that were likewise laden with supplies. My heart sank as I asked a question I knew the answer to. "What's with all the gear?"

"We're going back." Hanson squared his shoulders and looked to the east. "We have to see what happened there."

I looked around, then stood on my tiptoes to get as close to his ear as possible. He leaned down. "You know what happened," I hissed. "Going back there is suicide."

"Would you do any different?" He glared at me, but his expression softened slightly. "Sorry, Nate. I'm just…I know you know what I'm going through."

"I do," I insisted. "And so do most of the guys that were in that room with us. DiAngelo and Martinez and—and Jesus, poor Sanderson. He saw Charlotte vanish in a barrage of thirty nukes. Thirty!"

"Teledyne bastards." Hanson leaned over the other side of his horse and spat. "The only good that came out of this was getting to see their headquarters burn with the rest of Portland."

"Teledyne's the reason we survived here," I said, mirroring words spoken to me earlier in the evening. My heart wasn't in them, though.

"They won't get any thanks from me for that, and I imagine you feel the same, though you're too reserved to admit it." He sat higher in his saddle. "Sorry, Nate. We've got to do this. I talked it over with the men, and we're all in agreement."

"You told them? We were ordered to keep this secret!"

"What difference do those orders make? You think we're going to be able to contain this for very long? Everyone will find out soon enough. Better if they know the truth sooner rather than later. That's why we're going now. We have to see for ourselves."

He looked at his officers, who all nodded.

I stepped back. "I won't stop you, but I don't think you're making the right decision. We need to help the people here first, then go out to the neighboring towns and cities in force."

"*You* need to help the people here first. *We* have to go back to our homes and rescue any survivors." He hesitated. "If there are any survivors."

With that, he snapped his reins and started off at a trot. The other St. Louis officers fell in behind their leader.

I stared in the direction they headed, long after I couldn't see them anymore.

"What was that about?" Danny asked.

I jumped. When had he gotten there?

"Were they called back to St. Louis?"

"Yeah." Guilt from the lie made my shoulders sag. "Yeah, they were."

"I wonder if some of the other departments will get similar calls." He laughed. "Not that any of us are close enough to ride back in any reasonable amount of time. How long will it take them to get to St. Louis from here? Four or five days?"

"Two or three if the roads are clear and they push their mounts hard. St. Louis is about a hundred and thirty miles from here. And the Kansas City officers are just as close to home. It wouldn't surprise me if they head back, too."

"Well, I hope they stay," Danny said. "With the grid down and most vehicles disabled, we'll need all the help we can get to maintain order here."

"Yes, we will."

* * *

"Daddy!" Jason ran down the dormitory hall toward me.

I knelt just as he threw himself at me. His arms wrapped around my neck, and I scooped him up into a one-armed hug. "Woah, little guy! You almost tackled me!"

"Did not," he said in a tone of mock hurt. He punched my side with his small fist.

Helen hurried out into the hall. The worry on her face melted away and was replaced with a delighted grin. "You're both all right!"

"Of course, little lady," Danny said. He pulled her into an embrace and kissed the top of her head. "Nothing's gonna take out your old man, not as long as I'm with him."

"Then make sure you're always with him," a voice called from the dormitory set aside for the kids and me. Brother Stephen stepped out into the hall, a tired smile on his lips. "Welcome home. How was the food run?"

"Oh, that's right," I said with mock astonishment in my voice. I held up the bag that was in my right hand. "Who wants ice cream?"

"Me!" Jason screamed, his voice piercing in the enclosed space.

I laughed. Such a good, painful sound. "All right, then get off me so I can get this container open."

"But, it's so late," Helen objected, though the words were half-hearted. "We don't normally get ice cream at this hour."

I checked my watch. It was half-past ten. "Well, we had intended to feed you this earlier, but it's our fault we got back so late. So, just this once, we'll have an ice cream party, okay?"

"That's your Dad's way of saying he's hungry for some ice cream," Danny said with a wink.

As if on cue, my stomach growled so loudly there was no denying it. The kids burst into laughter, and I couldn't help but smile.

The days ahead would be dark, but for now there was light. And sometimes that's all you can ask for in this Fallen World.

That, and some double chocolate brownie fudge.

* * * * *

Chapter Eight

"Terry, you are a sight for sore eyes," Captain Jim Bradley said. He shook the hand of the older gentleman in uniform then turned to the rest of us in the auditorium. "Everyone, this is Terrence Welliver, Sheriff of Boone County, just in from a longer-than-planned visit to Centralia."

We stood and started to applaud, but Welliver waved it off. "Enough of that. I'm too old to waste time on that kind of ego-boosting." He folded his hands behind his back and assumed a parade rest stance that spoke of time in the military, either Corporate or government. Considering his age, I leaned towards governmental military. Welliver had to be pushing eighty, if the lines on his suntanned face were any indicator. Despite that, his back was ramrod straight, and his arms filled out his uniform shirt. He had muscle on him.

"Captain Bradley tells me you've all stepped up to the plate to help us in our time of need. I can't thank you enough for that. Especially you, Lieutenant Ward." He nodded in my direction. "The initiative you and your men took at the start of all this stopped a mass looting spree and allowed us to preserve vital food supplies."

"Thank you, sir, though I don't know that I'd call ice cream vital."

"Speak for yourself!" Captain Graham said. The rest of the room laughed.

Welliver smiled. "Regardless, it was just the kick we needed to get started. Your actions have been mirrored by several visiting departments over the last seventy-two hours. I'd especially like to thank those of you visiting internationally." He nodded to Captain Graham, Lieutenant Saleh, and Sergeant Mosher. The other international leaders, including Lieutenant Blackwood, were busy patrolling the university grounds or establishing defensive perimeters with student and civilian volunteers.

"As you can see, your efforts over the last few days have borne fruit." Sheriff Welliver turned to a tabletop map of the city. It had been divided into nine distinct zones, each color-coded to show who controlled what and how safe that area was. Four areas were outlined in green, denoting safe zones. Those areas included the University of Missouri, Teledyne Tower, the Country Hotel where the visiting Obsidian contingent was holed up, and the Three Rivers Renaissance Fair. Three other areas were yellow, which meant they were contested zones. Looting was a problem, but strides were being made with the police, Corporate soldiers, private citizens, or a combination of the three to pacify them. The remaining two areas were marked in red, and they were deemed no-go zones, at least at the moment. Gangs like the Emeralds and the Rubies controlled those areas, and Lord only knew what was going on inside those zones.

"Our positions are relatively secure here, so our next order of business will be to push into these red zones." He tapped each one in turn with a finger. "My deputies are stretched thin in other parts of the county, but I'm sending about thirty in to help with this." He smiled. "We don't have quite as many horses as you, but a few of us know how to ride. And those who don't can be taught, I assume?"

"Yes, sir," I said. "I'm setting up classes for Columbia and university officers who want to learn, as well as any private citizens who can secure a mount."

"Excellent." He tapped the red zones again. "We'll need all the help we can get to take these areas."

I chafed a bit at that. It would be all we could do to keep those zones from spreading, but it was something that had to be done. Some of us in the room had been in the command bunker that day. We understood that we might very well be the only city left in the United States that wasn't a smoking crater, and yet there were those trying to tear it to pieces. What was destroyed wasn't going to be rebuilt; not any time soon, if ever. We needed to secure those zones before things fell into complete chaos.

I felt that more keenly than anyone else in the room, save for Bradley and Sheriff Welliver. Both were locals, and I could only assume their families were here with them. My kids were here, too, and while that brought me no end of comfort, it also brought no end of anxiety. What kind of city was Columbia going to be at the end of all this? What would be left for them?

Maybe after this meeting, we would have an answer to that.

"If we're going to continue pacifying the city and bring it back to order," Welliver said, "we'll need to consolidate our forces. Right now we've got different safe zones under the control of different groups, and no real coordination between the good guys save for what's occurred in face-to-face discussions." He tapped the radio on his hip. "Most of our walkie-talkies are dead, and the city's communications system is in shambles. What we need is a way to quickly call in the cavalry." He looked around the room and smiled. "Literally, in this case."

"I may have a solution for that, sir." Captain DiAngelo opened a bag and removed a flare gun. "Spent quite a bit of time on my dad's boat in Long Island Sound, and we always had one of these to signal for help. Never needed it, thank Christ." He smirked. "Except as makeshift fireworks on the Fourth of July, that is."

He pulled out several canisters, each a different color. "Colored smoke. I figure we can develop some kind of simple code with these. We even have colored luminary flares for the graveyard shift."

"An interesting idea," Welliver said. He cocked his head to the side. "Where'd you get all those?"

The door burst open before DiAngelo could reply. Chief Ballantine strode in, his expression grim. "Ladies, gentlemen, we have a problem." He held up an envelope. "Orders from the mayor's office."

Welliver's brow furrowed. "You mean Teledyne Tower, right?"

Ballantine flinched, and handed over the envelope. "Orders are orders, Jim."

Welliver donned his reading glasses, then skimmed the letter. His expression darkened. "What's the meaning of this?"

"Exactly what it says. All officers are to stand down from their efforts to restore order to the city. Instead, we're supposed to protect the university grounds and the area around city hall."

"What about the food distribution?" Captain Phillips demanded. "What are we supposed to do about that?"

"It can be managed here, at the university," Welliver said, paraphrasing from the letter. "And only after everyone is properly vetted. We can't be seen supplying gangs and other undesirables with food that they'll just use to fuel more crime."

That part made sense, but not the rest of it. "Sirs, with respect, this is bullshit," I said. "We have a chance to restore order to this city, and we're just going to squander it?"

"I'm gonna go talk to the mayor about this." Welliver donned his hat and turned toward the door. "Bradley, finish the briefing and dismiss the boys and girls back to their posts."

"Now, see here," Ballantine objected. "You can't go around ordering my men—"

"Actually, old friend, I can." Welliver tapped his shoulder patch. "I'm the highest law enforcement authority in this county by the grace of God and with the endorsement of the citizens. Not even the mayor can overrule me, though I owe it to him to at least try and talk it out first. If you don't like it, run against me in the next election. Bradley, finish the briefing."

"Yes, Sheriff Welliver."

Ballantine glared at Bradley for a moment, then followed the sheriff out the door. "Dammit, Terry, get back here! We're not through."

"You heard the orders from the mayor," Bradley said. "For now, we'll halt food distribution except for city hall and the university. We'll keep our jurisdictions separate for the time being, as well: the university falls to the visiting units and the university police, while city hall and its surrounding neighborhoods belong to the Columbia PD."

I raised my hand. "Can we maintain our off-campus patrols?"

"Won't that violate the mayor's orders?" Saleh asked.

"Not really. We need to protect the university, right? What better way to protect it than to maintain security patrols beyond the property. If we keep the streets near the university safe, then it stands to reason the university will be safe."

Bradley chuckled. "Son, I like the way you think. Very well." He looked at the map and drew a wide circle around the university with his finger several times. "Extend your regular patrols up to three blocks in every direction from the campus and a mile into the southern woodland. There isn't much there except campers trying to rough it in 'the wild,' but you never know what could come creeping."

"Questions?" He looked around the room. "No? Then dismissed."

* * *

"Day-yum, something smells good out here!" Patrolman Jones sniffed loudly and let out a contented sigh. "Someone's cookin' up steaks!"

"And burgers and dogs by the smell of it," I added. My sense of smell wasn't the greatest in the world, but I always knew when someone was grilling hamburgers. "One of the best foods in the world, the hamburger. Wouldn't you agree, Countess?"

She snorted and pawed the ground. A definite no.

I patted her neck. "Maybe they'll have more popsicles for you."

Six of us rode today, all of them my boys and girls from the MPD. We were suited up in our riot gear, and our horses had their barding on as well. If not for the matte black of both human and equine armor, we'd have looked like a bunch of knights lost on their way to the Renaissance fair. We walked our horses single-file, their shod hooves clicking on the recently paved street. "Stay lively, everyone," I told them. "Keep your spacing, and be ready for anything."

"Be ready for what, LT?" Collins asked. "Seems just like an after-hurricane party up ahead."

"Can't tell you how many of those my folks have participated in," Jones said. He smiled. "Fun memories."

Pangs of homesickness hit me hard. My family had been suspicious the first time power was knocked out during a hurricane and neighbors came over to tell us we were welcome to help them eat their freezer stock. "Can't let all these ribs and steaks go bad, after all! Who knows when power will be back?"

We turned off University Avenue onto High Street and found ourselves on a wide road with a stand of trees and undeveloped property on one side and the high brick wall of a subdivision on the other. As with most streets in the city, disabled vehicles lined all four lanes with enough regularity that any working vehicles passing through would have to slalom through it. The sidewalks weren't wide enough for a car or truck, but our horses had no problem.

A brass plaque at the subdivision's entrance bore the words "Moss Creek Estates, Established 2046." I'd seen old maps of the city back at the university, but I forgot what had once been here. Individual homes, and maybe an apartment complex? They'd been torn down at some point during the city's restructuring, and this new subdivision had been born.

The entrance to Moss Creek Estates was a big flower and shrub garden. As we rode past it, we saw a common area at the end of the entrance lane, right where the road split to the left and right. The whole neighborhood appeared to be out there. Men huddled around several grills, women set up long folding tables and scores of chairs, and children played in any space available to them.

Some of the kids saw us first. "Horses!" one child shouted. "The police!" another cried. "The rodeo!" one kid called out.

"Rodeo?" Jones looked down at his uniform, then twisted in his saddle to look at everyone else. "We look like cowboys and cowgirls to them?"

"I've had the misfortune of seeing the pajamas you wear," I said. "Paint your face up just right, and you'd look like a rodeo clown, for sure."

"Oh God, don't say that, LT," Williams said. She shivered. "I hate clowns."

"You mean you're scared of them," Collins offered.

"No, I hate them."

"Why?"

"Because they creep me out!"

"Then you're scared of them."

"I'm not scared of them!"

"Hey, ladies," I said, turning around to look at them, "can the crap, would you? The public approaches."

The "public" was a group of about fifteen kids, ranging from four to ten years old. A few parents followed close behind, their expressions a mix of relief, interest, and trepidation. "Stay away from the horses' legs, honey!" one of the mothers called.

"I will, Mom!" a young girl in the lead shouted back. She slowed and stopped close to us, the other kids falling in line behind her. "Hi," she said with sudden shyness.

"Well, aren't you just the cutest little thing," Jones said, his dark face splitting into a toothy grin. "That dress you're wearing looks just like one my niece has! She's about your age, too."

God, I hoped Jones' niece wasn't in Mobile when it fell. I shook my head to clear it. "Hey, there, little miss. I'm Nathan, and this is Countess." I reached into one of my saddlebags and pulled out a carrot. "And she loves these. Wanna feed it to her?"

The girl looked at the carrot, then back at her mother, who by now had caught up to the children. The mother smiled up at me, then nodded.

She reached up and took the carrot from my hand, then held it out. "Make sure you hold it flat in your palm," I warned. "Keep your fingers clear."

Countess made a show of sniffing the carrot, then studying it with a critical eye from behind her helmet's faceplate. She then huffed a blast of air that made the girl jump.

"It's all right," I assured her. "That's a happy snort. Hold it out again. There, right under her nose. That's it."

Tentatively, the girl held the carrot out once more. Countess carefully took it in her teeth and gobbled it down. The girl giggled.

"Hey, you," Jones said to a young boy who had sidled up close to his horse. "Mine likes Three Musketeers bars, but he can't have a whole one." He fished one out of his pocket. "Want to split it?"

The other officers joined in on the fun after that, letting the kids pet and feed their mounts. Some of the adults who weren't needed to cook or set tables came over and talked about what was going on in the neighborhood. I listened attentively but couldn't keep the smile from my face. This seemed just like a normal patrol.

Then someone asked when the electricity and phone lines would be restored. The smile faded, I mumbled something about how the powers-that-be were working on it, and there would be a solution soon.

They offered to feed us, and I let the rest have a share of whatever they felt like eating. I stayed mounted, a little off to the side on the green, letting Countess graze on grass that hadn't been mowed in a couple days. I wondered how long it would be before everyone knew just what kind of situation we were in.

"Excuse me, Mr. Policeman."

The little girl who fed Countess looked up at me. She held up a plate of food and a plastic fork. "This is for you."

I reached down and grabbed it. It was loaded down with homemade potato salad, a hamburger dripping with juice, and a char-grilled Polish sausage dog, complete with bun. "Thank you, little miss."

She flashed her teeth at me, the expression so much like my daughter's, it hurt. I smiled back and dug into the food. "Oh, man. This potato salad is excellent."

"Thank you," another voice said.

It was the little girl's mother. She grabbed her daughter's hand and pulled her close. "That's for treating my daughter with such kindness. Not everyone's been that way lately."

"Ma'am, interacting with the community is part of our job. We want to have a good relationship with the people we serve and protect." I bit into the Polish sausage dog. A perfect mix of savory, salty goodness assaulted my taste buds. "We especially want to keep people who can make food this good safe, for our own sakes if no one else's."

She chuckled. "Well, we're happy to have officers like you patrolling our streets." She looked closer at my uniform. "You're…not from around here, are you?"

"No, ma'am. Our unit's from Mobile, Alabama. We were here for a mounted unit convention at the university."

"Just in time to lose power and the ability to communicate with the outside world." She shook her head. "Sorry to hear that. I bet you wish you could be anywhere but here."

Yes and no. I wasn't about to tell her what was going on, so I shook my head and said, "Ma'am, I can't speak for all the visiting departments, but I can tell you this: we're happy to serve wherever we are, in whatever capacity we can."

"It's appreciated, I assure you." She knelt down and pressed her daughter's cheek against her own. "With all the looting and shooting going on, we're all worried about whether we'll be next. It's good to know you're out there, keeping us safe."

Provided the mayor allowed it. Our orders from the morning still stood: keep the university and city hall safe, and to hell with the rest of the city. We were told Teledyne soldiers would patrol the streets, but there had been little evidence of that since this whole mess began, other than a lot of gunfire. And based on what I'd been hearing from other departments, they only cared about fighting the Obsidian folks whenever they ventured too far from their hotel.

Some things didn't change, especially in this Fallen World.

* * * * *

Chapter Nine

"Yo, Nate!" Danny called as we rode into the Francis Quadrangle. He and the other half of the Mobile contingent relaxed beneath the six towering columns that stood at the center of the quad. The pillars were all that was left of an old academic building that had burned down long ago. Now it was a gathering place for students, assemblies, and patrolling officers.

Dozens of students milled about with Danny's squad and with the officers and horses of a few other units. Some of the students enjoyed their lunches, some petted and fed the horses, and others were nose-deep in textbooks. Despite everything that had happened, much of the school still had electricity, which meant finals could continue. I had to shake my head at the futility of it, but then I remembered that none of them knew the true extent of the damage. And even if they did, was there anything wrong with trying to continue on as normal?

As we rode up to join Danny and the others, my brother gestured to an older officer standing next to him. "Nate, this is Deputy Powell, one of the few Boone County officers who can ride worth a damn. Powell, this is my brother, Lieutenant Nathan Ward."

"The Ice Cream Bandit!" Powell grinned at me from beneath a bushy mustache. "Good to put a face to such an accomplished deed."

"Ha. Ha. Ha." I slid from the saddle and held out my hand. "Glad to know sarcasm is alive and kicking despite the mess we're in."

"Because of it, you mean. My sarcasm has only grown stronger."

"How'd your patrol go?" Danny asked me.

I patted my stomach. "Filling. Yours?"

"Chased off a few punks trying to smash a grocery store's plexi-glass windows near 7th and Cherry, and lucky for them, too. The owner and his sons were up on the roof with shotguns, just waiting for the right angle."

"How about you, Deputy Powell?" I turned to the Boone deputy.

"Other than not having enough deputies who can ride, not too bad." He nodded at the mix of officers nearby. "My compliments to the Baltimore and New Orleans PDs for placing themselves under my command for the day."

"Well, you're the local, and you've got the seniority stripes to show you're no rookie. Where'd you patrol?"

"Escort duty. The university agreed to take in the Tiger's guests since their electricity's fried. They have running water, but no lights. And little chance of getting any of that back any time soon."

That was good news, as far as I was concerned. Half the vendors from the tradeshow portion of the mounted officers' convention had been staying at the Tiger Hotel. It would be good to have them on the university grounds, where we could keep them safe. "Has the hotel had any trouble?"

"Obsidian soldiers stopped by, wanting to use the building as an observation post, but management refused. They wish to remain neutral, and I can't say I blame them."

I also couldn't blame Obsidian for wanting that location. The Tiger Hotel was the tallest building in this part of old downtown, dwarfed only by Teledyne Tower nearly two miles away. "Will they let our men do it? It'd be good to have some eyes in the sky."

"No, for the same reason. They let us post officers in the lobby to protect against looters, but the rest of the hotel is barred save for emergencies." He shrugged. "We could force the issue, but Terry—Sheriff Welliver would rather not. He's still negotiating with the mayor, and the last thing he wants is to upset a wealthy constituent."

"Ah, politics." Danny chuckled. "Even in the midst of a city-wide catastrophe."

My expression soured. *If only you knew, Danny.* The Corporations and the mayor's office knew, yet they were still playing this stupid game.

Cracks, pops, and staccato sounds echoed in the distance. The officers around me fell silent as I tried to determine the direction. It sounded like it was coming from the east.

"Firecrackers?" one of the students asked, a tremor in her voice.

Not firecrackers. Lord knows I'd heard enough of those at New Year's and Fourth of July celebrations over the years to recognize the sound.

No, this was gunfire. Fully automatic gunfire. And it was a lot closer than I liked.

"Think it's inside our patrol zone?" Powell asked.

I took hold of Countess's reins. "Only one way to find out."

Powell bounded into the saddle with the energy of someone half his age. "Mount up!"

* * *

Thirty of us rode out ten minutes later. All of the Mobile contingent was there, under my command. The remaining fourteen came from the Bethlehem, Baltimore, and New Orleans PDs, with two of the six Tokyo police officers riding along as well because they wanted to know what was going on.

We hit University Avenue at a brisk trot. Powell rode on point, next to my friend Sergeant Beauregard of the New Orleans PD. They led us in the general direction of the echoing gunfire. "Spread out!" I ordered. It wouldn't do for all of us to be bunched up.

The squat buildings of old downtown gave way to trees and suburban sprawl. The few people we saw in the streets scattered when they saw us riding by. An old man waved a cane at us from his front porch and shouted, "Give 'em hell, boys!"

Danny chuckled and waved back as a young girl ushered the man inside. "Looks like gramps wants a crack at whoever's shooting up the neighborhood."

"I'd expected the gangs to reach the university at some point," Beauregard said, "but I hadn't expected it to be this soon."

"This doesn't sound like the gangs," Powell said. "Too much fully automatic fire. The locals don't have that kind of firepower. Gotta be the suits."

"Yeah, but which one?"

"Both?" He gave us an exaggerated shrug. "I'm not paid to think too deeply about this stuff."

"We're not paid at all at the moment!" Patrolman Jones said with a chuckle. "This is charity work!"

The other officers joined in the friendly banter, but it did little to steady my nerves. My patrol had just ridden along these roads on our way back to the university. I had a sinking suspicion about where we would find our firefight.

After another moment we rounded the corner at High Street. A pair of blacked-out executive sedans sat at the entrance to Moss Creek Estates, their doors opened wide. A corpse in a business suit lay sprawled next to one of them. The man's suited companions took cover behind the cars and fired across the street at a transport truck that hadn't been there earlier.

Teledyne soldiers and dirty men in green jackets crouched behind disabled vehicles and the cargo truck they had arrived in. They rose up long enough to shoot at the men behind the sedans. I didn't see or hear the round impacts, so I could only assume most of the bullets were going high, into the neighborhood beyond.

Right where the block party was still going on. I cursed myself for leaving when we did. "We have to put a stop to this, Deputy Powell!"

"We don't even know what's going on," Powell snapped. "Who started this? And why are the Emeralds with Teledyne?"

"Does it matter who started it? There are innocent men, women, and children in that neighborhood!"

"And in the street!" Danny pointed. "Look!"

A sedan rested in the center of the road, its windows blown out by gunfire. Glass fragments covered the asphalt around it. A pair of figures cowered beneath the vehicle: a boy and a girl. I recognized the girl as the one who had given me the plate of food.

"We have to do something, sir!" Jones shouted.

Powell hesitated. "Teledyne owns this city. We can't go up against them—"

A stray bullet skipped along the ground and blew one of the sedan's tires out. The little girl screamed as the vehicle listed.

Anger surged within me. I kicked Countess forward. "To hell with this!"

Some things just couldn't stand, especially in this Fallen World.

* * * * *

Chapter Ten

Countess broke into a run. The heavy armor draping her body didn't seem to slow her down a bit, and the added bulk made her already imposing size downright intimidating. "Police!" I shouted. "Drop your weapons!"

I drew my pistol and thumbed the targeting laser as a group of Emerald gang members turned toward me, weapons raised. I extended my arm and pointed the pistol as if it were my index finger. As soon as the red laser painted a chest, I squeezed the trigger. Seven rounds later, three of the green-jacketed thugs were bleeding on the ground, each with two holes in them. The seventh shot went wide.

Countess crashed into a knot of Emerald gang members who couldn't get out of the way in time. One was trampled underhoof, his screams cut off with a sickening crunch. The others scrambled away from us. One dropped his weapon and ran, but the rest turned to shoot. I fired at them point-blank, killing two and wounding a third before my pistol ran dry, the slide locking back on an empty magazine. I pressed the magazine release and dropped the empty mag into the dump pouch hitched to my saddle, then took a full magazine off my belt and slammed it home. I thumbed the slide release and took aim as the gun slid back into the battery position. I squeezed the trigger, and another thug died, the hollow point round ripping through his sternum and heart.

"At them, boys!" someone shouted behind me, then police officers charged through the gaps between the stopped vehicles, firing pistols or swinging nightsticks and expandable batons. Teledyne soldiers and Emeralds fell one after another, either shot or clubbed or trampled.

One thug scrambled up onto the roof of a disabled sedan and fired his sawed-off shotgun into Beauregard's face. The New Orleans officer's head snapped back, and he tumbled from his horse, his face-shield cracked and bloody.

"Yeah, get some, pig!" the thug shouted, as he pointed his shotgun at Beauregard's unconscious body.

Beaureguard's horse reared up and kicked its forelegs up at the man. Her heavy hooves struck his knee hard enough to twist his entire leg. He screamed and fell from the car.

As he fell, more gang members climbed onto nearby vehicles to get out of the way of our horses. I took careful aim and dropped one of the punks as he pointed his revolver at Danny.

A round struck the asphalt in front of us. Countess shied away from it, and her sudden movement threw off my aim at a second thug. I held my fire and was rewarded with the sight of the thug dropping from another officer's bullet.

I looked around. A squad of Teledyne soldiers had pulled back up the street and shot at us from the cover of more disabled vehicles. I dropped my pistol back into its holster and drew my pump-action shotgun from its saddle scabbard. I shouldered the shotgun, thumbed the safety off, and aimed down the ghost-ring sights. I lined my sights up along the center mass of one of them just as he turned his submachine gun my way. His eyes widened.

I squeezed the trigger.

Boom!

The shotgun rocked against my shoulder, the sight lifting off my target as the recoil carried the barrel upward. I racked the slide back and ejected the spent shell casing, then slammed a new round home as I dropped the barrel back on the soldier. I was just in time to see his limp form slam onto the hood of the car he had braced himself against. Blood poured from the exit wound in his back.

I fired at the next soldier, but the solid steel slug went wide and shattered the windshield and side windows of the van he stood behind. My next round caught him in the side as he tried to throw himself to the ground. He wasn't getting up again, at least not in this fight.

I pumped a fresh slug into the chamber, then dropped the shotgun into its scabbard. I drew my pistol again and snapped the reins. "Come on, girl, let's go!"

Countess spun around at my command, and we cantered around the morass of disabled vehicles until we were back on the sidewalk. I kicked her into a gallop, and we charged straight at the Teledyne soldiers.

The remaining soldiers had been so intent on their Obsidian targets, they didn't see or hear my approach until I was on them. Countess plowed into two of them, knocking them flat on their backs. One of them looked like the squad leader, so I leveled my pistol at him. "Police! Drop your weapons! *Now!*"

The squad leader started to raise his pistol toward me, then froze as three more officers rode up behind me. He eyed the weapons pointed at him, then dropped his pistol and held up his hands. "The Tower won't stand for this."

"Yeah, and neither will we," I said. "You and Obsidian want to kill each other, do it without innocents around."

"Collateral damage is part of the game." He smirked. "How many times have you officers done the same thing?"

A hail of bullets struck all around us, coming from further up the road. The smirking squad leader rolled up into the fetal position and shielded his head with his hands.

Teledyne Manager Strohl stood there, surrounded by his usual cadre of bodyguards, as well as soldiers in urban camouflage. He watched the battle with an unreadable gaze for a moment, then turned back to his waiting sedan.

I kicked Countess into a gallop. We crashed through a pair of gangbangers and leaped over an overturned garbage can. My focus was entirely on Manager Strohl's retreating back. If we could apprehend him, we could bring real justice to this Fallen World. "Strohl!" I shouted. "Halt!"

His bodyguards started shooting at us. I raised my pistol and took aim.

And then I was on the pavement, my lower back ablaze with pain from the equipment on my utility belt digging into me. Aster straddled me, clothed in urban camouflage and draped in armor plating. She pinned me to the ground with a petite hand on my chest. Her other hand wielded a long-bladed knife.

I grabbed her knife hand with my left, but it was all I could do to move her arm an inch. Her purple eyes flicked to my hand and focused on something there. She shook my hand off and pressed the knife to my neck, much as she had with Morris only days ago. She stared at me with a hard look, but the words she spoke were soft, almost pleading:

"Don't make me kill you."

And then she was gone, the weight of her small, ultra-dense body no longer on my chest and stomach. "Shoot her!" Danny shouted.

Aster bounded down the street, diving and rolling to avoid the bullets headed her way. Strohl and his bodyguards were gone, along with his executive sedan. The Teledyne soldiers in urban camouflage remained, and they fired snap shots in our direction to give Aster covering fire. One of the officers cried out, and a horse screamed.

Once she rounded the corner, her men fell back with her. Silence reigned, except for the moans of the wounded.

I sat up, my bruised ribs screaming in protest. My back felt raw, but I knew the armor I wore had absorbed most of the impact. If anything, it was light road rash. How my muscles would feel the next morning was another story.

Countess approached me, her head down to nuzzle against mine. Which would have been fine, except she was still wearing her plastic-and-steel face-shield. "Woah, girl, easy," I said with a laugh that turned to a pained gasp. Damn these ribs. Who knew a Specialist could be so damn heavy?

"Nate, you all right?" Danny asked. He knelt next to me and placed a hand on my shoulder.

"Yeah, I'm fine." I resisted the urge to pull my helmet off and wipe sweat from my brow. We were technically still in a firing zone, if the sporadic gunfire in the distance was any indicator. Last thing I needed was to take a stray bullet to the skull because of a little extra moisture under the helmet. "Help me up."

Once I was on my feet, I surveyed the damage. Dead and wounded gang members and Teledyne soldiers littered the street around us. Two officers were down, and each was being tended to by other officers with first aid kits. One of them was Beauregard, and I was surprised he was still alive after that shot to the face. These helmets really were made of tough stuff. "Any other wounded?"

"Beauregard's the worst," he said. "Carter took a round to the meat of his thigh. He's out of commission for a while, but he'll live. The rest are just scrapes and bruises. Kind of like you." He slapped me on the shoulder.

That sent a wave of pain through my chest and back. I grunted in pain, then slugged him, which sent more pain through my body. "Dammit," I groaned. "Why aren't you hurt?"

"Good luck, and God favoring me over you." Danny pointed. "He also favors those kids."

An officer knelt down in the broken glass and helped the two children get out from under the bullet-riddled sedan. The girl threw her arms around him and burst into tears, while the boy sniffled and called for his mom. A wave of relief washed over me. "Thank God they're all right."

"Lieutenant Ward!" Powell called. "We've got company!"

Six Obsidian bodyguards approached from the flower and shrub garden at the neighborhood's entrance. Each man held a short-pattern assault rifle at low-ready. I stood and drew my pistol but kept it at my side. Around me, the other officers did the same.

The bodyguards stopped close to their stricken sedans. Behind them, another pair of bodyguards escorted a woman in a low-cut dress, wearing more jewelry than I'd seen at a Mardi Gras ball. She placed a delicate hand on her partly-exposed bosom. "We can't thank you officers enough. I feared the worst before you showed up."

"Don't thank us just yet," I said. I pointed at the sobbing children and then past her. "What the hell did you think you were doing, shooting across an area filled with so many innocents?"

"Teledyne was the aggressor here, not Obsidian." She spread her hands wide. "Do you think I wanted to get into a shootout here, when I was making a social call to a friend of mine?"

"A friend of yours? In this neighborhood?"

"Oh, dear God, no." She put a bejeweled hand to her lips and laughed. "You think someone of my status would have friends in hovels like these? No, we were ambushed before we could reach our destination."

The two-story homes on half-acre lots had looked perfectly livable to me, but I wasn't an upper management type. "Ma'am, can I have your name?"

"Of course. Gwendolyn Greenway, Director of Public Relations for Middle America."

That brought me up short. Director Greenway had been the top name on Obsidian's endorsement paperwork for the mounted officer's convention since its inception. "You're a woman?" I asked, then immediately regretted it.

She made a show of looking down at her cleavage, then bent forward a little to look at her groin. "I've always considered myself one." She arched an eyebrow at me. "Would you like to confirm for yourself? You're handsome enough, I suppose."

My cheeks burned. "That won't be necessary."

Danny stepped forward. "How the hell can you be joking at a time like this?" he snapped. "We've got dead and wounded to deal with here, and who knows how many more beyond you in that neighborhood. We should bring you in!"

The Obsidian soldiers closed ranks around their manager, weapons up but not quite aimed at us. Yet.

"Danny, hold up." I placed a restraining hand on his shoulder and firmly pulled him back beside me.

He complied, but continued to glower at Director Greenway.

"Director Greenway, know this: Columbia isn't your playground. It isn't Teledyne's, either. Columbia belongs to the people, and *we* will keep it safe for them."

"You and your pony patrol?" Greenway threw back her head and laughed. "Oh, now that's rich." She looked at several of us in turn, then added, "And how many of you work for departments financed by Obsidian? Hmm? We own you, just like we will own this town. And you'd better remember whose side you're all on."

"We're servants of the public!" one of the New Orleans officers shouted.

"Yeah, we're not Corporate lackeys like you!" a Bethlehem officer called.

"Servants of the public?" Greenway shook her head. "And who do you think employs the public? Who do you think pays the public and, in turn, pays their taxes?" Her hand returned to her bosom. "I do. Obsidian does. Obsidian owns you because Obsidian owns the public."

I gripped the handle of my pistol so tight, its edges dug into my palm. That sounded exactly like what Manager Strohl had said back at the Renaissance fair. "Not here, you don't. And neither does Teledyne. Remember that as you slink back to your hotel."

Greenway's beautiful face twisted into a scowl. "What's your name?"

"Lieutenant Nathan Ward, Mobile PD, Mounted Unit."

"I will remember it." She started to climb into one of the sedans, then paused. "I wasn't joking about you being handsome enough for my bed. Call me if you want to discover just how much of a woman I am." She smiled. "I can fit you in between meetings."

My face grew hotter as the Obsidian bodyguards piled into the vehicles.

"Should we arrest them?" Danny asked Powell.

"For what?" Powell shook his head. "I know they're just as guilty as Teledyne, but in this situation, it looked like they were defending themselves."

The sedans slowly backed up to a clear portion of the street where they could turn around.

"Besides, we've got bigger things to worry about," I said. We had wounded officers to tend to, downed Teledyne soldiers and Emerald thugs to arrest, and a neighborhood to check for more wounded.

"You've got at least two big things to worry about, I believe." Danny cupped his hands in front of his chest.

"Shut up."

"Hey, I'm not the one blushing. That says a lot right there."

"Lay off!"

* * *

Aster trotted alongside Manager Strohl's sedan as it wended its way through the obstacle course of vehicles on its way back to Teledyne Tower. Even with the car moving at a steady twenty miles per hour with surges up to thirty, she kept pace with very little effort.

The rest of Section Nine wasn't faring as well, so they had fallen behind. Once Strohl was safely back inside the patrolled perimeter surrounding the Tower, she would fall back and rejoin her men. Until then, they would maintain contact with her through their radios.

She knew she shouldn't worry. The men and women of her "Party of Nine" were some of the best unaugmented soldiers Teledyne could afford. Still, they *were* unaugmented, and that meant they were far more vulnerable.

The rear window of the sedan rolled down, and Strohl leaned forward so he could see around his bodyguard from the middle seat. "You should have killed the officer you jumped. He pointed a gun at me."

"My orders from Maitre'D and Director Ingersoll are to monitor the mounted officers' convention and to pacify this city, respectively. Killing a police officer in this situation wouldn't have served either task."

"Those officers aren't helping us pacify Columbia."

"The areas they protect are the safest in the city."

"They're the enemy, Specialist."

"They're not Obsidian."

"They shot at our men. That makes them the enemy."

Aster hesitated. She didn't have an answer to that. When Strohl had pulled her and the others from perimeter security during the hunt for Director Greenway, she had seen the police attacking Teledyne soldiers and auxiliaries. Had they ridden in to protect Obsidian's master?

Or were they protecting the people *behind* the Corporate witch and her bodyguards?

"Was it because he's married?"

Aster started, then looked at Strohl. He smirked. "I remember Lieutenant Ward, the Obsidian mutt who took pity on one of our finest purebreds when she was covered in camel spit. And I've read your profile, even the parts that your doting 'Maitre'D' tries to conceal from the rest of us middle managers. The peculiar mercy you extend to family men is a liability, and one that could cost our company big. I'd suggest you refrain from such compassion in the future."

She clenched her jaw but kept her face neutral. "I'll do what must be done to pacify this city and rid it of Obsidian's taint."

"That's good to hear. Just remember that Maitre'D isn't here. He's back in Portland, or what's left of it. Unless he suddenly shows up or Director Ingersoll countermands it, you and your Section 9 are mine to control." He grimaced. "If only that young fool realized that."

Aster silently agreed. Ingersoll was a paranoid man, who didn't trust anyone outside his handpicked inner circle. Because Strohl and Aster had come from HQ for the specific purpose of monitoring the mounted officers' convention—and, more importantly, the Obsidian employees and subsidiaries in attendance—they had been met with suspicion. That hadn't changed, despite the severity of the situation and the fact that Aster and her team were now the Tower's greatest assets.

Strohl faced forward again, and the car window started to roll up. "Prove yourselves, and maybe the director will let me send you in to fight Obsidian on their home turf."

A rush of excitement flooded through Aster. *That*, she could get behind. Destroying Obsidian had always been her goal, and that wouldn't change, even in this Fallen World.

* * * * *

Chapter Eleven

"Six officers wounded, two of them badly." Sheriff Welliver took off his reading glasses and tapped the frames on the table. He set the report down, and Captain Bradley took it up and skimmed through. "Four horses injured, with one requiring surgery. On top of that, representatives from the mayor's office and both Corporations are banging on my door, demanding to know what in the world is going on, and why I allowed such a thing in the first place."

I stood in front of the table, alongside Deputy Powell and the unit commanders involved in yesterday's action against Teledyne and Obsidian. We were in the auditorium that served as a meeting room and as Welliver's office as of this morning. He and his deputies were no longer welcome at city hall or police headquarters.

"Anyone care to explain what happened?" Welliver demanded.

"Sir," Deputy Powell began, "it was all my—"

"It was my fault, sir," I said. "If I hadn't charged in, no one else would have."

Sheriff Welliver looked at me for a long moment. "And why did you charge in, Lieutenant Ward? You had been ordered by the mayor to stand down and leave both Corporations alone."

"Sir, there were civilians caught in the crossfire," I said. "Further, there were innocents behind Obsidian, and Teledyne's soldiers didn't care. We had to do something."

That neighborhood was burying four of their own, this very hour, in the green they had been barbecuing in the day before. Brother Stephen and Monsignor Owens, the NYPD's chaplain, were helping conduct the service. I wanted to join in, but with both Teledyne and Obsidian gunning for me, it didn't seem worth the risk.

"Had to do something." Welliver's eyes narrowed. "Exigent circumstances, you mean?"

"Yes, sir. We could not wait to receive new orders from the mayor's office or from you. We had to act quickly, or more lives would have been lost. I believe we did the right thing."

"As do I," Deputy Powell said. "Besides, I was the one who led the patrol out there. We had a good idea it was Corporate activity, and it was outside our established perimeter around the university. We could've let it slide, but it didn't seem right to. If Lieutenant Ward is going to take the fall for this, then I'll join him."

"Hmph. Didn't seem right," Welliver muttered. He ran a hand across his lined face. "Tell that to everyone who wants my head on a pike."

He was silent for a moment, then he chuckled. "Ah, fuck 'em. Never liked the assholes in Teledyne Tower anyway. Did you know there used to be a park where they put that ugly building of theirs? The Cosmopolitan Recreation Area. Beautiful golf course, too. That's still there, but they don't let us serfs have access to it."

"Terry, that ugly building's the reason we're still here," Bradley pointed out. "Or the missiles they had there are."

"That building's the reason Obsidian targeted us in the first place," Welliver countered. "If they hadn't set up shop here, Obsidian would've had no reason to send nukes our way." He crossed his arms. "And speaking of Obsidian, those assholes are no better. They rented out the whole Country Hotel, kicked out all the other guests, then set up their own perimeter security. No local law enforcement in or out, although that didn't stop Teledyne from demanding we set up surveillance. We had so many deputies watching that stupid hotel that we were shorthanded everywhere else."

"That's a blessing in and of itself, sir," I said. "It meant more of your deputies were on hand to help out here."

"Yeah, but at the cost of the county." Welliver ran a hand through his white hair. "There's a lot of farmland out there that needs protecting, now more than ever. I want to get patrols set up to keep those places safe, but how can I with all this infighting going on?"

"Sir, it's not our fault the Corporations can't play nice."

"Ward's right, sir," Powell said. "They showed their true colors when they started shooting at us. We wanted to protect those civilians, and the Corporate dogs couldn't abide that."

"I'll be damned if you're both not right." Welliver stood and walked around to the tabletop map. Some changes had been made to it since the meeting a few days ago, showing new boundaries around the different zones in the city. The areas around Teledyne Tower and the Country Hotel had been redrawn in red. "Our officers are no longer welcome anywhere near Corporate territory. Not unless we give up the officers who attacked them. The mayor's demanding that, as well."

Deputy Powell and I shared a look. "Sir," I began, "if you think it will help unify the city—"

"Didn't I already make my intentions clear? I said 'fuck 'em.' And I meant it. Teledyne, Obsidian, the mayor, all of 'em." He grinned. "You showed initiative out there, Ward. And you adapted to the sudden change, Powell. That's what I like to see in my officers, and that's exactly what we're going to need in this war. I'm not about to give either of you, or anyone else who was there, up."

A chill ran down my spine. "War?"

"Yes, son, war. That's exactly what we've found ourselves caught in the middle of. A war between titans too stupid to realize they're already dead." He placed his palm on the map, at Columbia's center.

"A war we will end right here, in this city. And to do that, we'll need to be more unified than ever."

"That's going to be difficult," Captain Bradley said. "Half the department's leadership has sided with the mayor's office."

"Yeah, but the rank-and-file are on our side, by and large. Tell any who want to join up I'll deputize them. I'm done playing nice with the mayor." Welliver turned his iron-hard gaze on me. "And the mounted troops? Where do they stand?"

"I think it's safe to say I can speak for everyone here," I said, with a glance at the other commanders. They nodded. "I can also vouch for the Border Patrol, Philadelphia, Jordan, and London units. As for the others, well, we'll need to discuss it. Keeping the peace against looters and gangs is one thing. Fighting the Corporations—"

"Is another thing entirely, yes. Well, like as not, we're stuck with that decision." Welliver held up a hand. "That's not an admonishment, Lieutenant, it's just the reality of it. That said, you need to step up to the plate and get as many of your officers on our team as possible, as well as private citizens. We'll need them all if there's going to be peace. And there must be peace, or there'll be nothing left to salvage in this Fallen World."

* * * * *

Chapter Twelve

"Sergeant Ward, I appreciate the situation you and the other departments find yourselves in, but I don't see how it affects us."

Danny tried to keep from glaring at Lieutenant Wendy Alexander, head of the Miami Police mounted unit. He had first met the woman from Florida at a Mardi Gras parade in '61. She had been a sergeant then, and a no-nonsense type at that. The two had hit it off.

Maybe a little too well, and then not-so-well. *Nate, I think you messed up sending me to do this*, he thought. "Lieutenant, it's going to affect all of us if we let this city spiral into chaos."

"And yet, we've been ordered to do nothing by the mayor and chief of police." She leaned against the wooden fence post, her back to the road. "Are you saying we go outside the chain of command and restore order to a city we have no jurisdiction over?"

"Sheriff Welliver is the supreme law of the land in this county, and he's deputizing anyone willing to fight the good fight."

"This *city* is owned by Teledyne." She waved a hand over her shoulder, in the general direction of Teledyne Tower. Though miles away to the west, its glass structure gleamed in the late-morning sunlight. "I respect the traditions of common law, but the reality is that the Corporations are the law in their territories."

Danny considered that. Unlike Mobile, Miami was firmly held in the grip of Obsidian, down to the manhole covers. Mobile was partially funded and run by Obsidian, but the town council still maintained some autonomy. In contrast, the Miami police force was completely financed by Obsidian, effectively making Alexander and her fellow officers Corporate security. They were Corporate dogs in anything but name.

With a sigh, he turned and placed his back against the neighboring fence post, making sure to keep his hands and utility belt away from the electrified wire that ran between the posts. He very much doubted there was electricity, but old habits died hard. "Wendy, don't you get sick of being beholden to the Corporations?"

He half expected her to object to the use of her name, but to his surprise she said, "I've been sick of it from the beginning."

She touched the shiny, brass badge pinned to her chest, her fingers touching the green palm tree on the center. "I always wanted to be a cop. To serve and protect. That was what I wanted to devote my life to." A bitter laugh escaped her lips. "It took a few years on the streets for me to realize who I really worked for. Who I was really supposed to serve and protect."

"That's what I'm saying," Danny said, hope surging in his chest. "If we come together here, we can show the rest of the country what real policing is. We don't do it for the Corporations. We do it for the people."

"Until the Corporations send reinforcements. You know what they're like. They're not going to let this city go that easily."

Danny hesitated. She had a point. One or both Corporations would eventually send help to the city. What would they do if they arrived and saw their fellow suits dead or in prison, and the citizens running the city the way he read it was once done? He had been a front-line soldier for several years. He knew what the Corporations were capable of doing to each other, and how bad the collateral damage could get.

"I was on the force for the riots of '57," she said, her husky voice dropping even lower. She nodded her head in the direction of the stables, where several of her men could be seen tending to horses or engaging in exercise. "The only one of my unit to be there, in fact. It was my first year on the force."

Danny smiled. "Hard to imagine you as a green rookie."

"Oh, I was." She chuckled. "Green in all the ways you could be and still manage to survive to the end of your shift." Her laughter died, along with the light in her eyes. "We couldn't contain it. No matter how much tear gas we launched and how many heads we cracked with nightsticks, they just kept coming. The poor, starving masses who just wanted food to feed their families.

"Obsidian stepped in then. They stepped in hard. They had us establish a perimeter around Coconut Grove, and they went in on their own."

"Agents?" Danny asked.

"Agents, soldiers, and Genos, too."

Danny's blood ran cold. "Genos? They sent Geno Freaks into Miami?"

"Thought it was just a Corporate myth, right?" Alexander's smile was back, but it didn't extend to her eyes. "I did, too. The great Obsidian, resorting to the use of failed science experiments to exert its will on a rebellious people. Only there was nothing failed about those experiments. It took thirteen hours, but at the end of it, the riots were put down, and we were sent in to arrest those who were left.

"Only there weren't any left." She hugged herself slightly, as if the warm May air had taken a sudden chill. "Those the Agents and soldiers didn't kill, the Genos ate. They *ate* our people, Daniel."

Danny shook his head. He knew Obsidian could be cruel, but he had no idea they had actually resorted to using Geno Freaks for suppression. The rumors of a secret division among the Corporate raiders had been true, then. "The Evidence Shredders," he whispered.

"Bingo." She shivered. "Now, you know why I'm hesitant to help in this admittedly noble endeavor. I have to think about my men and what will happen to them if we go up against Obsidian." She reached into a pouch on her belt and removed a portable rad-meter, which would check both the air and nearby materials for radiation. It clicked very slowly. "I'm amazed we're free of any fallout from that explosion."

"It exploded high enough in the atmosphere that all we got was the EMP."

"And that's bad enough. I haven't had a hot shower in nearly two weeks."

"All the more reason to come and join us at the university! Good food, hot showers, shared patrols. I don't see a downside."

She laughed. "You don't give up, do you?"

"It's how I ended up married." He winced as he said it, both because he missed Amy and because of his history with Wendy.

"How is Amy? Still a pilot?"

"Not as a career anymore, but yes. And she was fine, last I heard from her." He patted the pocket where he kept his fried cellphone. "Doing work on the USS *Alabama*'s restoration, in fact."

"That's awesome. It's been years since I've seen the Mighty A."

Danny turned to face I-70. As he did, movement down the road caught his eye. He squinted and visored his eyes with a hand. "Pair of riders."

Alexander opened a pouch on her hip and removed a sleek set of binoculars.

Danny whistled. "Fancy set of binocs. I wish Mobile had Miami's budget."

"I bought these with my own money," she retorted, then placed the binoculars to her eyes. She frowned. "It's a pair of uniformed officers. Can't tell from where at this distance, but they look hurt. One of them is slumped over in the saddle, and the other rider's horse is limping."

"Let's go get 'em," Danny said.

Danny, Alexander, and three of the Miami PD were in the saddle and riding hard within seconds. As they approached, the lead rider brought his horse to a halt and clambered off the saddle. He stumbled as his boots touched ground, then he fell to his knees and vomited.

Alexander held up a hand, and her men slowed to a halt. Danny stopped a little bit ahead of them, so he was between both parties. He turned back to the stricken man, who was about fifty yards away. At this distance, he recognized the uniform as belonging to the St. Louis PD. "Lieutenant Hanson?" he called. "Kevin! Is that you?"

The man looked up and waved. Then he doubled over and puked again.

Danny and Alexander shared a look. She fished out her radmeter and slowly approached Hanson. The device started clicking rapidly. "Shit," she murmured. "He's irradiated."

"Jesus, Kevin," Danny said. "How'd you end up like this?"

"St. Louis. We went back. There's…" He started to dry heave, but mastered it. "There's nothing left. It's gone. Just like everything else."

Danny's stomach knotted up. "Everything else? What do you mean?"

Hanson tried to respond, but no words came out. His eyes rolled back in his head, and he fell backward, the back of his head bouncing against the pavement.

* * *

"We're trying to leach the radiation out of him, Lieutenant Ward," Doctor Hollingsworth said through the intercom, "but he was hit with a massive dose days ago. It's a wonder he lasted this long."

I stood in front of a window in the campus hospital's cancer ward. On the other side of the thick glass, Doctor Hollingsworth skimmed the contents of a tablet while a nurse studied the readouts on a diagnostic machine. Both wore hazmat suits.

Behind them, Kevin Hanson lay in a bed, his wasted frame draped in a hospital gown. An IV ran into its arm, the bag filled with some kind of iridescent liquid.

"I'm the only one left," he murmured, his weak voice almost lost in the humming of machinery. *"My whole squad's gone."*

My heart went out to him. Patrolman McGraw, the man he'd brought back with him, had died before the medical team summoned from the hospital could apply first aid and preliminary radiation treatment. Both mounts had been put down on the spot, as well, mercy killings to end their suffering.

The officers who had first encountered them, including Danny and Wendy Alexander, had gone through decontamination. Their uniforms had been burned, and they were currently changing into fresh sets.

The door to my viewing room opened, and Danny strode in, Alexander a step behind him.

"*Lieutenant Hanson's case is strange,*" Hollingsworth said. "*The amount of radiation he was hit with could only have come from one of two places: inside a nuclear reactor or inside the blast zone of a nuclear bomb.*"

"They came from St. Louis," Danny said, his eyes flicking from the doctor's face to mine. "The lieutenant said the whole city was a smoking crater."

"It got hit with nukes the same day we were nearly hit," Alexander added. She glared at me. "Before he lost consciousness, he told us the whole country was like this."

"*Dear God.*" Hollingsworth's eyes widened. "*Is this true? This wasn't just a localized event? A missile launch gone wrong?*"

"Oh, it went wrong," I said. I looked at the three of them, then sighed. "Yes, it's true. We may be one of the only cities of our size in our current predicament, but that's only because most of the others were hit directly with nukes."

Danny suddenly grabbed me by the shoulders. "Even Mobile?" he hissed, then louder, "Even Mobile?"

I turned my head to avoid his gaze. "Yes."

Danny's hands went slack and then it was my turn to grab my brother, to keep him on his feet as his legs gave out. I helped him over to the only chair in the room. Danny put his head in his hands and sat there.

Alexander looked down at my brother a moment, her eyes full of concern. When she turned to me, her gaze hardened. "Miami?"

"We lost our satellite feed right as the big one exploded over us, so I can't confirm it." I hesitated, then added, "It didn't look good, though. Several missiles were headed that way."

She closed her eyes and released a shuddering sigh. "Damn," she whispered.

"I know."

"I'm sorry for your loss," she said after a moment. She placed a hand on my shoulder.

I reached up and placed my hand on top of hers. "And yours."

She nodded. We were both cops. Hope drove us as much as anyone, but often it was better to assume the worst in any given situation. Then you could be pleasantly surprised when things turned out better.

And if things were just as bad as you feared, well, at least you weren't disappointed.

That was an attitude all of us would have to adopt if we wanted to keep our sanity in this Fallen World.

* * * * *

Chapter Thirteen

"Why didn't you tell me?"

I shut the door to the dormitory suite Danny and I shared with Brother Stephen and the kids. The three of them were outside playing, leaving us to ourselves. The walk from the hospital to the dorm had been short, quiet, and awkward. The whole time I'd felt Danny's eyes drilling into the back of my skull.

Now those eyes glared at me, hard and bloodshot. "Why didn't you tell me?" he growled.

His hands clenched and unclenched every few seconds, a sign he was doing all he could to keep his rage in check.

No sense in sugarcoating it. If he wanted to fight, I'd let him hit me. Lord knew I deserved it. "Sworn to secrecy by Mayor Reynolds and Chief Ballantine. You've served long enough to know the whole 'need to know' rigmarole. Hell, you've been in charge of—"

"Never with you!" He slammed his fist against the wall, the sound reverberating like a gunshot. "Certainly never of this magnitude. My God, why didn't you tell me?"

"You think I didn't want to?" I snapped, my own anger rising. "You think I wanted to keep all this weight on my shoulders, without anyone to support me?"

"Oh, so that's how it is? Woe is you? At least you have your kids! My wife—"

"Is gone! Along with Mom and Dad and everyone we know." Tears brimmed in my eyes, but I was too mad to care. "I know what happened to them, and I know what happened to the rest of this godforsaken country, too."

I told him everything, from the moment Brother Stephen and I followed Aster into the command bunker to Mayor Reynolds' and Chief Ballantine's gag order. I also pointed out that it was Teledyne missiles that saved our asses, and that Obsidian was just as guilty. "If you want someone to be angry at, direct it at Teledyne Tower and the Country Hotel."

"Dammit, Nate, I'm not mad at you." He paused, then cracked a sheepish smile. "Well, not fully."

I returned the smile. "If it helps, I'm mad at me, too."

"I'm mad at the whole situation." Danny clenched his fists again, then forced them open. He pressed his palms against his knees and glared at the floor. "Teledyne and Obsidian and JalCom and all of them. Why'd they have to tear our country apart? What good did it do any of them in the end? Teledyne and Obsidian are going to Hell's boardroom, and they're dragging us with them. We're not even shareholders!"

"That's not what my 401k statements say, but I get your point." I crossed my arms and leaned against the windowsill. Outside, Jason and Helen ran around while Brother Stephen sat on a bench. The chaplain wiped sweat from his brow, and then Jason dragged him to his feet again. "I don't know why they did what they did, but we have to live in the aftermath of it."

We were silent for a time, each of us lost in the shared grief of the moment. My heart ached for my brother, but at the same time, there was an odd sense of relief. Now we both knew what had happened, and we could mourn together. We could rebuild together.

We could tell the kids together.

"My God, what will Jason and Helen think?" Danny muttered.

I laughed and scrubbed the wetness from my eyes. "You always could read my mind, man. We'll tell them after we've told the others. Maybe not even then. Not for some time."

Danny nodded. "Let them be kids for a little longer. This kind of news is gonna age them fast."

That gave me pause. "Them aging fast might not be such a bad thing, all things considered. They'll need to be able to protect themselves a lot sooner than either of us would like."

"Damn those Corporate bastards." Danny's face reddened, his hands clenched so tight his knuckles turned white. "I want them all dead. Every last one of the suited pieces of shit."

"You and me both, but we can't act out of vengeance. We're officers, and we need to remember that. What we're feeling, the men will be feeling. We can't give in to that."

Danny glared at me for a moment, then he sighed. "Yeah. Yeah, I know. It's just..." He reached into his pocket and pulled out his phone. He tried turning it on, but the screen wouldn't light up. "Thing's been broken since the explosion on the First. I should just—" He started to throw it to the ground, then stopped. "I didn't answer it when she called."

I grimaced. "When was that?"

"Right before Teledyne fired off its CBMs." His thumbs tapped the screen in an obvious pattern, and I realized he was typing Amy's phone number into the invisible number pad, over and over again. "All the guys were around, we had no idea what was going on, and that stupid ringtone..." He sighed and pocketed the phone. "I was preoccupied and embarrassed and, well, there it went. The last time I'll ever get to speak with her, this side of Heaven."

"There will be that, at least," I said, though it was small comfort in the present. I'd gone through the same thing with Regina, though the circumstances were quite a bit different. I patted him on the shoulder. "That's one thing this Fallen World can't take from us, man."

* * * * *

Chapter Fourteen

"Thank you all for assembling here." Sheriff Welliver stood on a dais at the rear of Devine Sports Pavilion, right in front of the yellow football goal posts.

Nearly six hundred police officers from various departments stood at attention in front of the dais, our boots pressing into the Astroturf floor. Two-thirds were mounted officers, with the remaining two hundred a mix of city police and county deputies. I was in the front rank, alongside Captain Phillips and Lieutenant Alexander, with more commanders to our left and right. Our subordinates stood behind us, and I didn't need to turn around to know all of them wore expressions similar to Alexander's: shock, grief, anger, or some combination of the three.

I noticed some people were missing from those assembled. In the three days since Hanson's arrival, word about the situation had spread like wildfire, forcing us to come clean about what we knew. No one had taken it well, but most were holding up. Shared grief among comrades was a beautiful, sacred thing. As I watched my fellow officers alternate between weeping, raging, and comforting one another, it made me realize just how resilient we could be if we worked together.

And yet there were a few who hadn't been able to cope. There were four suicides inside twenty-four hours, with another nine over the next two days. My own Patrolman Williams had slit her wrist, but

Corporal Ferris had caught her in time and applied first aid. Williams was recovering in the university hospital, along with two other failed suicides.

Danny and I had cleaned up the scene. It was a miracle Williams had survived, with as much blood as she lost. And yet, would that have been a bad way to go? Considering what lay ahead, I didn't know the answer.

And that scared me.

The remaining officers were now hyper-vigilant, and the unit chaplains and hospital psychologists were working overtime to prevent further casualties. I prayed there wouldn't be any more, but I knew we weren't out of the woods yet. Morale was lower than I'd ever seen it.

Maybe that would change today.

"At ease," Welliver said after a moment's silence. "I'll keep this short. By now, you've all heard the news. The extent of the nuclear attacks is a lot wider than initially reported. Many towns and cities across our great nation have been completely destroyed. Many of you are from those towns and cities."

I sucked in an unsteady breath. Alexander muttered a curse. Phillips remained silent.

"I'm blessed that my entire family is here in Columbia, but many of my deputies and fellow officers from Columbia have not fared as well. And for those with family in St. Louis and Kansas City, well, that hits hard. They're so close, yet there's nothing we can do for them.

"But, we can do something for the people here, in this town. I plan to take the fight straight to the Corporations. If it's their intent to make war in this city, they need to be stopped, no matter the cost."

Murmuring rose up behind me. I couldn't catch most of it, but from what I did hear, the sentiment was the same: how were we supposed to battle giants like Teledyne and Obsidian?

"I don't believe this is a lost cause," Welliver continued, as if hearing our thoughts. He chuckled. "I don't spend as much time in church as I should, but there has to be a reason for all this, don't you think?"

I frowned. Reason for what?

"There has to be a reason for all of you." Welliver spread his hands. "What are the odds that almost six hundred officers from so many departments would be here, in this city, on the day the world fell? And for you to be equipped with one of the very things we need to turn this ship around. We can't depend on vehicles to get us through, but we have man's oldest form of transportation in abundance. And we have talented, dedicated men and women who can ride them.

"I plan to use that asset to liberate this city from the gangs, whether they're in ratty green or red jackets or they're in tailored suits. None of these thugs have a right to this city. This city belongs to the people and to the men and women who would protect it. Who's with me?"

I stepped forward. "Sir, Mobile stands with you!"

"Miami stands with you!" Alexander shouted.

"Philadelphia is with you, sir!"

"The LAPD is ready to kick some Corporate ass!"

"Not before the NYPD gets a crack at it!"

The assembled men and women started shouting and cheering in a jumble that echoed through the pavilion. It hurt my ears, but it gladdened my heart.

We had our work cut out for us, but it finally seemed like we were getting somewhere in this Fallen World.

* * * * *

Chapter Fifteen

"**M**an, this brings me back," Jake Morris said from the front passenger seat of the Columbia PD SUV. "It's just like the good ol' days, right?"

I walked Countess next to the slow-moving SUV. I leaned over in the saddle to look at Jake, who sat in the front passenger's seat. "What's just like the good ol' days?"

"You know, all of us!" He gestured around the vehicle. "Danny, you, me—not you, Brother Stephen. Or you, Corporal Reed. Sorry."

"No need to apologize," Chloe Reed said, her head turned to look out the window as Danny slowly drove the vehicle toward the built-up area of New Downtown. She held her M14 tight against her armored chest. "That said, I don't know what the hell you're talking about."

"Same here." I maneuvered Countess around a wrecked truck, then trotted back up to the SUV window. Behind me, the dozen mounted officers who followed me moved through the bottleneck in pairs. "Last time we were all together in a vehicle like this, we were little kids being driven to a park by your Mom." I pointed at Countess. "And I don't think I was on horseback."

"Oh, don't be like that, little Nate," Danny said in a falsetto. "You won't turn out to be as good as my boy with that kind of attitude. Now, who wants to get a hot dog and some ice cream?"

The others burst into laughter, even Jake. "My mom didn't sound like that, dumbass!"

"She kinda did," I said, wiping tears from my eyes. "Though she never admonished me for not being as smart as you. Now, Danny here, he was the dumb one. Mom gave all the intelligence to me."

"Had to give you something to balance out your ugly face and horrible attitude," Danny retorted.

"Ha, ha. Just drive, Mrs. Morris."

"He doesn't sound like my mom!"

"Now, now, honey. I think someone's in need of a little sugar!"

We all laughed, maybe a little harder than the joke warranted. There had been so little to laugh about these last few weeks that we all latched onto any kind of humor. And, for once, it wasn't gallows humor.

"Nice to see someone is having fun," Lieutenant Saleh said. He and two of his camel riders marched behind me. Sergeant Mosher and two members of the Tel Aviv mounted police followed along, with another six men from the Mobile and Baltimore departments. We were all decked out in our riot gear, and our horses and camels were draped in barding and wearing protective boots. If the Corporations decided to attack us, we'd be ready.

We reached an intersection with a road running north on into the New Downtown area, and one running east toward residential neighborhoods on the city's outskirts. I waved at Danny and the others in the police SUV. "We'll see you back at camp! Call if there's trouble."

Danny patted the flare gun holstered on his chest rig. "Look to the sky for the smoke signals, my man. We'll be on the lookout for yours, too."

"Sounds good."

* * *

One thing you never really get used to is having guns pointed your way. I was reminded of that as I looked down the barrel of an old, bolt-action, hunting rifle. Its owner glared at me over the iron sights.

"Good morning," I said, and I hoped the smile on my face didn't show any of the nervousness I felt.

"It's afternoon, and what's good about it?"

"Sir, could you please lower the rifle? You can see we mean you no harm."

"You're armed, ain't ya?"

"You'd be a fool not to be," Patrolman Jones called out.

"True words." The man looked at the twelve of us a moment longer, then lowered his rifle a little bit. "Name's Jay. What can I do for ya?"

We had ridden up to the entrance of a big, fenced-in subdivision on the eastern end of town. The iron gate behind the man was locked, with furniture, sandbags, scrap metal, and other debris piled high against the black bars to keep them from easily being pushed in. The bars had been sliced clean near the center, and a steel door secured there. It made for one hell of a fatal funnel to whatever lay beyond.

Four men and two women crouched behind piled-up sandbags in front of the gate. Each was armed with a shotgun or rifle, but none had their weapons pointed at us yet.

"We're from the university," I said. "We're on patrol, looking to make sure everything's safe in and around the city."

"Looking to expand your territory, you mean." Jay hawked and spat tobacco juice at the asphalt between us. "Already had looters and gangbangers try the same thing, only they weren't so polite about it." He tucked the rifle into the crook of his arm and stroked the wooden stock with his free hand. "We ran 'em off."

"Sir, we're not looking to take over. We just want to make sure you're safe and see if there's anything we can do for you."

"With the Corporations fighting it out in the inner city, we need to come together," Lieutenant Saleh added. "There's strength in numbers."

"That a fact, camel jockey?" Jay squinted up at Saleh, then turned his attention back to me. "We are safe. Obsidian made the same 'request' of us, since their hotel's so close. Offered to take us all in, keep us fed and safe, provided we worked for them." He patted his gun. "Oh, and provided we turn all of these in. Not gonna happen. So, we ran *them* off."

"We have that in common, at least," I said. "We ran both Teledyne and Obsidian out of a neighborhood near the university a little over a week ago, and we're going to keep doing it."

"Mayor's office must be having a field day with that," Jay muttered.

"We work for Sheriff Welliver, not Mayor Reynolds."

"I voted for Welliver. Last four elections, actually. Good man. Knows how to keep the peace in the county."

"That he does," I agreed.

"And you're willing to do the right thing, are you?" Jay studied me for a long moment. "Well, I suppose we could at least sit out here and talk for a spell. You boys enjoy coffee?"

We all shared a look. "It's not my preferred drink, but—"

"Good, because there ain't any. There is sweet tea, though."

I grinned as I dismounted. "Well, I have to say there are still treats to be had in this Fallen World."

* * * * *

Chapter Sixteen

Danny fought hard to keep his anger in check as he drove down the street. Teledyne controlled the western end of the city, and now they were creeping into the northeastern fringes.

"Man, what a bust." Jake rested his chin on his hand. "Drove all that way, just for them to say no. Cowardly bastards."

"Now, now," Brother Stephen said, "we can't really blame them. Who knew Teledyne had spread that far north?"

Teledyne had taken over the Sheriff's office and jailhouse north of the city. Teledyne's goal had been the National Guard armory, but it was empty, courtesy of a mobilization last month to help suppress riots in Fayetteville, Arkansas. Even so, none of the neighborhoods near the armory or jailhouse wanted to do anything to draw Corporate attention, now that Teledyne had set up shop so close by.

"We'll just have to prove ourselves to them," Reed said. "We put the hurt on Teledyne, and the residents will come our way."

Danny looked at her through the rearview mirror. "I hope you're right, Corporal." He didn't hold out much hope, though. The subdivision they had visited had wanted nothing to do with them. "Teledyne's been supplying us with food for weeks," the head of the homeowner's association told them. "Where have you been?"

Damn them all. He gripped the steering wheel so tight the knuckles on his left hand turned white. He rested his right hand on his holstered pistol.

He tried to turn the SUV onto one of New Downtown's main drags, but found the intersection clogged with wrecked vehicles. He drove up to a side street and turned onto it. "It's times like this we could really use our horses."

"Yeah, no kidding," Jake agreed.

"You're not trying hard enough," Reed said. "We could've gotten around that with a bit more finesse."

"How come you didn't drive, then?" Danny snapped. "It's your department's vehicle, after all."

"I'm the only one with a select-fire carbine." She slapped her M14 for emphasis. "Would you rather I drive or shoot?"

"You could've given one of us the M14."

"Not on your life."

"We're all trained in its use," Jake said. "We didn't bring ours with us because, well... Hey, how come we didn't bring them?"

"Because we didn't think we'd be dealing with the end of the world," Danny said. "We mostly brought pistols and a few shotguns." For emphasis, he patted the parkerized Remington 870 in the vertical shotgun rack between him and Jake. "Same story for the rest of the mounted units, I'd imagine. And with the shotguns, we have more beanbags and rubber pellets than actual buckshot. We were training for parade security and riot suppression, not all-out war."

Reed chuckled. "We're a little short on parades, but we've had a fair amount of riots in the past few weeks."

"And more than our fair share of war and killing," Jake said in a quiet voice.

Danny grimaced. Jake wasn't exaggerating. Since the initial skirmish with Teledyne, police patrols had clashed with Corporate soldiers and employees at least ten times. And that wasn't counting the number of firefights they'd had with the Emeralds and the other gangs in the city. While the university and surrounding neighborhoods remained relatively untouched, it was only a matter of time before something happened. That was one reason why they had to expand their sphere of influence. Quickly.

"Hey, look at that." Jake pointed. "Smoke."

A black plume rose over the rooftops several blocks down the street. "Looks like a fire," Brother Stephen said.

It took a few minutes to maneuver around the tangle of disabled vehicles left abandoned after the EMP. Danny rolled down the windows as they approached the intersection the smoke came from. Shouts and screams pierced the acrid air. "That's not a good sign." He glanced at Jake and Reed. "You both ready?"

"Ten-four, Sarge," Reed said.

Jake drew his pistol. "Always."

"Brother Stephen, do your best to stay down." Danny moved around the last disabled vehicle between them and the intersection, then he gunned the engine. He sped to the intersection, then made a sharp left. Smoke and fire poured out of an apartment building two doors down the tightly packed street. A pair of Teledyne soldiers stood in front of the blazing building, their hands in the air. Three Obsidian soldiers had guns trained on them while a fourth patted them down for weapons. A fifth was busy stripping one of the prone women of her jewelry.

At their feet, several civilians lay prone, their heads down and arms outstretched. More than one appeared to be bleeding.

Hot anger coursed through Danny's body. More victims in this never-ending Corporate holocaust. *Not on my watch.*

He slammed on the brakes hard enough for the tires to squeal. He kicked the door opened and jumped out, shotgun in hand. "Freeze!"

One of the Obsidian soldiers aimed his gun at Danny, then dropped with a hole drilled through one of his eyes.

Jake fired again. His bullet struck another soldier in the hand. The man dropped his weapon with a curse. "Drop the weapons, or we'll drop all of you!"

Danny's hands trembled from the adrenaline surge, but he kept the front sight firmly on the torso of the soldier in front of him. Behind the man's visor, he could see eyes wide with fear. There was nothing quite like staring down the open end of a 12-gauge bore to get someone to contemplate mortality.

An audible click sounded from his left. Reed had exited the vehicle and sidestepped around him before presenting her M14. "Make my day, creeps. I'm just itchin' to try this baby on full-auto."

That was enough for the three remaining Obsidian grunts. Their weapons struck the pavement in a clatter as they raised their hands.

"Thanks for the assist," one of the Teledyne soldiers said. He started to lower his hands.

Danny shifted his aim. "Keep 'em up, bastard!"

The man's hands froze. His eyes narrowed. "Look, officer, we have no intention of fighting you. I'm Sergeant Rico of Section—"

"You're with Teledyne!" Danny took a step forward, shotgun aimed right between Rico's eyes. "That's all I need to know."

"Hey, Sarge," Reed said, a hint of nervousness cutting through her bravado, "dial it back a bit, all right?"

Before Danny could say any more, a loud rumble cut over the noise of the police SUV's engine. Jake cocked his head to the side. "Something big's coming our way."

Several somethings, if Danny's ears weren't failing him. He'd been around enough Obsidian vehicles to recognize the sound of APCs, and possibly a cargo truck or two.

A few seconds later, the first APC rolled through an intersection further up the road. It was a squat vehicle with a matte, black hull and eight wheels protected by an armored skirt. Its heavy machine gun turret faced forward.

"Yep, definitely not one of ours," Rico said, looking to the side. He glanced back at Danny's uniform. "I'd suggest clearing out, Sergeant Ward. It's about to get ugly."

The second APC to roll through had its turret turned away, to point down the opposite end of the street. Danny started to backpedal toward the SUV. If they were following the standard formation, the next APC would be aimed right at them.

One of the Obsidian soldiers dropped to the ground and scooped up his handgun. He pointed it at Jake.

The man staggered as several bullets struck his shoulder, neck, and face. He let out a wheezing cough and collapsed.

Rico held a small pistol in his hand. Where he'd drawn it from, Danny had no idea. "Get out of here, Sergeant Ward! This is a Corporate fight."

"I think that might be a good idea!" Brother Stephen called from the SUV.

Brother Stephen's voice broke through Danny's warring emotions. He cursed, then spun on his heel. "Out of the streets, all of you!"

"You heard the officer!" Rico shouted. "Get up! Get up, now!"

Danny jumped into the driver's seat and slid the shotgun back into its vertical mount. Doors slammed behind Jake and Reed.

There was no room to turn the SUV around, so Danny started backing up. He glanced at the rearview camera, then looked up just as the third APC came into view. Its turret faced their way, just like he'd suspected.

He stomped the gas, and the SUV rocketed backward just as the APC's turret opened up with a burst of machine gun fire. Most of the rounds went wide, but one blew out the windshield in a spray of glass.

Danny ducked and yanked the wheel. The SUV spun to the left as it cleared the intersection. He glanced back down the street. Rico and his partner were nowhere to be seen, and the three remaining Obsidian soldiers ran the opposite way, toward the approaching APC.

"Go, go, go!" Reed screamed.

Danny had no idea which way to go, so he floored it. He sped up the street and dodged downed vehicles like he was running a slalom. As he passed each intersection he looked for a side street to pull down, but the roads were filled with disabled and wrecked cars. There just wasn't enough space for the wide SUV to get through.

A crashing sound behind them brought Danny up short. "It's after us!" Brother Stephen shouted.

Danny glanced in the rear-view mirror. The APC slid around the corner and turned toward them.

He raced to the next intersection and turned left, onto a one-way street choked with vehicles. *Shit!* He threw it in reverse and flew back through the intersection. He looked to his left and saw the approaching APC weaving around a couple of broken-down sedans. The turret tracked them, and he tensed.

Then they were out of the intersection and racing backward up another one-way street. Danny tried to maneuver with the rearview camera, and found this street was just as stuffed with vehicles that would never drive again. He weaved to the left, to the right, onto the sidewalk. Sparks flew as he scraped against disabled vehicles, and one of the side mirrors was torn off.

They made it about halfway up the street before he had to slam on the brakes to keep from plowing into a delivery van. There was no way around it.

"It's here!" Jake shouted.

The APC rolled to a stop at the head of the street. The turret rotated toward them.

"Bail out!" Danny shouted.

All four doors of the SUV flew open, and three officers and a chaplain hit the asphalt just as the APC opened fire. Machine gun rounds tore through the SUV, shattering windows, blowing tires, and punching through the engine block. The vehicle gasped, sputtered, and died as oil and antifreeze spilled out of the engine compartment.

"Find cover!" Danny crawled back to the SUV. "A store, an apartment, something!"

He waited for the APC to stop firing, then he reached up and grabbed the shotgun from its mount. He threw himself flat on his back as the turret opened up again.

"Sarge, this way!" Reed called. She waved at him from the glass door of a brick building, the first level taken up by some kind of shop. The storefront was partly recessed when compared to its neighboring buildings, so she wasn't visible to the APC. Jake and Brother Stephen joined her.

Danny pulled the flare gun from its holster. He removed a red flare from his chest rig, popped it in the chamber, aimed, and squeezed the trigger. The flare shot into the air, a streak of red smoke trailing after it. He quickly ejected the spent shell and inserted another flare. Black smoke soon joined the red. *Please, Lord, let someone see that.*

He rolled onto his stomach and crawled away from the ruined SUV. The APC's machine gun fell silent again, and a new noise intruded on the sudden quiet: the sound of a hatch opening. He pulled himself into a crouch and scrambled between vehicles until he was in front of the building. Then he broke into a run. A shout and a burst of submachine gun fire gave him all the incentive he needed to get inside. Reed stepped in and slammed the door behind him.

Danny looked around. "Uh, Reed, did you intend to take us here, or was it an act of God?"

"It was the first building I saw that looked like it was out of the line of fire," Reed said. "Why?"

"Oh, nothing, really." A wave of giddiness hit him, and he chuckled. "It must be a cop's instincts. I mean, what are the odds we'd wind up in a doughnut shop?"

* * *

"Well, that don't sound good," Jay said.

I turned my head toward the city. Someone had a heavy machine gun, and it wasn't us. Where was the sound coming from?

And then a pair of smoke flares rose from a set of buildings in the New Downtown area not more than a mile away. Two colors, red and black. Together it meant "Officer in distress. All available units, respond immediately."

That was the direction Danny and the others had gone in.

"Jay, I'd advise you and yours to get inside and stay down," I said, turning Countess around. "We have to go investigate, but there's no guarantee the fighting won't spill out this way."

"Don't have to tell me twice." Jay motioned for those with him to head back behind the fortified gate. When they were gone, he walked up to me. "Think it's Obsidian or Teledyne?"

"Could be," I said. "We're going to go find out."

"And you expect to win against *that*?"

"That's the hope. Our people need us, and we're going to help." I looked down at him. "And that's the kind of help we'll offer to you, as well." I reached into my pack and removed a flare gun. "Blue smoke for daytime and blue luminous for night. Until we get our radios back up and running, this is the best way to reach us. Come by the university if you want us to extend patrols this way and share resources, but either way, we'll come running if you need us."

Jay took the flare gun and glowered up at me. "You know, we could avoid messing with you altogether until we need you. No need to share our resources or anything if you're going to help no matter what."

"Maybe, but it's the decent thing for us to do. And you're a decent man, Jay, no matter the kind of act you put on. I have faith you'll join us in our effort to retake this city and rebuild what was lost." I grinned. "No one who has a woman who can make sweet tea that good is a bad man in my book."

Jay laughed. "I like you, kid. Consider it a deal."

I touched the rim of my helmet in salute, then pressed my heels to Countess. We started off at a quick trot, Jay's laughter following us.

The others fell in beside me. "Should we head back to the university?" Sergeant Mosher asked. "Get one of the rapid response patrols to join us?"

"They're already on the way," I said and hoped I was right. The response team *should* be on its way, but the university was a lot farther away. And if things were bad enough that the black flare was launched, then whoever was out that way needed help, and they needed it yesterday.

"We'll go with what we have, but we'll be cautious. Observation, then hit and run tactics once we figure out what we're up against. Use our mobility to our advantage!"

A mix of "Ten-Four!" and "Yes, sir!" answered me.

I grinned. It paid to have brave comrades in this Fallen World.

* * * * *

Chapter Seventeen

"When the fuck did Obsidian get APCs?" Reed demanded. She held her M14 to her shoulder and crouched against one of the only solid walls at the doughnut shop's entrance, near the right corner of the room. Her small frame made her a difficult target for when the shooting started. "Were the bastards hiding them?"

"No idea, but they're here now," Danny said. "Jake, check the kitchen. There's got to be a back door." They couldn't stay here, not for long.

"On it!"

The doughnut shop had a sterile aesthetic; all the tables and chairs in the dining area were made of stainless steel, as was the counter that ran the width of the back part of the room. Parts of it looked pretty solid, too. Danny doubted it would hold up against that APC's heavy machine gun, but it would do against small arms.

Danny grabbed the nearest table and dragged it to the counter. Brother Stephen saw what he was doing and joined in, running toward the farthest table near the entrance.

A burst of machine gun fire shattered one of the storefront windows. Stephen ducked as he was showered with glass but continued pulling the table.

"No good, Danny!" Jake ran in from the kitchen. "Back door's blocked by something. Looks like there was a fire in the next building and part of its roof collapsed into the alley."

"Help us fortify the counter! We'll have to hold out until help comes."

"If help comes," Reed muttered.

Jake hurried around the counter and grabbed a table and hurled it against the counter with a resounding clang. "Damn, man, you been working out?" Danny asked.

Jake looked at his hands and shrugged. "Adrenaline does funny things to a man."

Once all the tables and chairs had been added to the fortification, the four of them crouched behind the counter. Reed and Danny aimed their long guns toward the windows, while Jake drew his pistol and braced it against the counter's smooth surface.

"Lord, shield us from the enemy's bullets," Stephen muttered. "Send your angels to protect us and to drive away the enemy."

"Amen," Danny said. He rested the shotgun against the counter long enough to draw his pistol and hold it out to Stephen. "Here, Brother. I know you know how to use it."

Stephen took the pistol in trembling hands. "I—" he began.

"You're a good shepherd," Danny said, and clapped the older man on the shoulder. "And a good shepherd always protects his flock, right?"

Stephen nodded and braced the pistol against the counter, much like Jake had.

"All right, boys and girl," Danny said, "let's give 'em hell and bust our way clear. I don't want to be remembered for my valiant last stand at the local doughnut shop."

Jake and Stephen laughed. "Shut up!" Reed snapped but then she laughed, too.

Another burst of gunfire shattered the rest of the windows in the storefront, and a pair of black balls were tossed inside.

"Get down!" Jake shouted. "Flashbangs!"

Danny ducked behind the counter just as the pair of stun grenades exploded. His ears rang, but his vision was spared from the blinding flash. "Get ready!" he shouted, his voice strangely quiet to his own ears.

As he raised his shotgun over the counter again, he took a quick glance to his right. Reed and Jake were ready. He glanced to his left, then did a double take. Stephen sagged against the rear of the counter, blinking furiously.

"Stephen, can you see?"

"A little." He squinted at Danny, tears welling and running from his red eyes. "Lots of bright spots, though. That grenade—"

"Stun grenades do that," Danny said. "Look, crawl back into the kitchen for the moment. Come back out when your vision clears, or—better yet—see if you can find another way out. Maybe a basement or attic Jake didn't see or a wall we can break through."

"Here they come!" Reed shouted.

Jake grunted an affirmative and cracked off three quick shots.

"Go!" Danny said and pushed Stephen in the direction of the kitchen.

Stephen crawled into the kitchen. Danny didn't expect the pastor to find anything, but at least he would be out of the line of fire.

Danny shouldered his shotgun just in time to see an Obsidian breaching team smash their way through the rest of the floor-to-ceiling windows in the storefront. There were five of them, one with a shield and pistol, and the rest wielding submachine guns. A sixth one lay slumped on the sidewalk, blood running from under his helmet.

Sighting in on the shield-bearer, Danny fired, racked, fired, racked, and fired in rapid succession. In less than a second, three steel slugs struck the shield one after the other. The clear ballistic plastic absorbed most of the impact, but the force of the rounds staggered the man, causing him to stumble back into his buddies.

One of the men reflexively sidestepped to avoid getting tangled up, and Reed lit him up with her M14. The heavy-hitting .308 rounds punched through his chest armor, and he tumbled to the sidewalk next to his fallen buddy.

Jake's pistol barked several times, laying down deadly, accurate fire. One of his rounds clipped the helmet of the shield-bearer, carving a groove through its rounded surface but not penetrating. The impact cracked the shield-bearer's resolve, and he started to back away.

As he did, he exposed one of the men behind him. Danny fired, and a slug struck the man in the pelvis, right beneath his hard chest plate. The soft, bulletproof armor beneath absorbed the fat slug without letting it penetrate, but the force of the impact shattered bone and ruptured tissue. The man fell to the pavement and screamed in agony.

The shield-bearer dropped his pistol on a lanyard and grabbed the drag-handle near the nape of the wounded man's neck and started hauling him away. One of his buddies fired a burst of submachine gun fire into the doughnut shop, forcing everyone down to avoid getting hit. Reed held her M14 over her head and fired blindly. One of the Obsidian soldiers cried out as a round hit home.

"Fire in the hole!" someone shouted.

"Shit, grenade!" Danny jumped up, shotgun tight against his shoulder.

He fired just as the soldier threw the grenade. Danny's slug slammed into the soldier's chest armor and knocked him to his knees, but the grenade was already on its way.

Jake leaped to the side and caught the grenade just as it sailed over the counter. Without hesitating, he flung it back outside. "Get down!"

Danny threw himself to the floor, Jake and Reed landing next to him.

The grenade exploded in a deafening blast. Fragments peppered the counter and walls of the doughnut shop, but nothing penetrated. Ears ringing, Danny picked himself up and surveyed the damage. The Obsidian insertion team had been reduced to a mangled pile of meat and armor.

The heavy machine gun from the armored vehicle opened up again, the rounds tearing through walls and what was left of the twisted, broken storefront. The angle wasn't in Obsidian's favor, though, because the rounds couldn't reach the counter.

"Well," Danny said as he thumbed more slugs into his shotgun, "the good news is they can't get that APC anywhere near us."

"Bad news is it can keep us from leaving," Jake said as he dropped his partly spent magazine and slammed a fresh one home. "There's no way we're getting out through that door with it still here."

Danny looked at the front entrance, with its shattered glass and broken frames. "What door?"

Jake chuckled. "Oh, right. What door, indeed?"

"How can you two joke at a time like this?" Reed snapped. Her dark hands shook as she tried to remove the magazine from her M14 and insert a fresh one. "My adrenaline's spiked, my hands are jittery, and I've got tunnel vision. It's a wonder I'm coherent, and you're both laughing away."

"This isn't our first rodeo," Danny said. "Been through plenty of firefights before this whole mess in Columbia got started." He looked up at Jake. "Damn nice throw back there. You're lucky it didn't blow up in your hand."

"Didn't have anything to lose by trying, right? We were dead either way."

Movement across the street caught Danny's attention. A squad of Obsidian soldiers crouch-walked their way between several disabled vehicles. "Well, shit. I think things are about to get worse."

Jake and Reed took their positions again, as did Danny.

"Danny!" Stephen called from the kitchen. He appeared at the door, his eyes wide. "I found an attic access!"

Hope surged in Danny's heart. "Is there a way out up there? Maybe a window that leads out back?"

"No, but there are windows overlooking the entrance."

The hope soured a bit, but then turned into something else: an idea. He looked back at the Obsidian soldiers taking cover on the other side of the street, then at Reed, who was performing tactical breathing exercises to steady her nerves and heart rate. "Corporal, how good are you on the range with that thing?"

"Ninety-five out of a hundred pretty consistently. Sharpshooter badge, but not quite good enough for Marksman." She cocked an eyebrow at me. "Why do you ask?"

"Follow Stephen up to the attic and wait for the right moment to strike at those bastards across the street."

"The right moment?"

"Wait until they're fully engaged with us and all the fire and fury's going down. Then light them up one-by-one. Start with the squad leader, then move on to the others. Pull back if you have to. And don't let that APC see you, or it's all over."

At mention of the APC, her eyes widened. She swallowed hard and gripped the M14 tightly enough for her knuckles to turn white. "On it, Sarge."

Danny clapped her on the shoulder and moved aside so she could get by. Then he took up position again. "Stephen, join us out here when you can!"

"It's right in there, Corporal," Stephen said from the kitchen. "Up that ladder." He then crawled out to where Danny was. "Yes?"

"How's your vision?"

"Much better."

"Good. I need you to help lay down fire on those pieces of crap out there." He pointed his chin in the direction of the street.

Stephen peered over the counter, then saw the mess of bodies in front. He gasped. "Dear God."

Danny grimaced. He wished his friend didn't have to see that, but there was nothing to be done for it. If he was lucky, that's the worst he would ever see.

Stephen braced the pistol against the counter. "I've never shot anyone before," he said.

"Well, if it makes you feel any better, you probably won't succeed in doing that today," Danny said. "I've seen you at the range, man."

"Just fire enough to keep their heads down," Jake said. "When Danny and I aren't shooting, you fill in the gaps. Keep them focused on us."

"Right." Stephen took a deep breath and let it out. "Right, I think I can do that."

"Good man, Brother." Danny lined up his sights on the front passenger window of the disabled sedan directly across the street. He had seen movement there just a moment before and—

A head peeked over the door panel.

Danny squeezed.

The head exploded in a shower of blood that painted the door panel and rear passenger window red. Several more heads popped up, along with submachine guns and rifles.

"I think you made 'em angry," Jake said as he fired. A soldier screamed and dropped.

Then Obsidian returned fire, and the three officers found themselves pressed to the floor. Bullets pinged against the thick counter and punched through the wall overhead.

Danny racked a fresh round into the chamber, then raised himself to fire. He fired four shells in rapid succession before ducking down again. Jake popped up next, firing several rounds. Even with the sheer volume of fire, Danny was able to make out a pained scream on the other side of the street.

As Jake ducked back down, Stephen popped up to shoot. Despite his clear reluctance to kill, he didn't hesitate to squeeze the trigger over and over again. He half-emptied his magazine and would have kept going had Danny not pulled him back down. A barrage of submachine gun rounds struck the wall immediately behind where Stephen had been standing.

"Stephen, stand up, fire a couple shots, then get back down again. It's like Whack-a-Mole, except we're the moles, and we've got teeth. But they've still got the hammer."

Stephen glanced up at the fresh bullet holes and grimaced. The man's usually tan face had grown pale, but his hands no longer shook as he held the pistol. That was a good sign in Danny's book.

"Your turn!" Jake said as he ducked down again.

Danny moved a few feet to the right of where he had stood last time and popped up, shotgun blasting.

His slug caught one of the Obsidian soldiers in the left shoulder. The man spun halfway around before steadying himself. He turned back, his weapon still tucked against his right shoulder as he aimed for Danny.

A bullet punched through the top of his helmet and flew out the back of his skull. Blood sprayed out of both wounds as he toppled to the curb.

Another bullet tore into the head of a soldier who was pointing their way and shouting orders. He staggered backward and slumped down against a lamp post.

"Looks like Reed's up there, earning her keep!" Jake said. He took aim and fired several more times, until his slide locked back on an empty magazine. "Reloading!"

"Pour it on them, Brother Stephen!" Danny said as he emptied his shotgun of the remaining slugs. The slugs tore holes into the sedan and winged more than one Obsidian soldier.

As he crouched down to thumb more shells into his shotgun's tube magazine, Stephen finished emptying the remainder of his magazine. Jake joined him in laying down as much fire as two handguns could muster.

Outside, the Obsidian soldiers screamed and died as Reed's M14 rained down fire and death from above.

Danny looked up and saw one of the Obsidian soldiers pointing up, toward their building. A round punched through the soldier's chest armor and neck, and he hit the ground, but he had gotten his message across.

They knew where Reed was.

The APC's heavy machine gun opened up, and overhead, glass shattered. Reed screamed.

Danny ran into the kitchen. If Reed had been hit, she'd need medical attention. Dammit, he should have been up there instead of her! As he reached the attic steps, he could hear Reed's screams much more clearly. "Reed!" He put a boot on the first step. "I'm coming—"

Suddenly Reed appeared at the trapdoor opening in the ceiling. She jumped, not even bothering with the ladder. Her petite frame crashed into Danny, and they fell to the floor in a heap.

"Oh, my God, my God, my God!" Reed shrieked.

"Are you all right?" Danny demanded from his place on the floor. "Are you hit? Where are you hit?" He placed his hands on her and felt around for any wounds her navy blue uniform might be hiding.

Reed threw back her head and laughed. "Oh, my God! That was insane! That was—" She blinked rapidly, then looked down at Danny. "Wait, Sarge, why're you underneath me?" Then her eyes narrowed. "And what's with your hands?"

Danny jerked his hands away from her as if he'd been burned. "Sorry. I—Well, you were screaming, and I thought you were wounded."

"If I'd been shot, do you think I'd be running around like a chicken with its head cut off, laughing hysterically?" She took a deep breath. "Man, what a rush that was. They were so focused on you, they didn't even see me at first. I was able to line up my shots perfectly." She pantomimed aiming and shooting with her arm. "Bam. Bam. Bam. One after another."

"Danny, Miss Reed, are you both all right?" Stephen crawled into the kitchen, took one look at them, then frowned. "Now, I can't say I approve of this, you two. We don't have time for these shenanigans."

"What shenanigans?!" Danny and Reed snapped in unison. Then they looked at each other and laughed. At least there was still humor to be found in this Fallen World.

* * * * *

Chapter Eighteen

I led my fellow mounted officers toward New Downtown at a trot, chasing the sound of the heavy machine gun. Suburban sprawl soon gave way to concrete jungle. Neighborhood entrances and abandoned strip malls turned into streets of office buildings, shops, and apartments. The buildings in New Downtown were never taller than ten stories, nothing compared to Teledyne Tower's forty stories. I couldn't help but smile at that thought. I'd spent a summer in Manhattan, and if there was a building that was only forty stories tall, it was considered a lightweight.

Then again, it was the same in Mobile. The tallest building there was still the old RSA Tower at thirty-five stories. Or, it had been.

I tightened my grip on the reins, and let out a breath through gritted teeth. *Focus, Nate. You're needed here and now, not in the past.*

As we drew closer, the chattering of the heavy machine gun was joined by short bursts from submachine guns, the pops of handguns, and the crack of some kind of long rifle. It was hard to tell where the gunfire was coming from, with the way the noise echoed and bounced off the walls of the buildings in New Downtown.

I continuously swiveled my head through each intersection, looking fully left and then right. Disabled, wrecked vehicles littered most of the streets, but the one we were on was surprisingly empty for a main road. Civilians peeked out of windows as we hurried past offices and apartment buildings. I waved, then turned my attention elsewhere.

The gunfire fell quiet for a few moments, and silence reigned but for the clattering of our horses' booted hooves against the pavement. I frowned. Where had that racket come from?

As we started to cross the next intersection, I turned my head to the right. Then the heavy machine gun opened up again, close enough to rattle my teeth.

I snapped my head to the left, and time seemed to slow down. Between one hoofbeat and the next, my eyes took in the scene: a number of men in Obsidian battle armor crouched behind a tall, eight-wheeled APC that faced down the street. Its turret blasted tracer rounds into the second story window of a doughnut shop about a hundred yards down the street.

My God, I thought, my mouth going dry. *Where did Obsidian get an APC?*

Several bodies lay in the street directly across from the shop. More Obsidian soldiers, dead and wounded. Chances were high our officers were inside, unless this Obsidian crew had stumbled upon a Teledyne patrol, which I doubted happened this far from the Tower.

One of the Obsidian soldiers turned toward us. He raised his submachine gun to fire.

Several of us fired at once. My pistol rounds couldn't penetrate the man's armor, but Saleh's AK-47 punched right through. The man fell without a sound.

The rest of the soldiers turned our way. The APC's machine gun fell silent, and the turret whined as it rotated toward us. I kicked Countess into a gallop. "Follow me!" I shouted.

We sped away from the intersection. Behind us, Obsidian soldiers shouted, and shots were fired. A horse screamed.

I turned in my saddle and saw Sergeant Mosher tumble off his mount. He rolled several yards and bounded back to his feet, pistol already blazing at the charging enemies.

Before I could react, Saleh wheeled his camel around and galloped back into the fight, flanked by two of his fellow Jordanians. "Allahu Akbar!" he shouted.

They crashed into the enemy soldiers before they could finish off the unhorsed Israeli officer. His camel stomped one man flat against the ground. Saleh leaned down and fired a burst of his AK-47 pointblank. The rounds shattered the Obsidian soldier's face-plate.

The second camel spat into the face of another soldier, blinding the man long enough for its rider to put a bullet in him. And the third camel plowed three enemies under, crunching bones and bursting organs with the tread of its heavy hooves.

Saleh stopped his camel near Mosher and offered his hand. The Israeli reached for the extended hand, then turned away. He walked over to his stricken mount, who kicked and convulsed as it tried to stand. Blood soaked the pavement.

Mosher touched the horse's head with his hand, and its thrashing ceased. The two locked eyes for a brief moment and then he put his pistol to its forehead and squeezed the trigger.

He holstered his pistol and took Saleh's still-extended hand. With a grunt, Saleh pulled Mosher up behind him. He and his fellow camel riders raced after us, turning in their saddles to rattle off AK-47 rounds. The Obsidian soldiers ran for cover.

"Scatter!" I shouted, hoping my voice wasn't lost in the gunfire. "Return to the university!"

Saleh led Mosher and their combined force of Jordanian and Israeli officers down one side street, while another four officers took the next. That left Patrolman Jones and Corporal Ferris with me. Up ahead, smoke wafted from a cross street. A building or vehicle fire? Regardless, we could use it to shake off our pursuers. I turned in my saddle to shout.

Then the APC rolled out into the street, its machine gun chattering.

We weaved through the downed vehicles in the street as machine gun fire tore through car bodies, windows, and pavement. Ferris pointed her flare gun behind her and fired. The flare canister struck a windshield and exploded into a cloud of blue smoke that blanketed the street. The machine gun fire stuttered to a halt momentarily, then started up again in random bursts.

"Now's our chance! Let's go!"

We charged into the cross street, my eyes and nose stinging from the smoke of an apartment fire. Figures moved through the haze, and as a gust of wind lifted it, I saw Teledyne uniforms.

I pulled back on the reins. Countess came to a halt, her boots skidding on the pavement.

The Teledyne soldiers looked up at me with wide eyes. One of them had laid aside his rifle and was tending to the burns on a small child. The second one had shouldered his rifle and was propping up a semi-conscious woman. The two men's faces were blackened with soot from the building fire behind them.

Countess danced about, breathing hard but not labored. I looked down at the Teledyne soldiers and what they were doing, then heard the rumble of the approaching APC. I came to a quick decision.

"Jones, Ferris, keep going!" I ordered my officers. To the Teledyne soldiers I said, "Get these people out of here!"

Without waiting to see their response, I wheeled Countess about and charged back out into the main street, flying straight through the intersection. The APC cleared the blue smoke, and its gunner let out a blast of machine gun fire. A round cracked past my ear. I ducked down against Countess's neck, both to make myself a lower target and to protect her body with mine. If she went down, we were both dead.

And then we were through the intersection, racing down the cross street opposite the burning building and the Teledyne soldiers helping the wounded. *That* shocked me, but I'd worry about that later. What I needed to do was get away from the APC.

I led Countess in a serpentine pattern down the cross street as the rumbling of the APC grew louder. I risked a glance back and saw it turning our way, its turret already aimed at us. It belched fire, and rounds impacted along the pavement and zipped through the air.

I turned Countess up another side street, and we ran past blown-out storefronts and burned-out husks left over from when the riots spread through the area a week or more back. I turned her up another street just as the APC turned in pursuit. I slowed Countess's pace just a bit to keep them on the hunt. I'd get them to turn up another street or two, then double back and join up with my men.

In the distance, back toward the area the APC had been guarding, more gunfire erupted along with a trumpet blast? I stood and twisted around in my saddle, straining to hear better.

The APC rumbled onto the street, and I had to focus on fleeing once more.

It chased me down two more streets, its machine gun firing in frantic bursts every time its gunner thought he had a proper bead on us. Countess's ears were flat against her scalp as we ran, and her focus was entirely on getting the hell away from the loud monster spitting fire at us.

I tried to lead her down another side street, but the machine gun raked the pavement to our right. I cursed and banked to the left, down a different street.

I skidded to a halt a dozen or so yards in. It was a dead end. I wheeled back around and snapped the reins and bent over Countess's neck as she broke into a run again.

The APC rolled to a stop just as we reached the intersection. The barrel on the machine gun turret whined as it lowered, but we were too close to it, and the gunner couldn't push it down enough to shoot at us. The gunner fired a frustrated burst, and the rounds sailed right over us.

I pulled Countess to the right, and we ran behind the APC and galloped back the way we had come. Behind us, the vehicle's treads dug into the pavement as it spun in a tight circle to come after us, its turret whining as it rotated our way.

An explosion startled both Countess and me. She let out a frightened whinny, and my heart skipped a beat. We kept on course, but as we rounded a corner, I risked a glance back and saw the APC slide to the right and crash into a building. Flames shot out of a hole in the turret, and a number of cracks and pops rumbled from inside. The unexpended rounds from the machine gun were cooking off.

What in the world had happened?

* * *

Aster leaned over the parapet to survey her handiwork. In the street, six stories below, the Obsidian APC burned merrily. One thing about that particular vehicle's design was the weakness of the turret's armor. Hits from the sides and ground were easily absorbed and deflected, but shoot a rocket or drop a satchel charge from above, and it was a different story entirely.

"They're coming out, ma'am," Lieutenant Paxton said. "Should we engage?"

A wave of anger washed over her as she watched the coughing, bleeding forms of Obsidian soldiers stumble out of the APC. She reached for her rifle. *No, let me take them out.*

The sound of hoofbeats made her pause. The rapid *clop-clop-clop* sound filled her enhanced ears. It was that officer and his horse that reminded her of a calico cat. The APC had chased him with single-minded intent, as if Obsidian had wanted him, in particular, dead. That didn't surprise her. Her superiors in Teledyne had made it known that Lieutenant Nathan Ward of the Mobile Police Department was a high value target, nearly as valuable as Sheriff Welliver and Captain Phillips of the Border Patrol. He was a ranking figure in the Police Rebellion, as their faction was known in the boardroom.

He was also a good man, from what she'd seen.

One of the Obsidian soldiers dropped his rifle and ran back into the APC. He staggered out a moment later, hauling the limp form of another soldier. One of his buddies ran to help, and together they pulled the man clear of the burning vehicle.

Her anger left her, as quickly as it had come. "No. Leave them. Wounded men use up resources."

"Yes, ma'am."

"Lady in Black, this is Lady in Red. We're positioned over the venue. The celebrities are about to make their appearance, but the paparazzi have shown up, in force."

Aster tapped her earpiece. "Red, Black. Drive the paparazzi away, then regroup at the Café."

"Roger."

"Is it wise to help the police out, ma'am?" Paxton asked. "Manager Strohl did say they were the enemy."

"Help them out?" Aster looked at Paxton with wide eyes. "Whatever do you mean? We engaged Obsidian soldiers and killed a fair number of them. We also destroyed one of the APCs they brought from St. Louis. And we suffered no casualties doing it." She slung her rifle over her shoulder. "I don't see that we did anything counter to our orders."

Paxton considered her words, then nodded. "Very well, ma'am."

"Besides," she added quietly, "he risked his life for Rico and Takahashi." She closed her eyes and let the sound of the calico horse's retreating hoofbeats fill her ears. It was hard to discern now that it was so far away and mixing with the sound of other horses in the vicinity. Horses and other four-footed creatures.

She opened her eyes and looked at Paxton. "He risked his life to lead that APC away from our men and the civilians they were attempting to treat. That has to count for something."

The skin around Paxton's eyes crinkled, a sign he was smiling beneath his ballistic mask. "Yes, ma'am. It does."

"Let's help Sergeant Rico treat the rest of those civilians. One more good deed accomplished in this Fallen World."

* * * * *

Chapter Nineteen

"I don't know who led that APC away," Danny said, "but I wish they'd taken more of these soldiers with them!" He stood up long enough to shoot his 870, then he ducked behind a disabled sedan's engine compartment as the air filled with return fire.

"You sure do make a lot of demands for a man getting rescued," Jake said. "Cover me!"

"We ain't rescued yet!" Danny pumped a fresh slug into his shotgun, shouldered it, aimed, and fired. Down the street, a soldier took the slug in the chest. His plate armor absorbed the impact, but it was still enough of a blow to knock him to the ground. One of his buddies stopped to drag him into cover behind a pickup truck. Danny cursed. They needed stronger weapons if they were going to deal with this kind of armor.

Reed leaned out from behind the trunk and fired a burst from her M14. "Get goin', big guy!"

Jake ran out from the cover of the bullet-riddled sedan they had all crouched behind and slid behind a truck about ten yards down the street. He leaned out from the other side and started shooting.

"Your turn, Brother Stephen!" Danny called.

Stephen murmured a prayer Danny couldn't hear, then the pastor jumped to his feet and scrambled in the direction of Jake's truck. Shots rang out, and bullets skipped along the ground after him, but Stephen made it without any problems.

They used this bounding cover tactic to leapfrog their way down to the next intersection. From there, they would make a break for it, leaving their pursuers in the dust. As Danny crouched behind a Jeep that crashed into a streetlamp, he looked for another storefront they could break into. The doughnut shop's lack of a usable back door had soured him on the idea of trusting a building with only one way out.

Machine gun fire echoed in the distance. Whoever had run off that APC was giving it a run for its money. He hoped they were able to shake it off soon, though. He remembered how chewed up the masonry of the doughnut shop had been and shuddered to think about what that gun could do to a man's body. Or a horse's, for that matter.

As he peeked over the crumpled roof of the Jeep, a shot pinged against the metal streetlamp. He ducked, then flung himself to the ground as another shot shattered the side mirror. He looked up in time to see a bullet strike a tire on the driver's side. It popped with a loud *whoosh*, and the vehicle sagged.

"Behind us!" Stephen shouted. "They're behind—Gah!"

"Brother Stephen!" Reed screamed. "He's hit!"

Danny rolled onto his belly and crawled to the cover of an electric coupe near the Jeep. It had one of those stupid, plastic body kits on it that made it look like a low-rider, so he couldn't see much underneath it. He crawled up to the curb and leaned his head out.

More Obsidian soldiers stood in the intersection they had been retreating to, mixed in with red-suited thugs from one of Columbia's gangs. He couldn't see the whole intersection, but he counted at least ten.

"How many you see?" he shouted to Reed.

"More than I'd like! Twenty or thirty!"

"Shit," Danny muttered. *What the hell were they going to do?* "How's Brother Stephen?"

"Patching himself up, the brave bastard."

In spite of the situation, Danny grinned. "Our chaplain's made of tough stuff. Jake, how's your ammo?"

"Oh, shit!" one of the gangbangers shouted. "It's the cops!"

"Shoot them!" a soldier ordered, and a tremendous amount of gunfire erupted from the intersection.

Danny raised himself up and saw that the enemy had turned to their left and were shooting at an unseen target. He aimed his shotgun, but a shot from behind him forced him to duck. He repositioned himself and tried to aim again.

A series of gunshots rang out from above, and several of the Obsidian soldiers hit the ground, blood pouring from new wounds. This threw the others into disarray. Half continued to shoot down the street, and then they all broke and ran as a wall of men and horses draped in red riot armor slammed into them. There were forty-eight in three ranks of sixteen, each wielding a long lance with a wicked looking point on the end. Most of the lances broke on impact, leaving long, jagged pieces of wood and metal stuck in their opponents' bodies.

Once the lances were discarded, the horsemen drew pistols from chest rigs or belt holsters. They aimed and fired into the enemy as they scattered and ran for cover.

"We're saved!" Reed said with a happy laugh.

"God bless the Mounties." Danny hadn't seen them gussied up in their new riot armor, but it was impressive. It looked a lot like their traditional uniforms, but it was heavily padded against blunt force trauma and small arms, with plates for stopping rifle rounds to the chest, back, and sides. The high collars had been replaced with armored gorgets to protect the neck and throat. And they'd given up their Stetsons in favor of black helmets with clear faceguards, much like the one Danny wore.

"Fall back!" someone shouted from behind, and Danny peeked over the hood of a car and saw the Obsidian troops who had been chasing them withdrawing.

Danny watched them go for a moment, then ran over to where he had seen Stephen and Reed. They were crouched down behind a delivery van. Jake was helping tend to Stephen, while Reed maintained overwatch. "Brother, how are you?" he asked as he slid down next to the wounded pastor.

Stephen favored Danny with a pained smile. He had cut away his left pant leg and was treating a wound in his thigh. "Bullet passed right through, thank God. Burns like the fires of Hell, though. Bleeding isn't too bad, so I think it just went through meat."

"Damn, how can you be so calm?" Reed shuddered. "If that was me, I'd be losing my mind."

"He was a paramedic before becoming a full-time pastor," Danny said. "He knows what he's talking about."

"I've got him," Jake said to Danny. "Go greet our rescuers."

Danny joined the RCMP officers in the intersection. He had to step over a number of dead and dying soldiers and gangbangers, many of which still had broken lance tips inside them, the jagged ends pointing into the air like trees broken in a hurricane. He smiled as he approached Captain Graham and said, "Looks like Hurricane Victoria blew through here." Graham chuckled. "Sergeant Ward, if I'd known it was you we were coming to rescue, I wouldn't have bothered. You and your brother have a habit of getting caught in the strangest situations."

"Yeah, but we have the most fun!" He spread his hands. "Damn fine work, by the way."

"Thank you. It's every horseman's dream to be in a cavalry charge." He held up the broken tip of his lance and frowned. "Though Mr. Reinhard at the Renaissance fair was right. These ceremonial lances weren't good for much."

"They were good enough, but you'll need more if you want to do this again." He studied the RCMP captain. "I take it you're joining us officially now?"

"It's not like we're going to be able to hide who did this from Obsidian," he said with a grin. "When your men get plowed down by a bunch of jumped-up redcoats, and there's only one unit of redcoats within a thousand miles, well, it's pretty easy to narrow down the suspect list, wouldn't you say?"

"Any wounded on your end?"

"Grazes only. This new armor is fantastic, and your man up on the roof gave us the distraction we needed just as we charged."

Danny frowned. "That wasn't one of ours. I thought he was one of yours."

He and Danny looked up at the roof they thought the shooting had come from. No one was up there now, or if someone was, they had hidden themselves from view. Someone from another department? A citizen who felt like joining in? Teledyne?

A flash of bitterness ran through Danny at the idea, and he shrugged it off. Why would any of those soulless bastards lift a finger to do any good? And if they had, should he be thankful? After what Teledyne had done?

He spat on the pavement, then jerked his head back toward the street. "We've got a wounded man. Our chaplain."

"We'll have our medic look at him, then get you boys out of here."

"Girls, too!" Reed called from her position behind the vehicles.

Graham looked at Danny. "One of yours?"

"No, but I'd take her if she wanted to switch departments. If you ever piss her off, make sure you run a serpentine pattern. She's wicked with that M14."

"Duly noted."

An explosion echoed from several streets away, and the rhythmic beat of the APC's machine gun fell silent.

"Someone has anti-tank rounds?" Danny asked.

"Not one of ours," Graham said. "I wish we did, though. You can't have too much firepower in this Fallen World."

* * * * *

Chapter Twenty

"Absolutely disgraceful!" Director Lloyd slammed his fist against the hull of one of the two remaining APCs he'd brought with him from St. Louis. "I'm not in this town for five minutes, and already there are screw-ups."

The crew of the destroyed APC stood at attention in front of him. Each man was covered in soot, and their uniforms had burn marks to show their close call with a fiery death. He glared at them. "Well? Anything to say for yourselves?"

"Sir, we don't know what hit us," the driver said. "We had just cornered this cop, and—"

"*One* cop? You pulled away from the infantry you were supporting to chase down one, lousy cop?"

"Sir, there were more at the time. On horseback—"

Lloyd laughed. "This just gets better and better. You mean to tell me that while the rest of the men were busy escorting me and the cargo—you know, doing their jobs—you were out playing tag with the local cowboys? Does that about sum it up?"

The driver couldn't answer that.

Lloyd shook his head. Why was it that idiots like these had survived the cratering of St. Louis, but some of his better men hadn't? He'd kill everyone in this parking garage and scuttle the remaining APCs if it meant he could have Agents Khatri and Jacobs with him, but Khatri was out on assignment when the bombs dropped and

Jacobs had died protecting Lloyd. The first missile had arrived suddenly, giving them only seconds to react. And the bombproof emergency elevator in Lloyd's office only had room for one.

He could still remember the look of fear on Jacob's face as the Agent's body did what it was conditioned to do: protect Corporate executives. That image had been burned into his mind as his escape car hurtled down the emergency elevator to the building's sublevels.

A good investment, that one. Much better than the losers he was now surrounded by.

"Don't be so hard on them," a voice said from the other side of the parking garage.

Gwendolyn Greenway, Director of Public Relations for Middle America and head of Obsidian in Columbia approached, flanked by four bodyguards in tailored suits. "Those cowboy cops are much bigger nuisances than you give them credit for. Especially the one your people were chasing." She crossed her arms beneath her breasts, a dark look passing over her face at the memory. "He's a dangerous man who he needs to be dealt with accordingly."

"Send a team into the university and kill him," Lloyd snapped. "Then you're done with the whole affair."

"His movements are too random. He and the other leaders—Sheriff Welliver, Captain Phillips, and Captain Bradley—spend as much time out on patrol as they do on the campus grounds. We don't know what buildings they meet, eat, and sleep in. We need more information before we can figure out a pattern."

Lloyd's anger subsided as his logical side took control. He stroked his beard. "And we can't fully commit to a hostile takeover of the university, otherwise Teledyne will attack us here." He looked up at the ceiling of the underground parking garage, as if he could see through the floor into the building above. "Nice place you got, by the way. Very luxurious."

Greenway flashed him a smile. "I have good taste." Her eyes flicked from one APC to the next. "Your arrival has helped balance the three forces, but only just." She then turned her attention to the other newly arrived vehicles in the cargo bay. "Is that going to tip things even further?"

There were three heavy cargo trucks lined up, one behind the other. Soldiers quickly unloaded food, ammunition, and a missile launcher from two of them, while a team of technicians carefully removed a large object shrouded in a tarp from the third truck. Lloyd smiled. "Yes, I believe it will."

It would also tip things in *his* favor. Miss Greenway outranked him, but that wouldn't last forever. Obsidian and the world at large were being restructured, and he didn't plan to be part of the downsizing.

He led her over to the cargo trucks, their boots clicking on the concrete floor. He had to give Greenway credit for trading in the heels she typically favored for boots. More than half the people he knew—men and women—wouldn't have had the sense to do that. Maybe she was more than just a pretty face and a big pair.

"Sir!" One of the technicians snapped to attention. "We're just about ready to inspect it."

Lloyd waved a hand. "Don't let us stop you."

The techs carefully pulled the tarp back, revealing a reclined chair with all manner of electronics hooked up to it. Greenway gasped. "An imprinter! I feared it was destroyed with St. Louis."

"It almost was. Our building took a direct hit, and it collapsed down to the fourth sub-basement." He nodded toward the machine.

"This was in the fifth sub-basement. Two techs were crushed when the ceiling partially caved in, but the others managed to get the imprinter broken down and reassembled on one of the untouched levels. They absorbed quite a bit of radiation, but they got us what we needed."

"Is the database intact?"

"It is."

"Excellent!" Her expression soured. "Now, all we need to find is an Agent, unless we want to imprint unaugmented employees."

"I wouldn't recommend that." Lloyd removed his tablet from his suit jacket.

Greenway reached into her purse and pulled out a tablet as well. "I've already checked the Agents' list," she said. "There are none within a hundred miles of us. They could show up at some point, but I'm not counting on it."

Lloyd brought up the Agents' list. It showed the names and current status—as of the date of the bombs dropping, before the satellite connections cut out—of Agents all across the country. She was right: no Agent on either the active or inactive list was anywhere near Columbia, or even Missouri.

He touched a button, then keyed in a password when prompted. A new tab appeared in the Agent locator app.

Greenway leaned over to look at this new list. Her eyes widened as she read the tab heading. "I thought that program was just a myth!"

"Only those directly involved in the project knew anything about it," Lloyd said.

Her eyes narrowed. "Need-to-know?"

"Not that it matters now." Lloyd held up the tablet. "What does matter is that we have an Agent in this very city. We just need to make contact, and this city is ours."

Greenway's smile stretched into a grin, revealing teeth that were just a little too white. She slipped her arm through his and pulled him close. "I think I could kiss you right now," she purred. "Shall we…take a break?"

He returned the grin. Even though he had every intention of taking her out as soon as the moment presented itself, she *was* quite beautiful. "Yes, ma'am."

One had to get pleasure where one could in this Fallen World.

* * * * *

Chapter Twenty-One

"**D**addy!" Jason shouted as we rode into the quadrangle. He ran full tilt toward me, a winded Helen following close behind.

I dismounted and held onto Countess's reins with one hand while I scooped up Jason with my other arm. "Woah, little guy, what'd I tell you before? You're getting too big for this!"

He pulled his head back from my chest and looked up at me. "Then you need to get stronger!"

"I don't think that's how it works," I said with a laugh. "Now, hold Countess's reins for a second so I can hug your sister, too."

"Okay!" He took the reins and rubbed Countess's nose. She snorted wearily and nudged his face with her nose. He giggled.

I knelt so Helen could throw her arms around my neck. "Daddy, I was so worried," she said, sniffling. "We heard all that gunfire. Are you all right?"

"It's the Mounties!" someone shouted, and a cheer rose up from the assembled officers, students, and administrators.

I straightened to get a better look. Across the green, a column of officers in red armor rode up the concrete path. Four of the horses carried two riders each, and it wasn't until they got closer that I realized who they were: Danny, Jake, Corporal Reed, and Brother Stephen. Danny looked a bit embarrassed, Jake was impassive, Reed's face held a mixture of excitement and fear, and Stephen looked like he was about to pass out.

"Keep an eye on Countess for me," I said to the kids and ran forward to greet them.

"Daddy," Jason said, a worried question in his voice.

"I'll be back in a minute!"

"But, Daddy—"

"Quiet!" Helen snapped. "He told us to wait!"

"Lieutenant Ward." Captain Graham smiled as he reined in near me. "I believe I have found some of your lost officers."

"I believe you have." I looked at Danny. "You were the ones who fired the flares?"

"Yeah. Where were you?"

"En route, but an APC got in my way. We couldn't get any closer."

"That was you?" Reed asked. "I could kiss you, sir! That APC almost got me."

"It won't get anyone anymore. Last I saw it, it was burning quite well."

Danny hopped down. "You took it out?"

"I wish. It chased me like it was in heat. Had me cornered at one point, but then someone hit it with a rocket or a satchel charge or something."

Danny and Graham shared a look. "We'll have to talk about this more later," the RCMP captain said. "For now, see to your wounded man."

Two Mounties helped pull Brother Stephen from the saddle. The pastor's usually tan face was pale and drawn, and it was only when he was laid on the ground that I saw the bloody bandage.

A pair of students with a stretcher rushed forward. A third student ran with them, bearing a medical kit and an armband with a red cross on it. The medical student inspected the tourniquet and bandaging, then motioned for the stretcher bearers to follow her.

I grabbed Stephen's hand as they lifted the stretcher. "Thank God you made it back," I told him. "How do you feel?"

Stephen's smile was more a grimace. "You should've told me bullets hurt this much, Nate. I might've thought twice about the whole police chaplain thing."

"He'll be in good hands," the medical student promised me. She pulled our hands apart. "But, we really have to go."

I nodded and stepped out of the way. She and the stretcher bearers trotted off toward the campus hospital. I'd go visit him as soon as we got the horses cooled off, brushed down, and fed. While I was there, I'd pay a visit to Kevin Hanson.

"Daddy!" a high-pitched voice shrieked.

I spun and saw Helen running toward me. "Daddy! Daddy!"

"Helen, it's all right," I called to her. "Brother Stephen's going to be all right! He—"

"It's Countess!" she shrieked. "She's hurt, bad!"

I looked past her just in time to see Countess stumble and fall to her knees. She then crashed onto her side. Jason threw himself on top of her and screamed.

Danny and I ran over to Countess, and it was then that I saw all the blood soaking her under-armor. My God, when had she been shot? Where? She'd carried us through that whole chase and the run back to campus without flagging.

The memory of Sergeant Mosher putting a bullet into his horse rose up, fresh and raw. "Get the vet!" I shouted. "Hurry!"

Tears stung my eyes as Jason wailed and Helen sobbed. I couldn't lose Countess, not like this.

* * *

"Countess is lucky to be alive," Doctor Lorio said. The veterinarian stripped off his blood-soaked surgical gloves and dropped them into the waste basket near the large stainless steel sink. He turned on the faucet, lathered his hands and arms with soap up to the elbow, then rinsed off in the steamy water. "I'm not sure how she made it here on her own legs."

"She's a tough mare," I said. "Survived more than one complicated pregnancy in her days as a breeder."

"And more than one Mardi Gras parade in her time on the force," Danny added.

"There's bad news, and good news with a caveat," Lorio said after he had dried his hands and arms on a towel. "The bad news is Countess isn't completely out of the woods. She'd lost a lot of blood by the time we got to her, and she has damage to her intestines and liver. The blood's been replaced, but the organ damage is more than we can handle with surgery. You both know how sensitive their digestive systems are, I imagine."

Despair filled me. I'd been with Countess since she was just a foal. She'd almost died from colic, but the vet had been able to save her. I knew exactly how sensitive their guts were.

"You said there was good news," Danny said. "Right, Doc?"

"It's good news with a caveat." Lorio walked over to a storage bin and opened it. He pulled out a tablet and turned it on. "I trust you both have heard of medical nanites?"

"Yeah, a little bit from my time at Obsidian," Danny said. "They're still in the testing phase, though, right?"

"Officially, yes. It's a known secret in the medical community that nanites have been in use for some time by the Corporations for various supersoldier programs. Obsidian's Agents, Teledyne's Specialists, JalCom's Juggernauts, Athenia's Phoenixes; you get the idea. One of the side effects of these nanites is a faster healing rate. It comes with the benefit of quicker blood production, so in the event of blood loss, the wound coagulates quickly, and new blood is produced to make up the difference. Cells in the body are constantly regenerating, as well, leading to longer life. And, more importantly, longer life in the *prime* of life. Imagine being in your eighties with the physique of someone in his twenties, thirties, or forties."

Danny stretched until something in his shoulder cracked. "Given the choice, I'll take my twenties. The thirties sucks."

Lorio smiled. "Wait until the sixties." He flexed and clenched his fingers. "Damn things are always so sore after surgery. Didn't used to be that way.

"Anyway," he continued, "the Corporations have been developing a toned-down version of these nanites for civilian use. Nanites that don't grant enhanced strength or bone density or whatever it is the nanites do for Specialists and Agents and the like, but they do grant faster healing and body restoration. And, like with any good research, they've been testing them on animals far longer than they have humans."

"Are you saying you can use these nanites on Countess?" I demanded. "On other horses we have that are wounded?"

"We can try," he said. "That's what I meant by good news with a caveat. Nanite introduction is hard on the body, even a healthy one. It's not recommended they be used on someone injured or frail due to disease or age. Nanites draw heavily on the body's metabolism to carry out their function. We can supply that body with fluid and nutrients, but if we don't keep pace, the nanites will draw on existing reserves in the body. When they are trying to repair massive internal damage, that draw could prove too much, and the host could die. That's where we're at with Countess. It's a slim chance, but it's the only chance she's got."

"Why didn't you let her die, then?" I asked, surprised by my own question. "Surely the resources you expended on her could have been saved for another animal."

"Above all else, I'm three things." Lorio held up a finger. "First, I'm a doctor, with a sworn duty to render aid and protect life. When I see a patient, I do everything I can to help, even if I know the odds of success are so slim it would take an act of God to succeed." He held up another finger. "Second, I'm an animal lover. I see a beautiful horse like Countess in pain, and my heart breaks like it would if it were one of my grandchildren on the operating table."

I smiled and scrubbed at my eyes. "I can relate to that."

Danny slapped me on the back.

"And third, I'm an American." Lorio grinned. "I love to root for the underdog." His grin faded. "So, I can't promise the nanites will save Countess. They may very well kill her. But, if we don't use them, she will die. And either way, if there is some small comfort, the attempted treatment will give us much needed research on what the nanites can do in emergency situations like this. I expect that is going to be an issue going forward, considering how dependent we all seem to be on horses nowadays."

"Where do you get these from?" Danny asked. "Aren't they in short supply?"

"We produce them on-site," Lorio said. "We received the necessary equipment through a joint grant from the federal government, Teledyne, and Obsidian. So long as the lights stay on, we can keep producing them." He shrugged. "Maybe with some luck—and the help of a skilled genetic engineer—we can fine-tune the nanites for human use, but at the moment, they're for equines only."

Danny and I looked at each other. He grinned, and I felt hope surge within me. "Do it, Doctor Lorio."

Sometimes good news with a caveat was the best you could hope for in this Fallen World.

* * * * *

Chapter Twenty-Two

"Gentlemen, this is becoming a real problem." Sheriff Welliver held up a pile of handwritten reports. "Six times in half as many days, our officers have clashed with Obsidian or Teledyne soldiers and affiliates."

More than just the unit commanders were in the auditorium this time. Each unit had brought at least three or four of their own, from corporals to patrolmen, who might have something to add to the discussion. And there was a lot to discuss.

Welliver walked over to the tabletop map of Columbia. In addition to the color-coded boundaries around sections of the city, four pieces of blue tape and six pieces of red tape had been placed in different areas. He pointed. "We won four of these engagements, if you can count holding our own with no ground gained as winning."

I raised my hand to object. "One of those successful engagements saw the destruction of an Obsidian APC that had several of our boys pinned down in a doughnut shop."

"The Last Stand at the DD Corral?" Welliver and a couple of the older officers laughed, but the joke went over my head. He waved the comment away. "Never mind. Reference to an old doughnut shop."

"We're never going to live that down, are we?" Danny whispered to me.

"Hey, you lived to tell about it," I said. "That's better than the alternative, right?"

"Getting back to the APC," Welliver said. "Lieutenant Ward, you and your team did not actually destroy it, did you?"

That deflated my ego a little bit. "No, sir. Someone helped us."

"Same here," Danny said. He looked at Captain Graham. "When the Mounties rode to our rescue in what has to be the coolest cavalry charge I've ever seen, they had fire support from the roofs. It wasn't any of my guys."

"Nor was it any of mine," Graham added. "We committed our full force to rescue Sergeant Ward and his men from their doughnut addiction."

"Dammit, not you, too," Danny grumbled.

The assembled officers laughed. Welliver's tough exterior cracked into a genuine smile before he cleared his throat. "Yes, that is something we need to consider. Who is helping us? And why are they doing it? We know Obsidian and Teledyne are fighting each other just as much as they're fighting us. Could the support have been Teledyne taking advantage of the situation to score a blow against Obsidian?"

"If that's the case," I said, "why not take us out at the same time? Whoever blew up the APC could've easily killed me while they were at it."

Danny nodded. "And if whoever was on the roofs had turned their guns on us, we'd have been fish in a barrel."

"And whoever took out the APC has a hell of a lot more firepower than we do," I said. "All I had was a pistol and my shotgun, neither of which was going to do me any good in that situation."

"Hell, my shotgun didn't do a whole lot of good in the doughnut shop," Danny said. "Even slugs can't penetrate Obsidian plate. They'll do damage, but they won't knock them out of the fight. If Corporal Reed hadn't had her M14 with armor piercing rounds, I think the Mounties would've been on funeral detail."

"Exactly right," Sheriff Welliver said. "What we need is to up our arsenal. Both Obsidian and Teledyne can outgun us, and now Obsidian can outmaneuver us with their APCs, as long as their fuel supply holds out."

"And that might last a while." Captain Bradley surveyed the tabletop map. "Obsidian has soldiers stationed at several gas stations around the hotel. If they want to, they can hurt us badly."

"They'll be more hesitant to send them out after the one was destroyed," Danny said. "It's their primary check against Teledyne's superior numbers in the city. They won't just roll them on top of us. If anything, they'll send infantry our way and keep the APCs in reserve to deal with Teledyne, especially considering they have Section Nine here." He shrugged. "It's what I would do if I were Obsidian."

Welliver picked up two APC figurines that looked like they came from someone's Warhammer 40,000 miniature collection. He placed them around the Country Hotel on the map, an area that was already crowded with infantry figures, each one representing a squad of ten or more men. There were at least twenty figures. Obsidian's ranks had grown considerably since reinforcements had come in from St. Louis.

"How'd they know to come here?" one of the officers muttered, just loud enough for half the auditorium to hear.

"Must've been the St. Louis PD," another said. "They rode out that way to look for survivors, right? Then came back here, glowing in the dark from all that radiation poisoning."

"And led them right back to us! Nice going."

A few chuckled. Danny slammed his fist on the table and glared in the direction of the voices. "Show some respect, dammit. Those are fellow officers you're jawin' about."

"Enough!" Welliver snapped. He picked up a green army truck with a canvas covering and set it down next to the hotel. "I only have one of these from my grandkid's toy chest, but imagine there are three." He tapped the truck. "Looks like they brought a lot of food and ammunition with them, and possibly heavier weapons. With these vehicles, they'll be more effective at raiding nearby neighborhoods for supplies. That's going to be a problem, but we've got other things to worry about at the moment."

He walked over to a whiteboard that had been set up behind his desk and wrote the phrase "Force Multipliers." Then he underlined it. "We need to up our game, gentlemen. From our estimates, we outnumber either Teledyne or Obsidian, but together, they outgun us by a significant margin. Further, they have less area to protect at the moment."

He walked back over to the tabletop map and circled the hotel with his finger, then the Tower. He then made a sweeping gesture around the rest of the city. "Put simply, we're spread too thin. Our power base is at the university, but even here we're spread too thin. The campus is huge, the size of a small town, with a population to match. We have a lot going for us, but we need to bolster our ranks if we're to mount an effective defense."

"Sir, a number of students and citizens who've taken refuge here have offered to help with the defense," I said. "The problem is a lack of weaponry. Many of the refugees brought guns with them, but not a lot of ammo."

"Can we requisition ammo from nearby gun stores or a National Guard armory?" another officer asked.

Sheriff Welliver shook his head. "The National Guard armory isn't going to work. Most of the unit was deployed to help deal with riots taking place down in Arkansas when all this crap hit the fan. We patrolled there a week into this and found that Teledyne had already raided the place."

A shocked murmuring arose at that news. Danny looked at me and shrugged. "It's what Obsidian would've done if they'd had the chance," he said. "These Corporations don't care about any laws other than their own."

"We learned from the surviving guards that there wasn't a whole lot for Teledyne to steal," Welliver said. "The deployed unit had taken most of the arsenal with them, leaving behind light munitions and ammo. Nothing they probably didn't already have."

I wondered if that's where the anti-tank rocket had come from. "Did many of the guards survive?" I asked.

"Surprisingly, all of them did," Welliver said. "Teledyne hit them fast, before they could mount any kind of response. Stun grenades, tasers, and shots placed to wound rather than kill. The team that did this knew what they were doing, and they wanted to minimize casualties as much as possible."

Don't make me kill you.

Aster's words—and the sad expression she wore as she pressed her knife against my throat—came back to me in a flash. "Section Nine," I murmured.

Danny leaned close. "My thoughts exactly. This sounds like the MO of the Battle Flower."

"We're working to trade with Tough Roughin'," Welliver said, referencing the big camp and shooting supplier on the southwestern end of town. "They've ridden out this entire mess with a well-executed defense of their store. Rooftop snipers, sandbag fortifications, and enough MREs and dehydrated food to last them through, well, the apocalypse. That said, all they have to trade is ammunition for the guns we already have. And the problem we're facing is a lack of firepower. We need bigger and better guns if we're going to fight the street gangs of the day. Namely, Obsidian and Teledyne." He smiled. "But, I think we may have a solution to that problem."

Captain Bradley stepped outside for a moment and returned with a man I didn't recognize, at least at first. He wore a business suit that looked like he'd been living in it for the last couple weeks. "Ladies, gentlemen," Bradley said, "may I present Harold Erland, Vice President of Combined Arms Conglomerate, and our new best friend in this Fallen World."

* * * * *

Chapter Twenty-Three

Cedar Lake Park was as lively as it had been the first day we drove into it, even considering the early hour. Bonfires blazed at different points throughout the fairgrounds. I shined my flashlight around, noting that there were a lot more tents than I'd originally seen here. Most of them were camping tents rather than the period-specific pieces required by exhibitors and vendors. It made the now-permanent Three Rivers Renaissance Fair seem a little dressed down and a lot more crowded.

And the tents weren't the only aspects of the fair that had gone casual. The reenactor outfits had mostly been replaced by T-shirts and jeans. The only exceptions were the SCA members in chain and plate armor. They stood guard at regular intervals along the fair's boundaries and marched in pairs and small groups throughout the shadowed camp, their presence marked by flashlight beams and lantern light.

"We had a bit of trouble a week or so ago," Richard Cates said as he rode alongside me. "One of the local gangs thought we would be a bunch of pushovers, since we're so far from the city proper." He nodded toward me. "You have my thanks for dispatching your squad here. Other than you, only Captain Graham has seen fit to grace us with any kind of protective presence."

"I don't know what good we've done," I said, a bit sheepishly. "Seems like you've done well enough on your own."

"We have very few firearms, save for handguns some of our vendors and visitors carry for self-protection, but they didn't pack enough ammunition to enjoy a day at the range, much less fight a sustained defensive battle." He rested his free hand on the pommel of his sword hilt. "We've had to return to what our ancestors once did to protect themselves."

Richard's horse moved a little too close to mine. My horse stepped to the side quickly, knocking me off-balance. I cursed under my breath and pulled the horse back into line. With Countess out of commission for the moment, I'd been forced to ride one of the remounts we brought. Watson was an excitable, red gelding. Even though he was nearly eight, he was new to the force, and thus had the least experience and riding time.

"Mr. Erland and Sheriff Welliver have both promised to share what we bring back," I said. "Your people are providing the means of transportation, after all. It's only fair you share in the spoils."

The means of transportation Richard's people were providing lay on the other end of the growing camp. Three sizable wooden wagons sat in a line facing west. Each had a driver and a Columbia PD officer riding shotgun, and each had at least two horses hitched to the front. One man rode in the back of the lead wagon, and after a moment I realized it was Harry Erland. He still wore his dirty suit, but he'd traded the jacket for a brown poncho. A scoped rifle lay next to him, within easy reach if there was trouble on the road.

"All I want to do is get back to my family," he had told us in the meeting two days ago. "Our factory and warehouse are just outside Boonville, about twenty-five miles from here. Help me make sure they're all right, and we'll get you stocked. Obsidian and Teledyne have gone after my company before, and I'd hate to see them try it again."

In addition to the three wagons, there was another wagon of the internal combustion kind: the white-and-woodgrain Roadmaster from the university. Its owner, the professor of creative writing, stood around a group of dismounted officers, filling disposable cups with what must've been sweet tea. He saw us approaching and waved. He wore a 1911 on his right hip with a spare magazine pouch on his left.

His wife, a professor of psychology, sat in the front passenger seat. I hadn't had a chance to meet her, but she looked like she meant business, especially with the stainless steel revolver hanging from her left hip in a cross-draw holster.

The backseat of the Roadmaster had been folded forward in anticipation of all the cargo it would be hauling. I also saw that a vertical gun rack had been taken from a squad car and screwed into the floor between the driver and passenger seats. A shotgun lay in the leftmost slot, and an AR-15 in the rightmost.

Danny was with the dismounted officers. He turned our way. "About time you showed up," he told me. "We've been ready to go for at least fifteen minutes."

"Had to shake the kids off," I said, and it was no lie. Jason and Helen hadn't wanted me to go on this trip. Countess getting shot had really shaken them up, but there was nothing to be done about it. Welliver's deputies needed assistance, and based on the new rotation we had put together, Mobile PD was up for that assist.

"You could've sat this one out," Danny said. "Kept the kids close for a day or two."

"Wouldn't have been right. I don't want to leave y'all high and dry like that."

"Who's watching them?"

"Stephen and Jake. Philly's on north campus patrol right now, so Jake offered to take them with him on at least one of the rides. I'm sure they'll have a good time."

"Well, once we're back, make sure you spend time with them."

"Will do." I nodded at the circle of officers. "Couldn't shake the professor, I take it?"

"And have one of us drive his precious wagon? Not on his life." Danny took a sip from his cup and smiled. "Not that I mind. Man knows how to make a batch of sweet tea."

"When it's all you drink, you get good, I guess."

We laughed, and it felt good. The pain of loss was still there, and it would be with us for months, years, or longer. But at least we had each other. That had to count for something.

Deputy Powell rode over to me, flanked by two of his fellow deputies. "Lieutenant Ward, good to see you this morning." He looked back at the Mobile officers trailing behind me. "This everyone?"

"I believe so." We'd mustered all twelve Mobile PD and Mobile Sheriff's officers. In addition, there were nine Boone County deputies, four Columbia PD officers riding in the wagons, Harry Erland, the three horse drivers, and the tea-swilling professor and his wife. We had a combined force of thirty-one armed men and women. "We're ready when you are."

Powell grinned beneath his bushy mustache. "That's what I like to hear." Then he raised his voice. "Mount up, everyone! We ride!"

* * *

Aster watched through a pair of binoculars as the caravan pulled out of the Renaissance fair. They rode west, following the headlights of an old station wagon. "I count thirty-one of them," she said. "Six civilians, twenty-four officers, and one soldier with a scoped rifle. Headed west."

"How can you see anything, ma'am?" Sergeant Rico peered through his set of binoculars and muttered a curse. "All I see are headlights and taillights."

Lieutenant Paxton aimed his night vision scope at the caravan. "I see 'em, but not with the same clarity her naked eyes can."

"That's a Specialist for you. Glad you're on our side, boss!"

Aster's lips twitched into a faint smile. "And I'm glad to have you both."

"What should we do about this, ma'am?" Paxton asked.

"Our orders are to observe and see where the rebel police are going. Wherever they're going, it's to receive cargo. Those wagons are empty."

"Lady in Black, this is Concierge," a female voice said over the line.

"Concierge, Black. What is it?"

"A new reservation has been made for you and your Party of Nine. Our Obsidian rivals are up to something."

A thrill of excitement ran through Aster. Obsidian was the real threat, not the police. Still, she said, "We just placed our order for western omelets. Should we leave before they're done?"

"We'll pick them up for you."

Another team would head west and continue surveillance. Aster glanced at the others and shrugged. "Roger, Concierge. We're on our way."

* * *

On a direct path, Boonville was only about twenty-five miles from the center of Columbia. Head straight west down I-70, across a bridge, continue a few more miles, get off at Exit 103, and go north. The CAC compound would eventually be on the left, and we'd know it when we saw it, according to Harry.

We weren't taking the most direct route, because we were starting from the Renaissance fair and we wanted to avoid attracting Corporate notice, especially Obsidian's. We had barely escaped the APC attack with our lives, and that was only because we'd had buildings and vehicle-clogged streets to maneuver around. If they caught us out in the open, it'd be open season on cops.

Deputy Powell rode up near the Roadmaster, as he knew the way. The rest of us followed the head and taillights of the station wagon. The high-beams burned bright in the darkness of a city mostly without electricity. The rest of us maintained light discipline. Our horses could see just fine at night, even if we couldn't.

"Don't look into the light too much," I ordered the men. "It'll mess up your night vision."

"Man, some night vision goggles would be good about now," Danny said. "Knew I should've kept my kit from when I was with Obsidian."

"It would've been fried in the explosion, remember?"

"I kept them sealed up in a lead-lined ammo can for just that reason. They'd have been fine."

"You think Obsidian and Teledyne have those now?" Corporal Ferris asked.

"It'd be best to assume so," I said. "If they're watching the Renaissance fair, they know we're up to something."

"Damn!" Patrolman Jones said. "You mean we could've slept in a few more hours? What a bunch of crap."

"Look at it this way," I said. "At least you'll appreciate your sleeping bag more tonight."

"That's true." There was a pause, then, "Oh, shit! I didn't bring it!"

"Well, you're not sharing mine!" Corporal Ferris said. "You're on your own, buddy!"

We all laughed.

The morning sun crested the eastern horizon around the same time we turned north onto Scott Boulevard. Subdivision entrances lined either side of the four-lane road, although the southernmost neighborhoods had been torn down. Only the sound barriers remained.

Powell led us onto W. Gillespie Bridge Road and straight into farmland. "All those subdivisions back on Scott will be this someday," Powell said. Then he grimaced. "Or, well, they would have been. Most of the houses back there have been gutted and were waiting for the final doze before cleanup, fill-in, and parceling out."

It wasn't long before we crossed the road's namesake. A sign leading up to the bridge read "Weight Limit 40 Tons." I glanced at Danny. "You think that thing's gonna hold the professor's station wagon?"

Danny snorted back a laugh. "Why don't you ask him? I'm sure it's not the first time someone's questioned his land barge's weight."

At the next set of farms, we saw people out in the fields, getting on with the days' labors. Most looked up as we rode past, and a few even waved. Others just stared, while a couple ducked down and came up with a rifle or shotgun of some sort. None pointed their weapons our way, and we made no move to do so either.

"We've been trying to spread our patrols out this way," Powell said as he pulled up alongside me. "The farmers are going to be the next ones hit once the gangs and Corporations run out of food in the city."

"That explains the ones happy to see us," I said. "What about the not-so-happy ones?"

"They're not unhappy. Just wary of anyone coming out of the city, and understandably so. They hear gunfire all day when they're tending their fields, and all night when they're trying to woo their women. Kind of ruins the mood when a machine gun opens up somewhere nearby."

"Oh, so they're pissed about not getting any," Jones said. "I can respect that, sir!"

Other than farmers, we didn't encounter another living soul as we turned north onto Highway 0 and followed it until it connected with I-70. We passed many disabled vehicles and had to cut over into the grass to avoid an overturned semi-trailer, its cargo of party snacks long since picked clean by animal and human scavengers.

We found our first body at the top of the Exit 117 onramp. The bullet-riddled corpse lay spread-eagle on the pavement, his body just beginning to decay. A vulture eyed us for a moment, then flew off in a huff, a strip of human meat in its beak. It circled overhead as we rode by the corpse.

Deputy Powell put a handkerchief to his face. "Damn. No matter how many times I come across something like this, the smell never gets better."

"Nor should it." I pointed at the van next to the corpse. "Looks like he was living out of his vehicle."

"Van's been cleaned out," one of the Boone County deputies said. "Back's empty, except for a sleeping bag."

"Hey, we found a sleeping bag for ya, Jones!" Ferris said, her mouth splitting into a grin.

"No way I'm using that!"

We all laughed, despite the grim situation. Or maybe because of it. The three wagon drivers looked at all of us funny, but that was to be expected. There was one thing cops and soldiers knew that a lot of civilians didn't: gallows humor could get you through the day, sometimes better than an encouraging word from a buddy.

Still, when we rode out of there, our guard was up. The people who had done this might have been long gone, but it showed how cheap life was in this Fallen World.

* * * * *

Chapter Twenty-Four

"What do you think?" I asked, looking ahead to the I-70 bridge we were about to cross. The four lane truss bridge spanned the Missouri River and was filled with disabled vehicles going east or west. From here it looked like the west-bound lanes were the clearest, but on horseback it was difficult to tell.

"Bridge is a natural choke point," Powell said. He held binoculars to his eyes and scanned the bridge, the hills, the tree line, and the other side of the river more than a thousand feet away. He returned his gaze to the bridge. "If someone's there, I don't see 'em."

Despite our early departure from Columbia, it was getting to be late morning by the time we reached the bridge. I had hoped we'd be past this point by now and almost to Boonville, but we had been forced to turn back after only a mile on I-70. Three tractor trailers had crashed into one another and caused a forty-car pileup that spilled across to the eastbound side. Further access was completely blocked. We returned to Exit 117, then followed West Old Rocheport Road as it ran parallel to the interstate.

Now that we were at the bridge over the Missouri River, I felt like we'd made it to the halfway point in our journey. If we kept up this pace, we'd be in Boonville close to early afternoon.

To our left, a rocky hill rose over the bridge. Powell pointed. "Let's get people up there and—"

A shot rang out, and Powell toppled from his horse. Blood poured from a hole in his temple.

Watson screamed and reared, and it was all I could do to keep from falling out of the saddle. More rounds struck the ground near me. "We're under attack! Find cover!"

The drivers moved their wagons behind the cover of a double-decker tour bus stalled in the right lane. The professors drove their Roadmaster forward and parked it behind a utility van.

I grabbed the reins of Powell's horse and pulled it along as I urged Watson behind the bus with the others. One of the Boone County deputies, a man named Stewart, looked at me. "Deputy Powell?" he asked.

"Took one to the head. He's gone."

"Damn." Stewart took the reins of Powell's horse and led him to the other Boone County deputies.

"I guess that puts you in charge," Danny said. "What're your orders to the troops?"

"We need to see who's shooting at us," I said. I dismounted and handed Watson's reins to Patrolman Jones. "Anyone have a pair of binoculars?" I shouted.

"Right here." Harry hopped down from the wagon he was riding in. He ran over to me, rifle in one hand, binoculars in the other. "Want to be my spotter?"

"I think I can manage that." I took the binoculars. "How do you want to do this?"

"In a way that ends with them dead and us alive, preferably." Harry thought for a moment.

After several minutes, Harry and I reached the summit of one of the hills. We crouched down behind a pair of trees and leaned out. I scanned the bridge with my binoculars. Had our bridge trolls shot at us a few minutes later, we would've been stuck on the bridge with no real cover to speak of save our own vehicles. Once past the bus, it was no-man's land. Someone up there had gotten squirrelly, which meant they were scared.

They were about to be dead, as far as I was concerned. I had Powell's blood on my face and uniform shirt, and that blood demanded justice.

"There's one," I said. "Peeking out from behind the trunk of that green sedan."

"I see him," Harry murmured. "What an ugly color." He adjusted his scope. "Range and windage accounted for. Squeezing, squeezing, squee—"

Boom!

I flinched at the sudden noise, but kept my binoculars fixed on the man I'd seen. His head snapped back, blood spraying out of the exit wound in his skull. He collapsed.

"Another one!" I said. "He just hopped up. Behind the red hatchback."

Boom!

This one spun in a half circle, his chest and backside ruined.

More figures popped up and started shooting toward the bus. They fired with wild abandon, sure that they were shooting at the right enemies.

Boom! Boom! Boom!

Harry's rifle cracked again and again. Each time he fired, another of the bridge trolls crumpled and fell, their guns tumbling from lifeless fingers. My mind filled in the noise of their weapons clattering to the asphalt.

After the fifth one died, the bandits broke and ran. They fled west along the bridge. Harry fired another couple of shots to empty his magazine, then we rejoined the others. "Mount up!" I said. "We need to take that bridge before they decide to come back."

I took half the force, and we rode hard to the bridge. There we found the five that Harry had shot dead. I wasn't sure what caliber Harry was using, but it had to be something meant for big game. The back of one man's head was nonexistent, his brain splattered all over the door and tire of the vehicle behind him. Another had lost a kidney and part of his spine, and the exit wound had exposed his internal organs to open air.

One of them clutched at a scoped rifle, his grip still tight, even in death. This had to have been the man who shot Powell, considering the range. He had nearly gotten me, too. Had Watson not shied away at the last second, I might've joined the deputy on the ground.

We spent the next hour clearing the bridge one vehicle at a time, but found no one else. At the center of the bridge was a makeshift camp around a broken-down RV. Tents had been set up, and some of the larger vehicles were obviously lived in. Judging by the number of sleeping bags and blankets, it looked like there were a lot more people here than those we had seen.

"You thinking what I'm thinking?" Danny asked.

"If it's that we should press on before all these bridge trolls come back, then yes."

You couldn't be too cautious in this Fallen World.

* * * * *

Chapter Twenty-Five

At a little past 2:00 PM, we rode up to a closed chain-link gate. Beyond that gate sat a large prefabricated steel building. A sign out front read "Combined Arms Conglomerate."

"Looks like this is the place," I said. "Harry, you're up!"

I looked back over the caravan as the wagons came to a stop in the driveway leading up to the gate. We had left the Roadmaster near the bridge with Danny and a group of volunteers to defend the professors and to keep an eye out. If those bandits came back, we would need to know their number. I wish I could've left enough men to secure the entire bridge, but that wasn't in the cards.

Harry walked up to stand beside me, then cupped his hands and shouted. "Everyone, it's me! Harry Erland! Open up. I've got some customers."

Bushes on the other side of the fence stirred, and several figures stepped out, each wearing camouflage and carrying some kind of rifle. A woman in her fifties squinted, then stepped closer. She glanced up at me, then spent a long moment studying my horse. She then looked down the drive at the wagons and other mounted officers. "Harry, you always come back with the strangest companions. I ever tell you that?"

Harry grinned. "All the time, Mom."

She returned the grin, then stuck her finger in a slot near the gate. Something beeped, and the gate slid open on well-oiled hinges. She leaned her rifle against the fence and threw her arms around Harry as he ran to her. She slapped him on the back. "Welcome back, son!"

Tears ran down their cheeks as they laughed and greeted each other. A hard, painful lump formed in my throat. A mix of happiness and pain flooded through me, and I had to fight back tears of my own. I loved seeing this kind of reunion, but it reminded me too much of what all of us had lost and would never get back.

My thoughts drifted to Jason and Helen and Danny, and I thanked God I had that much family left. So many of my men had nothing. Nothing but each other.

"Mom, this is Lieutenant Nathan Ward of the Mobile Police Department. Nathan, this is Elizabeth Erland."

"Mobile?" Harry's Mom frowned. "Alabama?"

"The very one, ma'am." I slid from the saddle and touched the side of my helmet. "A pleasure."

"Aren't you a long way from home?"

"Quite a bit, ma'am." I grimaced. "And getting farther every day."

She looked at me for a long moment and then she pulled me in for a hug as fierce as the one she'd reserved for Harry. "I'm so sorry," she said, and I felt her hot tears against my neck. "I'm so sorry we all have to go through this hell together. It shouldn't have been this way."

"No, ma'am." Unshed tears burned in my eyes as I returned the embrace. "It shouldn't be this way at all."

She went around and either hugged or shook the hands of every officer and wagon driver. When she returned, a smile was on her lips despite the redness in her eyes. "You've brought back a bit of my world to me, and I'm thankful for it. I thought my son lost when those officers rode through here a week or so ago, telling us Columbia was being torn apart by Teledyne and Obsidian, and it was only a matter of time before the whole city burned."

"Officers?" I asked. "Was it the Kansas City PD?"

"Yes, I believe so. They were riding back to see if anything was left, the poor dears." She shook her head. "I told them it didn't look good, that friends of mine who live close to the city saw the nukes hit it. Those friends are inside, if you want to talk with them. They only made it here by the grace of God. Days of travel on foot, looters and bandits, it's a mess out that way. I can't imagine anyone in the city survived, but if they did, they're not long for this world. The radiation's bad."

"It's the same in St. Louis," I told her.

"Harry, get these wagons situated in the loading yard. Nathan—can I call you Nathan?" Without waiting for my response, she continued, "Nathan, get your people and horses over to the barbecue pit on the other side of the parking lot. We're just serving up lunch now, and you must be hungry. The horses can have a field day in the grass. It's a lot higher than it should be." She looked at us, then put her hands on her hips. "Well? Get moving! Hop to!"

Harry and I hopped to. Some things don't change, even in this Fallen World.

* * * * *

Chapter Twenty-Six

Elizabeth knew how to set a table. The smells wafting up from the grills and smoker set my mouth watering, as did the cast iron pot of baked beans cooking over the open fire.

It had been my intention to wait until my people had been served, but Elizabeth had a different idea. She shoved a plate of food in my hand. "Come on, Nathan, I'll give you the nickel tour. You can eat while we walk; don't be shy."

I followed close behind her across the parking lot, munching on a plate of some of the best pulled pork I'd ever eaten. I studied the vehicles: a few pick-up trucks, a Jeep, and two sedans, along with an old utility van. "Any of these work?"

"The Jeep, but we don't really drive it anywhere. A working vehicle makes you a target these days, you know?"

I took one last look over my shoulder. The rest of my officers sat at or stood around the picnic tables with Helen's crew, a mix of family, friends, and employees who had gathered at CAC's headquarters to ride out the storm after the Fall. There were about thirty people total, and somehow they'd had enough food to feed more than double that. "Were you expecting us?" I asked around a mouthful of juicy meat and soft bread. "And is this bun homemade?"

"No and yes," Elizabeth said with a laugh. She pulled the ribbon out of her graying blond hair and let her locks fall around her shoulders. "Ah, that's better. Yes, the ladies and I make the bread ourselves. The store-bought stuff was gone within days, but we've got plenty of wheat put back for this kind of emergency, and a couple of Country Living hand-crank mills to keep us off the streets and out of trouble.

"We only break out the grills and smokers once every few days. We cook up just enough to pack our refrigerators. You got us on a cook day; lucky you."

"Lucky me, indeed." I took another bite. "You have electricity, then?"

She opened the door and let me into an office. "Yes, but not for much longer. Our propane generator was fried in the EMP, and we're running out of gasoline for our backup generator."

"Your roof is pretty flat. You have any solar panels?"

"We did, but they got fried, too."

"Dang. That's a shame, as this seems like it would be a very defensible position."

"It has been." We walked down a long corridor, passing offices and storage rooms on our right and left. "We've fought skirmishes against the Corporations in the past, though at the time, we had our full staff of around three hundred. If Obsidian or Teledyne hit us now, we'd be hard pressed to hold on to what we have. Especially if they sent any of their super soldiers at us."

"Yeah, they can be a handful," I said, remembering how quickly Aster had taken me down. "That's partly why we're here. We need better weapons if we're going to defend Columbia from the Corporations trying to tear it apart."

"In that case, you came to the right place." She opened the door at the end of the corridor and flipped a switch.

We stepped into a vast, dark chamber that quickly lit up as the LED bulbs thirty feet overhead came on. Crates and metal boxes lined the walls and filled the shelves. "We don't have as much as we did a couple months ago—big order sent out right before the poop hit the fan—but I think we've got enough to cover your needs."

* * *

"I think that's the last we can carry on this run," I said. "We don't want the horses to be too overloaded."

All three wagons had been packed with ammunition, select-fire rifles chambered in heavy hitting calibers like .308, 7.62mm, and even the devastating .50 Beowulf cartridge. In addition to this, we had been supplied with fifteen sniper rifles, nine light machine guns, one anti-materiel rifle, and a crew-served M2 .50 machine gun. "Go on, take it," Elizabeth had insisted. "My husband loved to collect them while he was still alive. We've got a couple others lying around."

"Ma'am, I really don't know how to thank you," I said, striving very hard to keep the grin off my face and failing miserably. "We didn't expect this level of generosity."

"Don't thank us just yet!" Richard called. He walked out of the warehouse with two long canvas cases in his hands. Three of his employees followed him. One carried two identical cases, while the other two carried big duffel bags. "We've got something extra for you."

Richard gently set his cases down in the wagon, then opened one of them. The open cylinder of some kind of bazooka peaked out at me. "RPG-7, post-Soviet production." He shrugged. "So, new in the sense that it was made fifty years ago rather than a hundred."

Patrolman Jones walked over and let out a low whistle. "Damn, now that looks sweet. May I, sir?"

"Be my guest," I said.

Jones pulled the RPG free of its canvas case and hefted it. "Lot lighter than I thought it would be." He placed it against his shoulder and aimed down the optical sight. "Think it could be fired from horseback, sir?"

Richard and I shared a look. "You planning to shoot it one-handed?" he asked.

"Trigger would need to be brought back to the rear handle," Jones muttered. He flipped the RPG around and examined it closely. "Would need to mind the backblast, too. I know ol' Rambo wouldn't mind the noise."

Richard grinned. "I guess you'll take them? You can have four, with twenty warheads. Nothing fancy. Just the old HEAT design. I don't know that they'll be able to defeat modern armor, but fire it into a building or a sandbag barrier and watch the fireworks."

I looked at Elizabeth. "Did I mention that I don't know how we'll be able to repay you for all this?"

"I told you before, didn't I?" Elizabeth placed her hands on her hips. "You brought back my son. That's worth his weight in gold. And you're trying to make sense of a senseless situation and restore some order. That's worth *its* weight in gold, too."

"This facility is worth its weight in gold," I said. "Once we set up in Columbia, we'll have to look into sending regular patrols out this way. Your ammunition and gun manufacturing abilities are things we'll need, for sure."

"You and everyone else." She shook her head. "We've already had the King of Boonville try to take this place over more than once.

Somehow, he just can't take the hint that fighting us isn't in his best interest."

"King of Boonville?"

"Tyrant of the town we're on the outskirts of." She hiked a thumb over her shoulder, toward the north. "They've got a bunch of well-armed thugs sittin' pretty in the center of town. They control the bridge running north and the main street running south. They wanted to control the intersection near us, but, well... We didn't much care for that, so they've pushed back into the town proper."

"Sounds like someone we'll want to deal with at some point," I said. I pulled out my notepad and jotted the information down for later discussion with Sheriff Welliver. "What does the sheriff of this county think about all this?"

"Oh, I imagine he thinks it's great, considering he's the King of Boonville."

My hand froze mid-scribble. "Come again?"

"It was him and his boys who took over the town. Killed the police chief and a number of good officers, then took anyone who wanted to serve him and made them part of his group. The Posse, he calls them. They have most of the guns, so they rule as they see fit."

Anger rose up in me, and I had to squash it back down. There'd be time to deal with him later.

Gunfire echoed in the distance, a lot of it. After a moment, a series of explosions ripped through the air. I cocked my head and frowned. It had come from the east, toward the I-70 bridge.

A few minutes later, the familiar white station wagon rolled into the driveway and stopped about fifty yards from the gate. "It's one of ours!" Harry called. "Hold your fire."

Elizabeth opened the gate, and the professors drove their wagon in. All four windows were rolled down. Danny and one of the Boone County deputies in the backseat held their rifles close at hand.

"What happened?" I demanded.

Danny stepped from the vehicle. "The bandits returned, and it's a good thing we weren't on the bridge."

"Too many of them?"

"Not as many as we feared. We could've dealt with them. The problem was Teledyne."

"Teledyne? What are they up to?"

"Tailing us, I imagine. They were trying to cross when they encountered the bandits. Big gunfight ensued, and Teledyne got pushed back. That's when they blew the bridge."

My mouth dropped open. "They blew up the whole bridge?"

"No, just a small section of it. They must not have had enough explosives to do the job. But, it was enough to dissuade any more pursuit from the bandits, and it's put a damper on us taking that route back."

"That may have been the point," I said. My stomach soured. "We'll have to think of a different way to cross."

"Shit," Danny said. Then he looked at Elizabeth. "Sorry, ma'am."

"I've heard—and said—worse." She looked from Danny to me. "Siblings?"

"Danny's my younger brother," I said absently, my thoughts on the problem at hand. "We need a new way to cross."

"According to the map," Danny said, "there's another bridge through Boonville."

I nodded. "The Highway 40 Bridge. Local sheriff controls it, though."

"We could negotiate with him—"

"He's a tyrant, according to Elizabeth. Killed the local chief, along with anyone interested in following the law, and took over."

"Motherfucker! Sorry, ma'am, but what the hell?"

"It's the same in Columbia," I said with a shrug. "The chief and mayor? Bad eggs everywhere, and bad situations help them rise to the top."

"Yeah, but they're beholden to Teledyne. I don't like it, but I can respect that. What this so-called king is doing is beyond the pale."

Harry walked over. "Mom, remember that bike trail Dad and I used to use all the time?"

"Yeah, what about it?" she asked. Then she snapped her fingers. "Wait, that's right! There's the Katy Rail Bridge!"

Danny and I looked at each other. "The Katy Rail Bridge?"

"It's a railroad bridge that crosses the river a little to the west of the Highway 40 Bridge. It hasn't had a train on it since last century, but the whole length of the rail line was converted into a hiking and biking trail decades ago." She stroked her chin, her eyes distant for a moment. "Yes, I think that might actually work."

"Would the sheriff have any men stationed on this bridge?" I asked. "If it's big enough for vehicles to cross, I'd imagine they wouldn't overlook it."

"Well, about that." Now it was Harry and Elizabeth's turn to share a look. She said, "This bridge is a little…special. They wouldn't have guards stationed on it in its present condition."

"That sounds ominous." Thoughts of a rusted out, rickety bridge, swaying in the wind, filled my head. "What kind of dilapidated shape is this thing in?"

* * *

"There she is," Harry said. "The Katy Railroad Bridge in all her glory."

Harry and I had ridden a pair of bicycles along the trail at an entry point near the CAC facility. He wasn't breathing hard as he alighted from his bike, but I was. Too much time in the saddle, not enough time at the gym. I needed to work on my cardio.

We stood behind some bushes near the break in the trail where it opened up to the river. The area around the bridgehead was cleared away to make room for any utility vehicles that needed to get in. There were also a few parking spaces for people who wished to park and ride from this point. A road ran along the river to the east, bound for Boonville town proper not too far away.

A small shed sat to the side of the bridge on our side of the river. "That's the engineer's shed," Harry said. "The motors that raise and lower the span are in there, as are the controls."

"It's manually driven?" I asked. "It wasn't automated when people wanted to cross?"

"No, it's lowered only at certain times of the day, in keeping with regularly scheduled shipping. It wasn't supposed to be lowered again until close to 1:30 PM. Then the bombs fell and, well, here we are." He pointed at the section of bridge that had been lifted high into the air. "There are ladders on either side that would allow us to climb up there and cross on foot, but that's not going to be of help to your horses and wagons. We'd also need bolt cutters to get through the locks securing the ladders."

"There's no manual release in case the span got stuck up there? Loss of power and the like?"

"Not that I'm aware of. I've only seen them lower it with motors. That section of steel weighs thousands and thousands of pounds. If you let it crash down without any kind of slow descent, it could ruin the whole bridge."

We definitely didn't want that. "All right, so we need to get the motor going somehow." I thought about it a moment, then grinned. "Say, your mom has that big ol' gasoline generator, right? The one mounted on the trailer?"

"I suppose she does." Harry returned the grin. "I think we can make that work."

Sometimes you needed a little bit of extra juice in this Fallen World.

* * * * *

Chapter Twenty-Seven

"Uncle Jake, how old are you?" Helen asked as they followed a group of Columbia and university officers down the concrete path between campus buildings. Only a few officers were on horseback, and Jake wasn't one of them.

"That's rude!" Jason said. "You're not supposed to ask someone his age!"

"That's only ladies! You can ask men."

"Oh. Really?"

Jake looked at the two kids and smiled. "I was born in 2033. How old does that make me?"

"Let me guess!" Jason scrunched his face up and focused so hard on math, he almost walked into a lamp post.

Helen pulled him back onto the pavement. "Stay on the path, dummy!"

"You're the dummy! Now, quiet! I'm trying to think." He scrunched his face up even harder, then said, "Fifty!"

"Where'd you get that number?" Helen shook her head. "No, you dummy, it's—"

"Don't tell me!"

"Thirty-four!"

"Gah! I told you not to tell me!"

"All right, you two. Settle down." Jake put a finger to his lips, then he chuckled. "Fifty. Do I really look that old?"

"No, just the opposite," Helen said. "You're two years older than Dad, but you look much younger. As young as—" Her voice caught in her throat, and she finished more quietly. "As young as Mom when she died."

"I never knew Mom," Jason said matter-of-factly. "She's in Heaven now, so I'll get to see her again someday."

"Yes, you will," Jake agreed.

Helen noticed that Jake's face clouded over at the mention of her mother. "Did you know Mom?"

"Not as well as I would have liked. She was a beautiful lady. Kind, sweet, and funny. And you're starting to look a lot like her."

Helen's cheeks flushed at the compliment. "Dad says that a lot, too. It makes him sad."

"He's sad that she's not here to watch you grow up," Jake said. "He's not sad because of you, or what you look like. Believe me."

Helen nodded and then grabbed Jake's arm and pulled herself close to him. She leaned her head against his arm as they walked. He felt solid and strong to her.

Jason hummed tunelessly as they walked along. The afternoon sun peaked out from behind a thick layer of clouds. It was warm, but not unbearably so, the perfect kind of weather for a long walk.

Helen kept quiet for a few minutes, and Jake seemed content to keep his silence, too. He occasionally looked down at her and smiled, but then he would go back to studying their surroundings. Just like Dad would do whenever he took them out for a meal somewhere. *I bet he also likes to sit where he can see the door*, she thought. Were all cops that way?

She recognized most of the officers with them, though she didn't know any of their names. They were local officers, from the city or university police departments. She had a hard enough time remembering the mounted officers' names, much less ones who didn't work with her Dad regularly. As she watched, she saw all of them studying their surroundings. What were they looking for? It seemed like a perfectly fine day for a stroll through Peace Park on the north end of campus.

"*Vrrrrrm,*" Jason said suddenly. He walked along behind Helen, his hands held up like he was gripping a steering wheel. "*Vrrrrm. Vrrrm!*"

"Jason, what are you doing?" Helen demanded.

"There's a truck nearby!" he said. "Can't you hear it? It's going *vrrrm, vrrrm!*"

"I don't know what—" Then she heard it. A very, very low rumble, almost outside her hearing. "You're right."

She felt Jake's arm stiffen beneath her fingertips, the muscle suddenly like iron. "So, it wasn't just me hearing things," he muttered. "Look sharp, everyone! We may have trouble!"

The other officers tensed, and one reached into the leather holster on his left side and drew a weird-looking, black gun. He broke it open and withdrew a pair of different colored tubes from another pocket. The tubes were the size of the shells that went into Dad's shotgun. Her shoulder ached just thinking about the time Dad had let her shoot his shotgun.

Firecrackers popped close by. One of the officers cursed and hit the ground, while the others dropped into crouches and drew pistols or unslung rifles.

Jake pushed her to the ground with that iron-hard arm of his, the force strong enough to squeeze the air from her lungs. She let out a pained squeak, and the pressure eased. "Sorry," he said. "Jason, get down, boy!"

Jason landed next to her, his eyes wide as he stared into hers.

Helen looked up just as the officer with the weird, little shotgun fired into the air. The shell shot straight up, a cloud of red smoke trailing after it.

"Cool, a flare!" Jason looked up, his mouth agape.

The officer broke open the flare gun, ejected the spent shell, and dropped another one in. This time the flare he fired was black.

She wondered what the different colors meant.

Something skimmed along the ground, just in front of her fingertips. She jerked her hand back.

"I'm hit!" an officer screamed.

Panic welled up inside Helen. She'd seen enough shows to know what was going on: this was a gunfight!

"Yay, fireworks!" Jason said with a giggle.

No, you idiot! She started hyperventilating. She wanted to shake him, to tell him what kind of danger they were in. They had to get out of there! Where was Uncle Jake? Where was he?

"They're coming around the right side!"

"Shit, APC!"

Several shots rang out really close to them. Helen and Jason covered their ears with their hands. The grin on Jason's face was starting to fade, and his eyes were growing wider by the second.

"Find cover!" Jake shouted. He dropped to a knee and pulled Helen into a crouch. "Take your brother and run back south." He pointed with his left hand. He held his pistol in his right. "That way. Run, and tell everyone Obsidian's attacking."

Helen stared at him, mouth agape.

Jake spun both children around to face south, then placed Jason's hand in hers. "Go!" He shoved them both. "Now!"

Helen stumbled forward. Her legs almost gave out on her, but she took another step, then another. She looked back over her shoulder.

"Go!" he shouted. "We'll hold them off!"

Helen started running. Behind her, Jake opened fire with his handgun.

More shots rang out. Loud booms, sharp cracks, and a sound like the chattering of teeth that could only be a machine gun of some sort. Occasionally something buzzed in her ear, and she ducked and tried not to scream.

"What's going on?" Jason shouted.

"Just keep running! Run, Jason!"

She shouted less for his benefit and more to block out the other sounds behind her: the gunfire, and worse, the screams of wounded and dying men. Tears burned in her eyes and threatened to blur her vision, so she blinked them away quickly.

A brick building stood off to her right. She pulled Jason that way. They would run behind it to get out of the way of the gunfire and then continue south.

Her lungs burned from the exertion. She'd never been much of a runner, not like Jason. She preferred horseback riding to being on her own two feet. But her horse wasn't here. She sucked in a painful breath and put on a burst of speed.

As she rounded the corner, she ran smack into a black-suited man and bounced back. Jason crashed into her, and the two toppled into a heap. Helen rolled onto her stomach and looked up.

The man she had run into looked down at her, as did three of his buddies. Each wielded a submachine gun of some sort. He put his hand to his ear. "Hotel, this is Baker Squad. We've got a couple kids here. Looks like they were with the cops. I—" He grimaced. "Roger. Only capture the cops. No other witnesses."

The others raised their guns. Fear paralyzed Helen as she stared up into the black barrel of the gun leveled at her face. *Daddy*, she thought.

She closed her eyes when the shots rang out. Something wet struck her face, but she was surprised there was no pain.

Next to her, Jason shrieked.

Helen opened her eyes. A woman in black armor stood between her and the four men with guns, blood dribbling from a wound in her side. The men lay on the ground before her, their weapons dangling from lifeless fingers.

Helen reached up and touched her face, and her fingertips came back red. Blood, but not hers.

Her focus returned to the dead men in front of her, and a wave of nausea threatened to overwhelm her.

The woman in black armor turned toward them. Her hair was stark white; what her Aunt Amy's magazines often called platinum or vanilla-cream blonde. And her eyes were a deep purple. It was then that she made the connection. "You're the camel punching lady from the Renaissance fair!"

The woman studied her for a long moment and then the corners of her mouth quirked up into a hint of a smile. She slung her short submachine gun and knelt. "Are you both all right?"

Jason pointed at the wound in Aster's side. "You're hurt," he said in a quavering voice.

"I'll heal. Are you all right?"

"Y-yeah."

Helen sensed movement and looked up in time to see a group of men and women clad in urban-colored camouflage similar to what Uncle Danny had in his closet. They flanked the camel punching lady, who continued to kneel in front of them.

She reached out a gloved hand to Helen. "Come with us. We'll keep you safe."

Tentatively, Helen reached out for that hand. She gripped it and felt a reassuring squeeze from the woman. She felt solid and strong to Helen.

She felt like she could be trusted, and that was a rare thing in this Fallen World.

* * * * *

Chapter Twenty-Eight

We rested the horses and men until later that evening, then we set the plan in motion. The entire column rode up the rail trail to avoid any of the main roads leading into Boonville. The plan was to avoid a direct conflict with the crooked king and his Posse unless we absolutely had no choice. I wanted to deal with the son of a bitch right here and now, but that wasn't the best of ideas.

It was slow going at first, as parts of the rail trail were starting to get overgrown from lack of maintenance over the last few weeks. Once summer was in full swing, this path would quickly get reclaimed by nature.

As we rode along, I noticed something in the wagon that Harry rode in. "What's in that case?" I asked, pointing at a black, plastic case about four feet long and two feet wide.

"Oh, that?" Harry made a face. "Experimental weapon the US Government was having us develop. We don't really have any use for it since it draws too much energy. Mom figured you might be able to use it. If not, well, it's pretty menacing looking in its own right. Maybe you can bluff with it or something. Mount it to that clock tower at the university and point it at Teledyne Tower until they leave."

An energy weapon? Sounded cool, if a little hard to believe. "Well, thank you. I'm sure we'll make good use of it."

If we get back to Columbia. I didn't voice the thought.

A commotion up ahead drew my attention, and I kicked Watson into a faster walk. The professors' Roadmaster had slowed to a crawl. An elderly man stood just beyond the wagon, his face shielded from the high beams by his hands. A couple of mounted officers had ridden forward to confront him, pistols drawn but not pointed.

I rode past the wagon and touched the side of my helmet in greeting to the psychology professor. She had her AR-15 tucked against her shoulder, with the barrel pointed toward the floor of the station wagon. "Ma'am, keep us covered, please."

"What's going on here?" I asked once I reached the man. "And move off to the side. We have an entire caravan moving through."

The man complied, and the three of us bracketed him so he couldn't run. I snapped on my flashlight and shined it down at him. He flinched away from the light, and I turned it away from his face. "Keep your hands where I can see them, sir, and tell me what's going on."

"Are you police?" the man demanded. "Real police?"

"He asked us the same thing," one of the Boone deputies said. "Not sure what he means by that."

I had an idea. "If by 'real' you mean not with the Posse, then yes. We're not with the king or whatever that crooked sheriff calls himself. We're from Columbia."

"Oh, thank God," the man said, his voice choking. "Thank God someone's here to save us."

"Save you from what? The crooked sheriff?"

"Yes! Some of the drifters he deputized are terrorizing my family. My name's Eddie Gale. They've got my daughter, Jess, and granddaughter, Lori!"

Anger boiled up in me. "Where are they being held?"

"In my house. The sheriff has been letting his men sleep wherever they please. The ones who live in the town have their own places, but the newcomers who drifted in crash people's homes, make off with possessions—" His voice choked off again. "Have their way with whoever they wish," he finished through gritted teeth.

I knew I shouldn't help. I needed to get the weapons home to Columbia, to put them into the fight against Obsidian and Teledyne, and to save a city of nearly a hundred and fifty thousand people. Helping would be the height of stupidity and arrogance. *You can't save them all, Nathan*, I told myself. *And you're a fool to think you can.*

But I could try, dammit.

"How far away is your house?"

Danny, six other volunteers, and I followed Eddie through the trees that separated the rail trail from the town. The rest of the group continued on to the bridge, with orders to get the motor hooked up to the generator. If we weren't back by the time they were ready, they were to get started.

With luck, we'd be back by then. If not, well, at least we'd create a good distraction.

We had dismounted to lead our horses by the reins, to give them a break and to keep from hitting low-hanging branches.

"They shoved me out of the house at gunpoint," Eddie whispered as he led us into the backyard of an abandoned house. It wasn't that late, and there wasn't a single candle lit. We turned our flashlights off and waited a moment for our eyes to adjust. "Told me I could come back in the morning." He pounded his hip with a fist, over and over again. "I should've fought them. I should've done something!"

I grabbed his hand before he could strike himself again. "You did do something. You ran to us. Let us take it from here."

The suspicious part of me worried this was some kind of trap, that this guy was working with the Posse to lure us in. They could've seen us arrive at CAC's headquarters, or seen Harry and me riding along the trail earlier, and set this up to see what we would do, to divide our forces.

The rest of me had to believe this man's tears of frustration were sincere.

We quietly approached the house indicated by Eddie. A single window was illuminated, up on the top floor. The window had been cracked, and in the silence of the night we could hear a combination of whimpers, moans, and an occasional slap.

"Come on, woman," a man called, "you know you like watching me do your daughter! Probably gettin' off on it, ain't ya?"

"Are we arresting these people?" Danny whispered, his eyes burning a hole in the window above us. He had his shotgun in his hands.

"If we can, yes. We might be able to get information out of them." I turned to Eddie. "How many were there?"

"Four of the bastards." He kept staring at the window, his face scrunched up as he tried to keep from crying. "God, what are they doing to my family?"

I placed a hand on his shoulder. "Your family's going to be all right."

Eddie quietly opened the front door for us, then he hung back with the three officers who held the reins of our horses. The rest of us stacked up on the door and slowly entered, Danny on point with his shotgun and me right behind, pistol held in one hand, braced against the hand that held my tactical flashlight. I kept the light off, thumb ready to depress the button the second we needed it.

The bottom floor of the house was dark and silent as we crept toward the stairs. Soft carpet gave way to the hardwood of the steps. My pulse pounded in my ears, and my breath came out in ragged gasps as loud as a rocket launch to my ears, but it wasn't nearly as loud as the sounds of pain and pleasure above us.

At the top of the steps, a hallway extended to the left and right. Danny moved over slightly so I could fit beside him on the wide stairs, and we leaned out at the same time, him sweeping to the right and me to the left. To the left were three doors, one of them open, revealing a bathroom. "Two closed doors," I whispered.

"One closed door," Danny whispered back. "The master."

That was where the light we had seen outside had come from. The other side of the house had been dark, but that didn't mean there weren't people in those rooms. I pointed to two of the three officers with us and motioned for them to cover the left side of the hallway. The remaining officer followed us as Danny and I crept down the corridor to the right. I hung just a step back, giving Danny room to step to the side if he had to.

As we reached the closed door, Danny stood a couple steps back so I could test the door handle. It wasn't locked.

Inside the room, the muffled sobs of the women and groans of the men grew in intensity. The three of us shared a look and nodded. It was time to end this.

I twisted the handle, flung the door open, and rushed in, pistol and flashlight raised.

Four men were in that room, in various states of undress, having their way with Jess and her teenage daughter, Lori. The expressions of terror and pain on the ladies' faces filled me with rage.

I thumbed on my flashlight and shined it in the face of one of the rapists. He shielded his face with one hand and reached for a pistol with the other. I lined my sights up on his bare chest and opened fire.

Three bullets pierced his torso. He screamed and collapsed onto the bed, his blood soaking into the sheets.

I sidestepped to the right, making room for Danny. My brother wasted no time in lining his shotgun up on his target, one of two animals raping Lori. He fired, and the man collapsed onto the teen, blood spurting all over her. She shrieked.

The third man drew his pistol. "Gun!" I shouted as I opened fire. I hit the man twice in the chest, then shifted my aim and shot him in the head.

The fourth man had picked up a rifle from the dresser, but he held it up and out, as if surrendering. I shined my light in his face. "Drop the weap—"

Danny's shotgun roared.

The man staggered back, a hole in his chest the size of an old half-dollar. He looked down, then back at me, his expression shocked.

Danny ran at him and smashed the butt of his shotgun into his face. He struck the floor so hard his head bounced. Danny clubbed the man again and again, until he ceased moving and his face was a bloody pulp.

The two women screamed. "Police, it's all right!" I shouted over them. "Police, it's all right! You're safe now!"

The pounding of feet coming up the stairs filled the house. "Jess! Lori!" Eddie shouted. "Are you all right?"

The bloody teen pulled herself out from beneath her headless assailant and threw her arms around her grandpa, heedless of the gore covering her naked flesh. She sobbed into his chest.

Eddie's daughter, Jess, got up from the bed and pulled the two of them into an embrace. She looked at Danny and then at me. "Thank you," she said, her voice coming out as a choked whisper.

"Were there any others?" I asked. "Or was it just these four?"

"No, that was all of them," she said. She took a shuddering breath, then laughed. "God, the whole room's a mess. I'm a mess. My daughter—" Tears rolled down her cheeks as she squeezed her family into a tighter embrace. "Lori, baby, I'm so sorry."

"No, it wasn't your fault," Eddie said. "I should've protected you. We shouldn't have given the guns up. We shouldn't have!"

Danny stared at the broken body of the fourth rapist, his expression unreadable. I pulled him out into the hallway to give the family a moment.

We quickly cleared the rest of the house. Eddie was right. There had been only four.

He met us at the bottom of the stairs, after he'd led Jess and Lori to the bathroom at the far end of the hall so they could get cleaned up and change into clothes taken from one of the other bedrooms. "There'll be repercussions for this. The king won't take lightly to his men being killed."

"No, I imagine he won't." I pushed open the front door, then turned back toward him. "Do you have anywhere you can go to?"

"Relatives on the other side of town. We're heading there as soon as they're cleaned up." His voice hitched on the last couple words, but he pressed on, "I really can't begin to thank you for what you've done for my family."

Shouts rose up in the distance, coming from the east. Eddie froze. "That'll be the Posse. Gunfire's not uncommon here, but they'll still want to investigate, especially if their men don't return."

"They weren't men," Danny spat, his face visibly red, even in the moonlight.

"You'd best be on your way. They'll be here before long." Eddie leaned in through the door and called up the stairs, "Jess! Lori! Hurry! We need to run to Aunt Sophia's place!"

"I have a better idea," I said. "Follow the rail trail south until you can cut across to Logan's Lake Road. You know where that is? Okay, follow it all the way to CAC's headquarters." I removed the badge from my chest rig and handed it to him. "Ask for Elizabeth Erland and tell her Nathan sent you. She'll see after you."

I was taking a gamble on her kindness, but I knew she wouldn't stand for this kind of treatment of her neighbors. She'd take them in and keep them safe from this Fallen World.

* * * * *

Chapter Twenty-Nine

By the time we made it back to the Katy Rail Bridge, a couple of Harry's employees had just finished running cables from the generator into the engineer's shed. "They'll be finished in a few minutes," Harry said. "That was quite a ruckus you raised behind us."

"If you're going to do it, do it right." I pointed at the towers. "Snipers?"

"Yep." Harry grinned. "I thought it wouldn't be a bad idea to have a couple of your men up in either tower."

Harry had also set up one of the crew-served .50s just behind the engineer's shack, facing the road but out of sight of the Highway 40 bridge. "Mom filled me in on the Posse's capabilities. A couple working pickup trucks and a squad car, but that's it. They bolted steel plates onto one of the pickups to make an armored vehicle, but I can't imagine it holding up to that bad boy."

"You've been busy."

"Man, I live for this stuff. My family's always been preppers, more so in the last decade with the Corporate wars heating up the way they have. Can't be too careful." His smile faded. "I just hope it's enough. I really don't want any of your guys getting killed."

I clapped him on the shoulder. "I understand that fear all too well."

"You've done good with what little we have to work with," Danny said. "Not much cover here, but you made the most of it. Our best bet is going to be keeping everyone's heads down on the 40 bridge." He lifted himself up in the saddle and peered to the east. "Speaking of which, any sign of activity?"

"A few minutes after the gunfire to the south—which I assume was you and your men—one of their pickup trucks started up and rolled off the bridge into town. Couldn't tell how many were in it, but I'd assume it was packed, so six or seven?"

"Any idea how many are left on the bridge?"

"None. Haven't seen any activity, so if we're lucky, it's empty."

"I don't like relying on luck." I nodded toward the bridge. "How long before it's down?"

"Couple minutes once we get the power restored." He frowned. "I really hate that you're having to take the generator back before you can leave."

"I appreciate you loaning it to us," I told him. "The least we can do is return it. We'll be able to hold here until they get back. Shouldn't be more than a few minutes."

"Thank you," Harry said. He held out his hand. "Always knew you were good people. Be sure to come back this way once you've cleaned up Columbia. Until then, give the Corporate bastards hell."

I gripped his hand tight. "Count on it."

The two CAC employees walked out of the shack and gave Harry the thumbs-up. "Looks like we're ready to go," he said.

"Then let's fire it up."

The generator was a lot quieter than I expected. Which is to say, it was about as loud as a regular diesel generator like the ones most of us have in hurricane country. It roared to life like the professors' station wagon did whenever they turned it on, and it rumbled loudly in the otherwise silent night.

Watson's ears flattened against his skull at the sudden noise. "Easy, Watson, easy," I murmured. He snorted.

If the generator was quieter than I expected, the lift motors more than exceeded my expectations in the loudness department. A deep warbling rumble rose up from the shed, then a squealing noise started as the span began to lower. I fished a set of earplugs out of my pocket and jammed them into my ears. I hoped the boys up in the towers did the same.

The lifted span of the Katy Rail Bridge slowly lowered amid the rattling of chains and rumbling of engines. Around me, officers petted and whispered to their nervous mounts. They had grown used to the quiet, but I had a feeling it was going to get a whole lot louder.

Over on the Highway 40 bridge, a pair of spotlights turned on, and their beams shined across the calm surface of the Missouri River. Whoever was operating the lights twisted them around until they shone directly on the bridge. One of the officers positioned in the tower closest to us placed a hand over his eyes and ducked down behind the aluminum parapet.

Gunshots rang out, and even at this distance, I could see the muzzle flashes from the Highway 40 bridge in the distance. Rounds pinged off our bridge and sank into the dirt near the engineer's shack.

Someone fired a shot from close by, and one of the spotlight beams suddenly veered to the right and up. "Pegged one!" an officer up in the tower called.

"Knock those lights out!" I shouted. "And keep their heads down!"

The officers in the towers traded fire with those on the Highway 40 bridge for another minute, until the span descended to its final resting position. It locked into place with a resounding thud.

Harry and his two employees hurriedly shut off the lift motors, then unhooked the cables connecting the motors to the generator. "We'll get the wagon back to you soon!" he said as he coiled up the cables and tossed them into a storage compartment in the trailer the generator sat on top of.

The familiar staccato of a machine gun rang out, followed by the rapid pinging of rounds punching into metal. "Shit!" one of the snipers shouted. "That was close!"

"Hurry," I urged Harry as Danny shouted, "Lay down suppressing fire!"

A few of the officers dismounted and grabbed the light machine guns out of one of the wagons, along with a few cases of belt-fed ammo. They ran along the now-descended span and set up at the base of each tower, where they had solid cover behind steel girders. "Can't see much from here," one of them called. "We're too low!"

"That'll be fine," Danny said. "Don't expose yourselves too much. Fire in bursts toward the muzzle flashes. The idea isn't to hit them, although it's good if you can. Just keep their heads down."

"Exactly," I added. "No one likes getting shot at!"

"You're telling me!" one of the snipers shouted as another burst of Posse machine gun fire raked the tower.

A gunshot rang out from the second tower, and the machine gun stopped. "Gunner's down."

"Sir, can we use the RPGs we got?" Patrolman Jones asked.

"Negative," Danny said. "We're almost outside the maximum range."

"Besides, we already lost one bridge over the Missouri, " I added. "We don't want to risk losing another." Who knew when we might need to cross again?

A second machine gun on the enemy bridge opened up, and the first one started shooting again. Our machine guns returned fire. Tracer rounds sailed back and forth across the river, looking like scenes from those old G.I. Joe cartoons I grew up watching.

The good ones from the '80s, not the crappy remakes from the '30s.

Just as I was considering moving the .50 out from behind the engineer's shed to lay fire on the bridge, a truck turned out of town and sped down the road. Two headlights and four lights mounted to the roof shined down toward us. Gunfire cracked, and rounds zipped through the air around us.

"Light it up!" I shouted to the officers on the .50.

The .50 roared to life, belching fire and lead. One of the truck's headlights exploded, and it veered to the side after the driver was hit. It crashed into a stand of trees, its motor whining as it died.

The officers fired another long burst into the side of the vehicle and then it fell silent. Nothing moved in the truck. When I shined my flashlight toward it, I saw why. The pickup truck had been chewed to bits. There were gaping holes in its doors and fenders, and most of the windows had been blown out. The paint looked to be blue, so I doubted the red color of the interior had anything to do with the upholstery. There wasn't much left of whoever had been inside.

"Must've thought they could flank us, the morons," Danny said.

"We should get to the other side," I said. "They may try the same there."

A barrage of machine gun fire came from the Highway 40 bridge. I didn't know how many people they had up there, but they were well-armed. Where had all those guns come from?

"Mount up!" I called. "We'll head off any attempts to flank us, then provide cover for the wagons to cross!"

The men jumped to obey, and in less than a minute we were ready to go. "Follow me!" I shouted and dug my heels into Watson's side.

Watson galloped across the bridge, his shod hooves clanging on the metal of the span. The rest of the bridge had been covered with concrete, but the lift span was fashioned of steel plates, its rail long-since removed to make a smooth path for foot and bike traffic.

I risked a glance to the right and saw tracer rounds coming our way. I pushed myself low in the saddle and fixed my gaze forward. Rounds zipped past my head.

And then we were over the bridge and on the other side of the river. I pulled Watson to a halt inside a stand of trees that offered concealment from the Posse. The others reined in behind me.

I pulled out my binoculars and studied the bridge. At this range and time of night, I couldn't make out much more than muzzle flashes, but I did spot flashlights moving from the center of the bridge to our side of it. They were trying to get a better angle on us and head us off.

We kept our flashlights off as we cantered along the grassy shoulder of Riverview Road to mask the sounds of our horses' hooves as much as to avoid the occasional disabled vehicle stuck in the middle of the lane. I scanned the bridge entrance with my binoculars and spied movement among the cars that had been pushed to the sides. Seven, no, eight men, all armed, their flashlights shining at their feet or out into the surrounding countryside. Some of those beams came our way, but the lights were too weak to make us out.

I slowed Watson to a walk and drew the assault rifle Elizabeth had given me. I hadn't had a chance to shoot it, but she had walked me through the mechanics and several dry-firing drills while we waited for dark. It was similar to the M4s we carried back in Mobile. The red dot that had originally been on it was fried in the EMP, but its front and rear sights had been painted in glow-in-the-dark tritium, making them highly visible, even in pitch darkness.

Watson snorted softly. I placed a hand on his neck and made soothing noises, like I had with Jason and Helen when they were young. The words didn't matter as much as the tone. Watson stilled beneath me, and his stance relaxed. "There, that's a good boy," I murmured. "This'll all be over soon."

I turned around and gestured for half the men to dismount, then hopped from the saddle and joined them. The others grabbed the reins of our horses. "All right, there are eight of them out there. Each of us gets one. I've got the lead, you have the next one, and you—" And down the line I went, assigning a target to each person. "I'll take the first shot. Open fire as soon as you hear me. Then we'll remount and charge. We have to put pressure on the bridge to buy time for the wagons to get by."

I put the rifle to my shoulder and lined the tritium sights up on the first target. I couldn't make out the man's features behind the flashlight he wielded, but I could see enough to know where his center mass was in relation to his hand. That's the danger of wielding a flashlight in a firefight, if you hold it up close to the body, as most people do. I traced the barest hint of a silhouette and centered my rifle on what I thought was the man's chest.

I took a deep breath and slowly released.

Just as my lungs emptied, I squeezed the trigger.

The rifle barked loudly, but the recoil against my shoulder was light. The .308 bullet sailed across the distance and smacked into my target. There was a cry, and the flashlight fell to the ground.

And then seven more rifles fired. Flashlights fell or flew into the air as the hands holding them jerked and spasmed. Men screamed, and their bodies crashed against vehicles or struck the pavement with audible thuds.

"Let's go!" I said, bounding up into Watson's saddle. I kept my knees tight against his flanks to maintain stability as Watson galloped down the road.

As we turned onto the bridge, a torrential blast of gunfire erupted from the Katy Railroad bridge. Someone had moved the .50 onto it. Tracer rounds chewed into the center of the Posse-controlled bridge.

Several men and women armed with guns stood close by on the bridge, their stunned gazes transfixed by the hellish display of fire superiority being unleashed on their buddies in the center. They didn't see us coming until it was too late. We opened fire at close range and gunned them down before they had a chance to respond.

One of the vehicles facing toward us came to life, or at least the headlights did. The sudden blast from the high-beams blinded me. Beneath me, Watson screamed and reared up.

"Kill 'em!" someone in front of me shouted.

I dug my heels into Watson, and the frightened horse broke into a run toward the light. I pressed the rifle tight against my shoulder and blinked rapidly, hoping my vision would clear before I was shot. I fired several rounds blindly, and managed to knock out one of the headlights.

Bullets zipped past me. A line of searing pain shot across my upper arm. I hissed and hunched my shoulders but urged Watson on. Behind me, a horse shrieked and something heavy crashed into a vehicle hard enough to break glass.

"What're you doing?" that same voice in front screamed. "Kill 'em! They're almost—"

And then the blinding light was past me on the left. The sudden darkness was near absolute after the intensely bright glow of the remaining headlight, but I could see well enough to make out shapes. I aimed for those shapes, firing two or three rounds at each before switching targets. Something appeared in the shadows directly in front of me, and I saw a glint of metal in the light of my rifle's muzzle flash. A gun, and it was rising toward me.

Watson reared up and stomped down with his forelegs. The figure fell beneath Watson's hooves, and there was a sickening series of pops and crunches as the thousand-pound horse trampled my would-be assailant to death.

"Good boy, Watson!" I said, shifting my aim to shoot at another figure in the shadows. "We'll make a police horse out of you yet!"

I shot at another shadow that moved toward me. It dropped. By now, my eyes were beginning to adjust again. Indistinct shadowy blobs resolved into the silhouettes of people, all members of the king's Posse. They tried to run back to the center of the bridge, but they ran into their own people fleeing our way.

We formed a ragged line and fired from our saddles at the twenty or thirty thugs and crooked cops running at us. The extra height gave them little room for cover on the bridge they had cleared of most disabled vehicles.

Our .50 had fallen silent, and a quick glance to my right showed me that two of the wagons were crossing. The third wagon had stopped near the .50, and the crew was breaking the big gun down for transport.

A cascade of gunfire had risen from the town, and the shots were drawing closer. I saw the headlights of a vehicle as it turned off the bike trail and started down the river road that connected the bridges. Guns fired out of the windows, and the tracer rounds of a machine gun came from the roof.

An explosion lit up the night sky, its source at the center of Boonville. "Woah, someone's having fun!" one of the officers called.

"Yeah, and someone else is having a really bad day," another said. "Like these jokers here."

My rifle bolt locked back on an empty mag. I dropped it into my hand and slipped it into my saddle bags, then drew a fresh magazine. I had to visually check to make sure it seated properly, then let the bolt slide home. "If they want to surrender, let 'em. If not, pour it on them!"

"What about that vehicle?" one of the men asked. "Is it theirs?"

"I don't think so." I grinned. "I think that's our backup."

As we continued to pour lead into the Posse members, the glow of approaching headlights grew noticeably brighter from behind them. A vehicle crested the top of the bridge and rolled down toward us.

"Cease fire!" I shouted.

Other officers took up the call, and after a few more expended rounds, the bridge fell silent. The noise of gunfire from the town center still echoed into the night sky. I pitched my voice to carry over it, "You Posse members best surrender! That vehicle pressing in from behind you is one of ours, and I've got another forty guys behind me ready to have another go at you."

That wasn't quite true, but all's fair in love and suspect apprehension.

The Posse members remained frozen where they stood, crouched, or lay prone, other than occasional looks over their shoulders at the approaching headlights.

One of them swore a foul oath and dropped his gun to the ground. With that, the fight went out of them. Weapons clattered to the ground as Posse members held up their hands, muttered curses, or shouted the usual, "It's not my fault! You don't understand!" that so many criminals love to utter when caught red-handed. One even had the nerve to burst into tears, a pretty young lady who should've been studying for college or having fun with friends, who shouldn't have been part of such a disgusting group as the Posse.

There was a very thin veil between civilization and barbarism, and that was all the more apparent in this Fallen World.

* * * * *

Chapter Thirty

The Roadmaster kept its high beams on as it pulled to a stop about fifty feet ahead of us, at an angle so its headlights could illuminate the prisoners huddled by the concrete median along the bridge. We had cuffed their hands behind their backs with zip ties and forced them to kneel. They weren't going anywhere fast.

I rode Watson toward the station wagon and shined my light at the roof. Sitting on the horse, I could see over the sandbags piled around the luggage rack. A familiar figure lay on his stomach, his hands on the pistol grip of a light machine gun that faced forward. "Didn't expect to see you come back to help," I said.

Harry grinned. "Yeah, well, I figured: what the hell? I can always walk home if I need to."

The sound of a machine gun tore through the night air. More guns rose in answer to that one, all of it coming from town. "What's all that about?" I asked.

"That'd be us stirring up some trouble." One of the rear passenger doors opened, and out stepped Elizabeth. She was kitted up in urban camo fatigues, a chest rig with armored steel plates, and a helmet complete with a night vision monocular. She had the monocular flipped up and out of her face as she grinned at me. "We couldn't let you have all the fun. Not after what happened to that poor family you sent my way. Here, this is yours." She tossed something at me.

I caught it. It was my badge. So, Eddie had made it. Good. "Is all that gunfire your doing?"

"No, we only started it. We— Go ahead?" She pressed a hand to the side of her helmet, and it was only then that I realized she was wearing an earpiece. "If they're in there and refusing to come out, send a few incendiary rounds in. We'll see how much they like the idea of burning to death."

A shiver ran down my spine. Elizabeth was one tough woman. "You serve at all, ma'am?"

"No, but my husband did, as did all my boys." She grinned. "I learned from the best. To answer your earlier question, most of the gunfire you hear is the townsfolk rising up against the king and his Posse." Her grin faded. "They're sick to death of what that man's inflicted upon them, but they had no idea what to do about it. Random killings, public rapes, and humiliations have a terrible effect on civilized people, people unused to seeing such atrocities. It cows them, turns them into sheep. And sheep don't typically fight back."

"But," Harry said, "get a few brave sheepdogs and shepherds into the mix, and even the sheep will fight when they have to. We have you to thank for that."

"Do you want our help?" I asked.

"I think you've done more than enough for one day, Nathan." Elizabeth nodded in my direction. "And I think your horse would agree with that."

Beneath me, Watson sighed and shuddered. He was exhausted. As I looked around at the other horses, I could see fatigue etched into their long faces. They were spent or would be soon. On the parade ground, these horses could run around for hours, but so many close calls with death over the last half hour had done for them what a day full of exercise couldn't do.

"No, leave this to us." Elizabeth walked behind the wagon and opened the rear hatch so two more of her men could climb out. "We should've cleaned up this town weeks ago, but we were afraid, just like the rest of these people." She grimaced. "More to our shame, because of all the munitions we sat on. If I had my entire company here, it wouldn't have been an issue, but with so few..."

"You did the right thing," I assured her. "Best not to pick a fight you might not win."

"Says the man who picked a fight with not one, but two, Corporations!" a voice said from behind.

Danny rode up, a big grin on his face. "You see that .50 in action? How'd I do?"

"That was you?" I asked, then laughed. "I should've known. You never pass up a chance to shoot a new toy."

"Neither do you. Besides, other than Collins, I'm the only person who's shot one."

"How is he?" I asked, sudden worry gnawing at my gut.

"Oh, he's fine. His loader got hit, though, when we were packing the .50 up. Boone deputy, can't remember his name. Knee's messed up, but Ferris patched him up while I continued firing. He should be fine until we get back, but he'll be riding in the wagons the rest of the way."

"Other casualties?" I asked. We had lost three horses on our charge. One officer died and another one suffered a broken wrist as he fell from his horse. The third unhorsed officer was fine, but understandably upset about his horse. We had to restrain him when we were cuffing the prisoners, as he'd wanted to put a bullet in the one who shot his horse.

"Just the loader," he said. "We made off easy."

"Yeah, we did," I said and was surprised I genuinely felt that way. Before the Fall, I would've considered the death of a fellow officer an earth-shattering tragedy, one that would be followed by an outpouring of public support, favorable media coverage, and a funeral parade a mile long.

Now it was "Just another day, and thank God we didn't lose more." It was amazing how quickly priorities and perspectives changed.

"What do you want to do with the prisoners?" I asked Elizabeth.

"We'll take them into custody," she said. "Though they'd probably be safer if they went with you folks. I can't imagine they'll get much of a warm welcome from the townspeople they helped oppress."

"It was the king's fault, not ours!" one of the men cried.

"Oh, shush!" Elizabeth snapped. "You screwed up. You picked the wrong side and gave in to your base desires. Be a man and accept what you did, you sniveling coward!"

"Fuck you! What do you know, you old bi—"

There was a loud crack, and the man's words choked off suddenly. Harry whipped the man again with his pistol, then pointed it at him. "Don't you cuss at my Mom."

"Like I said, we'll handle it from here," Elizabeth said. "We'll have this whole town cleaned up in no time."

"Very well," I said. "We'll do the same with Columbia."

"Now, that's the spirit! Go and give those Corporations hell!" She waved at us. "And y'all come back now, ya hear? We'll make Boonville the friendliest town there is in this Fallen World!"

* * * * *

Chapter Thirty-One

"Woah, this bed is huge!" Jason exclaimed. He climbed onto the queen-sized bed and started jumping. "It's as big as Dad's back home!"

"Stop jumping on it!" Helen snapped. "It looked like it was freshly made, and you're ruining it!"

"Aw, I'll fix it."

"Since when?"

"All right, you'll fix it!"

She sighed. She would have to, she realized. "Stop jumping on it. Beds are for laying, not playing."

"You're no fun." He stopped jumping and flopped down on it.

Helen turned away and looked around the bedroom that Aster had said was hers. A door led out into a dimly-lit but well-decorated hallway. The door was closed, but she knew two of Aster's men were standing out there. Helen had heard her say, "Keep them safe," which sounded to her like, "Keep them out of trouble."

They're not doing their jobs, she thought with a sidelong glance at Jason. *Boys.*

Helen had expected Aster to take her and Jason back to the dorm they shared with their Dad, but she had told them she'd been ordered to take them somewhere even safer than that.

Aster and her men had led them away from the gunfire and screams and back to the biggest tower in the city. "This is my room," she told them when she let them in. "I'll be back in a little bit. Make yourselves at home."

A small table sat in the center of the room, surrounded by four chairs. A desk and computer lay in the far corner. Other than the bed, that was all the furniture the room held. The desk drawers were locked when Helen tried to pull on them, and the computer started up, but it immediately demanded a password she didn't have.

Bored, she walked over to the two other doors in the room. The first led into a bathroom complete with shower and tub. The second was for a walk-in closet the size of a small bedroom.

Clothes racks lined the left and right sides of the closet, and a set of shelves was set along the rear wall. The racks to the left held numerous three-piece suits of different styles, though all were black. There were also several button-down shirts of varying, muted colors, with ties that matched each shirt.

The racks on the right held sets of military fatigues in various camouflage styles, from the urban camo she had seen Aster's companions wear, to forest green, desert tan, and arctic white. There was also the kind of dress uniform Dad wore for special occasions, at least up top. A black, knee-length skirt replaced the trousers. The outfit was completed with a peaked cap bearing the emblem of Teledyne.

As for the set of shelves at the end...

"Ooh, look, toys!"

Helen jumped and glared down at Jason, who had suddenly stepped up next to her. "Don't do that!"

"Do what?" He pointed. "Look, Helen, toys!"

"Don't—Oh, never mind." She harrumphed loudly, then looked closer at the shelves.

He was right. A wide variety of dolls, action figures, and figurines adorned the shelves at the far end of the room. A set of empty plastic boxes had been stacked to the side of the shelves, the kind meant for storage and travel. She imagined that this Aster lady had to travel a lot, and she took this whole closet with her.

But, why the toys? Sure, Dad had some toys from when he was a kid, but he'd given them to her and Jason. Didn't Aster have kids of her own she could give them to? Was she saving them?

She walked up to the shelf. Jason reached out to grab one from the lowest shelf, and she slapped his hand. "No touching," she hissed. "Not until we ask."

"Aw, that's not fair!"

"Would you like it if I touched your toys without permission?"

"No!" He looked aghast at the thought. "I don't want you touching my Legos at all!"

"See? That's exactly the same thing here. Maybe Aster doesn't want you to touch any of her stuff until you ask her nicely."

"Oh…that makes sense, then. Can we look at them, though?"

"Well, we're doing that already, aren't we?"

The two of them perused the shelves for a while without actually touching anything. And other than the occasional "Ooh!" and "What's this thing for?" Jason kept his mouth shut, which gave her time to think.

The toys covered a wide range: action figures and toy cars meant for boys, stuffed animals and dolls meant for girls, and for all ages. Some of the toys were immaculate, while others were falling apart. Some even looked singed or burnt.

And in the center of it all, on the topmost shelf, was the figure of a female knight in gold and blue armor. She was charging at an unseen foe, her blonde hair streaming behind her, her sword held low and ready to strike. One of her brilliant, blue eyes was covered with a black strip of cloth, and her mouth was opened in a scream of defiance.

She reached for it. "What's this?"

"Her name's Alice Zuberg," a quiet voice said.

Helen jumped, and Jason let out a squeak. Both kids spun on their heels. Aster stood there in the doorway, studying them with those purple eyes of hers. She had stripped out of her armor and was clothed only in undergarments. "She was my grandfather's," she continued as if nothing was wrong. "One of his favorite characters from an anime he loved."

Aster walked over to the rack with her shirts and reached into a cabinet Helen hadn't seen before. She pulled out a fresh set of underwear and pulled her sports bra off.

"Woah!" Jason said, then Helen covered his eyes.

"I'll just be a moment," Aster said. She dropped the bra to the floor. "Go on outside."

Helen started to lead her brother out, but froze as Aster turned toward her to look at her collection of button-downs. Round scars pocked her pale skin, from her abdomen up to her boobs. Dad had a similar scar on his side.

Then she noticed the bandage on her abdomen, where she had been bleeding when she saved them. "Miss Aster, are you hurt?"

Aster looked down. "Don't worry. I heal fast. In a couple weeks, even the scars will be gone."

Helen nodded, then led Jason out into the main room. "Why couldn't I look?" Jason grumbled.

"Because boys don't look at girls," she hissed. "Mind your manners."

A knock at the door startled Helen. Aster exited the closet, clad in dark gray slacks and vest, along with a lavender shirt and tie. She opened the door to the hallway and admitted a pair of servants. One carried a tiered tray filled with desserts, along with plates and forks; the other carried a tea set, a steaming pot, and a bottle of milk. They set these down on the table.

"Thank you," Aster said.

The servants nodded to her and left without a word.

Aster stared at the door for a long moment, then turned to the two of them. "Would either of you like some dessert?"

"Me!" Jason shouted.

Helen got Jason seated, then she sat down next to him. Aster took the seat across from them. Jason reached for the bottle of milk. "Milk and cake. Milk and cake!"

"I'll take tea," Helen said, snatching the bottle of milk before Jason could knock it over with his clumsy fingers. She twisted the cap off and filled one of the teacups halfway.

"Please, help yourselves," Aster said as she poured tea for Helen and herself. "The chiffon cake is very good."

"Chiffon?" Helen asked.

Aster pointed at what looked like a sponge cake covered in vanilla frosting. "This one. Also, the chocolate Doberge—" She pointed at a wedge that was a deep brown color, covered in a fudge topping, "—is my favorite."

"Is it as good as Pollman's?" Jason demanded. He eyed the chocolate cake with all the dubiousness a five year-old could muster.

"It's a bakery in Mobile," Helen said quickly. "They make really good birthday cakes, but Dad's favorite is their chocolate Doberge. It looks a lot like this." She picked up a fork and pushed a piece onto her plate. She took a small bite, and savored the delicious, rich taste of the fudge and moist cake. "Mmm, and it tastes just like this, too!"

"Let me have some!" Jason said, and he snagged a big piece with his fork before she could stop him.

"You're both from Mobile?" Aster asked.

"Yep! Born and raised!" Jason said, as proud as someone who'd accomplished a great deed.

"Oh." Aster's purple eyes grew sad. "I'm sorry."

Helen cocked her head. "Sorry? About what?"

Aster's eyes narrowed, then widened. "Oh. You don't know...?" She nodded slightly, then said, "I'm sorry, but I've never been to Mobile."

"That's nothing to be sorry about," Jason said. "You can come with us sometime! Our house is big. You can stay with us."

"Jason!" Helen hissed. "You can't just invite people to our home! What would Dad say?"

"But she's giving us cake. Dad would think that's cool. Hey, what's this one?" He pointed to a white cake with red and white swirled frosting.

Aster wrinkled her nose. "Peppermint. I've told the kitchen a dozen times I can't stand it."

"I love peppermint!" Jason crowed. He grabbed the piece and plopped it on his plate. He then licked the icing off his hand.

"Well, at least it won't go to waste today." Aster's lips quirked up into that slight smile she had displayed earlier, but her eyes had grown sad again. She used her fork to push a piece of cheesecake onto her plate. "Your father is Lieutenant Nathan Ward, correct?"

"That's right!" Jason said. "He's a cop!"

"You know Dad?" Helen asked. She sipped her tea and tried to hide her grimace. It was a little too bitter for her taste, but grown girls always drank their tea hot, so she had to get over it.

"We've met a few times since we've come to this city. Our work draws us together."

"But, you work with Teledyne," Helen said. "You're the bad guys."

"Bad guys don't give people cake!" Jason rolled his eyes. "Geez, Helen, get with it."

"Obsidian and their dogs are the bad guys." Aster set her teacup down on the saucer with a loud clink. "Teledyne has been trying to fix all the messes Obsidian has made throughout the country."

"Dad says both Corporations are bad," Helen said. "That both Corporations are the reason this city is as messed up as it is. That so many people have gotten hurt."

Aster was silent for a long moment. "Perhaps your Dad is right."

They sat in silence for a few minutes, except for Jason's happy smacking and slurping. Helen found that if she took a bite of her cake and then washed it down with the tea, the two tastes blended together nicely. Not too sweet, not too bitter. Chocolate and tea were a really good combination.

Helen had a thought. "Is there a reason you have those toys of yours?"

"Yes. They're all special to me."

"Like the Alice figure?"

"That's my first." Aster's eyes grew distant. "Grandfather always said I looked a lot like her."

"But, she has blonde hair and blue eyes."

Aster reached back and touched one of her white locks. "My hair and eyes weren't always this color. They are a rare side effect of the augmentation process."

Helen didn't know what that meant. "Who gave the other toys to you? Family?"

"Ooh, do you look forward to getting them each year?" Jason asked. "Like Christmas or birthdays?"

"No. I don't get them as often as I used to." She sounded relieved, which Helen thought was strange.

"That's no good!" Jason said. He grinned. "I know! I'll give you one of mine!"

Aster slammed a hand down on the table, hard enough to rattle the teacups and shake the tiered dessert tray. "No!"

Helen and Jason both recoiled as if slapped. They looked at each other, eyes wide.

"No," Aster said in a much softer tone. "I don't want any more. Never again."

A chill ran down Helen's spine. "Why not?"

"They're symbols." She took a sip of tea and set the cup down so gently, it didn't even clink against the saucer. "Symbols of the people I've failed to protect."

Jason and Helen shared another look.

Aster returned to eating. "I understand that children need to eat almost as much as I do, so have as much as you like. I can always order more." She smiled. "And I might."

Helen and Jason returned the smile, and they dug in with as much gusto as they could muster.

As they ate, it was Aster's turn to ask them questions. She asked what life was like in Mobile, what the two of them were learning in school, and how things were at the university.

Mostly she asked about their dad; what he was like; how he treated them; how he treated his friends and colleagues; how he treated his pets and horses; what he thought about police work; and what kind of faith he had. Jason mostly answered with nonsensical stuff that had Helen rolling her eyes, but Helen thought she answered the questions well.

"Why do you want to know so much about Dad?" she asked as she bit into a shortbread cookie. The rich buttery taste coated her tongue, and that paired really well with the tea. She was starting to see why the English loved their tea and biscuits so much. Even if their biscuits were nothing like Dad's southern biscuits and gravy.

"He seems like a good man," Aster said after taking time to finish her fourth piece of cake. She reached for a fifth. "He seems to care a lot about his men and about pursuing justice."

"That's what being a cop is all about!" Jason said. "Profiting and swerving!"

"That's protecting and serving, dummy."

"He swerves a lot in traffic!"

"That's different!" Helen rolled her eyes and looked back at Aster. "Dad's the best kind of cop. He does what he has to do to keep people safe." Her lower lip trembled as she added, "It scares me at times, but I know he's doing the right thing."

"Doing the right thing," Aster said quietly. "That's just what we need in this Fallen World."

* * * * *

Chapter Thirty-Two

We followed Highway 40 for about a mile before pulling into an abandoned gas station for the night. We corralled the wagons in a makeshift circle, and set up watches to keep an eye out for bad guys, as well as to keep an eye on the horses. We tied rope between two posts of the gas station's canopy, then looped the horses' reins around the rope.

The ride back to Columbia the next morning was uneventful compared to what had transpired over the last twelve hours. Space had been cleared in one of the wagons so we could carry the wounded and horseless officers. The Roadmaster had once again been packed with food, leaving the wagons to haul the ammunition and guns we had received from CAC. With such a heavy burden in each wagon, it was slow going for the horses.

We followed Highway 40 east for several miles, then turned south on Highway J. Highway J eventually crossed beneath Interstate 40 and merged with Highway O. As on the previous day, we didn't run into a single living soul until we hit W. Gillespie Bridge Road and all its farms.

I was on point in front of the Roadmaster when Danny pulled up next to me. "Sleep all right?" he asked.

"After all that adrenaline dumped out, I crashed," I said. "Soon as we had everyone else bedded down for the night and the first set of watches established, I was out until Jones woke me for my shift. You?"

"Nah." He shook his head. "Couldn't sleep too well."

I hesitated, then asked, "Have anything to do with that man you killed in Eddie's house?"

He flinched. "No."

"Uh-huh. I notice you didn't say 'which one' when you and I both know you bagged two."

"The man deserved it, Nate. They all deserved it! You saw what they were doing to those poor women."

"I was the first one in the door, remember? I was the first one to fire."

"Then you understand why I did what I had to."

"You didn't *have* to, and you know it." I turned my head to look him square in the eyes. "We're officers of the law, Danny. And that man knew he was beat. He was surrendering."

"He would've killed us if he'd had the chance!" Danny growled. "And the women, too."

"Maybe so. How many criminals did you and I bring down who would've done the same thing, if they had the chance? We didn't just execute them. We arrested them, so they could be brought to trial."

"What court exists anymore?" Danny jabbed a finger in my direction. "It's not that world anymore, man. This is a battlefield, in the truest sense of the word. No, in a worse sense. I never saw anyone in the Corporate battles do what those animals were doing to those poor women or to the countless others they terrorized in Boonville. I hope Harry and Elizabeth kill them all and hang their bodies from the streetlights. They—" He sighed. "Eddie's daughter Jess looks a lot like Amy."

A wave of sadness punched through my anger. "Yeah. Yeah, she does."

"I can't forgive them." He twisted in the saddle to look at me, the movement so sudden that Noir tensed. Her ears flicked back and forth as she tried to sense what upset her partner. "What those bastards did to my wife. To *our* family, Nathan."

"I understand," I said. "What Teledyne and Obsidian have done is reprehensible, and they haven't paid for those sins yet. There'll be a reckoning, brother. You'll see."

"I did the right thing," he muttered one last time.

I understood where he was coming from. Hell, I felt the same way when we broke into that bedroom and when I heard about what Obsidian and Teledyne had done to our world. But, to me, it didn't sit right. Maybe it was easier for him, since he'd fought as a soldier. I'd always been a cop, and the rules of engagement were vastly different between soldiers and police.

He was right about one thing, though. This was a war, and we needed soldiers if we were going to win. But if we gave up the codes and principles of the old world to win this war, would any of the old world be left once we were done?

He and I rode in silence for a long while, each of us lost in our thoughts.

* * *

"All right, Watson, we're almost home," I said as we left the Three Rivers Renaissance Fair behind. As promised, we had given Richard and his guards a cut of the weapons and ammunition, with the promise of more once we cleared the city and could establish a dedicated trade route with Boonville.

Once again, Danny and I were on point with a half-dozen other officers. The Roadmaster idled up Highway 163 with three wagons behind it. It must have been killing the professor to go that slow. On straight roads, his vehicle idled faster than the wagons moved.

As we turned onto Mick Deaver Memorial Drive, I caught sight of a white-haired woman standing in the road ahead of us. It was Aster, dressed in her full battle armor, with her FN-P90 hanging from its single-point sling. Two children stood next to her, each holding one of her gloved hands.

Jason and Helen? My heart skipped a beat. What were my children doing with Aster?

Part of me wanted to kick my horse into a gallop and barrel down on the Teledyne Specialist, but I'd seen what she could do. If she wanted to hurt my children, she could do it before I got close, then finish me off before the horror even registered.

I held up a hand to halt the officers coming up behind me. "Danny, put your weapon down!" I called, without looking.

Danny cursed. I heard the sound of a rifle dropping back into its saddle scabbard.

More Teledyne soldiers appeared from behind broken-down cars and trucks. They closed ranks around Aster. Manager Strohl stepped out of his executive sedan, flanked by a group of bodyguards.

"Lieutenant Nathan Ward?" Strohl asked. He studied me first, then smiled. "You owe Teledyne a great debt, Mr. Ward. Our good Lady in Black here saved your two children from Obsidian soldiers who attacked the university. We've had them in our protective custody since then."

"Helen!" I called and tried to keep the tremor of fear from my voice. "You all right, girl?"

Strohl looked annoyed and started to open his mouth.

Aster knelt down next to Helen and whispered something in her ear. Helen looked at Strohl, then back at Aster, who nodded. Finally she said, "Yes, Daddy! We're both fine! Aunt Aster saved our lives!"

"She likes cartoons, Daddy!" Jason said, a big grin on his face. "And cake!"

Relief flooded through me. It could all be some kind of ruse, some way for Aster and her soldiers to build trust with my children, but at least they hadn't hurt them, thank God. Aster turned to regard me with those purple eyes of hers. I nodded my thanks, then turned to Strohl. "Your Lady in Black certainly has my gratitude, but I owe Teledyne nothing. Now, what do you want?"

"We know you've returned to the city with weapons, enough weapons to tip the balance of power." Strohl spread his hands. "We would like to join you in this endeavor. Help us be rid of Obsidian for good."

"It wasn't Obsidian that nuked our hometown!" Danny growled.

Angry shouts of agreement rose up from the Mobile officers with us.

"Obsidian fired at us first!" Strohl snapped. "We had to retaliate."

"Is that the story you're going with?" I asked. "Last I checked, it looked like the blame could be cast either way. And I saw a lot more Teledyne nukes in the air than Obsidian missiles."

"Regardless," Strohl said, "we find ourselves at a crossroads, with one path leading to the destruction of all three of our factions, and the other leading to survival of the fittest. But, that will only work if one side joins the other. As it stands, all three factions are on equal footing. Join us. We'll bolster your defense of the university, and together, we can put down Obsidian and bring peace—real peace—to this city!"

"By using us as your frontline pawns?" Danny spat. "Meat for the grinder? Yeah, no thanks."

"How about we say to hell with both Corporations?" I placed a hand on my rifle. "Now, hand over my kids."

Strohl sighed. "Oh, I will hand them over. I always intended to. It's just the manner in which I did it that was in question. And it would seem you want them back a piece at a time rather than all at once. Inefficient, but I suppose it will have to do."

Aster stiffened noticeably. She very gently pulled her hands free from Jason's and Helen's grips and placed a hand on their shoulders. "That wasn't what we agreed on," she said.

"I don't recall agreeing to anything with you," Strohl said. "I told you to keep them safe, as in keep them in our custody. What we do with them is my business, not yours."

"You ordered me to protect them," Aster insisted. "And I will do just that."

Strohl's bodyguards tensed, as did the soldiers near Aster. Danny and I shared a look. What was going on?

"Yes, those *were* your orders, and you followed them to a tee. As a reward, you can carry out my next orders. Specialist Aster, I order you to—"

A gunshot rang out, and a round punched through the manager's throat.

Aster held a pistol in her hand that I swear wasn't there an instant before. She had drawn, aimed, and shot in less time than it took me to blink.

The manager grabbed his ruined throat, shock on his face, as blood poured between his fingers and stained his freshly pressed suit. He tried to speak, but only gargled gibberish came out.

"I'm sorry, sir," Aster said in that quiet voice of hers. "I couldn't make out what you said. What did you say my orders were?"

The bodyguards raised their weapons, but the soldiers who accompanied Aster fired first, ripping the suited men to shreds. One of the dying bodyguards got a round off and struck a soldier in the shoulder. Then it was over.

Jason and Helen cowered behind Aster, and it was only then that I realized she had pushed them behind her just before she drew her weapon. She approached the dying manager as he fell to his knees. She knelt next to him and looked him right in the eye. "Maitre D's file should've told you this: I don't hurt innocents. And if someone tries to order me to, I'll hurt them instead."

She stood up and turned away. Strohl reached out a hand toward her retreating back and then he fell flat on his face. He spasmed once and lay still, blood pooling around his neck and head.

She holstered her pistol and knelt in front of Jason and Helen. "It's all right," she said. "Go to your father."

Helen and Jason spun on their heels and ran across the pavement toward me. I jumped out of the saddle and knelt in time for them to leap into my arms. "Daddy, we were so scared!" Helen said between sobs.

"Scared? I wasn't scared!" Jason said. "Well, maybe a little. But, it was okay. Uncle Jake kept us safe and then Aunt Aster gave us cake!"

"Yeah, but Uncle Jake was taken by Obsidian!" Helen buried her face in my chest. "We couldn't do anything to protect him!"

My heart sank. At least he had been taken and not killed. I'm sure some of the other officers weren't as lucky. "It's all right now, guys," I whispered. I kissed the tops of their heads. "It's all right. I'm home, and I've got what we need to win this war."

"Nate," Danny said in a warning tone. "They're still here."

I looked up. Aster still stood there, flanked by her men. There were about twenty of them. Nervous murmurings rose up from the officers behind me. Aster, alone, could probably take on all of us, but with her famed Section Nine at her back, we didn't stand much of a chance if they wanted a fight.

"Maybe they want to join us?" I asked Danny.

"How can we trust them?" he hissed, his eyes never leaving Aster. "They're Teledyne!"

"Not anymore," I said with a pointed look at the dead Strohl and his bodyguards.

"It could all be a trick."

"That's a pretty lethal trick." Still, he had a point. How could they trust someone who had been a thorn in their sides? What was her real motivation?

Jason broke away from my embrace and looked up at me. "Aunt Aster's a good person, Dad. You'll see!"

And with that, he spun around and ran back across the pavement toward Aster.

Aster's eyes widened, and she knelt down again as Jason flung his arms around her neck. He hugged her fiercely, then scrambled up onto her back and sat on her shoulders. "She's real strong, Daddy! Look!"

Aster tried to look up at Jason, and the move nearly pitched him backward. He flailed his arms, then clamped his hands on her forehead. His fingers pressed into her scalp and pulled at her eyes, giving her an almost angry look. She sighed.

I couldn't help it. I laughed. And with that laughter, all the tension I'd felt these last couple days melted away. I laughed until tears ran down my cheeks and Helen looked at me funny, but that just made me laugh harder. She cracked a smile and started laughing. Then Jason laughed.

"I'm surrounded by weirdos," Danny muttered. Then he chuckled.

I stood up and scrubbed my eyes with one hand. I took Helen's hand with my other. "Come on, you can properly introduce us to your 'Aunt' Aster."

It may not be the right decision, but sometimes you have to take things on child-like faith in this Fallen World.

* * * * *

Chapter Thirty-Three

"Lieutenant Ward, the other commanders told me you were the kind of man who delivers," Sheriff Welliver said, "and they weren't wrong. Is that a .50 on that wagon?"

The sheriff had ridden out to greet us as our caravan turned into the university's southwestern entrance. With him were a number of Boone County deputies on foot, Lieutenant Blackwood and his Londoners on horseback, and Saleh and his Jordanians on camels. "Quite the international presence you've got there, sir," I said. "Expecting trouble?"

"Our spotters saw you coming up 163, then we heard the shots when you turned onto Mick Deaver. Figured you could use the backup…" His voice trailed off. "What have we here?"

Welliver stared at Aster as she came into view. She and her men marched in the center of the procession, surrounded by mounted officers. The Teledyne soldiers had surrendered their weapons, but that was small comfort where Aster was concerned.

"They're on our side," I said. "I think, anyway."

"You think?" Welliver raised an eyebrow. "I suppose you have a good reason?"

"Two good reasons. She saved my kids from Obsidian, then from Teledyne when her manager wanted to torture them to get to me."

"Jesus." Welliver shook his head. "Torturing kids? What's the matter with those people?"

"I don't know, but Aster did right by me. Gunned the manager down right in front of me, and her men finished off his bodyguards."

Welliver's eyebrows raised. "That does merit some consideration. We'll keep them under surveillance until I can meet with them."

"Keep her away from my men." Saleh glared at Aster. "I remember what she did to Corporal Hamdan's camel, and I don't want a repeat of it with mine."

"What about the weapons you obtained, Ward?" Welliver asked. "How'd it go?"

"Very, very well." I grinned. "I think you and the others will be pleased."

"Well, let's see," Welliver said. "We could do with some good news today."

He rode past to inspect the wagons. The others followed suit. Saleh hung back long enough to place a hand on Nathan's shoulder. "I feared for your children. Allah be praised."

Blackwood turned to look back. "Lucky turn, that. Glad they're safe, Nate!"

A lump formed in my throat, so I just nodded in response. It was good to have friends and comrades like them.

* * *

We met in the auditorium a few hours later, after weapons and ammunition had been distributed among the various units. Everyone with the rank of sergeant or higher who could be spared filled the auditorium to near capacity. I sat with Danny, Deputy Stewart, and Brother Stephen, who had limped in from the infirmary when he heard about the meeting.

"Pastor," Welliver said, "would you open our meeting with a word of prayer. We're in sore need of guidance today."

Stephen jumped to his feet and wobbled a bit as he put too much weight on his wounded leg. He steadied himself, then said, "Of course, Sheriff. Let's pray." He bowed his head. A number of other officers did as well, including me. "Lord, we thank you for the blessings you've bestowed upon us these last few days. Guide our discussions this hour, so we can make best use of the weapons provided to us by the good people of Boonville. Help us restore order to this city and carry out Your will here, on Earth. It is in your Son's Holy Name we pray. Amen."

"Amen," I murmured and heard the word repeated through the room.

"And thank you for painkillers," Stephen added as he flopped down into his chair.

I chuckled and patted Stephen on the shoulder as the rest of the room erupted in laughter.

Once the merriment died away, Welliver said, "Gentlemen, the last couple days have been eventful, to say the least." He pointed at the tabletop map, and I noticed how much things had changed. Both Obsidian's and Teledyne's territories had grown, spreading out and away from their respective headquarters. Obsidian controlled the northeast side of Columbia, and Teledyne the west. Both territories butted up against one another now, and lines had been drawn along that boundary to show how contested it was.

Their territories had also crept south. "Lieutenant Ward, you and your two travel companions may not be aware of this, but Obsidian really stepped up its game after you left." He picked up one of the APCs sitting near the Country Hotel and pushed it through the town, then out onto I-70, leading west from the city. "We believe they drove one of their APCs dangerously close to Teledyne Tower, hoping to intercept you before you reached the I-70 bridge."

"Man, was everyone tailing us?" Danny muttered.

"But they were held up in a skirmish somewhere along here." Welliver indicated a point on the map. "They were forced to turn back after engaging Teledyne soldiers. While that was happening, they sent their remaining APC to the north end of the university. Several Columbia and Philadelphia officers were captured."

And Jason and Helen were almost killed. A chill ran down my spine at the thought. I owed Aster more than I could ever hope to repay.

"The good news is that we've already agreed to trade our prisoners for theirs." He checked his watch. "We should have our officers back within the hour."

"It better be a five-to-one exchange in our favor!" one of the Columbia commanders shouted. "We're worth a lot more than any of those Corporate pukes!"

"My Miami boys will be there to facilitate the exchange," Lieutenant Alexander said. "I'll be joining them as soon as we're done here."

"Since their raid on the university, Obsidian has pulled back. The lack of pressure against us is worrying, but it may be because of what Teledyne's up to." He made a sweeping gesture of Teledyne's enlarged sphere of influence. "They now control the roads leading out of the city to the west and the northwest, and they're pushing into neighborhoods that—up to now—had been neutral and wanted nothing to do with any of us. More than one envoy has arrived requesting police protection." He smiled. "Isn't that how it always is, though? No one wants the cops until they need them."

"It's the same overseas, too!" Lieutenant Blackwood said amid a chorus of chuckles. "How about it, Saleh? You deal with that much?"

"Not to my face, no," Saleh said. "Then again, if you insult me, you insult my camel. And when you insult my camel, my camel spits. A lot."

The chuckles turned into outright laughter. Welliver smiled, but held up his hand for silence. "With the weapons Lieutenant Ward and his men requisitioned, our options have opened up quite a bit. We're now on equal footing, and that's got Teledyne and Obsidian nervous. I like when our enemies are nervous, as it shows they're weak. But, nervous people do stupid things, and that doesn't change at the Corporate level."

"What about the Specialist?" a sergeant from Lancaster called. "We hear she's on the university grounds."

"Yeah, what are we going to do about her?" another officer said. "It's making my people nervous!"

Welliver looked up at me for a moment, then said, "That's something for the captains and me to discuss. Let's just say we have it on good authority that she and her men have turned in their Corporate badges without the courtesy of a two-week notice."

The room erupted. Welliver held up his hand for silence. "Now, as for whose side they're on, that's anyone's guess. Like I said, the captains and I will discuss it soon. For now, she and her men will be kept under guard at the campus hospital while one of her soldiers is treated for a gunshot wound.

"More important than that," Welliver continued, "is that we now have a chance in this war against the Corporations. Return to your men and get ready. We're about to make a difference in this Fallen World."

*****

Chapter Thirty-Four

"I appreciate you coming along," Wendy Alexander said as they rode up the street. She stroked her horse's black mane. "Candace agrees."

Candace snorted.

"It's no problem at all." Danny's words came out harsher than he intended. He smiled to soften them. "Some fresh air will do me good."

"Haven't you had enough fresh air over the last few days?" She wrinkled her nose. "Well, fresh as it can get with horses around. Sorry, girl."

Candace snorted, and this time Danny could have sworn she sounded indignant.

"Hey, I think horses smell great." He leaned down and got a whiff of Noir's mane. "Mmm."

Alexander wrinkled her nose again. "Yeah, no thanks. I love animals, but never cared for their odor. It's why I don't own any dogs or cats. Dogs stink when they're wet, and litter boxes are gross."

"We'll just have to agree to disagree."

"So, what's the real reason you're out here?" Alexander leaned toward him. "Is it to get away from that Teledyne woman and her lackies?"

He looked at her, then chuckled. "I swear, you're as bad as Amy. She can always—*could* always—read me like a book."

She winced. "Sorry. I didn't mean to make you think of her."

"What doesn't make me think of her?" He sucked in a deep breath and expelled it in a rush. "It's all right. I'm slowly coming to terms with it."

They rode in silence for a couple minutes, the hooves of their horses and those of the men behind them clopping against the pavement.

"I don't trust her," Danny said after a moment. "She saved my niece and nephew, sure, but to what end? I doubt it was out of the kindness of her cold heart. And how do we know it wasn't a setup?"

"You think Teledyne let one of its middle managers die just so one of their people could infiltrate our ranks?"

"Life is cheap to the Corporations." He waved his free hand around to encompass the abandoned buildings, shattered storefronts, and bullet-riddled signs and masonry. "Case in point."

"Point taken. And just so we're clear, I have no love for the woman or her men either. I have two officers recovering in the hospital because of them, and I know I'm not alone." She grimaced. "It pains me that they're holding her in the same building."

"A soldier's courtesy. One of her men was wounded saving Nathan's kids." He looked around. "Now, where is this meeting supposed to take place again?"

"There's an abandoned comic shop near the corner of 10th and Walnut. It's big enough to carry out this kind of exchange, with all the empty floor space. We should be seeing it pretty soon."

They rode through a couple more intersections, past brick buildings ranging anywhere from three to eight stories in height. Danny scanned the upper story windows for threats. He spied movement in the window of an apartment building, then realized it was a little kid. The kid waved down at them. Danny smiled and waved back.

"My God," Wendy whispered. "Who is that?"

A figure stumbled toward them from further down the street. He was covered in blood from head to toe, but even with all the gore, Danny could tell he had a police officer's uniform on. He stumbled along as if drunk and dragged another officer by the collar of his uniform with his left hand. His right hand held a pistol, the slide locked back on an empty magazine.

As he got closer, Danny realized it was Jake Morris. He didn't recognize the officer he was dragging, but he knew they both needed help. He reined Noir in and dismounted. "Jesus, Jake, what happened?"

Morris looked up at him with dead eyes. "Danny? What's going on?"

"You tell me, brother." Danny knelt to examine the fallen officer. His shoulder patch identified him as a university officer. He was still breathing, but he looked pretty messed up. "Medic! Got one who needs your services, now!"

Danny led Jake to the bumper of a sedan and sat him down. He pried the pistol from his hands.

Alexander pulled Candace over next to him. "Is he one of the prisoners?"

"Yeah," Danny said.

"What happened? Where are the others?"

"Dead," Jake looked down at his bloody hands. "All dead."

"And the officers that came to do the exchange?"

"Them, too."

Alexander snapped her reins. "H'yah! Go!"

"Wait," Danny said. "Wendy, wait!"

She galloped down the street, her five Miami officers close behind. Danny waited long enough for the medic to dismount and begin tending to the fallen Columbia officer, then he climbed into Noir's saddle.

Up ahead, Alexander screamed.

"Stay with them," Danny said to the Philadelphia officers. He dug his heels into Noir's side.

He turned down Walnut and rode past a café called Ernie's. The comic shop was in the next building over. It took up the entire first floor and possibly the second, though from where he was, Danny couldn't tell. Three of the Miami officers who had accompanied them sat astride their mounts on the grass near the front door. Each held the reins of one of their comrades' mounts.

Noir's ears flicked back and forth. She snorted and backed up a step. Danny clicked his tongue and guided her forward. She grudgingly complied. He couldn't blame her for being nervous. Even he could smell the blood from here.

Danny slid from his saddle and handed his reins to one of the other officers. As he stepped onto the path to the front door, a fourth Miami cop stumbled out of the comic shop and vomited. Danny hesitated a moment, then stepped through the door into a scene of absolute carnage.

Blood soaked the carpeted floor, dripped from the ceiling, and splattered the walls. Rows of bookcases lay on their sides, their former contents spilled and soaked in crimson. The remains of God only knew how many men and women lay scattered all over the place. It would take a forensics team a week or more to match the parts and get an accurate count. Those that had died had been ripped apart, like rag dolls in the hands of a vengeful child.

Alexander knelt in the center of the room, amid a sea of severed limbs and spilled organs. Blood had soaked the knees of her pants through to the skin, and her hands were drenched where she had planted them in the wet carpet.

Danny's boots squelched on the carpet as he walked up beside her. He crouched down and placed a hand on her shoulder. The stench of blood and death nearly made him gag, but he mastered himself and said, "Wendy, come outside. You don't need to see this."

"It's Miami all over again," she said, her voice a whisper. Tears rolled down her cheeks. "This is what *they* did."

The hair on the back of Danny's neck stood on end. "Who?"

"Dear God, my men. My poor men." She started to place a hand to her mouth to stifle the sob that was about to come.

Danny grabbed her hand before she smeared blood all over her face. "Come with me, Wendy. You need to get outside."

"I should've been here with them!" The words came out half-strangled. She sucked in a deep breath, then broke down into sobs. "I should've been with them."

Rage built inside him. Obsidian had committed all manner of atrocities before, but this was beyond the pale. And the last straw had been seeing a fellow officer he respected, and even admired, reduced to this. "You didn't fail anyone, Wendy. It was Obsidian that did this, not you. We'll talk to Jake and figure out exactly who—"

"I know who did this!" She yanked her hand out of his grip and stared down at the blood on them. "It was the same then, Danny. This is what it looked like right after the Evidence Shredders came through."

A thrill of fear shot through Danny. If Obsidian had brought Geno Freaks with them from St. Louis, the cops were in for a world of hurt. Some of them were said to be more powerful than the nastiest imprinted Agents. "You really think they brought them here?"

"Look at this!" She pressed the clean backs of her hands against her eyes and scrubbed furiously. "And if it wasn't the Genos themselves, then it was their Agent handlers. The Agents—" She pressed a hand against her mouth and squeezed her eyes shut.

Danny hauled her to her feet and turned her away. "Let's get you into some fresh air," he said. "Before the stench gets to both of us."

She let him lead her toward the door. "The Agents—" She pressed the hand to her mouth again, and it was clear she was trying to keep from vomiting. "The Agents would do something like this to get the Genos' blood up. Get them excited and ready to tear into flesh. Once they were in a frenzy, they'd be unleashed. The Agents in charge had us on perimeter security in case any of their targets escaped, but none did. Not at any of the sites we guarded." She waved a hand over her shoulder, in the direction of the bodies. "That's why."

"My God," Danny said.

He led her across the street and sat her down on the high curb. He took his canteen from his saddlebag, along with a roll of paper towels, and helped her rinse her hands.

She had stopped crying, but he could tell the grief was still there, bubbling just below the surface. "I should've been there with them," she whispered.

Danny didn't say anything. He wanted to tell her that was silly, that she would've died, too. But, he knew he would've felt the same. If something happened to his brother or any of the men and women from Mobile, he'd want to be there with them, even if it meant sharing their fate.

Especially if it meant sharing their fate.

Danny walked back over to the Miami officers. "Guys, I'm really sorry any of us had to see this. We'll make Obsidian pay, don't you worry."

The officers mumbled agreement.

Danny took Noir's reins from the officer holding them. "Give the lieutenant a minute. Then we need to link back up with the others and get the two surviving officers back to the university. They both need medical attention."

He mounted and turned back to where Jake was. "Damn the Corporations," he muttered. "Damn them, and damn this Fallen World."

* * * * *

Chapter Thirty-Five

"It was awful, Nate." Jake sat on the edge of the hospital bed, idly picking at the IV needle stuck in his left hand. "They had us all in that store together, waiting for our boys to show up with the Obsidian prisoners."

I leaned against the wall. "So, the Miami and Philadelphia officers showed up with the Obsidian prisoners and then what?"

"That's where it gets a little fuzzy." Jake pressed his right hand to his forehead. "Things were real tense for a moment as the Obsidian soldiers guarding us counted us and compared our number to the number of prisoners Miami and Philly brought. There weren't as many Obsidian prisoners as there were cops.

"Then there was shooting and screaming and so much blood. Patrolman Wilson got hit and then the Obsidian soldier who shot him was killed."

I crossed my arms. "Was that the gun that was in your hand when Danny found you?"

"It certainly wasn't mine. I lost that when we were first captured." He rubbed his forehead. "That part's a bit fuzzy, too. I remember yelling for Jason and Helen to run, and then—" His eyes widened. "Are they all right? Nate, did something happen to your kids?"

I held up a hand. "They're fine, man. Relax."

His shoulders slumped, and he sighed. "Thank God. I don't know what I would've done if something had happened to them. Did they run for help?"

"Actually, no. They were cornered by a few Obsidian soldiers, but Specialist Aster saved them at the last second and took them into Teledyne custody." I held up my hand again. "Relax, they're fine. A Teledyne manager wanted to cut them into pieces, but it turns out the Lady in Black isn't keen on child mutilation and torture, so she handed the manager his severance package and released the kids to me."

"Shit." Jake shook his head. "Never thought I'd be grateful to a Teledyne Specialist, but I owe her a debt." He looked at me sharply. "So, where is this Specialist? Back at the Tower?"

"She's—"

The door flung open, and Jason ran in. "Uncle Jake!"

I intercepted him before he could throw himself at Jake. "Woah, there, cowboy. The man's injured. If you see someone in a hospital gown, you need to be gentle."

"Gown?" Jason wrinkled his nose. "That's for old ladies!"

Jake laughed. "Well, little guy, I feel like an old lady right now." He rubbed his eyes. "I'm exhausted."

Helen stepped into the room. "Hi, Uncle Jake," she said in a quiet voice. She smiled. "I'm glad you're all right."

"And I'm glad both of you are all right." He held out his arms. "Come on, give me a hug. But mind the IV."

I smiled as my kids embraced Jake. It was good to see him back. He and Patrolman Wilson were lucky to be alive after all they went through.

I needed to learn more about what happened while he was held captive, and what happened in that bookstore, but not with my kids around. Danny's description of the comic shop massacre was enough to make me sick, and I'd seen a lot in my years as a cop. I didn't want that for my kids. They'd seen enough already.

There would be time to discuss it when the other commanders got here. An emergency meeting had been scheduled after Jake requested that everyone attend so he could go over some critical information he learned during his captivity. He had always had sharp ears, and they had grown sharper during his time as an Obsidian soldier and then as a cop. And it looked like Obsidian had big plans for the city.

Jake spoke with Helen and Jason for the next several minutes. He told them a little bit about how he had been held captive and that their Uncle Danny had bravely rescued him from the clutches of some bad guys. "I got to beat up a couple of them, but Danny was the real star of the show," he said. "And his horse—"

"Noir!" Jason exclaimed.

"Noir even bit someone!" He placed a hand on his backside. "Right here, on the bottom!"

Helen laughed. "Ew, that's gross!"

I'd have to make sure Danny knew about this story so he could back it up. I smiled. Having kids was a lot of fun.

Helen turned for the door. "I'll be right back. I wanted to stop by the restroom on the way up, but *somebody* wouldn't let me." She glared over her shoulder at Jason.

Jason stuck his tongue out at her. "Get a bigger pee bag!"

I laughed. "Pee bag? It's called a bladder."

"What's the difference?"

"Well, nothing, I guess."

"Then it's a pee bag."

Helen rolled her eyes. "Boys." She slid the door shut and stomped off down the hall.

Jason sat on the bed and looked up at Jake. "So, did you kill anyone, Uncle Jake?"

"Jason!" I snapped. "You *never* ask someone that!"

Jason lowered his head. "Sorry," he mumbled.

Jake placed an arm around Jason's shoulder and pulled him close. "It's all right, little guy. It's natural to be curious. And when you're older, we can talk about those kinds of things, okay?"

"Okay," Jason said with a sniffle.

There was a knock, and the door slid open again. Several officers stood outside, including Sheriff Welliver, Captain Phillips, Captain Hsu, Captain DiAngelo, Captain Graham, and Captain Bradley. "Glad to see you're all right, Morris," Hsu said, a big grin on his face. "Unit's not the same without you keeping everyone in line."

"Yes, we're very glad you made it out of there," Bradley said. "And thank you for keeping Wilson safe. He's still in surgery, but the doctors are confident he'll pull through."

"Glad to hear it, sirs," Jake said. He had let go of Jason and had a hand to his forehead again.

I took Jason by the hand and helped him off the bed. "Sirs, give me a few minutes to hand my son off to my daughter, and I'll be right back."

"Very good, Lieutenant Ward," Welliver said. "We'll wait for you."

"I appreciate that. Excuse us."

"Aw, but I want to stay—" Jason started to whine.

"Hush." I pulled him out into the hall and shut the door. I glanced to the right. The hallway continued another thirty feet, ending in a window that showed the darkening sky. "Come along. Let's go find Helen, and the two of you can hang out in the lobby. Then we'll get dinner in the cafeteria."

Jason's expression brightened immediately. "The cake lady's down there! We can say hi!"

Cake lady? He must've meant Aster. I hadn't realized she was down in the lobby. I still wasn't sure how to feel about her. Even though she'd saved my kids' lives twice, she had turned her gun on my fellow officers before she turned it on Strohl. "If she wants to spend time with you, she will, but don't pressure her."

"Okay!"

Muffled shouts filled the corridor, followed by a hair-raising scream of pain and fear. I spun on my heel, pushing Jason behind me as I did.

The door to Jake's room exploded outward, followed by the headless body of one of the commanders. Judging by the uniform, it had to be DiAngelo.

"Run, Jason!" I drew my pistol and charged toward the room as more screams rose. Several gunshots rang out, but they ended abruptly with a loud ripping sound and a gargled scream.

I slid to a halt in front of the mangled doorway, weapon raised, focus on the front sight as I scanned the room for threats.

Sheriff Welliver lay on the ground, left hand clutching the stump of his right arm. It had been ripped from his body at the shoulder and lay discarded like a mangled piece of meat in the corner of the bloody room. Bradley lay in two halves nearby, his unmoving body torn apart at the midsection. And Hsu hung halfway out the broken window, unconscious.

Captain Graham leaned against the wall, pistol hanging from its lanyard, as he clutched at one of his eyes. The other eye was squeezed shut from pain.

In the center of the room stood Jake Morris. His hospital gown was spattered with blood, and his fingernails were caked in flesh and fabric. He flexed and contracted his fingers, and even over the sounds of the moaning officers, I could hear the joints popping. "Jesus," I whispered, a mixture of fear and revulsion flooding through me.

Captain Phillips swung his shock baton. Jake took the blow on the shoulder and flinched slightly as the buzzing baton arced electricity through him. Then he snatched it out of Phillips' hand with enough force to break his wrist. Before Phillips could register the pain, Jake turned the baton back around and stabbed it through Phillips' stomach and pressed the trigger.

The baton buzzed loudly, and Phillips screamed as thousands of volts shot through his body cavity.

"Jake!" I shouted. "What the hell is this?"

"Oh, Nate, good." Jake watched as Phillips slumped to the floor, then turned to face me. He grinned, but the expression didn't reach his cold, dead eyes. "I'm glad you came back, so I don't have to hunt you down." He bunched up his legs to spring at me.

I lined up my sights on his chest and started to squeeze the trigger—

"Stop!" a little voice cried.

Jason ran into the room, heedless of the blood and gore around him. "Uncle Jake, what are you doing? Stop!"

"Out of the way, Jason!" I shouted, my voice coming out as little more than an adrenaline-fueled squeak.

Jake Morris looked down at Jason. Gone was the kind, compassionate expression he had worn when talking with my kids just a few minutes ago. Now his eyes looked like I imagined someone's did when they regarded something beneath their notice, like an insect or a rodent.

He moved faster than I could see, the back of his fist slamming into Jason's chest with a resounding crack. Jason flew backward and smacked into the wall a few feet away. His tiny body struck hard enough to crack the sheetrock and then he fell flat on his face, where he lay, unmoving.

Before I could open my mouth to scream, Morris had cleared the distance between us. I twisted to avoid the fist aimed at my sternum and took it in the left shoulder. Morris's hand struck like a hammer blow. Something in my shoulder popped as I spun and crashed on top of DiAngelo's headless corpse.

The pain in my shoulder was enough to make my head swim. I raised my pistol and tried to squeeze off a shot, but he knocked it out of my hand. The gun sailed down the corridor. I reached for my ankle gun, but he already had it in his hand. I tried to go for my boot knife with my left hand, but my arm refused to move.

"Wanted to kill me with this, did you?" Morris asked. He shook his head and made a tsk sound with his tongue. "You're gonna have to be punished for that." He turned back toward the hospital room, the weapon aimed at Jason's unconscious form.

Fear jolted through me, dulling the agony in my shoulder. I tried to push myself to my knees, but my right hand slipped in Jackson's blood, and I crashed to the floor again. I cursed and tried again. "Don't go near him!" I shouted.

He looked over his shoulder at me. "Come on, Nate, I promise it won't hurt—"

And then a small, white-haired form tackled him. It was Aster!

Morris and Aster flew down the hallway. Morris fell flat on his back but managed to kick her off him and jump to his feet. She landed on all fours in front of him. He raised my backup revolver and emptied the five .357 magnum rounds in a blink.

Aster leapt out of the way of the bullets and sprang off the nearby wall. Her boot struck Morris in the face. He slid back several feet. She bent down and scooped something up off the floor. It was my duty pistol, sitting where Morris had knocked it a moment ago.

Morris danced back down the hall as Aster fired. Whereas he had tried for the quick kill at pointblank range, Aster was more deliberate. She still emptied the fifteen-round magazine in less than a few seconds, but she took the time to aim at her retreating target.

One of the .45 rounds struck Morris in the shoulder. He spun on his heel and sprinted down the hall. Another of Aster's rounds tore into his back, but it didn't slow him a bit. He held his arms over his face and jumped through the glass window at the end of the hallway.

Aster ran after him as the sound of shattering glass filled the air. She aimed the pistol out the window and fired five more times, until the slide locked back on an empty magazine. She dropped the gun and put her hands to the broken-out window frame, as if she were going to jump, too.

I sat up and groaned at the pain in my shoulder.

Aster hesitated, then turned and ran back toward me. "I knew he reeked of Obsidian," she said as she extended a hand to help me up.

I waved her off and pointed into the room. "Get the doctors," I said as a fresh wave of pain struck me hard enough to make my head swim. "The others need more help than I do. Jason—"

At mention of Jason, her head snapped to the left to look in the room. Her eyes widened, and her mouth opened. "No," she whispered.

In the blink of an eye, she was at my son's side. She felt up and down his body, particularly around his neck. She then rolled him over onto his back and peeled back his shirt to examine his chest. His entire torso was one big mass of purple skin. Blood ran down his side, and it was only then that I realized one of his rib bones was sticking out.

She scooped him up and ran out of the room and down the corridor, each bound of her tiny legs eating up yards instead of feet. "Medic!" she screamed. "Medic!"

I stood and started to follow, but stopped to look in the room. I hesitated, then reached into a pouch on my gun belt. Aster would get Jason to the right people, and she'd get help for the commanders. At the moment, I was all the commanders had.

"Please, God, keep him safe," I whispered as I withdrew a tourniquet from the pouch and approached Welliver. "He's one of the only people I have left in this Fallen World."

* * * * *

Chapter Thirty-Six

"Dad!" Helen ran into the room, followed closely by Danny. He tried to grab her, but it was the nurse checking my vitals who intercepted her.

"Honey, you need to give your daddy some space," she said in a soft, soothing tone. "He's been hurt, and he can't have you hanging off him like I know you'd like to. Can you go easy on him?"

Helen looked from the nurse to me, her eyes wide. She nodded. "Okay."

"That's my girl." The nurse patted Helen on the head.

I shrugged at her, then grimaced. My left arm hung in a sling. I could actually move it now, but it hurt like hell to do so.

"Your shoulder's been reset, Mr. Ward." The nurse leveled a finger in my face. "Don't go messing it up again, or the doctor won't be pleased. And if she's not pleased, none of us nurses are pleased. And that means none of our patients are gonna be pleased." She leaned close, her eyes narrowing. "You don't want that."

"Yes, ma'am," I said, shrinking back slightly. Why were some nurses so aggressive? "Can I go see my son?"

"You can sit in that bed until you're told you can leave," she snapped. Then her expression softened. "I've left instructions for the surgeon to call me as soon as he's finished. Jason's condition is serious, but he's improving by the minute. I can assure you of that."

"Thank God." My shoulders sagged with relief.

Aster stepped into the room, quiet as a mouse. Danny looked up at her sharply, but said nothing. He placed himself between Helen and Aster, his body canted so that his gun was well out of reach of the Teledyne Specialist.

"Amen," the nurse said. She smiled and looked around the room. "I'll leave you to your family."

"Oh, I'm not—" Aster started to say, but the nurse was gone, moving fast enough to keep pace with the Specialist, it seemed.

"Thank God you're all right, man," Danny said. He gripped my good shoulder. "When we heard what happened, we thought the worst."

"Is Jason okay, Dad?" Helen asked. She started to climb up into the bed, then remembered the nurse's admonition and stood back.

I leaned over far enough to take her hand and squeeze it. "Jason's going to be fine," I said, with more assurance than I actually felt at the moment. I prayed the Lord wouldn't turn me into a liar.

"Is it true Uncle Jake hurt him?"

I sighed. The truth would come out sooner or later. "It's true. Something's not right with Uncle Jake, and he did some very bad things to some very good people." I pointed at my shoulder. "I got off easy compared to the others."

She sniffled, and tears started to run down her face. "Why would he do that? He's such a nice man!"

Danny grimaced, an expression I knew I must've worn on my face, too. "He's sick, honey," was all I could think to say.

She sobbed and threw herself into Danny's arms. He pulled her into a tight embrace and smiled. "Easy, girl. Easy."

I smiled. Despite everything, it was good to see Helen. For a brief moment, in that hallway, I'd been sure I'd never see her again.

Aster had remained in the corner of the room, her right hand crossed over her body, gripping her left arm at the elbow. She looked like a lost puppy.

"Helen, it was Aster who saved me." I pointed. "She swooped in and chased Uncle Jake off before he could hurt us any further."

Helen looked at Aster, her eyes wide. Then she sobbed and wrapped her arms around Aster's waist.

Aster stroked Helen's hair. "It's okay," she whispered. "It's okay. I won't let him hurt any of you ever again."

Danny leaned in close. "Did she really help?" he whispered.

"I'd be dead without her. So would Jason and the other commanders. He meant to kill all of us."

"Why would he do that?" Danny demanded, his voice suddenly loud. He looked back at Helen, but the girl still had her face buried in Aster's chest. "Why would he do that?" he asked in a quieter voice.

"That's what I'd like to know," a voice from the door said.

Captain Graham leaned against the door frame. One of his men had provided him with another uniform shirt, which he'd buttoned up to the collar. Heavy bandages wrapped the right side of his head, covering the eye damaged by the IV needle. "Should you be up and about?" I asked. "Lack of depth perception and all that?"

"I've walked into a few things, but I need to get used to it." He touched the bandages and frowned. "Doc says I'll be wearing this for a while. They extracted the needle, but they're waiting on the specialist to arrive and examine me before doing anything else. That could be a couple hours, and we need action."

Helen sniffled loudly, and Graham turned his head fully to the right so he could see Aster. "Ma'am, we owe you our lives. Thank you for what you did."

"I should've been faster," Aster said. "I should've kil—I should've dealt with him weeks ago, when I sensed what he was."

"What is he?" Danny demanded. "What did those bastards do to him when they captured him?"

"He's an Agent," Aster said.

"Impossible." Danny shook his head. "You can't become an Agent overnight."

"He's always been an Agent." She looked from Danny to me. "Have either of you noticed anything strange about his behavior or abilities? Unnaturally quick reflexes, overly keen senses, amazing accuracy with firearms, an insatiable appetite?"

"Well, he's always had an appetite," I said. "And sharp hearing. And he's a crack shot. But, he's always been that way! Ever since we were kids. Right, Danny?"

"Yeah," Danny muttered, his eyes distant.

"Besides," I went on, "he was only at Obsidian for four years before joining the PPD. Would they really let an Agent go after so short a time?"

Aster didn't say anything. She just continued to stare at Danny, who chewed his lower lip for a moment before saying, "The Slipped Mask. Shit." He glanced at Helen, but she didn't seem to have noticed.

"Slipped Mask?" Graham frowned. "Is that supposed to mean something?"

"Code for a secret project of Obsidian's." Danny crossed his arms and leaned against the wall. "Years back, there was this JalCom facility we raided, or tried to. Met a lot of fierce resistance, and it turned into a siege. Things got bad, and we requested the intervention of an Agent. I overheard my commander talking to HQ, and HQ mentioned something about an Unknown Mask about to be activated.

"We held back, and after about fifteen minutes, we heard a lot of gunfire coming from inside the compound. We stormed the place, only to find most of the enemy dead, killed by an Agent of ours who had infiltrated the facility. We would've shot him, too, as he was wearing the uniform of a JalCom security platoon commander."

"A spy or assassin?" Graham asked. "That matches what Specialist Aster was saying about Lieutenant Morris."

My stomach twisted. "Are you saying Jake was always working with Obsidian? This whole time?"

"Well, that's the weird thing," Danny said. "The Agent in the JalCom uniform held up his hands and surrendered to us. At first, we thought he was just another enemy officer, and we treated him accordingly. Then this suit from high up the ladder arrived and pulled him aside. She whispered something into his ear, and suddenly his whole demeanor changed. He broke the manacles we had him in like they were nothing and left with her without a glance in our direction."

"A sleeper," Aster murmured. "We always suspected Obsidian had sleeper Agents."

"What do you mean?" I asked.

"Agents who have their personalities suppressed until they're triggered. Intelligence theorized they were used for deep undercover ops, as well as for experimentation to see just how far imprint technology could be pressed."

"Yeah, exactly," Danny said. "At the time, I thought the Agent was just jerking us grunts around. But another time, when we were escorting some eggheads from Corridor 13, one of the advanced science departments, they were talking about this very thing."

Graham chuckled. "You overhear a lot of things, Sergeant."

"It pays to hear things. Those on the higher rungs often forget about us at the bottom. And when they don't tell us something, it's our asses that get burned."

Helen looked over at him. "Language, Uncle!"

"Sorry, girl."

"It's okay." She sank to the floor and pulled Aster down with her. Then she leaned back into the Specialist's lap. She looked at him beneath heavy lids. "Just don't say it again."

"I'll try. No promises, though." To the rest of us, Danny said, "The researchers were talking about the possibility of completely splitting an imprint's personality from the personality of the host body. The technical aspects of the discussion were way above my pay grade, but it sounded like they wanted to keep the host's personality intact while the imprint was active, to see what sort of memories were retained when an Agent was active." He looked down at Aster. "I imagine you would know more about all that."

"A little," she said. "Specialists and Agents go through a very similar augmentation process, but the similarities end with the physical. Imprinters allow Agents to learn new skills immediately and to trade personalities. Specialists learn much like any other soldier or martial artist. We train, we study, and we apply those skills." She squared her shoulders. "We don't cheat like Obisidan scum, in other words."

"I can appreciate that," I said.

Aster looked down at Helen's sleeping form. "Based on the brutality of the attack, Morris is either a Berserker or an Assassin. And he was sent back from Obsidian with the express purpose of luring most or all of the police commanders into one location so he could kill them." Her eyes narrowed, and she clenched her fists. "If only I'd been there. If only I'd had my weapons."

"It wasn't your fault," Graham said. "We didn't trust you enough for either, yet." He glanced at me. "I'm still not sure we do, at least as a whole. Regardless, you have my thanks. You took a bad situation and kept it from getting worse. That counts for something in my book."

Danny looked away, a dark look on his face.

A wave of fatigue hit me suddenly, and I leaned back against my pillows. Graham must have noticed, because he said, "We'll talk more about this later. I'm going to arrange a meeting with as many of the remaining commanders as I can muster, but not until you get some rest. I also need to see if that surgeon's back yet and find a pirate outfitter." He tapped the bandage lightly. "I have a feeling I'm going to need a kick-ass eye patch. Sorry, Helen."

"S'okay," Helen slurred sleepily. "Pirates are cool."

Graham chuckled. "On that, we agree."

"I need to see to my men," Aster said. "Morris could be back at any time. It's likely he retreated to Hotel Obsidian, but we can't be too careful."

Danny reached down and took Helen from Aster's lap, then set her in the chair next to the bed. She stirred, but didn't wake.

I closed my eyes and was out like a light.

* * *

Danny stayed in Nathan's room long enough to tuck his brother and niece in, then he stepped out into the hallway. He nodded to Patrolman Williams and Corporal Collins, both of whom had volunteered for guard duty outside their commander's room. "Keep them safe."

"Will do, Sarge," they said in unison.

As he walked, he tried to undo the knot of emotions sitting deep in his chest. So much had changed in just a few, short hours. His nephew was on the operating table, in critical condition. His brother was wounded and in a hospital bed. Several commanders he had grown to respect and call friends were dead or grievously injured. And all of this had been carried out by one of his and Nathan's best friends.

And if all that wasn't bad enough, the only person they could rely on at the moment was a Teledyne attack dog.

He stopped and slammed his fist against the wall. The sound reverberated through the corridor, loud enough to make a nurse jump and drop the clipboards she was carrying. She glared up at him. "Hey—" she started to say.

"Sorry." He stomped past her and entered the stairwell. He trudged down to the ground floor, his boots echoing in the stairwell. He clenched his teeth so tight that his jaw ached.

He stepped out into the lobby and saw *her*. There was no mistaking the white hair, the gray-and-blue urban camo fatigues that clung very nicely to her curvy frame, and the intensely purple eyes that roved across the room, assessing threats, angles of attack, and avenues of retreat. She stood near an empty set of benches, one hand pressed to her ear. She spoke so quietly he couldn't make out what she was saying, but he knew she had to be talking to her men.

At least someone still had radios, but that posed a problem. If she had one, chances were the rest of Teledyne did too. Lack of reliable communication had plagued the officers for weeks, and the enemy had had good radios the whole time. He clenched his teeth even tighter.

Damn them. His hand strayed to his pistol. *Damn her.*

He glared at her for a long moment, and he feared his rage would boil over beyond his control. He knew he wouldn't be able to kill her, and that fueled his anger even more. He couldn't stop her if she suddenly showed her true colors, just like he couldn't protect Nathan when Agent Morris had shown *his* true colors. Nor had he been able to protect his nephew or his niece when they were attacked by Obsidian.

Damn me for not being there.

His anger fled in a great rush, like a balloon deflating. His gun hand relaxed, and he took a deep breath.

He stepped over to Aster as she dropped her hand from her ear. She studied him, and his pulse quickened. Had she sensed his killing intent? It had been so strong, he could practically taste her blood.

"Ma'am," he said, "I want to thank you. You saved my brother's life, and my nephew's."

Aster's eyes narrowed, and she clenched her fists. "No. I was too late. I heard the screams, but I couldn't run fast enough."

"You were in the lobby, four floors down." Danny chuckled bitterly. "I'd have only made it to the first landing by the time it was all over. Same with the rest of us. We would have arrived in time to bag bodies." That was the story of a cop's life on some days.

"I should've protected him," Aster whispered. "I promised I would keep him safe. Him and Helen."

"You really care for them," Danny said. "Why? You barely know them."

"I don't want Obsidian to destroy any more families." Her expression hardened. "I don't want anyone else to go through what I went through."

Danny felt a pang of guilt. He had never been part of any action that directly targeted civilians, but he knew there was often collateral damage in urban engagements, and a lot of Corporate actions took place in cities. "Corporate raid that went bad?"

"Or good, depending on the side you're on. Obsidian attacked my family's apartment complex when a Teledyne upper manager was visiting a neighbor. They leveled the whole building and wiped out half the city block during their extraction." She looked down at her hands. "I was only eight at the time. My whole family was killed, and I was saved by a Teledyne soldier. He took me in and taught me how to fight. Two years later, I joined the company's security force and eventually entered the Specialist program."

So, that was how the Battle Flower had bloomed. Danny knew she was the youngest to ever successfully complete the treatment and training to become a Specialist, but he'd had no idea about the rest of her past.

A bright light flashed in the distance, illuminating the darkened cityscape. Seconds later, a deep rumble rattled the waiting room windows. Patients and visitors looked up, and more than one pointed and screamed.

"That's Teledyne Tower," Aster said, her eyes fixated on the inferno.

"Obsidian?"

"Without a doubt." She pressed her hand to her ear. "Yes, I see it. The penthouse? Was Director Ingersoll inside? Understood. Rico, monitor the situation on the encrypted tac network. They'll probably change the frequency soon, so get as much information as you can. The rest of you, stay vigilant. This could be a diversion to let the Agent infiltrate again."

"Your men are guarding the hospital?"

"As well as we can without weapons," she said with no hint of reproach in her tone. She looked at him. "You may want to inform your commanders that Director Ingersoll has been assassinated."

"No shit?" Danny whistled as he watched the fireball in the distance. "Well, thank Heaven for small favors in this Fallen World."

* * * * *

Chapter Thirty-Seven

"You have some balls," Manager Kazama said. The Teledyne official crossed his arms and stared down his nose at Lloyd. "You attack our Tower, then want to negotiate?"

"That was just a wake-up call for a fellow business rival," Lloyd said. "Did Director Ingersoll get my message?"

The two men stood about thirty feet away from one another, in a parking garage equidistant between Teledyne Tower and Hotel Obsidian. Each was surrounded by a squad of their toughest fighters. Well, almost. Lloyd had left Agent Morris back at the hotel to recover from his gunshot wounds. He would be healed by the time their operation took place in a couple of days.

But, before that could take place, Lloyd had one more deal to close.

"I'm not authorized to answer that," Kazama said after a moment. He adjusted his glasses with his middle finger. "Especially not to you."

No need, I already know he's dead. Lloyd was in such a good mood, he let the rude gesture slide without complaint. He had seen the missile's camera footage. It hadn't been fired until it was confirmed Ingersoll was in his bedroom, balls deep in the ass of one of his pretty little legal aides, as he had liked to call his floozies. They'd aided in something…

Lloyd felt a small bit of remorse for the woman's death. Not out of any sense of chivalry, of course. Worrying about the weaker sex wasn't profitable, in money or in life. But, no one deserved to die with a disgusting little weasel like Ingersoll breaching her backdoor. At least her body had been burned up in the inferno.

"So, am I to assume you're in charge until Ingersoll is no longer indisposed?" Lloyd asked. "Can I negotiate my proposed pact with you?"

"Proposed pact?" Kazama looked incredulous. "With you? Whatever for?"

"Why, to wipe out the police holding the university, of course." Lloyd spread his gloved hands. "They've been a thorn in both our sides for weeks, keeping us from wresting control of the city. It's bad business for two obviously superior rivals to have their dealings constantly interrupted by petty amateurs."

Kazama smirked. "Those *petty amateurs* turned back your recent assault on the university, if I recall."

Lloyd felt a flash of annoyance. "We left because we wanted to." Then he returned the smirk. "And what about you? I hear you lost one of your upper managers the other day, to your own Specialist, no less. Where is she now? Keeping an eye on us? Or is she at the university, sucking the long dick of the law now that you lost your hold over her?"

"Again, I'm not authorized to tell you."

That confirmed Agent Morris's report and explained why the elite Berserker had only partly succeeded in his mission. Still, he had carried out his orders to the letter: pursue the targets unless resistance was so stiff there was a chance he could be killed. Then, he was to return to base and prepare for the next mission.

If he had wanted to, Lloyd could have ordered Morris to fight until he was literally cut into pieces, much like how he left his victims. And Lloyd relished that kind of power. More than money, more than exotic vacations, and more than a night of carnal bliss with the most beautiful women, what he loved most was power. And not just the power to command thousands of Obsidian employees on a whim. That kind of power was cheap, something even lower level managers at Obsidian had access to. But, the power to order an individual to take his own life, to dismember his own body, or to dismember the bodies of his closest friends and family members, and to have them thank you for the privilege and honor of the task? *That* was real power. *That* was the kind of stuff that made him hard enough to drive nails.

He looked forward to the day he could order Morris to do just that, but that wouldn't be for years to come. Agents weren't as plentiful now as they had been a few weeks ago, and if he wanted to maintain and grow his power base, he would need Morris and any other Agents he could acquire. It really was a shame the ones with him in St. Louis had died in the Teledyne strike.

Kazama shifted uncomfortably. Lloyd smiled but kept his silence. He had found there was strength in quiet moments, especially in aggressive negotiations. The tension from both sets of bodyguards was palpable.

At last, Kazama broke the silence. "What would this pact entail?"

Gotcha. "Working together to wipe out the police in one fell swoop. There was an incident late yesterday afternoon, and a number of their leaders were killed or so badly injured they might as well be dead.

"That's…promising." Kazama tried to hide his excitement, but the way his shoulders tensed and his eyes widened slightly told Lloyd all he needed to know. "So, we work together to eliminate the cops. And then what?"

"We'll continue our war the way we always have."

Kazama laughed. "Are you always this honest in your negotiations?"

"Only with people I respect."

Kazama scoffed, and for a moment, Lloyd thought he had pressed too far. Then Kazama said, "I think we can make this work. If we both know the fight will continue the moment the last cop dies, we won't have to worry about a doublecross happening."

"Exactly. We can work together with full understanding. And I think you know who our primary target should be."

"Specialist Aster." Kazama grimaced. "She will need to be dealt with immediately."

"Once she's gone, the police lose their ace in the hole." *And once she's gone, I can send Morris in to kill all of you.*

Kazama thought about it for a moment, then nodded. He walked forward, his guards hanging back a few steps.

Lloyd walked forward as well, and they met between both groups of guards. Kazama held out his hand, and Lloyd grasped it. The Teledyne manager's grip was firm and sure. "Deal," Kazama said.

"Pleasure doing business with you," Lloyd said. He tightened his grip. "Now, come with me, and we'll earn us some blue scalps."

Kazama's eyes widened. "With you? I'm needed back at the Tower."

Lloyd raised his other hand, and a dozen Obsidian soldiers appeared, their weapons trained on Kazama's surprised guards. "Director Greenway insists you pay her a visit. The two of you can coordinate our joint strike together from the comfort and safety of the Country Hotel."

Kazama glanced around the garage, a look of outrage on his face. Then he sighed. "If you insist, very well. I wouldn't want you to beg."

Lloyd grinned. Sometimes amicable business deals could still be had in this Fallen World.

* * * * *

Chapter Thirty-Eight

Countess trotted out of the stable, dragging the poor stable hand along with her. She slammed into me with her head and knocked me off balance. I groaned at the pain in my shoulder, then laughed. "Easy, girl, easy!"

Countess didn't go easy. She hooked my shoulder with her chin and pulled me in for a fierce hug. I wrapped my good arm around her neck and squeezed. She nickered softly, then backed away and butted me with her head again.

"Stand still a moment, girl. I want to get a good look at you." Countess obeyed, and I took a moment to walk around her. Her coat of calico hair practically gleamed in the morning light. When I squatted down and looked at her stomach, I couldn't see any trace of the wound that had nearly killed her. Even the parts of her abdomen that had been shaved for surgery were now covered in white and brown hair.

"Damn, those nanites really do their job," I said.

"They sure do, sir." The stable hand grinned. "Seen 'em in action a couple times before, and the results are amazing." He looked to the left, and his mouth fell agape. "It's *her*."

Aster walked across the yard between the three stables. When she was about thirty feet away, Countess broke free of the stable hand's grasp and cantered toward the Specialist. Aster froze, her purple eyes growing wide.

"Countess, get back here!" I jogged after the horse. Memories of a camel getting punched in the face rose in my mind. "Aster, it's all right! She won't hurt you!"

Countess slid to a stop inches from Aster and bent down to smell her. Aster backed away, and Countess followed, nostrils flared.

I caught up to them, grabbed Countess's lead rope, and put myself between the two of them. "Countess, back off. She's a friend, but she doesn't like it when you get too close." To Aster, I said, "Sorry if she startled you." Then I realized how silly that sounded. This was Aster we were talking about. Nothing ruffled her feathers.

Aster backed several feet away. "Th-thank you," she stammered.

Was she nervous? "Are you all right?" Realization hit me. "Wait, did Countess really startle you?"

Aster's alabaster cheeks colored. "No. I just don't like horses."

I cracked a smile. "Sounds like you're afraid."

"I'm not afraid!"

"Then why don't you like them?"

Aster crossed her arms and looked down at her feet. "They're big."

"Have you ever ridden one?"

She looked up at me, aghast. "That's way too high up."

Now it was my turn to look aghast. "I've seen you leap more than thirty feet through the air, and others said you can scale the side of a building like you're Spider-man."

"That's different!"

I couldn't help it. I laughed. This was not the way I expected this conversation to go.

Her face burned a brighter shade of pink. "When you're done laughing, we have something important to talk about."

That brought me up short. "Sorry. It's just...I didn't expect you to be afraid of anything."

Her hands clenched her biceps. "I'm afraid of many things. Like our chances of surviving the next forty-eight hours if we don't act now."

I let the stable hand take Countess's reins. "What do you mean?"

She tapped her earpiece. "We lost communication with the Tower a short while ago, but not before hearing about a new deal. Teledyne and Obsidian have joined forces for the express purpose of wiping you out. If we don't respond aggressively, we will lose."

"Shit," I muttered. "I had wondered if they would get desperate enough to team up. Strohl certainly seemed to realize it was a good idea."

I asked her, "You said 'our chances.' I take it you and Section 9 want to join forces with us?"

"If you'll have us." She frowned slightly. "We should have joined up with you a long time ago. For that, I'm sorry."

"Let's go see Captain Graham and come up with a plan. We have a meeting in an hour."

"Very well." She paused. "How do you suppose your fellow officers will take this?"

I sighed. "I have a good idea of how they'll react."

* * *

"She put Jerry in the hospital!"

"Her men shot up one of our only remaining squad cars!"

"She hamstrung my horse and nearly killed me!"

Aster stood next to me on the auditorium's floor, her feet shoulder-width apart and hands clasped behind her back in a perfect parade rest stance. She stared straight ahead as the officers seated above hurled accusations her way.

I'd known they would react poorly to her presence in the strategy session, so I gave them time to vent. Captain Graham sat behind me at Welliver's desk in a chair to the side of the wounded sheriff's empty one.

After a moment, I held up a hand. "I understand everyone's concerns. Believe me, I do. But, the fact of the matter is Aster has gone above and beyond in the last twenty-four hours to aid us."

Graham stood. "I'm living proof, as is Lieutenant Ward." He touched the bandages swathing the right half of his face. "If not for her, I'd be missing more than an eye."

The room fell silent. Even the officers with legitimate complaints against Aster had nothing to say. Word had spread like wildfire about Jake Morris's betrayal and about her intervention in the assassination of the police commanders. No one could argue. "But, it still doesn't change the fact that her people have shot at us," Lieutenant Wendy Alexander said.

"She has a point, LT," Danny said. He stared down at us, a hard look in his eye. "It's not enough that she shot her own manager and switched sides, nor is it enough that she saved some of our commanders. She still needs to prove herself."

"She shot her own manager?" one of the officers muttered.

"I thought what she did to us was bad," another whispered. "How can we trust someone who shot her own commander?"

"Aren't all of you under similar oaths?" Aster asked, her quiet voice cutting through the rising murmur. "To honor and uphold what is right, and to not follow an unlawful order?" She lifted her chin to look at her accusers. "I did what was right, nothing more."

Don't make me kill you. The words and the look in her eyes came back to me again, stronger than it had before. "I think she can be trusted," I said.

"Lieutenant Ward," Saleh said, "I appreciate your position, considering she was the one who saved your children. But, that doesn't change the fact that—"

"It's not just my kids," I said before Saleh could go on or anyone else could jump in. "Back when we first fought against Teledyne and Obsidian, I tried to bring down her boss. She knocked me off my horse and put a knife to my neck. She had the chance to kill me right then and there, but she didn't. And of all your complaints, not one of them involved the death of an officer or an animal at her hands or the hands of her men. They only fought us when we attacked them."

"Are you saying we're in the wrong for shooting Teledyne's soldiers?" Blackwood asked. "That we started it?"

"No, I'm not saying that at all. What I'm saying is that Aster's actions to this point have been purely defensive." I looked around the room. "Has Aster killed any of us? I can't recall. As far as I know, the only people she's killed have been Obsidian soldiers and that piece of crap Teledyne manager who wanted to *carve* my children up into pieces to get me to side with them in their stupid, insane war against Obsidian.

"I'm not saying we should blindly trust her or her people. But, their actions to this point lead me to believe we should give them a chance. And more importantly, we need them if we're going to defeat the combined might of both Corporations."

"Combined might?" Saleh frowned. "What do you mean?"

Aster reached up and tapped her earpiece. "They've joined forces. Manager Kazama of Teledyne and Directors Greenway and Lloyd of Obsidian. They mean to make a move against the university in the next two or three days, once Agent Morris heals."

An uncomfortable silence descended on the room. Officers looked around at each other, and more than one muttered, "Well, shit."

"Teledyne has the numbers, and Obsidian has their APCs and, now, an Agent," I said. "If we wait until they've consolidated their forces, our attack will fail and we'll die. If we wait here and try to wage the battle defensively, we'll die." I walked over to the tabletop map and placed my hand on the Country Hotel. "Our only hope is to strike while the iron is hot. Take the hotel, capture Obsidian's leaders, and force them to stand down. Then we either negotiate with Teledyne or we take the fight to them."

"And you're saying we need this Specialist to help us with this plan?" Saleh asked.

"She will act as a check against Agent Morris once he reveals himself." A wave of bitterness hit me, but I pushed it down. "It's her job to neutralize him, whatever it takes."

"For what it's worth," Graham said, "I agree with the plan." He held up a document. "Captain Phillips, Captain Hsu, and Sheriff Welliver were briefed in their hospital beds, and all three have given their blessings to this plan, as have I."

That forestalled any further objections. "Ladies, gentlemen," I said. "This is our chance to really take the fight to the enemy. Our goal was always to bring down the Corporations and restore order to this city, and now we can. Let's get this done and bring true justice to this Fallen World."

* * * * *

Chapter Thirty-Nine

"Excellent work getting the Teledyne leadership under our thumbs." Director Greenway held up a half-full wine glass in salute.

Lloyd held up his own. "Ma'am, you honor me. I was just closing a deal, nothing more. A deal that will end up with us controlling the whole city." *And with my controlling a whole lot more.*

Greenway drained her glass, then held it out to the side, her finger pointed at one of three bottles in the room: one chilled in a bucket of ice, one resting in a bucket of warm water, and one sitting on a table. A servant snatched up the chilled white wine and refilled her glass. She swirled the clear liquid as she gazed at Lloyd, her expression inscrutable. "So, when do you plan to betray me?"

The guards standing at her back tensed. A thrill of fear shot through Lloyd. Had he been so obvious? He put on his best smile. If honesty had worked with Manager Kazama, then it could work here, too. "You would be a casualty I could easily explain away to the men. Teledyne backstabbing, a stray round from the police. Something to get your most loyal servants' blood up so I could send them into the meat grinder."

Greenway threw back her head and laughed. "I appreciate your forthrightness. It's a rarity the higher one gets in this company." She sipped her wine. "Stand with me, and we'll rule this land together."

Lloyd's mind raced at the possibilities. He certainly could make great strides as her second-in-command. Once his plan was set in motion and the police and Teledyne dealt with, they could establish a power base in this city, expand out into the wild, and unlock the secrets JalCom had left here. It could be a very good partnership.

There was just one problem. Why should he be subordinate himself to her and not the other way around? The one with the most power should rule, and the one with the most power was the one with the most knowledge. And that person wasn't Gwen Greenway.

Of all the managers and executives in this city from either Corporation, Lloyd was the only one who had any knowledge of JalCom's prior activities and investments in Columbia, and he'd only learned of them after interrogating a former JalCom employee they had found hiding out in St. Louis. The poor bastard had been killed in the Teledyne strike, much to Lloyd's annoyance. The man hadn't told them everything he needed to know, only that there was something—

The door burst open, and a guard ran in. "Ma'am, trouble!"

Greenway's hand froze with the glass at her lips. She arched an eyebrow over the glass's round rim.

The guard took that as a signal to continue. "It's the police! They're massing just beyond our west perimeter. Dozens of them on foot and a few in vehicles—" He pressed a hand to his ear. "And just as many on horseback coming from the south and east!"

Lloyd ground his teeth. They'd acted a lot more quickly than he thought they would. It should've been days before they had the stomach to fight, not hours.

Greenway looked at him. "I'd say your timetable is a little off, wouldn't you?"

Was she a mind reader? Lloyd took a deep breath and nodded. "I'll have Kazama mobilize his people, then get Agent Morris ready."

"And I'll head upstairs and see to the defenses." To the guard, she said, "Don't let them inside the hotel. Use the APCs, the missiles, whatever you have to stop them."

"Yes, ma'am!"

"Oh, and Lloyd? When you're done with him, send Kazama to me." She indicated her bodyguards. "It wouldn't do if something happened to the Teledyne manager if he's left to his own devices."

Lloyd pulled his phone from his coat and dialed Kazama's number. It was time to show these cops who was really in charge of the city.

* * *

I trotted Countess down the empty street, flanked by Lieutenant Wendy Alexander, Corporal Collins, and Patrolman Jones. A mix of about forty Mobile, Miami, and Los Angeles officers rode behind us, with Danny and Lieutenant Cassandra Martinez riding in the rear. If something happened to Alexander or me, Martinez would take command of our ad hoc platoon.

All of us were decked out in riot armor, and barding covered our horses from nose to flank. None of us would win the Triple Crown, but our mounts should be able to shrug off all pistol calibers and any but the heaviest rifle calibers. More than one of us had a bulletproof riot shield hanging from the saddle, ready to grab at any time. I had mine hanging off Countess's right side. My left arm didn't have the strength to hold up the twenty-pound shield for very long, not with my shoulder numb from painkillers.

Gunfire rang out ahead of us. Countess snorted, the noise muffled behind her helmet. I placed a gloved hand on her white mane to steady her. She'd recovered so fast it was hard to believe she had nearly died a few short days ago. I silently promised to keep her safe.

"Sounds like it's getting' hot up ahead, sir!" Jones shouted. He reached back and patted the RPG-7 slung across his back. "Reckon I'll get to use this?"

"I reckon it wasn't a good idea to load it beforehand," I said, "but I imagine you'll have the chance to use it. Just make it count." *And try not to blow us up.*

We had given the remaining three RPGs to Section 9, but Jones had refused to give his up, not after he'd gone and modified it for one-handed use. I didn't want to try and separate the giant from his newfound toy, subordinate or not.

"This will be our most ambitious operation yet," I said into the headset I wore beneath my riot helmet, courtesy of Section Nine's radio man, a former engineer from Bose Corp. "All unit leaders, sound off."

"Londoners, here." Lieutenant Blackwood's voice crackled over the line.

"Joint Desert Patrol, reporting," Lieutenant Johnson of the Border Patrol said. He had taken over for Captain Phillips and currently rode at the head of a column of Border Patrol officers, Jordanian camel riders, and Tel Aviv cops. *"Ready to kick some ass, then let our horses munch grass."*

"Pennsylvania squad, ready for some payback," growled Lieutenant Harriet Stalling. Her Philadelphia officers had combined with the Bethlehem, Lancaster, and Baltimore units to form a platoon of around forty.

"Brazilians, here!" called Sergeant Berengár Silva. *"Just give us the word, and we'll plow these* capangas *under our buffalos' hooves!"*

And on down the line it went, with each of the mounted units sounding off their status. There hadn't been enough headsets or radios to hand out to all the squad and unit leaders, so the decision had been made to combine units. I tried to pair up units based on the cohesion I had witnessed in training exercises prior to the Fall and in patrols during the days after.

"Columbia, here," Chief Ballantine said. With his friend Bradley dead, the chief had quickly decided it was high time Obsidian be expelled from the city. *"All my squad leaders report they are in position and are now engaging the enemy west of the Country Hotel."*

I kicked Countess into a canter. "Roger that, Chief. We're beginning our southeastern assault now."

"Godspeed, Commander Ward."

I wasn't sure how I felt about that title, but it had been agreed upon by all the other leaders. Since it was my plan, the other lieutenants, and even Captain Graham and Chief Ballantine, had agreed I should have command. So, in the interim, I wasn't a lieutenant, but a commander.

"Remember, the rules of engagement are simple!" I drew my rifle from its saddle scabbard. "If the enemy has a weapon, shoot him!"

"And if the enemy doesn't have a weapon, shoot him anyway!" Danny said, and several of the men whooped their approval.

"And if you see Agent Jake Morris, do not engage him in close combat. Stay at range, and let Section Nine know. Aster will have to take him on."

Speaking of which... "Lady in Black, what's your status?"

"Party of Nine is spread out among Restaurants Q, T, and Z," she said, her quiet voice filling my helmet. *"Q and T were empty, while Z was unu-*

sually full for the hour. We had to ask a few guests to leave, permanently. It'll be a few minutes before the M2 is in position."

Q, T, and Z were code names for three of the taller buildings in the vicinity, on the outskirts of the park surrounding the Country Hotel. From there, Aster and her men had clear views of the hotel's upper floors, as well as the connecting streets. They couldn't see most of the ground level, but there was a narrow view of the main entrance.

An explosion resounded up ahead. *"The hotel is now open for business,"* Sergeant Rico said. *"Left door is wide open."*

"Ten-four. Any sign of the guest of honor?"

"Negative, but we're ready. He'll get a warm welcome, no matter where he shows up."

No one had seen Agent Morris since he fled the hospital. He had been shot up pretty badly, if Aster's testimony and the bloody crater he'd made beneath the fourth story window were anything to go by. We could only hope he was incapacitated, but each minute we delayed was another minute he could heal.

And with Agents, sometimes that was all the time it took.

Obsidian soldiers appeared in the street up ahead. They crouched behind vehicles and dumpsters and opened fire with rifles and submachine guns. The air filled with the buzzing and snapping sounds of bullets passing by. A round skimmed along Countess's helmet, leaving a streak in its painted dome. She snorted, but didn't shy away. If anything, she picked up speed.

I thumbed the rifle from safe to semi-auto and shouldered it. I stood in the stirrups and bent my knees in counterpoint to her galloping strides. With my aim steadied, I opened fire.

My first round missed my intended target, instead shattering the windshield of the vehicle the man was crouched behind. He stayed in his position, intent on killing me or one of my men. He fired a long burst from his submachine gun before my second shot struck him in the torso. The .308 armor-piercing round punched through the steel plate and soft under-armor. The man tumbled to the asphalt.

The other officers opened up with such a volley of fire that the Obsidian soldiers ducked or threw themselves to the ground. The few who tried to keep shooting wound up on the ground anyway, peppered with holes.

"Close ranks!" I shouted.

Danny, Alexander, and Martinez pulled in tight on either side of Countess, and we charged straight past the gap in the Obsidian position. Behind us, a few of our officers reined in long enough to wipe out the defenders, then they raced to catch up to us.

Obsidian soldiers fired at us from the windows of the apartments and offices around us. We returned fire as we could, while other officers shot flares modified to explode on contact with a hard surface. Soon, a haze of multi-colored smoke hung over our heads, and the fire from the upper stories ceased.

Periodically, I received updates over the radio from the other units. The Pennsylvanians had penetrated deeply along Hoke Street and had driven most of the Obsidian soldiers back. Silva's buffalo riders had yet to encounter anyone and were chomping at the bit. And Blackwood's London boys had stumbled across fierce resistance along Martin Street two blocks over. *"Machine gun nest in the brick apartment building, fifth floor bay window! Could use some help!"*

"Londoners, this is Lady in Black. Request confirmed."

The thunderous crack of a high-caliber sniper rifle rang out once, twice, and again.

"Enemy machine gun nest neutralized," Section Nine's Lieutenant Paxton said.

"This is Ballantine. Teledyne officers have attacked our flanks. My officers are turning around to face them."

"Shit," I muttered. We expected it, but it still wasn't good. We needed to crush Obsidian quickly, then turn our attention to Teledyne. "Captain Graham, can you get your men into the fight? Columbia's foot patrols could use your help."

"I think we can manage that, Commander." I could hear the wry smile in Graham's tone. *"We know a thing or two about fast, brilliant maneuvers, after all. Just ask your brother."*

I grinned. "I'll be sure to do that."

"APC!" Johnson called. *"Enemy APC along Justine Street. Taking fire!"*

A heavy machine gun opened up to our right. I shivered. That was the same kind of gun that had nearly killed Countess and me.

We passed beneath Building Q as a pair of rocket-propelled grenades sailed off the roof and whistled through the air. A series of explosions rang out, and the machine gun's staccato beat vanished.

"APC is disabled, but not out of the fight," Sergeant Rico said. *"Reloading for a second—"*

A missile sailed over our heads. I looked back in time to see the top floor of Building Q explode in a shower of broken glass and torn metal.

"Rico!" Aster screamed over the radio. *"Rico, Jamieson, answer me!"*

Aster was up on the roof of Building T, directly across the street from Q. I watched as she leapt the fifty-foot divide. Her jump arc dropped her through a window three floors down from the burning rooftop. She disappeared inside. *"Rico! Jamieson!"*

And then the second Obsidian missile slammed into the building. Glass shards and office debris flew high into the sky. Flames poured out of the blown-out windows, and the building's top half listed to the side. The roof gave way first and then the entire top half of the building collapsed into the street below. Huge pieces of masonry rubble crashed into nearby buildings and tumbled to the street.

The radio went crazy. The Section Nine squad leaders in Buildings T and Z called out to their comrades in Q. *"Rico? Jamieson? Lady in Black? Please respond! Lady in Black!"* And then the police commanders started, their words a jumbled rush: *"What's going on? What was that explosion? What happened to the Specialist? Is the Specialist all right?"*

"Commander, what's happened to Lady Aster?" Captain Graham asked, and the line quieted. *"Has she been taken off the board?"*

"I'll go back for her!" Danny shouted. He wheeled around, and ten other officers peeled off with him. "If anyone can survive a building dropping on her, it's that crazy Teledyne witch!"

"Sergeant Ward is seeing to that now, Captain," I said. "The missile strike didn't hit her position directly, but she's not responding. Could be radio damage or—" I left the thought unfinished.

"If she's dead," Blackwood chimed in, *"what do we do? We need her to beat this Agent, don't we?"*

"It's our fault, sir!" Johnson said. *"If we hadn't needed the support—"*

"We can play the blame game later," I snapped. "Specialist Aster did what any of us would have done if our men were in need of assistance. We continue the mission, with or without her. We're kicking in Obsidian's door and apprehending their executives. It's our only chance now. This is all-or-nothing."

And it was starting to look like nothing. I glanced at Danny's retreating back. "Please, God, let her be alive," I whispered.

Then I looked forward as more Obsidian soldiers fired at us from windows and behind disabled vehicles. I shouldered my rifle and took aim as smoke flares exploded above me.

Sometimes all you could do was charge straight into Hell in this Fallen World.

* * * * *

Chapter Forty

What am I doing? Danny repeated that thought as he raced to the pile of rubble that had filled the street he and his brother had just galloped through. *We should just press on with the mission. Time's of the essence. We need to get those executives—*

And yet, he couldn't just leave Aster, not with a chance she was alive. He knew how tough Agents and Specialists were. Barring a shot to the brain or complete loss of blood, very little could kill the monsters. If she was alive, she could turn this whole thing around and save a lot of officers' lives.

He slowed Noir as he reached the rubble. Chunks of masonry and broken pieces of steel littered the street, with the central pile nearly ten feet tall. Small pieces of debris continued to rain down, and glass fragments struck the pavement with a tinkling sound. The air was heavy with smoke and dust, enough to make him thankful his helmet had a respirator.

A figure rose up from the rubble, and for a brief moment he thought it was Aster. Then the dust cleared a bit, revealing a bloody, dirty Sergeant Rico. He looked up and waved at Danny. "Help me! She's trapped beneath all this!"

Danny dismounted and hurried over, followed by a few officers. The rest stayed on horseback and set up a perimeter.

"She shielded me," Rico said, looking down at the debris below his knees. "Rode down the rubble with me in her arms, then she threw me out of the way as all this shit came down on top of her."

"Is she still alive?" Danny demanded.

"If anyone is, she is."

That was enough for him. He dropped to his knees and helped Rico pick up a heavy section of brick wall. With a grunt, he tossed it out of the way and reached for another.

"We've got company, Sarge!" one of the mounted officers shouted.

Gunshots rang out, and rounds zipped past Danny's head. He let go of the piece of masonry he held and unslung his rifle. He put it to his shoulder and fired at the Obsidian soldiers appearing through the haze. One fell, while two others ducked down and shot back.

One of the bullets struck him in his chest armor. The bullet didn't penetrate, but the force of the blow knocked him onto his butt. He grunted, shrugged off the pain, and fired. The man who shot him went down, and his buddy ran off.

"More to the west!" another officer called.

"Friendlies!" someone cried. "We're friendlies!"

"What department?" Danny demanded and wished he had one of the headsets Nathan had.

"Columbia! Lieutenant Jefferson's squad!"

Danny recognized the voice. "Chloe?"

"That you, Sergeant Ward?"

"Get over here and help us! We need to get Specialist Aster out of the rubble!"

Corporal Chloe Reed jogged through the gloom with five Columbia officers behind her. All of them were dirty and bloody, but they seemed ready to fight. Danny didn't see a lieutenant's bar on any of the uniforms. "Where's Jefferson?"

"Dead. Teledyne sniper got him." She tapped her M14. "The bastard didn't get much time to celebrate."

"With you behind the scope, I don't doubt it." Danny looked down the street. "Were you pursued?"

"As a matter of fact—" Bullets impacted the rubble around them. Reed and Danny ducked. "Yes."

Shots rang out from the east, and more bullets zipped past their heads. "Well, isn't that great?" Danny muttered. "We're the meat and cheese of a Corporate sandwich."

"The meat and cheese is the best part." Reed grinned. "Where do you want us?"

"If a few of you will assist with the digging, we'll get to the defense." Danny mounted Noir and faced west. "Let's let Teledyne know we're here. Come on. H'yah!"

* * *

We raced past the trees, shrubs, and overgrown grass of Country Club Park on either side of the street. Beyond the park sat the imposing form of the Country Hotel. It was twelve stories of elaborate stonework, with a giant steeple that would have looked more at home on a cathedral than a luxury inn. The steeple's clear windowpanes gleamed in the morning light. What looked like a castle gatehouse stood in front of the lobby entrance, and stairs led up to a pair of arched doorways. The right set of double-doors were closed, but the left set had been blown apart by one of Section 9's RPGs during the beginning of the assault.

A machine gun on one of the upper floors opened up with a barrage of tracer rounds that tore into the pavement. Behind me, horses screamed and more than one rider struck the ground. I gritted my teeth and pressed on. No time to look back.

More Obsidian soldiers shot at us from the windows and from the lobby entrance. I let my rifle drop on its sling and slid my arm into the shield's straps. I held it up as Countess and I charged headlong through the intersection and into the hotel's parking lot.

The booming chatter of a heavy machine gun sounded from behind us. Tracer fire raked the upper stories, shattering windows and punching through masonry. *"M2 is now in position,"* Lieutenant Paxton said. *"Sorry for the delay."*

A rocket from one of Section Nine's buildings sailed through the air and destroyed the machine gun nest in a fireball. Smoke poured from the gaping wound in the hotel's façade.

"Not a bad idea!" Patrolman Jones slung his rifle over his left shoulder, then pulled the RPG-7 from his right. He peered through the optical sight and squeezed the modified trigger.

Whooosh!

The rocket shot out in a brilliant flash of light and sound. In less than a second, it sailed up into one of the windows we were taking fire from. Glass, masonry, and more than one body rained from above. Jones had been right: Rambo didn't flinch at all, even though I suspected the RPG's backblast had singed his tail.

Countess was another story. She slid to a halt and reared up. I leaned forward in the saddle to keep from getting tossed by the sudden move. I kept my shield raised as I loosened my grip on the reins. "Easy, girl, easy!"

A bullet struck my shield, the impact reverberating through my arm. I grimaced at the pain, then cursed when a second bullet struck. "Girl, we're sitting ducks out here!"

A third bullet struck Countess's barding. That was enough for her. Her booted hooves struck the pavement with a resounding clatter, and then she broke into a gallop again. Jones and Collins were only a short distance ahead of me, and the rest of the platoon was right behind us as we charged up the concrete steps.

Once we cleared the last step, I dropped my shield back into its rest and took up my rifle. I thumbed it to burst-fire and shouldered it just as we charged into a vast, open lobby. An atrium reached all the way to the cathedral-like steeple, with balconies extending all the way up to the twelfth floor. Sunlight streamed in, bright enough to illuminate a good section of the chamber.

A group of Obsidian soldiers ran toward the entrance, presumably to reinforce the fight outside. They saw us coming and scattered. Some threw themselves over the concierge desk, while others tried to get away.

I gunned down one soldier as he raised his weapon toward me, then winged another as he tried to shoot Jones, who fumbled with trying to hang the empty RPG on his right shoulder while pulling his rifle off his left. "Let the thing go, Jones!"

"Not on your life, sir! This thing's great!" He finally slung the RPG and pulled his rifle free. "Besides, they don't make them anymore!"

"Good point!"

The lobby ran the entire length of the hotel's first floor. A circular concierge desk took up the center of the room, while shops and restaurants lined the outer wall with glassed-in partitions to give everything an open appearance. No enemies had taken positions in these shops and cafes, but plenty of Obsidian soldiers and their auxiliaries from the local gangs were coming off elevators and exiting stairwells. We raced around the circular room, blasting away like we were shooters in a video game.

As we rode back around to the lobby entrance, a group of about forty enemies armed with rifles and light machine guns waited for us, their backs to the arched portals. The doors that had previously been closed now hung open. Had they come from outside?

Their commander raised a hand and opened his mouth.

Then the horned Hussars arrived.

All twelve Brazilian buffalo riders crashed into the mass of bad guys. The hulking beasts sent men into the air with tosses of their curled horns. Other soldiers fell beneath the buffalos' massive hooves. The enemies' armor didn't protect them from nearly two thousand pounds of beast and armor. Their shrieks mingled with the cracking of bones and squishing of internal organs.

A soldier wound up impaled on Sergeant Silva's mount. The buffalo roared and swung its head left and right, shaking the man until he flew off and skidded across the marble floor.

We fired at the enemies who didn't have the sense to run. I was tempted to follow Danny's advice and kill them all no matter what, but I didn't have the stomach for that, or the time. We needed to get upstairs and capture Directors Greenway and Lloyd before Agent Morris joined the fight. "Surrender, or you will be shot!" I shouted.

One Obsidian soldier aimed his weapon at me. I shot first and gunned down the man next to him. The remaining soldiers and thugs dropped their weapons and held up their hands. "All right," their leader said, "we surrender. Just don't kill—"

His head vanished in a spray of blood that coated the men around him. Before anyone could react, three more soldiers struck the ground, their bodies torn to shreds.

Agent Jake Morris stood in the blood and guts of his former comrades, his Obsidian uniform somehow untouched by the gore. He cracked his knuckles and popped his neck. "It's so hard to find good help these days. One little cavalry charge and running of the bulls, and it's quitting time." He grinned. "Well, not for me."

"Murderer!" Lieutenant Alexander shouldered her rifle and fired.

Morris jumped out of the way, then lunged at Alexander. In one move he pulled the Miami officer clear of Candace's saddle and held her close, their faces inches apart. "Now, now. That's not a very nice way to treat a man who saved your department's bacon back in '57. I wish I had my beautiful Genos to help me here, but sadly, you'll have to make do with me."

Alexander tried to break free, but his hold on her was too tight. She stared at him, eyes wide with fear.

"Don't worry, Wendy, I won't kill you. Not until I've finished your friends off, anyway."

Morris let her go, then leaped onto the back of the closest buffalo. He knocked the rider off, then plunged his hand down into the buffalo's back. With a jerk, he ripped a chunk of the beast's spine out. It collapsed without a sound.

The cops opened fire, but Morris was already on the move. He jumped about randomly, killing men and maiming horses with his bare hands. I tried to track him with my rifle, but he moved too fast, and there were too many good guys between him and me.

Then Morris landed next to me. I twisted in the saddle and tried to bring my rifle to bear, but I knew I wouldn't make it in time. He looked up, his bloody fist poised to strike at either Countess or me.

Our eyes locked, and a flicker of recognition passed through them. In a split-second that seemed like an eternity, I expected him to give me a smug smile before he killed me.

Instead, he frowned.

"LT, look out!" Corporal Collins shouted.

Everything snapped back into real-time. A bullet struck Morris in the side, punching through his soft armor. He staggered, and a pained growl escaped his lips.

Collins fired again, but Morris dodged and leaped at him. Collins screamed as he was dragged from his saddle and slammed into the ground with enough force to shatter the marble beneath. Morris flung the Mobile officer's broken body fifty feet across the room where it crashed through the concierge desk.

Anger surged within me. I switched my rifle to full-auto and squeezed the trigger. Around me, a half-dozen other officers did the same.

Morris danced his way through the gunfire, avoiding every round as if he could see them. With an Agent's enhanced reflexes, maybe he could. I tried to stay ahead of his movements, but he was a blur as he retreated from us.

My rifle bolt locked back on an empty magazine. I pressed the mag release and reached for a fresh one. Around me, other officers ran dry as well.

Morris spun and jumped straight into the air. He grabbed onto the second floor balcony railing and used it to fling himself up to the third floor and then the fourth. He changed directions each time he jumped to avoid our gunfire.

He rolled over the banister of the seventh floor. A second later, he peeked over the railing about forty feet away. "You should've come sooner, Nathan! I was bedridden about twenty minutes ago! Your man Collins hit me pretty good, so you've got a little time, maybe!"

Obsidian soldiers appeared on the balconies of several floors and rained fire down on us.

Once again, I let my rifle drop on its sling and took up my shield. "Get away from the atrium!" I shouted. If we clung to the sides of the lobby, we would be out of the line of fire from the upper floors, at least.

We regrouped on the left side of the lobby, behind thick support columns and a small marble fountain. Obsidian soldiers on the second, third, and fourth levels could still shoot at us. Bullets chipped the marble floor and tore out chunks of the columns. "Smoke flares!" someone called.

"I've got a better idea!" Patrolman Jones dropped from Rambo's saddle and slid another rocket into his RPG-7. "Stand clear, y'all!" he shouted as he took a knee, aimed, and squeezed.

The rocket shot across the lobby and struck the third floor balcony right where some soldiers were setting up a crew-served machine gun. The explosion tore through three levels of balconies and destroyed the walls to several rooms. Broken bodies and splintered furniture crashed to the lobby.

Countess snorted, but she maintained her footing. I stroked her neck. "Good girl."

"My God, he's here." Alexander stared up at the high ceiling, her eyes wide. "He's really here."

"How the hell are we supposed to fight that?" one of the LAPD officers demanded. "He killed ten guys like it was nothing, including his own people!"

"Man, fuck that!" Patrolman Jones returned the RPG to its canvas case and hooked it to Rambo's saddle. "He killed Corporal Collins. We gotta get through these guys so I can get my hands around the bastard's neck."

If only it were that easy. Jeremiah Jones was big and strong, but even he had nothing on an Agent. Hell, I didn't even know if Aster could take him in a toe-to-toe fight. "We knew there was a risk he would be in the fight," I said. "It doesn't change our mission. If we can take Directors Greenway and Lloyd, we can get them to order the Agent to stand down." If we put guns to their heads, it wouldn't matter how fast Morris was.

"We're with you, Commander Ward!" Lieutenant Martinez popped a fresh magazine into her rifle, then slid out of the saddle. "Let's end this."

I dropped to the ground, as did most of the other officers. Lieutenant Alexander stayed in her saddle, her eyes still searching the ceiling for signs of Morris. "Alexander, you and your boys stay here and secure the perimeter."

"No." She hopped from the saddle and stumbled as her knees gave out. She steadied herself against Candace. "No, I'm coming with you. I owe it to my men."

"You owe it to your men to make sure Obsidian doesn't get away to fight another day," I said. "Stay here and run them down if they try to escape." I leaned close. "I need people to keep an eye on our horses, and I want someone I can trust to keep Countess safe for me."

She let out a sigh and nodded. "Very well. We'll stay put."

"This is Commander Ward," I said into my headset. "We've taken the lobby. Preparing to ascend. What's everyone's status?"

"Londoners, still bogged down on Martin Street!"

"Desert Force, moving to assist the Londoners. Once we free them, we'll secure the hotel perimeter."

"Party of Nine, still maintaining hotel overwatch," Lieutenant Paxton said. *"We can't see the street from here, but we've got their snipers busy on the upper floors. The approach should be easy."*

"Commander Ward, Chief Ballantine. We're sending help your way."

A rumbling sounded from outside. I froze, afraid it was the last of Obsidian's APCs about to plow into the lobby. Jones cursed and reached for his RPG while others scrambled back into their saddles.

A vehicle did plow through the broken remains of the exploded doorway, but it wasn't an Obsidian APC. It was an armored SWAT van from the Columbia PD. It pulled up near us, and ten men in full battle rattle clambered out of the rear hatch. The driver and two passengers in the front bench climbed out next, for a total of thirteen. All of them, save for the driver, took up positions near the atrium and started firing into the upper floors.

The driver was an older man with a gray mustache. "Commander Ward?"

I slid out of the saddle and approached. "That'd be me, Lieutenant—?"

"Gerald Ferguson, SWAT leader. The chief figured you could use some breach-and-clear expertise." He looked around. "Though, you seem to be doing a pretty good job of that on your own."

"We won't say no to more help," I said, relief flooding through me. I wasn't sure what a few dozen mounted officers could accomplish in a building this big, but maybe with the SWAT team, we could quickly reach the top. "Bring any more people with you?"

"As a matter of fact…"

Three full squads of Columbia officers jogged in. They were decked out in bulletproof riot gear and wielded everything from shotguns to assault rifles. That brought our combined assault team up to just under seventy men and women.

"There are four stairwells in this building, so we'll need to break into four groups," Ferguson said. "I'll divide my team among each group. We've raided this hotel a couple times in the past, once as a drill and another for real. We know the layout better than anyone."

"Excellent," I said. "Would you like to be on point?"

"We would love it." He grinned. "I've always wanted to evict an entire Corporation."

I chuckled. "Well, it looks like someone's going to get their wish in this Fallen World."

* * * * *

Chapter Forty-One

"There she is," Rico grunted. He tossed a chunk of masonry out of the way.

Danny knelt down and saw Aster's head. She lay under a couple more feet of rubble. Her helmet had been split from dome to jaw, exposing part of her face. Blood had run down her nose and around her open mouth. He couldn't tell if she was breathing.

A burst of gunfire rang out, and one of the horses screamed. An officer tumbled from the saddle. "I'm hit!"

Noir lay against the wall of a nearby building, her head resting on the pavement. She'd taken a ricochet to the leg just as they were forming up for another charge. The leg had given out on her, and she had gone down. Her fall was soft enough that Danny could safely get out of the saddle, but she wasn't going anywhere on her own. She looked at him now, her dark eyes full of pain. *Wish I could help you, little lady*, he thought. *But, I don't think we can help ourselves right now.*

His mounted unit had been cut in half over the last several minutes. He'd led a few charges against Teledyne and Obsidian, but their combined force was too strong, their crossfire too withering. He had hoped they would stop shooting once they realized the cops were sandwiched between them, but that had only spurred them on more. Both sides must have wanted the other dead, as well.

The Columbia officers with Corporal Reed fired from what cover they could find, but there was precious little of it except for the mound of rubble Aster was buried beneath. "Reloading!" Reed shouted. "Last mag!"

They were running out of time, Danny realized. And they didn't know if the Battle Flower was dead.

Danny reached down and smacked Aster's helmet hard enough to make the split deepen. "Wake up!"

"What are you doing?" Rico objected. "She's hurt!"

"She can also take a beating better than any of us, and you ought to know that." Danny struck her helmet again, then reached between the widening split to thump her forehead. "Get up, Aster! We need you!"

She stirred slightly, but her eyes stayed shut.

"She's alive!" Rico picked up another piece of rubble and hurled it aside. "Come on, clear this away from her!"

With a renewed burst of energy, Rico, Danny, and one of the Columbia officers dug into the rubble with their bare hands. Around them, guns blazed, men and horses screamed, and the shouts of approaching Obsidian and Teledyne soldiers grew closer.

The Columbia officer helping them took a bullet in the leg. He fell down, clutching the wound. Danny pulled a tourniquet from a pouch at his waist and tossed it to the officer. "You got that? Good." Then he got back to digging. "Come on, Aster! Wake up! We need you, girl!"

He and Rico moved the last big piece of masonry out of the way and then they each grabbed an arm. Danny pulled and was surprised at the weight. "Damn Specialists," he muttered. "Always so damned dense."

Rico laughed. "You don't know the half of—"

A bullet punctured Rico's faceplate. Blood splattered the inside of the glass, and the Section Nine soldier fell into the hole on top of Aster.

Danny reached for his rifle, then froze. Four Teledyne soldiers stood no more than twenty feet from him. Behind them, a mix of Obsidian and Teledyne soldiers stepped into the intersection, weapons leveled at the still-living officers.

A man in a Teledyne officer's uniform stepped out of the haze. He looked around at the dead cops and soldiers and shook his head. "It didn't have to come to this, you know. You could have let the Specialist and her fellow traitors die while you nobly charged into oblivion, but you've left us no choice. We can't have witnesses to our shame." He raised his hand.

A blur flew from the hole, and the four soldiers closest to Danny went down in a heap of broken bones and severed limbs.

Aster stood there, Rico draped over one shoulder. Blood from the sergeant's head wound covered her face and drenched her hair. She carefully set his body down on the ground, then stood up. "How many more?" she growled.

Blood soaked her arms to the elbow and dripped from her fingers as she stepped over the bodies she had just eviscerated. Her purple eyes seemed to glow as she glared at the Corporate soldiers pointing weapons at her. "How many more orphans must I make before you're satisfied?" Her lips peeled back from her teeth in a snarl. *"How many more?!"*

"Kill her!" the Teledyne officer shouted, his voice cracking from fear.

With a shriek, the Lady in Black charged.

* * *

"It seems that the Specialist isn't dead," Lloyd murmured. He took the headset off and placed it on the desk in the cramped security office. Three soldiers stood or sat with him, and another fifteen stood guard in the basement garage. So far, the police hadn't breached the garage's wrought iron gate or shown much interest in it, and he hoped it stayed that way. The imprinter was down here, loaded up and ready to move.

Gunfire and explosions echoed through the Country Hotel. Even without the headset on, he could hear the panicked chatter coming from squad leaders all over the compound and in the streets. With one APC disabled and Teledyne's reinforcements stymied by the police, it would only be a matter of time before the building fell.

Agent Morris could still turn the tide, but that was if Lloyd could find him. The bastard was easy enough to order around face-to-face, but he'd lost his earpiece when he engaged the cops in the lobby. Lloyd had witnessed the performance on a camera feed. It always thrilled him to watch an Agent in action. There was something mesmerizing about a master working his craft.

But then Morris had been shot, and he'd retreated, presumably to protect Director Greenway in the safe room.

Lloyd ground his teeth. Morris should've been keeping *him* safe, but his programming forced him to defer to the person of higher rank. And if the choice came down to protecting him or her, Morris would choose her without a second thought.

"Show me the stairs," he said to the soldier at the controls.

The high definition monitor switched from the lobby to eight separate camera feeds. In three of them, officers ascended the concrete without any problems. In three others, Obsidian soldiers positioned themselves on an upper floor landing and aimed down. And the final two cameras caught both sides of a firefight near the twelfth floor landing in the northwest stairwell.

No sign of Morris anywhere.

"Get the vehicles ready," he ordered one of the soldiers.

Sometimes you needed to know when to cut your losses in this Fallen World.

* * * * *

Chapter Forty-Two

Bullets rained down from the twelfth floor, and I pressed myself up against the wall. One of the officers on the stairs across from me screamed as he was hit. He tumbled down the steps, taking two others with him. They rolled to the ninth floor landing in a heap of moans and curses.

"I hate stairwell fights!" Corporal Duffy of the Columbia SWAT shouted. He reloaded his assault rifle. "Unless we're at the top shooting down, and when does that ever happen?"

I switched my rifle to burst fire, leaned out, and squeezed the trigger. With each squeeze, the rifle belched three rounds in a fraction of a second. An Obsidian soldier cried out as my bullets struck him. I shifted targets and fired three more bursts. I don't know if I hit anyone, but they stopped shooting at us.

We advanced, a few of us leaning out to shoot while the rest ran to the next landing, then they covered us as we ascended. We stopped long enough to check the access door to each floor for ambushers, then we moved on. The real fight was up above.

They tried dropping grenades on us a couple times, but the gap between landings was so narrow they couldn't get a good angle on us. The grenades dropped right past us and exploded on a lower level.

The stairwells between floors eleven and twelve were twice as high as the others, with four landings between them rather than the usual two. The two floors were the most luxurious part of the hotel, which meant they must've had luxuriously high ceilings to match. My knees were starting to ache from the climb, and more than once, I wished Countess could gallop up these stairs like she did the lobby stairs.

The deadliest part was the intermediate landing just before the top floor. It was mostly exposed, and the defenders had an L-shaped platform to shoot from. Part of that platform would be directly behind us as we tried to cross the intermediate landing to the final set of stairs.

Two SWAT officers went out first, one with a shield and Corporal Duffy with his assault rifle. The shield man sidestepped across the intermediate landing, his revolver spitting lead. His partner walked backward alongside him, his rifle aimed at the strip of landing that was right above where I stood. He fired a burst, and I heard someone scream.

The remaining Obsidian soldiers on the top floor landing fired. Rounds impacted the officer's shield and staggered him, but he kept his footing. His partner shifted his aim and fired.

Patrolman Jones and I stepped out next, and after a deafening exchange of gunfire, the stairs fell silent except for a last few rounds of expended brass pinging as they struck the concrete walls and floors.

The shield man turned to grin at me. "Well, that was exciting."

Something black flew out of the twelfth floor doorway. It bounced against the far wall and skipped down the stairs to our landing. "Grenade!" I yelled and pushed Jones down to the floor.

The shield man dove on the grenade, his shield between it and his body.

The grenade exploded with a muffled *whumph*. The shield absorbed most of the impact, but the force still blew the SWAT officer a few feet in the air. He crashed on top of his shield and then rolled onto his back, groaning. "Medic!" I called, and a Columbia PD officer down below called an affirmative.

Corporal Duffy led his remaining SWAT members up the steps. They stacked up on the closed door and pulled it open. Gunfire rang out, and the SWAT officers returned the favor with a cascade of fully automatic weapons fire. They paused long enough to reload, then pushed into the hall.

I popped a fresh magazine into my rifle and hurried up the steps, the rest of the Mobile and Columbia officers on my heels. We entered a long hallway that continued to the other side of the building, with an adjoining corridor intersecting from the left about twenty feet ahead. Obsidian dead littered the hallway. Duffy and the rest of his SWAT members stood at that intersection, firing straight ahead or leaning out to shoot down the left corridor.

The bulk of the twelfth floor was comprised of a series of multi-room suites that lined the building's outer walls, giving every occupant a sitting area and bedroom with a view. The interior portion of the floor held a restaurant that surrounded the atrium's balcony and a small lounge, both of which were only accessible to the guests on that floor.

"Commander Ward, this is Lieutenant Ferguson. We hear a lot of gunfire above us. That you?"

"Yeah," I answered. "We just breached the twelfth floor. Meeting heavy resistance."

"We were slowed at the tenth floor, but haven't encountered anyone since. We're about to breach. We'll let—"

A shriek pierced the connection, and I winced at the sound.

"*Shit, he's behind us!*" an officer screamed through Ferguson's connection.

"*Calm down!*" Ferguson shouted. "*He's just one man. He's just—Dear God in Heaven. Shoot him! Shoot him!*"

The connection cut out, but even without it, I could hear the gunfire echoing from the other side of the building.

"All units," I said into the comms, "be advised: we are breaching the top floor of the Country Hotel. Guard all exits, and don't let any reinforcements from outside into the buildings. If you see Directors Greenway or Lloyd, detain them immediately."

I clapped Duffy on the shoulder as he reloaded his rifle. "We have to hurry! Ferguson's in trouble, and we're running out of time."

"The suits are holed up in the restaurant." Duffy pointed forward, then jerked his head in the direction of the intersecting corridor. "Bunch of them retreated through either door, but there are four doors total."

"Agent Morris could be opening up a path for the Directors to escape," I said. "We'll need to cut off all four entrances if we're to seal them in." I keyed my mic. "Lieutenant Martinez, Sergeant Lipton, status?"

"*Martinez here. About to breach the twelfth floor. We'll be to you soon.*"

"*Lipton here,*" the Columbia PD sergeant called. "*We're stuck down on seven. The stairs above us are a fucking mess. Looks like a rocket partially collapsed them. We'll move to assist Lieutenant Ferguson's squad.*"

Damn, I thought. Already our strength on the top floor was cut in half, but we couldn't afford to wait any longer. And neither could Ferguson and his people. "Martinez, as soon as you reach the twelfth floor, hit the restaurant hard. We'll see you inside."

"Ten-four!"

"Duffy, you take SWAT and half the Columbia PD to the left. I'll take the rest to the door straight ahead of us." I waited long enough to check my ammo, then said, "Watch your sectors and keep an eye on the suite doors, but our goal is the restaurant. Let's go!"

We ran, weapons held at low ready. As we ran past the first set of suite doors, my shoulder blades itched in anticipation of a bullet. We were taking a huge risk, but we didn't have time to clear every room. All I could do was go by my gut, and my gut told me Directors Greenway and Lloyd would be wherever their guards were thickest.

Glass shattered off to the left, followed by a hail of gunfire. I slowed as I reached the glass door on my side of the building and peeked inside. Tables and chairs had been arranged around the circular atrium balcony to give diners a view of the steeple above and the lobby far below.

Obsidian soldiers ducked behind the long bar that ran along an interior wall that led to the lounge Duffy had mentioned. Most of them fired at the door the SWAT team was attempting to breach, but one soldier looked my way.

I stood back, raised my rifle, and fired a three-round burst. The door disintegrated, and the man dropped behind the bar.

Patrolman Jones jumped to the other side of the door, and together, we poured fire on the soldiers. Most of them ducked, but one sprayed bullets our way. We threw ourselves on the ground as rounds punched through the sheetrock walls.

"Frag out!" I heard someone yell, and my stomach clenched.

Several soldiers cried in panic and then there was a loud boom and a blinding flash of light. The screams intensified.

I jumped to my feet just as Corporal Duffy and his team stormed the restaurant. They fired as they ran forward, showering the bar with bullets. One Obsidian soldier jumped to his feet to return fire and was hit with twenty or more rounds before he collapsed.

Movement to the right caught my eye. Soldiers had appeared from the kitchen on the other side of the circular balcony. I stepped out into the restaurant and fired. One bad guy dropped to the ground, clutching his stomach. Patrolman Jones stepped in behind me, followed by the rest of the men. Together, we laid down enough fire to push the Obsidian soldiers back to the kitchen.

The door on the far end of the restaurant shattered, and Lieutenant Cassandra Martinez and her squad ran in. "Did you save any for us, Nate?" she called across the divide.

I waved, then frowned. So far, we'd encountered only about a dozen soldiers in the restaurant. Did we miss them?

Corporal Duffy and his men finished off the last of the soldiers behind the bar, then stacked up on the heavy wooden door that led into the lounge. One of the men fished out a flash bang and flung it through the small passthrough between the bar and the lounge area.

Once it went off with a muffled explosion, Duffy kicked open the door and charged in. Gunfire and screams echoed from the dimly lit room.

I left a few Mobile officers to watch the kitchen, then the rest of us hurried to back up Duffy and the others. I crept up to the door as it slowly swung back on its hinges and pushed it open again.

Spatters and pools of blood coated the dark tile floor in the center of the room, but Duffy and his men were missing. We fanned out, rifles pointing every which way. As with the restaurant behind us, tables and chairs took up most of the floor space, and some low couches lined the far side of the room. Black-and-white photos from the 1920's hung from the walls, showing antique cars and then-famous celebrities living the good life.

A bar lined the wall to the right of the doorway, parallel to the one in the restaurant area. Blood had dribbled on the polished wood surface.

Behind us, the door to the lounge locked with an audible click.

Corporal Duffy flew out from behind the bar. He rolled along the floor until he struck a table. His arms and legs hung at odd angles. He stirred, and groaned.

"He's a resilient one!"

Morris stood behind the bar, holding a severed arm and leg in either hand. "His buddies, though... They don't make them like they used to, I guess."

We opened fire. Morris jumped out of the way and disappeared behind the bar again.

"Ward, what's happening?" Martinez barked.

"It's Morris! Keep your men outside!"

When Morris reappeared, he held a nightstick. He dove over the bar and struck a Columbia cop so hard the stick snapped. The officer flopped to the ground, his neck broken, his helmet split in two.

"Damn you!" Jones shouted. He swung his rifle like a club. Morris's eyes widened in surprise, but he dodged and caught the weapon in his hand. He smiled. "Finally, someone who understands the beauty of a good melee. I like you, Officer Jones!"

He ripped the gun free from Jones's grip and swung it at him. Jones twisted, but the stock still connected with his side. The big man crashed into a table so hard, its sturdy legs broke. He struggled to get back to his feet.

Someone pounded on the door. *"Nathan!"* I could hear Martinez's voice from outside and through my headset. *"Nathan, open the door!"*

We tried shooting again, but Morris just danced out of the way like it was nothing. If Collins had slowed him down at all, he'd long since healed from the bullet wound. He snatched Patrolman Winfield by the neck and held him up as a shield. "I'm trying to have a match with Jonesy over here, Nate," he said, his voice full of mock hurt.

"Shit!" Martinez snapped. *"Does anyone have a breaching round?"*

"Martinez, stay outside!" I tried to keep the rising panic from my voice as I fumbled to reload. I took a deep breath. "Cassandra, find Directors Greenway and Lloyd. Search the rest of the floor! They have to be here!"

Morris chuckled as Winfield struggled to free himself. "Greenway's a lot closer than you think."

Jones drew a knife from his boot and charged at Morris.

"That's the spirit!" Morris dropped Winfield and met Jones's charge head on. He caught Jones's knife hand and wrenched the blade free. He threw it past me, and it buried itself to the hilt in the sheetrock wall.

Jones threw a flurry of punches at Morris, who dodged and blocked every strike. "This is what I like to see!" Morris shouted. "Not enough martial arts in a world of guns, wouldn't you agree?"

"Shut up!" Jones growled. His dark skin glistened in the dim light, and his breath came in ragged gasps. "And stay still!"

"All right, give me your best shot!"

Morris stood perfectly still, arms wide. Jones roared and slammed his fist into Morris's face. The Agent's head snapped to the side, and he stumbled back. Jones stepped forward to strike again.

Morris sidestepped the next punch and grabbed Jones by the arm. "My turn," he whispered.

He flung Jones across the room. Jones bounced against a table, crashed into the far wall, then hit the floor as pieces of sheetrock and a broken picture frame landed on top of him. The big officer groaned and tried to get to his feet.

In a blink, Morris stood over him. He put a boot against Jones's side and rolled him into the center of the room.

Martinez pounded on the door again. "Nathan, help's on the way! Just hold on!"

"Dammit, Martinez!" I shouted. "Get the Directors!"

"Oh, come on, Nate!" Morris laughed. "Why hog all the fun for yourselves?" He held up his hands and clenched them into fists. "I'll take on any challenger! Big or small, I'll fight them all!"

The damaged wall behind Morris exploded in a shower of wood splinters and powdered sheetrock. Aster flew out of the hole, her alabaster face covered in dust, her white hair stained red with the same blood that drenched her arms. Her eyes glowed with purple fire.

It was the most terrifyingly beautiful sight I'd seen in this Fallen World.

* * * * *

Chapter Forty-Three

Morris spun to meet Aster's attack, his fist aimed at her face. She twisted midair and slammed into his chest with her shoulder. The blow staggered him, but he recovered and aimed a jab at her side. She dropped her arm and blocked his strike, but the impact knocked her several feet away.

She pushed off the wall and swept her leg out at his temple. He threw his head back to avoid the kick and reached for her leg, but she pulled back and launched another kick at his midsection. Her boot connected with a crack as loud as a gunshot.

Morris grimaced, then chuckled as he hopped from one foot to the other. "You know, I actually felt that one, little lady."

The two circled one another. I motioned everyone back against the walls. I didn't want any of us mere mortals to be caught up in this clash between Corporate titans.

Aster lunged at him, her tiny hands a blur of motion. He blocked her strikes and tried to strike her, but she dodged and leaped at him again. Back and forth they went, their movements too fast for me to follow. I couldn't line up any kind of shot without risking hitting Aster.

As they danced around the room, Morris laughed. "First Jonesy, then you? I'm on Cloud Nine, girl. How about you?"

"I'll kill you for what you did to Jason," she whispered.

He froze, and his grin turned to a scowl. "You didn't even know him!" he shouted as he leaped at her.

Aster turned his fist aside and punched him in the gut. Morris ignored the blow and grabbed her by the collar. She tore herself free and swept his legs out with a low kick. He caught himself on a chair but still landed on his butt. With a roar, he threw the chair at her.

She stepped out of the way, and the chair exploded against the back wall.

Morris snatched up another chair and threw it at her, and then another. She dove and jumped out of the way of each.

"Shoot him!" I said, and we opened fire.

Morris took a bullet in the side. He snarled and hurled another chair at Patrolman Harris.

Aster jumped in front of the officer and caught the chair. She flung it back at Morris, who dodged and then cocked his head at her.

Before we could do anything, Morris snatched up a pistol from one of the downed officers and aimed it at Jones, who was still on the ground. He squeezed the trigger.

Aster slid between the two men, her arms crossed in front of her face. Most of the bullets struck her torso armor, but one grazed her hand while another pierced her forearm. She then launched herself at him, her fists a blur.

"Oh, ho." Morris grinned as he avoided each strike. "So, if I can't hit you directly, I just need to target someone slower than you." He drew a knife from his belt and flung it at one of the Columbia cops.

Aster caught the blade midair and started to throw it back at him.

Morris slammed his boot into her stomach. She flew over the bar and crashed into a shelf full of bottles. She bounced off the bar's wooden surface and crashed to the floor. She groaned but jumped back to her feet.

Patrolman Harris shot at Morris, but the Agent rolled out of the way. He came up with an assault rifle that he aimed at me. I didn't hesitate. I held down the trigger and emptied my gun's thirty-round magazine.

Morris jumped back and fired. The round went wide, and no more rounds came out of it. None of my bullets had hit Morris, but one had punctured the rifle's magazine. He snapped the rifle in half with a frustrated sigh. "This is why I hate guns, Nate."

Aster's fist connected with his jaw. "Your fight's with me, Obsidian dog—"

Morris dropped the rifle and grabbed Aster's right arm. He twisted her around and slammed her into the floor with enough force to crack the tile.

Something in Aster's arm popped, and she screamed.

Morris lifted her by her torso armor and drove her into the floor again. The subfloor splintered.

When he raised her up a third time, Aster hung limp, her arms and legs dangling. I let my rifle go and drew my pistol. He saw the movement and grinned. "Want to stop me from killing your girlfriend, Nate? Let's see which one of us is the fastest!"

Aster moved first.

She struck Morris in the face with one of her knees. Blood sprayed from his ruined nose, and his grip on her loosened. She hooked her legs around his neck and dropped forward. She struck the ground, but the powerful muscles in her legs tugged Morris with her. She flipped him over onto his backside with enough force to shake the room.

When he tried to sit up, she latched onto his back. Her legs coiled around his midsection and pinned his arms to his sides. Her right arm hung uselessly, but she hooked her left arm around his neck and squeezed.

Morris strained against Aster's vice-like grip. The muscles in his neck and shoulders bunched and strained, and his breath came in short gasps through a restricted windpipe. He tried to spread his arms and managed to move Aster's feet an inch.

"Shoot him!" Aster shouted. "I can't hold him for long!"

My hands shook as I tried to keep the laser sight on Morris's head. Aster had him in a perfect headlock, but the slightest twitch of my fingers could send a .45 ACP round into Aster's brain. "Get your head out of the way, Aster!"

"I can't!" she hissed.

Morris broke enough of Aster's hold to grab her injured arm and twist. She screamed and coiled around him even tighter. "Shoot him already!"

Morris tossed his head back and forth and growled like a rabid dog or a man possessed by a demon. My heart sank as I considered that. Jake Morris *was* possessed, brainwashed by Obsidian's dark science. He wasn't like this normally. He was my best friend, for God's sake!

"Shoot him!" Aster shouted again. "Do it for Jason!"

Morris froze, and he and I locked eyes. "Nate?" His voice came out as a choked whisper. "God, Nate, what have I been doing?"

"Jake?" I lowered the pistol slightly. "Is that you?"

Jake tried to shake his head, but Aster's hold on him was too tight. He squeezed his eyes shut. "Something...controlling me. Nate...Kill me."

"Maybe we can fix you!" A wild hope flared in my chest. "Danny and Aster said they used an imprinter on you. If we can just get you to it—"

"No time!" Morris suddenly strained at Aster's grip, then stilled once more. "No time. Kill me!" Tears rolled down Morris's—no, *Jake's* cheeks. "Please."

I took a steadying breath and aimed once more.

"Jason," Jake mumbled. His eyes widened. "Oh, God. Jason. Is he...?"

My throat grew thick and pained. "You hurt him, Jake, but he's going to make a full recovery."

Aster whispered something into Jake's ear, then ducked out of the line of fire. He closed his eyes. "Thank you."

I squeezed the trigger.

The silence that followed that gunshot was absolute. Jake slowly slumped to the floor. Aster slid out from under his bulk and tried to stand, but she dropped back to her knees. She cradled her right arm with her left and examined it. "That's going to take a while to heal."

"What did you say to him?" I asked. I cleared my throat and scrubbed my eyes. I needed to radio in that Jake Morris was dead, but I needed a moment, too.

"I told him he's the reason Jason's alive." She studied me, her purple eyes glowing in the dim light. "If the Berserker persona had fully been in control, your son would have been ripped to pieces."

More tears threatened to spill over, and I blinked them away. I cleared my throat again and walked over to her side. "Let me help you up."

"I'm heavier than I look," she warned. She reached for my hand.

Then the floor beneath us gave way, and we crashed into the room below.

We landed in a lounge that looked identical to the one above us, in the midst of a group of scared managers, soldiers, and bodyguards. Gwendolyn Greenway stared at me from across the room, mouth agape. To my left, Teledyne soldiers surrounded Manager Kazama, the current leader.

A hidden speakeasy! That explained the 1920s décor upstairs. If it were any other situation, I'd think it was the coolest thing ever, but I had bigger problems.

Before her guards could do anything, I aimed my pistol at Greenway. I felt a hand on my leg, then Aster pointed my backup revolver at Kazama. The Corporate goons leveled their weapons at us, but no one made a move. "Call off your goons and surrender, Greenway," I said into the silence. "Your Agent's dead, and our men are surrounding this place. You can't win."

"We won't know unless we try," Greenway said with a smug smile.

"You won't know at all." I thumbed the targeting laser and painted a red dot on her face. She flinched as the beam struck her eyes. Then I lowered it to her ample bosom. "I may have qualms about shooting a lady, but I just had to kill my best friend because of what you fuckers did to him, so I think I'll get over it."

"And I have no such problems killing a little weasel like you, Manager Kazama," Aster said.

There was movement upstairs and then my officers positioned themselves around the hole above us, their rifles and pistols pointed at the Corporate soldiers.

We stood there for a long moment, no one daring to move. In the silence, my radio crackled. *"This is Paxton. Enemy APC and a heavy cargo truck made a break for it from the parking garage. The APC got away, but we blew up the truck."*

"Sounds like someone decided to get out of Dodge while we were busy up here." To Greenway I said, "Backup ain't coming, honey."

Greenway scowled. "Damn that man," she muttered.

"So, you have a choice: you can both stand down and help us try to rebuild this city, or we can kill each other here and now." I cocked my head. "You may get me, but I'll be damned if I don't send you to Hell first."

"You won't get me," Aster added quietly. "I'll kill every single one of you, though it'll be messy and slow with only one arm to work with. A lot of you will die screaming."

That sent a shiver down my spine. "You heard the Lady in Black. Now, hurry up and make your decision. We have a lot of work to do in this Fallen World."

* * * * *

Chapter Forty-Four

"**D**amn them all," Lloyd growled.

He sat on one of the steel benches in the rear of the APC. Sweat ran down his face from the heat, and the noise of the vehicle's engine was deafening in the enclosed space. The vehicle suddenly turned to the right, and he almost fell off the hard, unyielding bench. Then the APC turned left, and he slammed back against the armored hull.

Six soldiers sat across from him, and four more hunched in the narrow lane that ran down the center of the vehicle. The four grasped handles built into the low ceiling, and they did a far better job maintaining their balance than Lloyd could. All ten of them looked everywhere but at him.

Three more soldiers accompanied Lloyd, one in the gunner's seat and two up in the driver's compartment. A far cry from what he'd brought with him from St. Louis. "Damn them all," he muttered. This wasn't the end of it. Even with the imprinter gone, there were other options. There had to be. He'd survived setbacks worse than this.

His tablet chirped. He pulled it from his coat pocket and examined it. Somehow, satellite reception had briefly been restored and the Agents List had updated before it cut out again. He skimmed over the list of names and locations and then grinned. One of the locations wasn't too far away. He grabbed the radio next to him and gave the driver a set of coordinates to head toward as soon as they were clear of the city.

He would be back, this time with overwhelming force.

* * *

Danny and Reed crouched behind a bullet-riddled pickup truck. Both had discarded their rifles in favor of handguns. "Shit, I wish the Specialist had stayed around a bit longer," Reed muttered.

"Now you're just asking for too much." Danny dropped the magazine to check his ammo. Four more rounds. He shoved it back home.

Around them, the remaining mounted officers and Columbia cops fought a losing battle against Teledyne and Obsidian's soldiers and thugs. If backup didn't arrive soon, they'd be taken out.

Aster had stuck with them for a few moments and had killed more than a dozen men with her bare hands but then she ran off into the smoke. "He's up there!" was all she said.

A bullet skimmed along the hood of the truck and struck the telephone pole right behind Danny. He ducked down even lower.

Gunfire and explosions echoed from the direction of the hotel for several minutes and then died away. The next thing Danny heard was the clatter of weapons being dropped.

Reed poked her head over the hood of the car, her eyes wide. "What the fuck…?"

Danny glanced up, then did a double-take. The Obsidian and Teledyne soldiers had dropped their weapons and now stood, hands behind their heads. "We've been ordered to surrender!" one of them shouted.

Danny and Reed shared a look, then Danny said, "No shit? Well, good! Stay there! We'll arrest you in a minute."

Reed laughed and threw her arms around Danny. "We did it! We did it, Sarge!"

Before he could react, she planted a quick kiss on his lips before hugging him even tighter.

Danny had no idea what was going on, but he returned the embrace and laughed. Sometimes all you could do was celebrate a surprise win in this Fallen World.

* * * * *

Chapter Forty-Five

Thunder rumbled across the hazy sky, promising the first of the summer rains.

Sixty-seven fresh holes lay in a growing patch of Hinkson Field set aside for burials. Wooden crosses and other grave markers had been staked into the grassy soil at the head of most of the graves, with each person's name, rank, affiliation, and date of death carved into the attached plaques. Behind them lay graves that were older by a matter of weeks: officers, students, refugees, and other university denizens who had died since the Fall. The new cemetery already contained over two hundred deceased, a far cry from what had befallen the rest of Columbia's population, but still a terrible number.

We stood in a long line on the grass divide between the sidewalk and roadway. Many of the officers were mounted, except for those too wounded to sit in the saddle and the Columbia officers in attendance. Every department also had a riderless horse in attendance, a pair of boots turned backward in the stirrups to symbolize fallen riders.

I stood at parade rest along with the rest of the officers on foot. I was under medical orders to avoid any "horsing around" until fully healed, so Countess had stayed in the stables with the remounts. I wore my dress uniform, the look marred by the fact that my left arm was back in a sling. The painkillers had worn off shortly after the battle in the hotel, and I realized my shoulder was a lot worse than

I'd thought. The doctor and nurse had wanted to kill me, but they had settled for fixing my shoulder in as painful a manner as possible. It still ached two days later.

Aster stood next to me. She wore a black military dress uniform, its gold buttons polished so they gleamed even in the morning gloom. Her long hair had been pulled around her shoulders, so that it flowed out from her peaked officer's hat and down her back. Her right arm had been sealed in a hard cast at the elbow, then placed in a sling so it was tight against her body.

"Are you sure you should be here?" I asked.

"A number of these men died for me," she said quietly, "including two from Section Nine. I owe it to them to be in attendance."

"What about your arm?"

She glanced at me. "What about your shoulder?"

"Touché."

"*A-ten-hut!*" a voice boomed.

I snapped to attention, as did everyone around me. Brother Stephen walked down the first row of open graves, alongside Monsignor Owens, a man wearing the vestments of the Episcopal Church, an Imam, and a Rabbi.

Behind them came a long line of litters bearing flag-draped bodies, each carried by two officers in dress uniforms. The officers would be buried in body bags, as coffins had already become a rare commodity in the month since the Fall.

Nineteen of the litters were accompanied by an officer carrying a cloth bundle in both arms, filled with the remains of that officer's fallen horse. We couldn't spare the meat, so slain mounts were being buried in the way racehorses were: their heads, hooves, and hearts would be buried with their partners, but the rest would be consumed.

A further thirty-eight mounts, including three water buffalo and one camel, would be buried on their own in a separate part of the field, as their human partners had survived.

I saluted and held that position as each litter passed by. Most of the flags were American, but mixed in were Canadian, Brazilian, British, Jordanian, and Teledyne flags. Aster hissed as the first of the Teledyne flags passed us. I turned my head slightly. Aster stared straight ahead, her body rigid. Her lips were pursed, as if she were biting the inside of her lip. Sweat beaded her brow. "Are you all right?" I asked. She had to be in agony from her arm, even with the nanites.

"I can't salute." She grimaced. "I can't even honor my men properly."

"Your arm in that cast is salute enough. Bear that wound proudly until it heals. You saved a lot of lives, and the men who died saving you didn't do so in vain."

A tear spilled out of her eye and ran down her cheek. She nodded almost imperceptibly.

I turned forward again as the long procession continued. Behind our line, student onlookers, family members of the local officers, and city officials waited. Save for the muffled sobs of the grief-stricken, all was quiet.

Once all sixty-seven bodies were in position, the bagpiper started a slow rendition of "Amazing Grace." The flags were removed and folded, then the pallbearers gently lowered the bodies into the holes. My throat felt raw. I hadn't known all these officers personally prior to May 1st, but in the month since, that had all changed.

The honor guard stepped forward, rifles raised.

We fought together.

"Ready! Aim! Fire!"

We bled together.

"Ready! Aim! Fire!"

We went through the crucible together.

"Ready! Aim! Fire!"

They were my brothers and sisters in blue in this Fallen World.

* * * * *

Chapter Forty-Six

A few days after the funeral, Sheriff Welliver called the leadership into a meeting. Since neither he nor Captain Phillips had been discharged from the hospital, the meeting took place in one of the university's operating amphitheaters. We had just finished settling into the seats above the operating room when both commanders were wheeled in on their beds. Their nurses positioned them so they could look up and address us through the glass partition.

Welliver looked much better than he had when I'd first seen him after his surgery five days ago. His arm had been reattached, but it would take months to heal, and many months of physical therapy awaited him after that. Even then, the doctors weren't sure he'd ever have full use of the arm again, given his age. He'd asked about a cybernetic arm, but the belief was that it wouldn't hold up long-term.

Phillips still looked like he was near death's door. I didn't know the extent of his injuries, but he had died twice on the operating table and again after they stitched him up. He looked up at us through half-lidded eyes, and at first, I thought he couldn't see us. Then his eyes fell on me, and he nodded weakly.

"We'll keep this short so we can get our beauty rest," Welliver said, his raspy voice coming through the amphitheater's speakers loud and clear. "A provisional government has been established, with city hall serving as headquarters. In the absence of an actual mayor who's anything more than a Teledyne puppet, the town is to be ruled by a joint council of four: President Oakford of the University of Missouri, Richard Cates of the Three Rivers Fair, Obsidian Director Gwendolyn Greenway, and Teledyne Director Ichiro Kazama."

That raised a bit of murmuring. A flash of annoyance went through me, but I squelched it. I didn't like the idea of Teledyne or Obsidian having any say in the city's affairs after they'd spent the better part of a month tearing it up, but I had given them the choice. And this was the price of that choice. I only hoped I didn't end up regretting it.

"While not officially on the council, a fifth faction has been given the power to act as the tiebreaker vote and to veto all but unanimous council decisions in the interests of city security." Welliver smiled. "That would be us, for those of you slow on the uptake."

Several men whooped, and a few of the lady officers laughed and high-fived one another.

"You deserve no less," Welliver said. "You are the glue that held this city together through thick and thin. Some of us paid the ultimate price for that, and I'm sorry I wasn't there to see those honorable men and women laid to rest."

The mood turned somber again.

"I intend to join the council for these sessions as soon as I am able, with Captain Phillips at my side as my second-in-command. That said, it will be a while before either of us are up and mobile again. To that end, we have asked Captain Graham to sit in on the council in the weeks ahead, along with someone to organize our collective units into a combined force that can effectively defend this city and the surrounding farmland, which we will all be dependent upon in the coming weeks. Captain, what is your decision?"

Graham stood up from his chair in the amphitheater. The bandages were gone from his face, and he wore a black patch over his right eye. He snapped to attention. "Sheriff, I would be honored."

"Good. Lieutenant Ward, please stand."

I swallowed hard and stood.

"Due to your experience as a trainer and tactical leader, we ask that you spearhead the organization of this cobbled-together unit of departments into a cohesive fighting force. Even after Captain Phillips and I are able to resume our duties, we will need you to train the men and carry out actions as a tactical commander."

Trepidation filled me. I wasn't ready for this kind of thing. What happened in and around the Country Hotel was me flying by the seat of my pants. And men had died. A lot of men.

And yet, what choice did I have? There was a job that needed to be done, and I'd been asked to do it. I snapped to attention. "Thank you, sir. I would be honored."

"Now, let's open the floor," Sheriff Welliver said. "The council demands that our 'faction' have a name. Are there any ideas?"

"The Blue Bobbies!" one of Blackwood's boys called.

"How about the Blue Knights?" a Columbia cop asked.

Saleh scoffed. "Are we crusaders now? Would you like it if we were the Blue Janissaries instead?"

"Jani-what?"

"What about the Blue Rangers?" Danny offered.

"What is this, the Power Rangers?" another demanded.

"'Power Rangers' is a great show, you jackass!"

"What about the Constables of Chaos?"

As the discussion continued to grow more heated, a team of nurses wheeled Sheriff Welliver and Captain Phillips out of the chamber. I think I was the only one who noticed. I leaned back in my chair and smiled. It was good to see everyone as lively as ever, despite all we'd gone through.

It gave me hope for the future that my kids would inherit.

* * *

Helen slid the hospital room door open and grinned. "Aunt Aster! You're not at the meeting?"

Aster studied Helen, a sad look in her purple eyes. "Good morning, Helen. No, my men and I were excluded from the meeting, so I wanted to stop by." She held up a bag with her left hand. "I brought some sweets. Please share them with Jason."

Helen took the bag, then grabbed Aster's left hand. "Come on in! We'll have them together."

"Oh, no, I really shouldn't—"

"Jason, Aunt Aster's here! We're going to have candy together!" She tugged on Aster. "Geez, you're heavy!"

"You're not supposed to comment on a lady's weight," Jason croaked from the bed. "That's what Daddy says."

"That rule's only for boys," Helen said.

"Oh. Okay."

Aster let Helen guide her to Jason's bedside. She looked at the machines hooked up to him, at the IV in his arm, and then at his bandaged body. Her brows furrowed, and the skin around her eyes crinkled, like she was about to cry.

Helen didn't like seeing Aster so sad. "He's going to be all right! The doctor says he'll be healed in a few months. Isn't that great?"

"A few months?" Aster winced and touched her right arm in its sling.

"Is your arm hurting?" Helen asked.

"No. Well, yes, but—it's just that my wound's only going to take a few weeks to heal, not months like him. It...it doesn't seem fair."

"Wow." Jason looked up at her, his eyes wide. "You heal fast, Aunt Aster."

"It's the nanites in me."

"Na-what?"

"Never mind," Helen said. She opened the bag and pulled out a box. "She brought cookies!"

"Yay, cookies!" Jason grimaced and grabbed his chest.

Aster reached for him, then froze, her left hand inches away. "Are you all right?" she asked, withdrawing her hand and setting it by her side.

"Yes. Just can't talk too loudly." He touched the bandages beneath his hospital gown. "Ribs hurt."

"Oh. Well, please speak quietly, then."

Helen pressed the button on the side of the bed to raise the mattress to an upright position, then they dug into the cookies. The three ate in companionable silence for a few moments. Helen relished the soft chocolate chip, oatmeal cookies. Part of her wondered if there would be many more meals like this. She'd heard the adults talking about food growing scarce. She remembered the grocery stores being empty in the days after Hurricane Patricia, but everything was back to normal a few weeks later. Surely that would be the same this time, right?

Helen opened her mouth to ask about it, but Aster asked, "What are these?"

She pointed at Jason's action figures. Dad had brought a pile of them from their dormitory, something to keep him occupied. He didn't yet have the strength to play with them, so Helen set them up for him however he liked. That way his imagination could do the rest.

Today, a group of fantasy warriors battled a pair of dragons: one black, the other blue. A shirtless, muscle-bound warrior with shoulder-length black hair and a long sword stood with his back to a fur-cloaked woman with long red hair and a sword of equal length. Their allies stood in a circle around them as they fought the dragons on either side of the nightstand.

"Do you like them?" Jason asked. He pointed at each figure in turn. "The robed priest is Brother Stephen—have you met him? I think you'd like him. The hooded man with the crossbow is Patrolman Jones. He's a great shot. The knight is Uncle Danny. The man with the black hair and big muscles is Daddy, of course."

"Daddy's muscles aren't that big. And his hair isn't that long!"

Jason stuck his tongue out at her. Then he pointed at the fur-cloaked woman. "She's you, Aunt Aster. Go on, pick her up."

"Me?" Aster picked up the figure and examined her. "You think she looks like me?"

"Yep! Even down to the hair."

Aster frowned. "My hair?"

Helen's cheeks flushed hot. She leaned close to Aster. "I saw you when they brought you in the other day. I sort of told him your hair turns red when you fight." She smiled. "You do look a lot like Red Sonja, though. You have her figure."

"Oh." Her eyes turned up, as if trying to see the hair on her head. Then she looked down at the vest and shirt that clung snugly to her frame. "I see."

Aster started to put the figure back, but Jason said, "Keep her."

She froze again, the figure an inch from its former resting place. "What?"

"Jason!" Helen hissed. "She said she didn't want anything from you, remember?"

He looked down. "I want you to keep her. Daddy says you saved my life." He smiled. "She's a gift for that."

She stared at him and then at Red Sonja. She was silent for a long moment. "I...don't know what to say."

"Daddy always tells me to say 'Thank you' when someone gives me a gift," Jason said in a know-it-all tone.

"I see. Well, um, thank you."

Helen's annoyance at her brother disappeared as she saw the smile spread across Aster's lips.

"Thank you, Jason." She pressed the Red Sonja figure to her chest. "I will cherish it always."

Good things still did happen, even in a Fallen World.

* * * * *

Epilogue

"All right, what's the emergency?" Dr. Schneider yawned as he walked into the powerhouse control room. "You do realize it's 3:30 AM, right?"

"Sorry, sir, but I didn't think this could wait," the tech supervisor said. "We've got an electrical problem."

Schneider's grogginess disappeared at once. His mind raced at the possibilities. They had started rationing electricity back in May to buy time for them to find a source for natural gas, so they should have a few weeks left. "What's the problem? Generator malfunction?" Then he looked at the control panel. "Dear God, man, why are we running at full power? It's the middle of the night! We're wasting fuel!"

"That's the thing, sir," the supervisor said. "We're not wasting fuel. In fact, we're not using any."

Schneider blinked. "Come again?"

"I wish I could explain it, sir, but I can't. Earlier this evening, we noticed that the pressure gauges on the tanks hadn't gone down any. And then just a few minutes ago, the generators went to idle. They're not running at all."

Schneider cocked his head. Now that he listened carefully, the generators did sound quieter than usual. "But the lights are still on." His eyes narrowed. "If we're not powering the university, what is?"

# # # # #

ABOUT THE AUTHOR

By day, Benjamin earns his bread as a necro-cartographer (which is a fancy way of saying he makes digital maps) for a cemetery software company, and by night, he writes about undead, aliens, and everything in between. *Blue Crucible* is his first novel. Other works include short stories set in Chris Kennedy Publishing's Four Horsemen military sci-fi universe, and the Sha'Daa dark fantasy/horror universe by Copperdog Publishing. He had stories that were Baen contest finalists in 2018 and 2019. He is working on the sequel to *Blue Crucible*, as well as a Four Horsemen novel, both of which will be finished by the end of 2020.

* * * * *

Connect with Benjamin Tyler Smith Online

Website: http://benjamintylersmith.com

Facebook: https://www.facebook.com/BenTylerSmith

Twitter: @BenTylerSmith

Did you like this book?
Please write a review!

* * * * *

Connect with Blood Moon Press

Get the **free** prelude story **"Shattered Crucible,"**

join the mailing list, and discover other titles at:

http://chriskennedypublishing.com/

Facebook: https://www.facebook.com/chriskennedypublishing.biz

* * * * *

The following is an
Excerpt from Book One of The Devil's Gunman:

The Devil's Gunman

Philip Bolger

Available Now from Blood Moon Press

eBook, Audio, and Paperback

Excerpt from "The Devil's Gunman:"

I eased the door open and braced for gunfire or a fireball.

I got neither. I swept the entryway with my rifle's sights. Nothing more offensive than some high school photos glared back at me, and I didn't hear anything running down the hallway or readying a weapon. There were no shouts from police or federal agents, either.

What I did hear, from the living room, was incessant chatter underscored by the occasional interjection of a laugh track. The chatter was accompanied by the soft peripheral glow of my television. Whoever had broken into my house was watching a sitcom.

"I'm unarmed," a man's voice rang out. "So put down the rifle, and let's have a talk."

"The fuck we will," I shouted back. "You broke into my home!"

I moved down the hallway, keeping my rifle on the opening to the living room.

"That's part of what we have to talk about," the voice said. I peered around the corner and saw a young Caucasian man. His pale features and dyed blue hair did little to mask the malicious smirk on his face. He was dressed in an oxford shirt and slacks with a skinny tie, as though he couldn't figure out if he wanted to look like he'd just joined a band or an investment firm. He wore a silver tie clip with a red blood drop on it.

I stood there with my rifle sights on his head.

"I'm here as a messenger," he said and flashed his teeth. I saw pointed incisors. That was enough for me. "This is peaceful, Nicholas. No need to be violent."

I lowered the rifle. I didn't like the prick's condescending tone; he sounded like he enjoyed the sound of his own voice. Those types were always eager to give up information.

"Okay, let's talk. Who's the message from?" I asked.

"I hold the honored post of Emissary of the Lyndale Coven," he said politely, examining his nails. "We've taken a professional interest in you, and Coven leadership sent me."

"Oh yeah?" I asked. "What for?"

"To dictate the terms of your surrender," he said, locking eyes with me. His hands twitched, then curled slightly. I imagined him leaping off the couch and knocking me down. I fought the urge to bring the rifle to bear, keeping it at the low ready.

"Thought your kind needed an invite," I said.

The man snarled.

"We both know who built this house. I have a standing invite. The coven master says that the Duke no longer wants you, so you're fair game. Our agreement, which I have right here, has the details."

He pulled a no-shit scroll out of his suit jacket and put it down on my coffee table. I glanced at it. The Lyndale Coven seemed to be under the impression that I belonged to them. I read the word "slave" once, and that was enough for me to decide I wasn't interested.

"No dice," I said.

"These terms are much more charitable than those the Coven Master wanted," he said, warning in his voice. "Oath breakers aren't normally given this kind of clemency."

I didn't have much idea what he meant about oath breakers, but I wasn't going to play ball with this pompous fuck.

"Not charitable enough," I said. "Why do you guys want me? Running out of blood from young clubgoers and runaways?"

The young vampire smiled again, flashing his teeth with what I'm sure he thought was menace.

"It'll certainly improve our coven's standings with the Duke if we prove we can clean up his loose ends. I'm sure you'll make an excellent blood thrall. We'll be taking a pint of blood every month, as—"

I raised the rifle and sighted in on his head. He sighed, and rolled his eyes.

"Look, you primitive ape, guns won't—"

I fired three times, the rounds earth-shatteringly loud in such a tight place. He screamed in pain and terror as the holy rifle's bullets tore through him, the wounds leaving bright blue caverns of light.

His screaming echoed in my head, so I kept shooting. I fired the rest of the magazine until there was nothing left but a corpse, riddled with holes and glowing softly, and me, standing there in my gunpowder-fueled catharsis.

I dropped the mag and slapped in a fresh one, savoring the sound of the bolt sliding forward and knowing that if the emissary had any friends, they too, would be introduced to the kinetic light of St. Joseph.

"Anyone else here? I got more."

* * * * *

Get "The Devil's Gunman" now at:
https://www.amazon.com/dp/B07N1QF4MD.

Find out more about Philip S. Bolger and "The Devil's Gunman" at:
https://chriskennedypublishing.com/philip-s-bolger/.

* * * * *

The following is an
Excerpt from Book One of The Shadow Lands:

Shadow Lands

Lloyd Behm, II

Available Now from Blood Moon Press

eBook and Paperback

Excerpt from "Shadow Lands:"

The combatants, for lack of a better term, were both resting at the edges of the dance floor. To the left was a very butch-looking blonde in what looked to be purple leather, along with her entourage, while to the right, a petite, dark-skinned Hispanic in a princess outfit stood, surrounded by meat popsicles wrapped in leather. Vampire fashions make no damn sense to me, for what it's worth. There were a few 'normals' huddled against the far wall, which showed signs of someone's face being run along it, repeatedly. Sure enough, the London 'Special' was in the DJ booth. He killed the sound as soon as he realized we were standing there.

"Ladies and gentlemen, may I introduce the final players in our little drama, the Reinhumation Specialists of the Quinton Morris Group!" the Special said into the mike.

"Fuck me running," I said.

"With a rusty chainsaw," Jed finished.

The two groups of vampires turned to face us.

"Remind me to kick Michael in his balls when we get back to the office," I said.

"You're going to have to get in line behind me to do it," Jed replied.

"You can leave now, mortals," the blonde said with a slight German accent. She had occult patterns tattooed around her eyes, which had to be a bitch, because she would have had to have them redone every six months or so. Vampires heal.

"Like, fershure, this totally doesn't involve you," the Hispanic said, her accent pure San Fernando Valley.

"Jed, did I ever tell you how I feel about Valley Girls?" I asked, raising my voice.

"No..."

"Can't live with 'em, can't kill 'em," I replied, swinging my UMP up and cratering the Valley vampire's chest with three rounds into the fragile set of blood vessels above the heart. Sure, the pump still works, but there's nothing connected to it for what passes as blood in a vampire to spread. On top of that, company-issue bullets are frangible silver, to which vampires have an adverse reaction.

With that, the dance was on. The damn Special in the DJ booth at least had the good sense to put on Rammstein. *Mien Teil* came thundering out of the speakers as we started killing vampires. Gunny ran his M1897 Trench Gun dry in five shots, dropped it to hang by a patrol sling, and switched to his ancient, family 1911. I ran my UMP dry on Valley Vamp's minions, then dropped the magazine and reloaded in time to dump the second full magazine into the Butch Vampire as she leaped toward the ceiling to clear the tables between us and the dance floor. As soon as Butch Vamp went down, the remaining vampires froze.

"Glamour," the Special called, stepping out of the booth. "I can control a lot of lesser vampires, but not until you got those two randy cunts thinking about how much they hurt."

"You. Fucking. Asshole," I panted.

Combat is cardio, I don't care what anyone else says.

"Yes?" he replied.

I looked him over. He was wearing a red zoot suit—red-pegged trousers and a long red jacket with wide shoulders over the ubiquitous white peasant shirt, topped with a red, wide-brimmed hat. He even had on red-tinted glacier glasses.

I felt his mind try to probe mine, then beamed as he bounced off.

"My that hurt," he replied.

"You know, we don't work with Michelangelo for nothing," Jed replied. Apparently the mind probe had been general, not specific.

I went through the messy side of the business—staking and beheading—assisted by Capdepon. Crash helped Jed sort out the normal survivors, followed by prepping the live lesser vampires for transport. The Special leaned against a wall, maintaining control of the lesser vampires until we could move them out. Once all the work was done so the cleaners could move in, and the lesser vampires were moved out of Eyelash, I stepped wearily to the Special.

"What's your name?" I asked.

"You can call me," he paused dramatically, "Tim."

I kicked him in the nuts with a steel-toed boot. Even in the undead, it's a sensitive spot.

* * * * *

Get "Shadow Lands" now at:
https://www.amazon.com/dp/B07KX8GHYX/.

Find out more about Lloyd Behm, II and "Shadow Lands" at:
https://chriskennedypublishing.com/imprints-authors/lloyd-behm-ii/.

* * * *

The following is an
Excerpt from Book One of The Darkness War:

Psi-Mechs, Inc.

Eric S. Brown

Available Now from Blood Moon Press

eBook and Paperback

Excerpt from "Psi-Mechs, Inc.:"

Ringer reached the bottom of the stairs and came straight at him. "Mr. Dubin?" Ringer asked.

Frank rose to his feet, offering his hand. "Ah, Detective Ringer, I must say it's a pleasure to finally meet you."

Ringer didn't accept his proffered hand. Instead, he stared at Frank with appraising eyes.

"I'm told you're with the Feds. If this is about the Hangman killer case..." Ringer said.

Frank quickly shook his head. "No, nothing like that, Detective. I merely need a few moments of your time."

"You picked a bad night for it, Mr. Dubin," Ringer told him. "It's a full moon out there this evening, and the crazies are coming out of the woodwork."

"Crazies?" Frank asked.

"I just locked up a guy who thinks he's a werewolf." Ringer sighed. "We get a couple of them every year."

"And is he?" Frank asked with a grin.

Ringer gave Frank a careful look as he said, "What do you mean is he? Of course not. There's no such thing as werewolves, Mr. Dubin."

"Anything's possible, Detective Ringer." Frank smirked.

"Look, I really don't have time for this." Ringer shook his head. "Either get on with what you've come to see me about, or go back to wherever you came from. I've got enough on my hands tonight without you."

"Is there somewhere a touch more private we could talk?" Frank asked.

"Yeah, sure," Ringer answered reluctantly. "This way."

Ringer led Frank into a nearby office and shut the door behind them. He walked around the room's desk and plopped into the chair there.

"Have a seat," Ringer instructed him, gesturing at the chair in front of the desk.

Frank took it. He stared across the desk at Ringer.

"Well?" Ringer urged.

"Detective Ringer, I work for an organization that has reason to believe you have the capacity to be much more than the mere street detective you are now," Frank started.

"Hold on a sec." Ringer leaned forward where he sat. "You're here to offer me a job?"

"Something like that." Frank grinned.

"I'm not interested," Ringer said gruffly and started to get up. Frank's next words knocked him off his feet, causing him to collapse back into his chair as if he'd been gut-punched.

"We know about your power, Detective Ringer."

"I have no idea what you're talking about," Ringer said, though it was clear he was lying.

"There's no reason to be ashamed of your abilities, Detective," Frank assured him, "and what the two of us are about to discuss will never leave this room."

"I think it's time you left now, Mr. Dubin," Ringer growled.

"Far from it," Frank said. "We're just getting started, Detective Ringer."

Ringer sprung from his seat and started for the office's door. "You can either show yourself out, or I can have one of the officers out there help you back to the street."

Frank left his own seat and moved to block Ringer's path. "I have a gift myself, Detective Ringer."

Shaking his head, Ringer started to shove Frank aside. Frank took him by the arm.

"My gift is that I can sense the powers of people like yourself, Detective," Frank told him. "You can't deny your power to me. I can see it in my mind, glowing like a bright, shining star in an otherwise dark void."

"You're crazy," Ringer snapped, shaking free of Frank's hold.

"You need to listen to me," Frank warned. "I know about what happened to your parents. I mean what really happened, and how you survived."

Frank's declaration stopped Ringer in his tracks.

"You don't know crap!" Ringer shouted as Frank continued to stare at him.

"Vampires are very real, Detective Ringer." Frank cocked his head to look up at Ringer as he spoke. "The organization I work for...We deal with them, and other monsters, every day."

Ringer stabbed a finger into Frank's chest. It hurt, as Ringer thumped it repeatedly against him. "I don't know who you are, Mr. Dubin, but I've had enough of your crap. Now take your crazy and get the hell out of my life. Do I make myself clear?"

The pictures on the wall of the office vibrated as Ringer raged at Frank. Frank's smile grew wider.

"You're a TK, aren't you?" Frank asked.

"I don't even know what that is!" Ringer bellowed at him.

"You can move objects with your mind, Detective Ringer. We call that TK. It's a term that denotes you have telekinetic abilities. They're how you saved yourself from the vampire who murdered your family when you were thirteen."

Ringer said nothing. He stood, shaking with fear and rage.

"You're not alone, Detective Ringer," Frank told him. "There are many others in this world with powers like your own. As I've said, I have one myself, though it's not as powerful or as physical in nature, as your own. I urge you to have a seat, so we can talk about this a little more. I highly doubt your captain would be as understanding of your gift as I and my employer are if it should, say, become public knowledge."

"Is that a threat?" Ringer snarled.

Frank shook his head. "Certainly not. Now if you would…?" Frank gestured for Ringer to return to the chair behind the desk.

Ringer did so, though he clearly wasn't happy about it.

"There's so much to tell you, Detective Ringer; I'm afraid I don't even know where to begin," Frank said.

"Then why don't you start at the beginning, and let's get this over with," Ringer said with a frown.

"Right then." Frank chuckled. "Let's do just that."

* * * * *

Get "Psi-Mechs, Inc." now at:
https://www.amazon.com/dp/B07DKCCQJZ.

Find out more about Eric S. Brown and "The Darkness War" at:
https://chriskennedypublishing.com/imprints-authors/eric-s-brown/.

* * * *

Made in the USA
San Bernardino, CA
27 April 2020